the
PRISONER

Also by Carlos J. Cortes

Perfect Circle

Books published by The Random House Publishing Group
are available at quantity discounts on bulk purchases for
premium, educational, fund-raising, and special sales use.
For details, please call 1-800-733-3000.

the
PRISONER

Carlos J. Cortes

BALLANTINE BOOKS • NEW YORK

A Spectra Mass Market Original

Copyright © 2009 by Carlos J. Cortes

Published in the United States by Spectra, an imprint of The Random House Publishing Group, a division of Random House, Inc., New York.

Spectra and the portrayal of a boxed "s" are trademarks of Random House, Inc.

Excerpts from *The Divine Comedy of Dante Alighieri: Inferno: A Verse Translation* by Allen Mandelbaum. English translation copyright © 1980 by Allen Mandelbaum. Reprinted by permission of Bantam Books, an imprint of The Random House Publishing Group, a division of Random House, Inc.

Excerpts from *The Divine Comedy of Dante Alighieri: Purgatorio: A Verse Translation* by Allen Mandelbaum. English translation copyright © 1982 by Allen Mandelbaum. Reprinted by permission of Bantam Books, an imprint of The Random House Publishing Group, a division of Random House, Inc.

Excerpts from *The Divine Comedy of Dante Alighieri: Paradiso: A Verse Translation* by Allen Mandelbaum. English translation copyright © 1984 by Allen Mandelbaum. Reprinted by permission of Bantam Books, an imprint of The Random House Publishing Group, a division of Random House, Inc.

ISBN 978-0-553-59163-7

Printed in the United States of America

www.ballantinebooks.com

9 8 7 6 5 4 3 2 1

To Shawna

acknowledgments

Most books, I have discovered, are collaborative efforts, drawing on the wisdom of a host of clever people, and this novel is no exception. I would like to thank:

S. J. Thomas for reading the arcane of my early draft and straightening it with her editorial guidance, comments, and endless revisions that only a talented writer can suggest. That her belief and insight never flagged is beyond me. Thank you for being there.

Everyone at Spectra. Anne Groell, besides being a *gran bruja,* proved herself an editor worthy of her towering reputation. Kathy Lord, my copy editor, has the patience of a saint and the eyes of an eagle. Stacks of their notes that I pile on my desk silently remind me what a lucky writer I am.

Kristin Lindstrom for her support and frequent scolds. She's simply the best agent a writer can hope for.

Perry Lindstrom for guiding me through the maze of the American government and sharing Rioja, cheese, friendship, and dirty jokes.

Luis Cano for his computer savvy and his encyclopedic knowledge of hacking.

Jim Giammatteo, scientist-headhunter extraordinaire and fellow writer, for his advice.

Luis José Jacobo for his hospitality and priceless gossip on issues relating to the Dominican Republic.

I'm especially indebted to the fearless fraternity of urban explorers on three continents, and those who read the sewer chapters to offer priceless insights, in particular:

Max Action, from Actionsquad, in Minneapolis. I not only picked his brain for countless details about sewer networks but also shamelessly stole a word he coined: "snotsicles." Thank you, Max.

Steve Duncan from Undercity for his precious knowledge of rats, roaches, and the atmosphere of deep sewers.

Greg Luzteka from Silentuk for sharing the finer aspects of brickwork.

Erik Norris, aka Umbra, from The Vanishing Point for pointing out the right terminology and countless other details.

My guides to the Barcelona, Rome, and Paris sewers: Jordi Salas, Enric Bonet, and Carlos Parra.

My everlasting gratitude to the Lord of the Moscow sewers and the rest of the Russian gang who need to remain anonymous.

The Prisoner is a work of fiction, but the science underlying human hibernation exists.

Teams of scientists, both in the United States and in Europe, are at present actively engaged in human hibernation research.

Just like the discovery of fireworks led inevitably to the cannon, human hibernation, if conquered, will most likely change the world as we know it.

the
PRISONER

day one

||||

Inferno, Canto III: 7–9
*Before me nothing but eternal things were made,
and I endure eternally.
Abandon every hope, who enter here.*

The Divine Comedy, DANTE ALIGHIERI

chapter 1

17:02

"Remain calm and follow the instructions."

Laurel Cole sniffed. *Calm? How can anyone about to die remain calm?*

The truck's enclosure had a subtle smell ingrained in its polished steel surfaces and expanded metal grilles—a smell no amount of steam and disinfectant could remove. It was the odor of fear, of sweat tinged with a whiff of feces and vomit.

There was a shudder, a hollow thud, and the hiss of hydraulic bolts locking; the rear of the truck had coupled against the building. Overhead, the speaker continued its monotonous mantra. "Remain calm."

Laurel blinked. Although it was outside her field of vision, she knew every step to dock the vehicle against the admissions entrance of the prison complex. Shepherd had explained the procedure more than once and with the matter-of-fact tone of firsthand experience.

Do people scream? In retrospect, it had been a foolish question, but Laurel had asked her trainer—the man she knew only as "Shepherd"—anyway. He didn't know but offered a warning instead: *Whoever opens his or her mouth before they're told to, or departs from instructions in any way, risks another year.*

Another year? *In for a penny*—No. Laurel checked the thought. Once you're dead, it shouldn't matter for how long: elastic time, darkness, and nothingness. But it did. How long you were dead was important, and the thought of an extra minute would be enough to drive anyone insane.

Will I dream? Another stupid question. She pushed the tips of her fingers through the wire mesh fronting her cage and narrowed her eyes as a panel behind the truck inched upward, blinding light pouring through the widening gap at its base.

"Stand away from the doors."

Laurel disentangled her fingers and pressed her back against the side of the cage. It wasn't a question of stepping back but simply leaning. Her enclosure, two feet wide and eighteen inches deep, didn't have enough space for a step. Twenty-four enclosures to a truck. Twenty-four new inmates on their way to hell.

A blue-white glare lit the truck's interior. Tiny stars shone on the wire grille, perhaps a few specks of dust. The light must be UV heavy. *We don't want germs, do we?* In the pen across from her own, Laurel peered at a bright orange shape. It was an old man, his shaven head glistening under the glare. Cold sweat. His mouth opened and closed like a goldfish in a bowl. Or, better still, like the face in Munch's *The Scream*.

A snap, and the door to her enclosure swung open smoothly on its hinges.

"Five-one-five-eight-five-three-one-six, exit your compartment. Remain calm."

How thoughtful. Ladies first. After standing in the same spot for several hours, the metal floor outside her pen felt cold. *No shoes?* Nerves had probably triggered her questions, since she already understood the horror, but Shepherd had answered anyway: *No. No shoes. What for?*

"Walk out of the truck and into the adjoining room."

Laurel stepped forward, darting a glance back at the pens, each with an orange outline inside—like gaily wrapped mummies, tucked into as many catacomb niches. "Remain calm. Stand inside the circle at the center of the room."

Behind her, she heard the truck's rear panel slide back down, its bolts ramming home. No witnesses, nothing to give the other twenty-three prisoners a clue.

"Undress and drop your clothes inside the circle."

She pulled a T-shirt over her head, tore at the strip holding the trousers around her waist, and stepped out of the cloth as it pooled around her feet. Cold. She maneuvered both feet over the garments. No underwear. No need. Warmth seeped through her soles. Her warmth, soon to wane.

The room, a perfect cube perhaps ten feet by ten feet, was featureless, with white polymer walls, floor, and ceiling. No openings, no anything. It was empty but for a gray circle and a terrified, naked woman standing on orange clothes. She didn't notice when the wall facing her started to rise. The continuous floor and lack of features played tricks with her perception.

"Advance into the next room."

Although it was difficult to estimate time—there was no urgency to the process—the wretches in the truck would get a glimpse of eternity. Laurel was sure that, year or no year, some would scream. Perhaps that was the designer's idea. She stepped forward. The building probably consisted of blocks, every room a carbon copy of the previous one. No, wrong cliché. No carbon here; a snow copy.

Another circle.

"Walk to the center of the room and stand inside the circle."

The wall behind her must have been sliding closed, as Laurel sensed more than felt movement. She glanced at the ceiling and an approaching circular gap. The circle where she stood rose, becoming a platform.

"Remain calm. Don't move."

No. We wouldn't want me to fall, would we? I might hurt myself. When her shoulders cleared the space separating the levels, Laurel blinked. She feasted her gaze on the left-hand wall. In its center, there was a small square niche, large enough to stand a vase with a bunch of wildflowers, though there was nothing there now. On the floor, right under the niche, there was a gray semicircle. *Now what? Remain calm. Walk to the semicir—*

"Remain calm. Step over to the opening on the left wall and keep inside the gray area."

The programmer must have felt verbose.

At the base of the niche were two trays with slimy green things inside. She leaned forward a fraction. Not trays, but slight hollows. Laurel knew what came next, and the thought filled her with dread.

"To your right are earplugs. Hold one by the larger spherical end and insert the pointed end into your left ear."

The plug felt like a blob of jelly, like the candy her mother used to make. Laurel tried to push her auburn mane out of the way and froze when her hand encountered air. There was not a hair left on her body. The blob fell to the floor and jiggled a little before coming to rest. The training had been one thing, but the reality was far more horrifying.

"Remain calm." A click, then a different voice, this time female and with a warm Hispanic lilt. "Pick it up and try again, five-one-five-eight-five-three-one-six. No punishment for the accident. The floor is sterile."

Laurel recovered the plug. The programmer hadn't recorded instructions for this eventuality. It could be her imagination, but the new voice had a whiff of humanity, assuming the fallibility of fumbling fingers. After pushing both plugs into her ears, she waited until the voice sounded inside her head. It had switched to the implant in her neck.

"Continue with the nose plugs. Hold the spherical end and insert the pointed end into your left nostril. Breathe deeply."

She held the nose plug, also green but much softer than the earpieces and long, at least three inches. It looked like a fat worm with a bloated ass. When Laurel pushed the tip into her nose, the slimy object slipped from her fingers and rammed deep into her, almost of its own accord. Then it fizzed and expanded, leaving a ball-shaped blob resting on her upper lip. She jerked her head back, panic gripping her muscles in an age-old terror. *I won't be able to breathe!*

"Remain calm. Repeat with your right nostril."

Calm. Calm. Calm! Her legs trembled, but she contracted her calves and bunched her toes. Almost over. Almost. With ears and nose plugged, the cold jelly feeling predictably alien, she stood motionless before the empty niche and tried to control her shortening gasps. Her tongue dried to a barky texture, like a piece of beached driftwood.

"Step into the next room."

Laurel did a quick double take. The wall to her right had vanished and now opened into another room, its center occupied by a sinuous form.

"Lie down on the bed."

Bed? Like an abstract white sculpture, the form grew seamlessly from the floor—a shape that reminded her of a sofa dreamed by a stoned avant-garde designer: a formless shiny mass dipping in its center. Laurel sat down and swung her legs over. She adjusted her anatomy to the shape, her shaking legs hampering her movements.

"Remain calm."

For once, the voice made sense.

Gradually, the bed softened. Like an enormous amoeba, the shape absorbed her body. Laurel felt a powerful suction under her buttocks as the sculpture molded to her back and limbs.

She scrunched her eyes, terrified of what she knew would follow. The bed continued to move, adjusting, rearranging, softening and hardening in places, molding to her anatomy, and robbing it of any capacity to move. Her legs flexed at her knees and rose, her body adjusting to a child-delivery position. Then her head started to sink. She opened her eyes and tried to straighten out, but her head seemed caught in a vise.

Her head continued to fall. Now her toes must be pointing to the ceiling, and her head arched back almost to her spine, her throat stretched.

"Remain calm."

Laurel rotated her eyes frantically. They were the only things she could move besides her gaping mouth, which drew in short gasps. The tips of her nose plugs tickled the back of her throat. Most would scream at this point, definitely, or at least whimper, or empty their bowels.

She detected movement on the fringe of her vision. A thick phallus-shaped green mass neared her face. She saw its tip approach her eyes and pause before the blobs projecting from her nose. This was it: the real thing, the truth. Somewhere deep in her mind, a voice screamed.

"Remain calm."

Then the hoselike object rammed past her lips and slithered down her throat, sizzling, expanding, digging deep into her.

Then the lights went out, or she passed out, or died, and Laurel didn't care anymore.

chapter 2

||||

17:08

Impressive. His fears didn't melt away—he *was* risking his neck—but the tension twisting Lukas Hurley's gut into a painful knot relaxed a notch. He twiddled a joystick and zoomed a pin camera for a closer look at the woman's expression. Yes, there was horror in the disfigured face, her mouth open wide to accept the long green cylinder into her throat. Horror, revulsion, and fear, but she'd done a good job of mostly masking all three. Donald Duck, the woman's boss, had selected his people well. Lukas thought the moniker he'd chosen apt. His only contact had been a quacking voice on a phone.

Money could be a powerful enticement and Donald Duck had paid him a truckload already, with a second installment due before the end of the day. The problem was, if the Department of Homeland Security caught him, Lukas could look forward to a similar truncheon down his throat on his way to a tank. His hands felt clammy. He rubbed his palms over the front of his lab whites, then reached down to a drawer and removed three plastic envelopes. He rested them on top of a wastepaper basket he'd positioned to one side under his desk.

Flat on his work surface, a tablet PC displayed an inmate's restricted file of a type he'd never seen before. Prisoners bound for hibernation in the central area of the tanks arrived at his station without personal records or names, only numbers— long numbers and a bar code. Lukas peered at a holograph of a serious-looking bald woman with a row of numbers superimposed on her chest. *Laurel Cole, 26, 5′3″. Caucasian. Lawyer. 913. Center.*

No term of sentence—not that Lukas expected to see one.

Center inmates didn't merit hope. Yet he knew the courts had sentenced the woman and her colleagues to only a two-year stretch. Someone had doctored their files with the *Center* tag. Someone from Donald Duck's team, and that spelled clout.

The operators outside the fishbowl, as workers called his office, could follow inmates past the intubation room all the way to the hibernation tanks. But not all the inmates. Those earmarked with only a number and a bar code faded from their screens after intubation. There was a rumor that the inmates sent to occupy the center spaces in the tanks were test subjects, willing guinea pigs to improve hibernation technology in exchange for a lump sum paid to their families. But Hypnos, the corporation running the hibernation penal installations, had never confirmed that, and Lukas didn't believe a word of it anyway. He'd never seen any testing involving center inmates, only oblivion. Supervisors like him were the only ones with clearance to escort these rare souls on their voyage—a task made more palatable by a modest bonus each time they donned the cloak of eternal ferryman. Lukas, a modern-day Charon with a Christian evangelist's name—a supreme paradox.

During hibernation, inmates were suspended in concentric rows inside tanks measuring thirty feet square and nine deep. A cross-shaped, six-foot-wide empty area bisected each tank to simplify maneuvering the bodies in and out of their allotted positions and up to the maintenance labs above.

When engineers at the Department of Homeland Security had studied the layouts, they complained about the wasteful arrangement. *Can't we pack inmates closer? Why the empty corridors and centers?* Eventually they had seen the sense in the corridors, because they were necessary for operation, but insisted Hypnos find a use for the center of the space and increase the tank capacity by four, from 136 to 140 inmates. Hypnos Inc. obliged and produced a design to populate the central areas. Yet the blueprints presented to Congress were the original ones: 136 inmates to a tank and an empty middle. An empty space that didn't show up in any statistic and didn't appear occupied in any of the scant published diagrams available to the public. And such spaces were always deserted in the tanks the DHS inspectors were allowed to see. Congress approved the untouched arrangement—a clear sign of someone's powerful and anonymous footwork. Lukas suspected the unknown someone or someones used the extra room to store enemies.

In his ten years at the company, he'd accompanied a dozen wretches into areas that didn't exist in the station's formal layout or its architectural drawings. It was a clever ploy. Where to hide a tree? In the woods, of course. Where to hide a body? In a tank full of them. Yes, the C area looked innocent enough, but it was a limbo for anonymous souls.

Lukas pecked at his tablet PC and the holograph grew. Laurel. The Spanish name of a splendid Mediterranean shrub: *Laurus nobilis,* bay. He tasted the name of the woman in the photograph, pondering that Romans used bay's aromatic leaves to make triumphal crowns for victors. *Laurel—what an encouraging name.* He'd risked storing the files Donald Duck had supplied on his tablet to learn the faces and names he otherwise would have never known.

The first time he had heard the quacking voice on his cell phone—obviously filtered through a distorting circuit—Lukas thought someone was having fun and severed the call. That was before two men pushed him into the back of a car as he was leaving for work, drove him to an abandoned warehouse, and made him stand before a quacking speaker. He'd never met the voice's owner, but it belonged to a persuasive man. A few days after his abduction, Lukas fielded a call from Cuzco, Peru, to learn from his awed bank manager that Donald Duck was not only persuasive but also true to his word.

After selecting one of his files, Lukas placed it on standby. During the minutes following an inmate's intubation, the program locked on to a routine to coax his or her body into deep hibernation—a tamper-proof routine coupled to scores of fail-safe sensors. Once the inmate was stabilized, the program looped into its maintenance subroutine; this was the spot where Lukas had to slip the patch provided by Donald Duck's men. The lines of code would override the maintenance program, hiking the Thermogenin dosing into Laurel's bloodstream—a protein to uncouple the electron transport chain from the reaction producing adenosine triphosphate. As a result, her body would produce heat by thermogenesis and ward off the onset of hypothermia. Then the rogue patch would loop yet again into the reanimation sequence. When Lukas finished, he adjusted Laurel's mixture of gases and set a timer to launch his patch for ten minutes after immersion in the fluid. A tiny set of numerals appeared on the top of the middle screen and remained static.

Lukas bit his lower lip and ran his hands down the front of his lab coat again. Within a few hours, he would be on his way to Peru with Elena. In the land of the Inca Empire and Machu Picchu, they would build a big house and settle as wealthy landowners, to her family's chagrin. "He's a loser; a jailer," her brothers had insisted. "And twice your age." Or perhaps they said a jailer and a loser, but the order of words didn't matter. Her father had spat at his feet and had slapped Elena's face. That had mattered, had stuck in his gut like a branding iron.

Over the three plasma panels on his desk, Lukas glanced through the bubble isolating his office from the main control room. He weighed the expressions and postures of his staff. Normal, routine faces, a tinge of boredom here and there. He looked at an expanse of synoptic boards, counters, and the myriad screens of the network controlling the station. Normal. No flashing lights out of sync. From Lukas's vantage point, the control room could have been in any power station. At desks bristling with overrides, screens, and communications terminals, four men and a woman followed the automatic processing of inmates into the station. From a peak of over thirty thousand, occupation had halved in less than ten years, so there was plenty of room.

After processing and during their sentence, the inmates remained suspended in a fluid. At intervals of four to six weeks, the computer would remove them from the tank and coax their body temperature to normal for a few hours, triggering extensive protein synthesis. Since chemical degradation of macromolecules piled up—although at a slower rate in low temperatures—periodic arousal was necessary for their bodies to repair and flush organs, tissues, and cells. Of course, the inmates remained deeply sedated during these periods, to prevent psychological damage.

His central screen offered a view of an empty room clouded by the steam from high-pressure lances, which were sterilizing the bed Laurel had just left. Lukas turned to another screen, where a young black man inserted plugs in his ears and nose with an expressionless face. Again, impressive. On his laptop, Lukas scrolled down to a file. *Bastien Compton, 28, 5'11". African–American. Lawyer. 913. Center.*

Lukas keyed a string of instructions onto his keyboard, and a screen on his right flared to life with a layout of tank 913. Less than half full, and its center occupied by a single inmate: Eliot Russo, a long-term resident. Why him? Eight years in hibernation? It was too long. It occurred to Lukas that the costly ploy to spring the man from 913 was a waste of time. He was bound to be raving mad after eight years in a tank. An unlucky tank with the number 13. Then Lukas frowned and added the digits of tank 913. Doubly unlucky. A tank with two 13s. But that wasn't his concern. By the time Russo regained consciousness, if he ever did, Lukas would be out of the country.

Once in the nonexistent zones, center inmates waned into oblivion; it was as if they'd never existed. But not quite. The subroutine in the computer program that roused all inmates every few weeks and hoisted them to the medical labs for maintenance included center residents. Yet, a few years back, by mere accident, he'd noticed that Russo had remained in the tank—very much awake on account of the fluid rippling around his suspension wires—although the rest of its occupants had been taken to the labs in batches. Thinking it could be a glitch, Lukas had raised the director of the medical team, only to be fobbed off with a curt "I know. With some test inmates we carry out maintenance from here. A new technique." Lukas had forgotten the event. But later, after Donald Duck enlisted his help, he'd pondered the issue. No scrubbing of the prisoner's system, no maintenance, no repair. A death sentence, in truth.

On another screen, Lukas followed Laurel's inert body. It

was dangling by thin wires from an overhead conveyor, like a carcass in an abattoir, stopping over the expanse of liquid in tank 913. She was cocooned in a net of transparent green cords fastened to a large doughnut around her neck. Not loose but not too tight, the flexible net allowed for a degree of movement in limbs, triggered by the computer to prevent muscle atrophy. The machine lowered the body next to the edge of the tank, barely disturbing the patent leather gleam of its surface.

When fluid closed over Laurel's head, only thin wires and a hose—the umbilical cord keeping her alive—marked the point where she had sunk under the liquid. Lukas eyed the timer as it sprang alive and started its countdown to zero. *Ten minutes to reanimation.* He turned to the second screen.

After swallowing the coupling plug, Bastien lay inert on the molding bed. The shape holding Bastien went through a series of movements, contorting the body so that mechanical arms could strap a sling with wire supports around his chest and shoulders while another pair of arms secured protective goggles over his eyes.

On his left screen, another young man stepped onto the gray floor pad on his way to plugging. *Raul Osborne, 28, 6'1". Caucasian. Lawyer. 913. Center.* All impressive, and all accounted for. Lukas tweaked Bastien's mix, set another timer, and ran the complex schedule ahead in his mind. Once more, he glanced out of the fishbowl, this time to peer at a digital clock centered over the control panels: 17:17.

Standing straight, Lukas unbuttoned his lab whites, recovered the envelopes from the top of the wastepaper basket, sucked in his stomach, and slipped them under his belt.

After he finished tweaking Raul's intake of chemicals and gases, it would be 17:20. Forty minutes later, the central computer would loop into the daily backup routine. The carrier truck would slam shut and processing would stop for ten minutes. Life support ran independently, and the computer shutdown wouldn't affect it. His staff would stretch, perhaps walk out onto a catwalk to snatch a toke from a joint or grab a cup of coffee.

Lukas would have ten minutes to step outside, nod at

Josh or Martin, smile at Sandra, leisurely make for the rest rooms, and, once in the main corridor, run like hell toward tank 913.

chapter 3

||||

17:27

"We've read the documents you sent and watched the film several times. Haven't we, dear?"

Dear made a wry movement with his mouth and nodded.

Dr. Floyd Carpenter hated this aspect of his work. He attempted a reassuring smile and nodded at the couple sitting in his office. He would have chosen nearness and the sofa, to offer them some warmth for what might be the most difficult decision in their lives, instead of hiding behind a desk. But the company insisted on a protocol: Clients prefer sitting across from a doctor in a white overcoat.

"But there are some details we don't understand. Right, dear?"

Dear didn't move this time. The man was fading. Unless they reached a quick decision, there would be nothing left to hibernate.

Floyd glanced at the screen on the surface of his glass desk. Sarah Ward, 66, and her husband, John, 70—the latter dying of a fast-spreading bone metastasis. He checked the time: 5:28 P.M. By six o'clock the labs would be deserted. Then he would have perhaps two hours to prepare a little-used operating theater and a reanimation vessel for a private patient due at around eight o'clock. No witnesses and no help. Plenty of time, he hoped. "That's what I'm here for."

"We are simple people," she started. "I mean, all this technology is a little over our heads."

Floyd had to agree with her caveat. Their business was

simple magic, not science. John's tales of Theodore the Turtle, Tiberius the Gecko, and Bernard the Squirrel—lovingly illustrated by Sarah—had filled generations of American children with wonder.

"Will he dream?" she asked.

Simple folk ask unsimple questions, as his father used to say. "Yes, he will. A live mind needs the exercise, but we select a proper mixture of sedatives to guarantee"—he was about to say *pleasant dreams* but corralled his tongue in time—"a peaceful slumber."

"How long?"

Floyd leaned forward. "How long?"

Sarah darted a glance to her husband. John's head lolled like a stalk of ripe corn before a breeze. The cocktail of sedatives and painkillers he swallowed six times a day must be playing hell with his biorhythms. "Yes. How long will he be in hibernation?"

"I'm afraid nobody knows." Floyd slid a neat sage-green file across the glass, flicked it open, and pointed to a form. "That's the reason we accept not monthly or yearly payments but a fund to guarantee your husband's upkeep almost indefinitely."

"But . . . can he die?"

Simple folk ask unsimple . . . Floyd swatted away his dad's memory and tried marshaling words to reduce the unexplainable to simple terms. "We all die, Mrs. Ward. Hibernation is a form of energy conservation. We lower the patient's metabolism but don't stop it. Patients age at a much slower pace, but they age, and their bodies continue to decay. Nyx Corp has the most advanced hibernation installations anywhere in the world—"

"Better than Hypnos?"

He would have to tread carefully. "We work under their license. They developed and own the technology, but there are differences. Hypnos runs the penitentiary hibernation stations and built their installations for economy, with large tanks to house many inmates. Our capsules hold a single patient, surveyed day and night by medical personnel—"

"Instead of wardens?"

"I didn't—"

Sarah shook her head. "I'm sorry, Doctor. I keep interrupting."

"Don't worry. What I was trying to explain is that we've designed our installations to arrest your husband's decline and hope that science discovers a cure for his ailment within a reasonable time." He raised his hand a fraction to ward off her next question. "How long is 'reasonable'? We don't know. We're in a race against disease. At this station, we hamper cell destruction, buy time." Floyd drew a rigid finger across the glass. "But there's a line beyond which your husband's body will not recover. If he reaches that line before science can help, John will die."

She nodded. "Thank you for your candor."

John's breath had deepened into a soft snore. Sarah tried to tug the hem of her skirt over dimpled knees encased in fine silk stockings. Earlier, when she sat, Floyd had caught a glimpse of a garter and mulled over the strange habits of some women. A girlfriend had once explained that garter belts were damn uncomfortable—okay for fun and games but not for every day. Sarah didn't seem racy but, quite the contrary, almost demure. He puzzled over the contradiction.

"As I said before, we've watched the video, but could you explain the procedure again?"

Sarah had read the documents, probably knew every word by heart, and had watched the slides, films, and diagrams a thousand times. Floyd held her gaze. She must have been stunning in her day and was still a beautiful woman, not flashy but with a certain poise. With just a hint of makeup, her face had the serenity of a long-distance runner, in for the long haul with her chosen companion. Despite John's harrowing predicament, Floyd felt a pang of envy. Her amber-colored eyes sparkled under a film of tears. Yes, though she knew everything, she needed to hear it in a voice modulated through living membranes.

"After admission we place a small sensor, the size of a hazelnut, below the skin in the patient's neck—a procedure lasting a few minutes under local anesthesia." From a tray on his desk, Floyd picked up an oval object similar to a bird's egg, its glossy surface rippling under the strong light, and laid it on the glass. "This sensor collects information from the body and relays the data to our computer via a receptor on a ring around the patient's neck. After a battery of tests, we sedate the patient, seal his nose, mouth, and ears to prevent fluid entrance, and place a net of conducting jelly around his body. The net will ensure he can stretch his limbs and exercise his muscles thanks to the impulses delivered by the computer. This will prevent muscular atrophy."

"Will J—a patient be able to stand after . . ."

"Yes. The procedure mirrors that of some hibernating animals. But your question is a good one, since a human wouldn't be able to walk after a few months of lying in bed. However, just consider, by contrast, that a ground squirrel can be up and running quickly after six months of hibernation." Floyd blinked, appalled at his tactless choice of example. He could have chosen chipmunks or raccoons among scores of hibernating animals rather than a squirrel, which was almost impossible to disassociate from one of their creations: Bernard, a squirrel decked out in a black-and-white-checkered waistcoat. "Our technology mimics such natural mechanisms."

She reached for her sleeping husband and covered his hand with hers. John, her squirrel. Sarah's lips didn't move, but Floyd could have sworn he spotted the words flashing across her irises.

"After that, we immerse the patient into a capsule, holding fluid slightly above the freezing point, and lower his core temperature to between five and ten degrees Celsius—say forty to fifty degrees Fahrenheit. We use a harness and wires to handle his body. Once in the fluid, the wires relax, since the hibernation liquid has a precise density to guarantee the patient's weightlessness. He's ventilated through a tracheal cord and supplied regularly with lipids, minerals, and whatever else he may need. This stage we term *torpor*, as opposed to *arousal*."

"Why do you wake them up every so often?"

Floyd didn't answer at once. It had just occurred to him the garters were a gift to her squirrel, perhaps for the last time, and the thought left him speechless.

"We must periodically carry out repair and maintenance of organs, tissues, and cells. Chemical degradation of macromolecules increases over time, and each patient needs conditioning and dialysis regularly. From torpor, we promote an endocrine reaction and hyperventilate the patient to increase the oxygen in his blood. And to reduce carbon dioxide concentration, we must raise the body temperature from a nonshivering stage. Shivering begins above twenty degrees Celsius. We then increase the rate of warming until the patient reaches normothermy." Floyd bit his lip; he was lapsing into jargon. "I meant normal temperature."

Sarah blinked and her eyes smiled. "Will he wake up?"

"Of course not!" Floyd's voice raised a fraction. Consciousness between the stages of torpor and arousal had almost doomed hibernating technology, until scientists understood its effects. Back in the thirties, during the first clinical trials, a few of those hibernated for extended periods suffered acute mental imbalances, paranoia, and dementia. Dr. Nemecio Chavez and his team at Caltech had discovered that, before the onset of hibernation, technicians should sedate patients with a carefully metered mixture of gases to guarantee a gradual loss of consciousness. The patient would then sink into torpor with a smooth brain-wave signature. Otherwise, after arousal, the gases dissolved in the patient's bloodstream would interfere with the chemical equation. As a result, the patient entered torpor excited, his brain signature choppy and riddled with spikes. This triggered nightmares. "During periodic arousal and return to torpor, we change the mix of gases the patient breathes to ensure he doesn't come out of his placid slumber. The issue shouldn't concern you, Mrs. Ward. From the beginning to the end of hibernation, your husband will be in deep, tranquil sleep."

Sarah Ward closed her eyes and breathed deeply, as if gathering strength. Then she caressed John's hand for an instant, just a flicker of fingers, before straightening.

Floyd peered into her eyes and felt the hairs on the back of his neck prickle. There was uneasiness to her expression, and something else he once saw on a little girl's face when she couldn't find her mom.

"Please, tell me where I should sign."

She was giving her squirrel away.

chapter 4

||||

17:34

Awareness didn't return at once. At least, it didn't feel like consciousness but rather the distant sensation of being in a long tunnel. Laurel shied away to slip back into nothingness, but beeps of increasing volume prevented her. It took her a few slow heartbeats to realize the sound was in her head.

She jerked awake. Rollers of panic pushed out from the corners of her mind. Her hands jerked to entangle in a web of slithering worms encasing her body. Cold slime, thick as snot. Her fingers drew back. The worms drew tighter, suffocating. They were everywhere. She felt them on her thighs. On her legs. On her back. The beep blaring in her head matched the erratic tattoo beating in her chest. She tried to scream, but her mouth was full of gunk.

Laurel kicked, but the worms held her fast. Darkness. She was blind; she couldn't open her eyes. The worms gripped her feet, dug under her arms, and brushed her crotch to lift her through the slime. She fought, jerked, and kicked, but the worms held tight. Then, somewhere, a tiny light flickered. She reached for it, projected, streamed through the mass of worms to the light. She needed the light. *I'm Laurel Cole,* the light whispered, *and I'm alive.*

Shit, I'm in hibernation.

Laurel sucked in greedily with a deep motion of her stomach. *Hyperventilate. I need to hyperventilate. I need to drag more air from the hose.* But she came up empty until the machine delivered her next breath. She thrashed in panic. *I need more air.*

The sensation of weight increased. She was being hoisted from the tank.

The whirlwind of spinning details slowed to a stop. Laurel tried to relax as Shepherd's voice echoed in her mind. *By the numbers. You must go by the numbers. Remove your eye protectors.*

The sensation on her skin had changed; her face tingled. In small stages, she hiked her right arm through the tangle of jellylike cords to stop at a thick lump wedged into her mouth. She explored the object. Higher up, the lump rounded and became a hose. *I'm still intubated.* She sucked greedily at the next delivery of air from the machine.

After you're intubated, a machine will attach eye protectors. Remove them.

Laurel's fingers reached behind her left ear and found a strip of elastic material. She hooked a finger around it and pulled it up. Light flooded her eyes. She closed them as a sharp stinging sensation flared. Then she blinked repeatedly to clear them as her irises adjusted.

Your body will produce heat by chemically induced thermogenesis. For a while, blood vessels close to your skin will dilate to promote irrigation, but it will wear off soon.

Laurel eyed her arm and flexed her fingers. Red like a boiled lobster. Fighting an insane urge to yank the coupler from her throat and breathe at a faster rhythm, she rolled her eyes sideways to get her bearings.

She was dangling in midair, in a forest of wires that disappeared into the gloom above her head. The wires attached to her harness shuddered, and her cocoon moved past scores of gleaming cables sinking in the fluid beneath her feet. Laurel knew it was a fluid, but it looked solid, its surface bright. A drop fell from her toes, and the surface distorted for an instant but didn't ripple, like crude oil.

When her wires cleared the maze, unseen robotic arms veered her cocoon over a catwalk and slowed to a standstill above an empty platform clad in the institutional white polymer surrounding the tank. The robotic arms must have been in need of fine-tuning or the programmer hadn't given a damn, because the wires slackened a tad too fast. Laurel dropped the last foot unceremoniously onto a mess of jelly net, but the solid surface beneath her butt felt good.

The wires snapped free and disappeared into the heights as she felt a tremor in her throat. *Oh, shit!*

Laurel's stomach protested with involuntary contractions as the never-ending hose pulled from her throat. She tried to stand and follow the motion to arrest the overpowering movement, but she failed. With a wet slurp, the plug yanked free and vanished upward. At once, she rolled over, convulsing inside her slimy cocoon, and retched blobs of pink-tinged bile until her gag reflex calmed, leaving a thin thread of saliva dripping from her lip. Then she filled her lungs to capacity with air redolent of chemicals.

Her jaw ached. *Give head? Never again. Never.*

A few yards away and to her left, she eyed a square pool—an expanse of black glass, its unmoving surface pierced by pairs of wires and fat green tubes.

By the numbers, you must go by the numbers. Get out of the protective net and remove the plugs.

When she could control her greedy gasps for air, Laurel reached to the back of her neck, explored the thick ring surrounding it, found the quick-release catch, and pressed it. The doughnut sprang open. Pulling with fingers and toes, she disentangled herself from the slippery net. When she was free, she pulled out her nose and earplugs, ran a sticky hand over the smooth dome of her head, and huddled on the floor to enjoy her recovered senses and peer at the mass of green cords, slowly flattening over the hard floor like a beached jelly-fish. Laurel eyed her knees, stretched her legs, and wiggled her toes. *Like a boiled lobster.*

She closed her eyes and took a deep breath, shocked at the sudden euphoria shooting through her body. Laurel remembered hearing tales of how Napoleon, Caesar, and Alexander had each spent a night in the funerary chamber of the great pyramid at Giza—a large room, perhaps thirty by fifteen feet. Half the size of Hypnos's standard tanks, and with a large sarcophagus dead center on the floor. They had experienced an everlasting night, alone in complete darkness, where it soon became difficult to decide where fingers ended and air began. They claimed the pinnacle of the experience was not the entrance or even the stay but the exit. The return to the outside, walking along a narrow gallery in darkness and toward the light, was like a rebirth.

Everyone who had undergone such an experience was changed. Fear of death was forever lost. Laurel felt similarly reborn.

When she heard a high-pitched whine, she glanced upward but couldn't find the source of the noise. Suddenly she spotted movement out of the corner of her eye. At the edge of the tank, the surface broke and another cocoon started to emerge. *Raul or Bastien.* She narrowed her eyes and smiled at the glossy ebony skin inside the net. Bastien. *Let's see how you fare when they yank the plug from your mouth, buster.*

chapter 5

||||

17:41

Nineteen minutes to computer shutdown.

Lukas held his breath as the wire harness pulled the woman clear from tank 913, dreading an explosion of blaring alarms, but nothing happened. The subroutine he'd slipped into the station's computer when he started his shift had worked like a charm. Donald Duck had said it would and, so far, the quacking man had been true to his word. Obviously, only someone familiar with Hypnos's internal procedures could have written the code. During the daily backup routine, when the machine connected with the mainframe at the corporation's headquarters, engineers would probably detect the rogue program. Then all hell would break loose. But by then he hoped to be out of the reach of the DHS's long arm.

With another ten inmates left, processing the new arrivals was only halfway done. At three minutes each, he and his team couldn't deal with all the new guests before the computer would start its backup. After a moment's hesitation, Lukas turned to a squat gray cordless box on his desk and blinked to bring it online. The box turned dull red.

"Instruction to all controllers," Lukas said.

The chameleonic box changed to green.

"Please continue processing for twelve minutes, until seventeen fifty-three, then prepare to shut down until backup is complete. Secure all unprocessed inmates." He paused. "Lukas Hurley, supervisor."

The box seemed to shrink as it returned to its gray standby status.

He could have scheduled another inmate, or two, but he didn't want to tempt fate. If any of the inmates struggling through the admission freaked out—and a few did—it would add minutes to the schedule. They would have to seal the room where the wretch happened to be at the time, then, after sedating the prisoner with gases, a security crew would have to carry him physically to the intubation bed. The procedure would add a good three minutes to the schedule. No. There was no need to risk cutting it too close.

A man's image filled the center screen. Lukas frowned. The guy must be pushing seventy. Thin as a rake, he shook like a tree caught in the crosswinds. The nose plugs had slipped twice through his fingers. If he carried on, they would have to use the gas. *Damn!*

Again he blinked toward his communications console. "Audio."

"Relax. Bend over, let your arms hang loose, and breathe deeply. Relax. Breathe deeply once more. Good. Relax. Again, breathe deeply. Relax." Lukas listened to Sandra Garcia's soft voice issuing from the yellow box and nodded. She had overridden the computer and was coaxing the old man through the plugging. *Come on, Granddad. Stick the plugs up your nose. Piece of cake.*

The inmate straightened, reached for a plug, and rammed it up his nose.

"Attaboy! Now the other."

After a short delay, the thin man staggered toward the intubation bed, both green balls dangling over his upper lip.

"Control Room."

A pause.

"Line to controller Garcia."

Lukas straightened his back and looked over his screens to a station where a young woman swiveled in her seat to look in his direction.

"Excellent job, Sandra."

She gave him a thumbs-up.

The screen on his right zoomed in on the old man as he swallowed the coupling plug. *Douglas Stern, 72, 5' 2". Caucasian, Retired executive. 50 years, 761.* Lukas scrolled down his pad to Douglas's holograph. He remembered the face from the news. The little old man had drowned four cats, a Labrador dog, and his three grandchildren—aged six, three, and eighteen months—in the family's bathtub.

He turned to the left screen. No wonder the man was nervous. Fifty years was a death sentence. Although Congress had abolished capital punishment in 2046, prisoners served their terms in full. With sentences often running to hundreds of years, the abolition was a farce. Many inmates entered hibernation knowing they would never walk again. At least not in this valley of woe.

Down by tank 913, the woman had discarded the protective net and, after a stint of heaves, was on all fours watching the black man pop up from the tank. Lukas zoomed in on the crawling figure. Red as a beetroot. Nice ass.

He darted a look at the clock: seventeen fifty.

Suddenly a white line at the bottom of the screen started to flash. Lukas jerked. "Holy mother—" He felt his gut clench. The line froze and changed to an angry red.

chapter 6

17:50

The cocoon with Bastien inside maneuvered through a swarm of wires almost to the far edge of the room before turning and heading in Laurel's direction, like a strange hive at the end of a sagging branch. The ceiling over the tank was a grid of metal rails and guides holding square plates, each fitted with two suspension wires and a greenish tube. Laurel watched the moving plate shunting past other squares, guided by a thick cylinder, probably a hydraulic arm. After more clicks and whines, the mess of jelly cords with Bastien inside traveled overhead along the platform surrounding the tank, leaking steady dribbles of clear fluid.

She waited—as one waits for the last strain of an organ note to die out before leaving church. A few paces beyond the heap of her discarded netting, the bundle slowed to arc in sluggish swings, as if buffeted by unseen winds. Glistening threads stretched to pool on the floor below. Then it lowered. Laurel gathered her legs and tried to stand, her eyes intent on Bastien's upturned face, distorted by thick lips stretched around the green tube. *Why doesn't he yank his goggles off?* Her toes gripped the textured floor.

With a loud click, clasps fastening the wires to Bastien's harness snapped and his body sagged onto the floor. Rather than standing, Laurel edged toward Bastien on all fours, her arms and knees wobbly.

The green hose tightened, lifting Bastien's head a few inches from the floor before sliding from his throat. As the tube contorted toward the machinery above, Bastien's head thumped back onto the polymer floor.

Laurel lunged over to him, reaching behind his head for

the fastener holding together his jelly net and tugging at his protective goggles. His eyes stared, fixed, unfocused, to a point somewhere over their heads.

Oh, no, you don't. She yanked his neck ring and tore at the net, but she couldn't remove it without lifting his slick body. "You bastard!" she screamed. He was too heavy to maneuver out of the jelly mess. With quick movements, she removed his nose plugs and lowered her ear to his gaping mouth. He wasn't breathing. She rammed her fingers into his neck to check his carotid pulse; nothing. She pulled back one of Bastien's eyelids, but his pupil didn't react.

"You bastard," she insisted. *Chest compression is more important than ventilation.* Laurel strained to remember the precise details from a first-aid course she'd attended several years before. Swinging a leg over his body, she straddled Bastien. *One, two, three . . .* She lowered her weight and rammed her stacked hands on his sternum. *At least one hundred a minute. Ten, eleven, twelve . . .* Laurel jerked her head, scanning the bare walls for a defibrillation station. Nothing. *Twenty-one, twenty-two, twenty-three . . .* At thirty, she stopped. He needed a shock to restart his heart.

Again, she glanced quickly around the room for anything electric, a service outlet she knew wouldn't be there. Still nothing. *One, two three . . .* A whine and two sharp clicks. Something moved overhead. *Seven, eight, nine . . .* Time for Raul. Laurel pushed and counted, her stomach twisted into a painful knot. Stopping again at thirty, she peered into Bastien's unseeing eyes and started over.

Either Bastien had suffered a cardiac arrest or something had malfunctioned in the life-support equipment. She knew there was someone helping them out from the inside, though she didn't know his identity. But their plan hinged on the helper's ability to bypass a high-level program and insert a subroutine to slip in a few lines of code. Perhaps the rogue program had conflicted with other computer instructions. It was a miracle she was alive. She darted a glance to the center of the tank—the limbo of forgotten souls—and to the twin wires separated from the others. Their goal. Laurel shuddered, her mind torn with conflicting emotions. For more than eight years, Eliot Russo had floated under those wires, kept in the perfect form of bondage by a sadist. Eliot Russo, a man she'd never met but had learned to hate the moment she discovered his existence. A man probably insane after his ordeal. Yet, insane or not, he was proof of the system's criminal abuse by the government. Laurel had sworn to expose the corruption in the Federal Bureau of Hibernation, but doing so by springing out the man she knew only as Eliot Russo was the ultimate paradox. Resentment burned her stomach.

There were more whines and clicks as the hydraulic arm moved to raise another sac of sinew and bone from hibernation. What if Raul was dead or unconscious? She might as well dive into the icy fluid and breathe deep—anything but hibernation for life. *Thirty.* Again, she leaned to peer into Bastien's eyes and, grinding her teeth with rage, resumed the cardiac massage with renewed vigor.

The clicks stopped and the fluid rippled before Raul's head surfaced. Underneath, the liquid boiled and lazy wavelets radiated from Raul's torso. His enmeshed arms thrashed at the net, and a hand snaked through to reach for his goggles.

Laurel closed her eyes as a wave of relief washed over her. She paused and drew in a deep breath, looked once more at Raul's writhing shape, then resumed the compressions.

Even before the wires supporting Raul had snapped free, he was already releasing the neck ring and tugging at his ear and nose plugs. When the hydraulic arm removed the mouth plug, Raul rolled on the floor as he tore out of the gelatinous mess, lurching heavily from side to side, then crawled toward her.

"Move," he croaked. "Let's get this mess off him."

Good old Raul; no questions. In the short flight over the tank, he'd pressed through his horror and assessed the problem.

Raul pushed both hands under Bastien's head and jerked the unconscious man to a sitting position to free the net so Laurel could slide it down.

"Take over chest compression. I'll do the mouth-to-mouth," Laurel said.

"How long has he been like this?" Raul started pounding away at a good rhythm.

Laurel had lost count of the maneuvers. "Six or seven minutes." Keeping his airway free, she breathed hard into his mouth. It tasted of hibernation fluid—metallic with a hint of sweetness.

Still no reaction. Laurel blew into his lungs again. The window for successful bridging until defibrillation was ten to eighteen minutes. They were running out of time.

Raul compressed Bastien's chest with vigor, eyes darting around.

"Don't bother. I checked. No defibrillator," Laurel said.

"Bastards!"

"It would be needless overkill. The machines hoist the meat straight up to revival labs above us. Why should they have emergency equipment around the tanks? This is a clean room, sterile. To handle emergency life support outside the tank, you'd need real people with real germs."

"What about maintenance?"

"Automatic. Only a major breakdown would bring anybody here through the personnel corridors and service galleries."

"Which way is the entrance?"

She cocked her head. "Behind me, but you can forget it. Shepherd's notes were clear; it opens from the other side and won't work until Russo surfaces and our contact joins us."

When Raul paused, Laurel lowered her head and tried to breathe life into Bastien's inert body. Raul continued pushing and heaving. Her mind raced. The machine would pluck Eliot Russo from the tank any minute now. Then they would have ten minutes to grab him and run before the alarms went off. They would never make it.

"What went wrong?"

"The program or his heart. Does it matter?"

She scowled at his bleak look, and his eyes lowered, disappearing into shadow.

Bastien's muscled body rippled under Raul's onslaught. She'd read of people reviving after lengthy revival maneuvers, but not under such conditions. Laurel eyed Raul, his face grim, determined, slamming down onto Bastien's chest like a battering ram, *twenty-nine, and thirty*. She leaned over, fastened her lips to Bastien's cold mouth, and blew. Pause. Another breath and Raul resumed his pounding. She ran a hand over Bastien's shaved head, following the ridges of his left temporal bone, cold and slimy.

Throughout her life, Laurel had attached herself only to cherished scenes, hoarding them like amulets against disaster. An image flashed through her mind now: Trees burned in the autumn sunlight, ablaze in a riot of red leaves, and the three of them—Bastien, Raul, and her—lounged on the grass, drinking Sonoma Riesling straight from the bottle. Bastien had a serious expression. "At a monastery, the prior asks a novice to replace an almost exhausted candle in the chapel. The young man forgets. After prayers, the prior sends for the novice and confronts him with a spluttering wick in a pool of molten wax. 'Where's the candle?' he demands, and the young monk replies, 'Yes, it does, doesn't it?'" Raul had shot a confused look at Bastien. Then the penny dropped—"*Wears* the candle?"—and they all roared with laughter. *Thirty.* She leaned over one more time and blew anger into Bastien's lungs. *Breathe, my friend, breathe.* Laurel peered into Bastien's face. His eyes had dulled. She closed his eyelids.

Raul looked up, as though to speak, but his mouth froze. Laurel followed his gaze and saw a shadow shifting overhead.

A whine and clicks. Laurel closed her eyes, grief welling in her chest. Bastien's candle had worn down and guttered into darkness. Now it was time for the man they had come to spring from this hell.

It was time for Russo.

chapter 7

17:59

Mocking the immutable laws of science, time became softer—stretching into a distorted reality, viscous like molasses. Liquid air transformed unconscious breathing into strenuous labor. Lukas stared at the red digits framed high over the control panels: 17:59. They hadn't moved in hours. With glazed eyes, he queried the frozen numerals, his tongue pressed against his teeth. Hard lumps dug into his belly. Under his belt, the envelopes seemed to have lost their padding, and his usually tame bladder screamed for release.

Lukas lowered his gaze to the angry red line blazing on his screen. Once more, the program supplied by Donald Duck had done its job. No alarm had triggered, and it was obvious nothing had shown on the screens of the operators outside his office. As the drama unfolded at tank 913, he'd watched, transfixed—not with anxiety but with detached calm. The man . . . what was his name? Bastien. Lukas had spotted his metabolism flatline as it happened. The man had died of heart failure. To the pair battling to revive their friend's corpse, it was an inexplicable piece of bad luck, but Lukas knew better. Cardiac arrest was a common event when undergoing reanimation. Naturally Hypnos had kept the plethora of side effects hidden. Full return from torpor, unlike partial periodic arousals, needed supervision by expert medical personnel with an awesome array of revival equipment at their disposal. Technical wizardry and human intervention ensured that the casualties remained at a reasonable two percent. But outside a surgical theater and in the dreary conditions of the platform surrounding a tank, Bastien's chances were almost nonexistent. If the plan was thorny to start with, now it was almost impossible: The woman, however well trained, couldn't replace a strong man, and Lukas was no match even for her. But there was no going back now.

Lukas forced his gaze back to the clock. Suddenly the light grew to flood the control center in blinding clarity, sound thundered in his ears, and the slothful numbers dimmed to configure a new reading: 18:00. Then whatever machine had caused the time warp meshed into gear and time raced. In a blink, the clock moved to 18:01.

Holding on to his desk to buttress his shaking legs, Lukas stood to glance at controllers leaving their posts for their short break while the computer entered the backup routine. A haze of fear threatened to void his bowels. Lukas made it to his office door, carefully dried his sweaty fingers on his lab coat, offered his finger to the lock for a full biometric scan, and exited to the corridor.

"Hi." Sandra's voice had a cheerful ring. "I thought the old guy was gonna croak on the spot."

Lukas fought an impulse to check his watch and stopped beside Sandra. A few paces farther on and leaning over the guardrail of a fire exit corridor girdling the tank blocks, Frank, another controller, dragged on a misshapen cigarette.

"New look?" She nodded to his feet. "I've never seen you wear sneakers before. I like it."

"You did a great job with that old guy." He made a face of dire discomfort and nodded to a door opening thirty feet ahead. "You mind? Tacos for lunch. Went right through me."

Sandra nodded in understanding.

He strode toward the salvation of the door, repressing an urge to break into a run.

"Do you want anything? A cup of tea?" Sandra asked.

"Yes, please." Without turning his head, Lukas slammed down the handle and hurtled through the door to the echo of Sandra's laugh.

Past four doors opening right and left, each marked with unisex pictograms, Lukas stopped at the entrance to the service area, flashed his ID card past an open slot, and leaned over for a retinal scan. A red light changed to green and the lock clicked open. When the door snapped closed, Lukas was already one hundred feet away, barreling ahead as terror gripped his gut. *901*. A panel marking the entrance to a hibernation tank flashed by. In seven minutes, the computer would be online and his unauthorized entry logged. Then a chain of events would unfold with clockwork precision—and not in slowed-down time but the real stuff. A signal would flash to maintenance. *902*. The workers on duty would run a trace to confirm the access. That would take thirty seconds. After confirmation, a second signal would flash to security. The officers there would analyze his heat signature and plot his movements from the instant he'd entered the service area. *903*. Lukas had seen it before in tests and exercises—a three-dimensional hologram with a red line snaking along the route followed by whoever had breached security. That would take another thirty seconds. At 18:11, the mother of all alarms would go off and unleash the computer program to seal every door. Tight. *904*.

In the ten years since the hibernation stations had replaced obsolescent prisons, there had never been a breakout. Vlad Kosmerl, the head of security—a weird Slovak with a milky eye—would now have the opportunity of a lifetime to make a name for himself and prove his knowledge of the system by thwarting the breakout. *905*. He would grab it. His first order would be to power cameras and passive security mechanisms: gas, induction fields, high-voltage beams, concussion explosives, epilepsy-inducing lights, and scores of sophisticated toys designed to stun, maim, or kill. *906*. Then he would fire the alarms and arm the hair triggers of hundreds of heat and motion sensors. Moving—even breathing—would be suicidal. Once the alarm tripped, only the inmates immersed in their cold fluid would be safe.

907. Lukas pumped his legs with more energy, vaguely aware of his dismal style, knees rising almost to his chest, arms moving like pistons, and huffing to rival Emil Zátopek, the long-distance runner they'd dubbed "the Czech Locomotive" over a century before. Although he'd tried to get in shape for his race through the corridors, training mornings and evenings for the past two months, Lukas was rapidly reaching the end of his endurance. *908*. His ribs ached, and the staccato of his heartbeats fused into a continuous roar.

His lab coat ripped when one of his pockets caught on the edge of a water fountain outside the access to tank 909. He tore it open and shrugged his arms free without breaking stride. He careened around a bend in the corridor, smashing his shoulder into the wall. The tearing pain released fresh supplies of adrenaline into his bloodstream, and Lukas sprinted ahead. He glanced at the numbers overhead. *910.* Another three hundred feet to go.

When a man turned fifty, most of the decisive events of his life were behind him. It was often too late to start over. For most people, life was just a new comedy with old and tired actors. Only a few got a second chance, and Lukas Hurley wanted to be one. His legs pumped harder.

When he reached the access to tank 913, Lukas couldn't focus his eyes. His breath came in ragged gasps, his lungs screaming for air like the first time he'd visited Cuzco in Peru, at more than 11,000-feet elevation. Lukas fumbled his card in the lock's slot but missed. Through blurry eyes, he peered at his shaking hand. He was falling apart. After two more tries, the card slid into the slot and the door snapped open. Five minutes left.

Raul and Laurel jerked in unison when a loud snap sounded at their backs. Laurel swiveled her head and froze. *I know this guy!* She stared at the man slowly bending in two at the far end of the platform, his back against the closed door. Slight and with thinning red hair, he looked like . . . *Where have I seen this guy before?* The man seemed on the verge of collapse, hands cupped over his knees and heaving, his ragged breath whooshing like punctured bellows.

"Into the tank," he wheezed.

Raul leaned sideways with measured movements and lifted the leg straddling Bastien's body. When he could plant his feet on the floor, he rose to face the man. "What?"

Laurel turned her head to follow a shape moving behind Raul. The hydraulic arm maneuvered the jellylike net with Eliot Russo inside.

"We must get into the tank," the man groaned. He neared with an unsteady gait, a hand digging into his left side. In his mid-fifties, with a large nose and sad bloodhound eyes, he—

"What's your name?" Laurel asked.

The man panted, reached with his other hand to massage his shoulder, and winced. "Lukas."

She frowned in disbelief. *Woody Allen!* With tan slacks, sneakers, and a white shirt, Lukas resembled the bygone genius, without eyeglasses. But Lukas probably wore implants.

You will have minutes to recover. Then help one another out of the mesh. Check for damage. Russo will rise last. Leave his net intact; it will give him a measure of protection during transport. Your contact inside the station will join you. You don't need to know any more about him. Follow his instructions. He will guide you through the station's secure spur to the sewers. Once in the sewers, follow your plan.

"Look, mister—" But Raul stopped mid-sentence when Lukas darted a glance over his head. Propping a hand on the wall for support, Lukas fished a black matte card from his back pocket and inserted it in an almost undetectable slot a few feet away from where they stood.

His tone changed. "Get Russo over here. Don't remove his protective net."

Laurel turned on her heel and stepped toward the descending bundle, careful to avoid the fluid spills. The machine lowered Russo's cocoon with its characteristic harshness and removed the flexible life-support tube. The bundle stirred. As she squatted and reached to remove Russo's goggles, Lukas yelled, "Don't!" in a curious high-pitched tone. "Drag him over here."

She waited for Raul. On a silent prompt, they gripped Russo's neck ring and dragged an emaciated, squirming body with surprising ease over the film of fluid oiling the textured floor. Laurel flinched after checking the wasted figure inside the net. *He's all skin and bones!*

"Three and a half minutes," Lukas announced. His voice had recovered a little color. His hands moved inside a niche that had appeared on a seemingly featureless wall. He paused, reached inside his belt, and yanked hard. Then he dropped three padded envelopes on the floor and returned to whatever he was doing inside the niche.

"One contains stabilizing pads. Stick one on your lower back. In another envelope, there are two ultrasonic syrettes. Push the one with the red cap into Russo's neck. In the last, there are LAD lamps. Recover your discarded goggles and clip the lamps to the strip forming the nose bridge, then slip them over to dangle from your neck."

It sounded as if Lukas was reading a manual. He must have memorized the precise words of the plan. Laurel stole a glance past Lukas's hands. A screen. He must be keying instructions into a computer.

You will have a ten-minute window to leave the station. That's how long it takes for the main computer to back up. The machinery and maintenance runs on a separate computer.

Whatever Lukas was doing had to do with equipment.

Raul recovered the crumpled envelopes and tore one open, tipping two thin cylinders like pencil stubs onto the floor. He picked up the one with a red cap and handed it to Laurel.

"What's this?" she asked.

"A muscle relaxant and a sedative. He could die if he reaches full arousal in his present state."

"Like our friend?"

Lukas slammed at something inside the recess and a panel slid down, the hollow disappearing. "Yes, like your—Bastien. A common accident."

Laurel put the syrette by her feet and had finished peeling the protective cover from a skin pad the size of a playing card when she froze. "Common? How common?"

"Common enough. About one in fifty of the regular inmates and most of the—illegals."

A powerful whine fired and the floor trembled.

"Into the tank. We're running out of time."

Something moved. Laurel swiveled toward the tank. Its surface rippled and the level dropped. She'd always been comfortable with her body, but she suddenly felt vulnerable being naked before a stranger. She handed another pad to Raul, slapped hers at kidney height, and turned her butt toward

Lukas. After a short delay, she felt a cold hand patting over the pad to ensure good skin contact.

Laurel eyed Lukas as he turned to Raul and continued with the patting routine, then he leaned over Bastien to reach for his discarded goggles. Laurel pushed the syrette into Russo's neck and flicked the release lever. The tube emptied with a hiss and the bundle stopped squirming.

"What's the other syrette for?"

"A stronger dose of the same mix, in case he starts convulsing."

Raul neared, grabbed Russo's neck ring, and dragged him over to the tank's edge.

The tank looked like a collage of Hieronymus Bosch's paintings composed by de Sade. The level in the nine-foot-deep tank was dropping fast. A sea of upturned faces with dark goggles and fluid up to their necks stared toward the ceiling like monstrous insect pupae dangling from green hoses. In the center of the fluid expanse, a dimple formed, sucked down by what must be a powerful eddy.

Her eyes fixed on the revolving expanse of fluid, Laurel understood, and her spirits sank even lower. It all made sense now. The drainpipes must link with the spur line for flushing the tanks during periodic maintenance. *We're going down the drain!*

Raul padded over with the other goggles, already clipping on a hazelnut-size LAD lamp: a new generation of light amplifying diodes.

Lukas glanced at his watch. "Two minutes." He darted a glance around and jumped on the nearest inmate suspended in liquid up to his chest. He gripped onto the jelly net as his face contorted into a mask of shock. His jaw started chattering at once.

"Ju-ump!"

"What about him?" Raul nodded to Bastien.

Lukas's eyes widened. "He's dead."

"Can he be resuscitated?"

"He's dead!" Lukas insisted.

Raul's voice sharpened. "Watch my lips, mister. Can your people revive him?"

Silence.

Laurel could read Raul's expression, and she felt her stomach contract involuntarily.

"I don't—know. Maybe. But he would be a vegetable. He's been down too long."

Raul wedged the spare syrette between his teeth, turned on his heel, and squatted by Bastien. Slowly, he ran a hand over the dome of Bastien's head, like a mother caressing her newborn. Then, face set and his profile cast in stone, Raul gripped Bastien's head and jerked his hands. The report of bones snapping echoed over the whine of motors.

Laurel's shoulders sagged. Honor was an aesthetic idea for some. Not for Raul. They had been like brothers. Through a haze of tears, she saw Raul's shadow near and felt the tips of his fingers brush her cheek. Then she heard a sharp intake of air and, instants later, a splash when Raul jumped into the tank.

"Pass—Russo—over." Lukas's voice sounded muffled.

Laurel followed the sound. A quivering Lukas, wisps of red hair plastered to his forehead, reached to remove the syrette from Raul's mouth. He was pale. She squatted, threaded the fingers of one hand through the slippery mesh, and hauled Russo's neck ring with the other.

Raul swung, one hand gripping the net of a young man— almost a child—then caught the cords cocooning Russo and pulled.

It all happened too fast. As Laurel squatted by Russo, her hand gripping the jelly cords, a powerful force dragged her forward. She lost her footing and plunged headlong into the tank, still holding on to Russo.

The shock astounded her. A forest of needles skewered her skin with icy cold. A hot pincer seared her neck and jerked her head upright. She screamed. Laurel thrashed in the liquid ice until she felt something solid beneath her feet. She planted her soles and bolted straight, one hand flying over her face to remove the viscous liquid slithering over it, while the other reached blindly for the nearest jelly mesh. She started to shake.

"Just a few seconds. It will wear off in a few seconds." Lukas's voice droned somewhere to her left.

Unable to keep her chattering jaw steady, she rubbed stinging eyes with her free hand. The fluid was level with her midriff. In the center of the tank, the liquid turned lazily around a wide depression. Around her, scores of nets held inmates, their skin pruned like alien larvae, some thin, their ribs protruding like so many grates, others padded with flabby skin like shar-pei dogs. The wretches jerked an arm or a leg here and there; necks twitched, their mouths stretched as they suckled the tits of a machine. Laurel's stomach heaved, but she had nothing to throw up.

Raul and Lukas stood on the bottom of the tank, each holding on to one of the dangling inmates to offset the powerful pull of the rapidly draining fluid. Lukas kept Russo's head above the liquid with a grip to his neck ring, and Laurel suddenly realized the burning sensation on her own neck came from Raul's other hand.

The lights dimmed an instant, as if an automatic relay had rearmed after a power surge.

"The alarm," Lukas announced.

"Now what?" Raul asked. He removed his hand from Laurel's neck and grabbed Russo's ring.

"Too much fluid yet. When the level drops down to six inches, we can go."

Laurel lowered her head. The fluid was level with her knees. Raul had not asked Lukas how they would reach the sewers. He must have figured it out, like she had.

"How long?" Raul demanded.

"Thirty seconds, tops."

The conflicting sensations were almost unbearable. Her body burned, but her legs and feet seemed encased in a block of ice.

"Feetfirst." Lukas nodded to a manhole-size opening in the center of the tank. "It's a tall drop, twenty feet vertical to a smooth bend, then fifty or sixty feet horizontal until we hit the secure spur line."

"It'll tear our skin off!" Laurel complained.

"No, it won't. These conduits are smooth-walled, designed for special cleaning machines and kept spotless, without incrustations or excrescences. The secure spur line uses a more aggressive cleaning procedure because it handles solids. These conduits," he nodded to the drain on the floor, "are for fluids only."

"Where's the secure spur line?"

"Underneath us. It runs parallel to the city sewers, but it's independent, clean, and secure. Computers control all exits."

Laurel didn't ask how they would reach the city sewers if all exits were secure. *Your contact knows how to get you out. Follow his instructions.*

From all four corners of the tank, strobe lights started to flash a slow cadence.

"They've armed the stunners," Lukas said. "In thirty seconds, the condensers powering these lights will be on full charge. There are heat sensors overhead, and we're warmer than anything else. As soon as we're detected, these lamps will fire a sequence that will trigger epileptic fits. But don't worry."

"Why not?" Laurel asked.

Lukas checked his watch. "The bottom valve will close in twenty seconds. I'll go first." He pointed at Russo's neck ring. When Raul had a grip on it, Lukas splashed toward the hole like an ungainly duck and jumped.

"You next," Raul said.

Laurel was about to protest when Raul interrupted. "I need you down there to arrest Russo's drop. He'll fall like a sack."

He was right. She gripped his arm and, refusing to think about what she was about to do, covered the distance to the hole in long strides and jumped feetfirst into the drain.

When darkness swallowed her, Laurel braced for the impact, but it never came. She dropped for a long time, her mind feebly registering that Lukas must have lied. The chute must be hundreds of feet long, even thousands. Then something hard and slimy touched her shoulders and butt, pressing harder and harder until she had to release the breath she'd carefully held. Her legs and arms shot up the walls of a smooth cylinder, its surface racing under her touch. She surrendered to gravity and momentum, choking a gasp when sharp pain radiated from her left buttock. Then a pinprick of light below her pierced the gloom. The light grew, with it she saw a rapidly approaching circle and, beyond, a figure with a striking likeness to Woody Allen. She almost laughed, but in the next instant she cannoned out of the tube, slammed down a couple of feet into a much larger cylinder, and climbed halfway up its wall before crumpling down into a heap in four inches of liquid flowing along the curved floor.

"Who's next?" Lukas sounded impressed.

"Russo."

"We had better try to grab him as he exits. He'll be much faster. Switch on your flashlight and aim it inside the drain."

She picked herself up and stumbled to the mouth of the tube, fingers fumbling at her flashlight.

Lukas aimed his light into the drain, illuminating a ball form hurtling rapidly toward them. "Here he comes."

They stood on either side of the opening, one hand each stretched to catch him.

In a flash, the bundle barreled from the drain, dragging them to the opposite side of the sewer. A loud thump echoed from the mouth of the drain. Laurel froze. It wasn't a good sound.

"That's the valve closing," Lukas said. "Within four or five minutes, the tank will be full again. An automatic security routine to prevent the inmates' core temperature from rising."

Had Raul made it? She had no way of knowing. The seconds stretched. What could she do with Woody in the sewers? Despite Russo's slight weight, neither she nor Lukas was strong enough to carry him any distance. *Do we leave him?*

An instant later, Raul followed, his light blazing around his neck. He slid sedately the last few feet to the point where the drain met the main sewer and stayed seated on its rim, surveying their tangle of arms and legs. "A hell of a ride."

Laurel reached to her left buttock, then checked her bloody fingers.

Lukas trained his flashlight on her and she instinctively shrank back. "Let me have a look," he said.

She felt soft fingers, then pressure, then a sharp stab. "Ouch!"

Lukas held something small between thumb and forefinger. "A toenail. They drop off the inmates." He flicked it aside, stood, and checked his watch. "We have twenty-nine minutes to leave this tube and a mile and a half to cover. We'd better get going, fast."

Laurel darted a look to Raul.

Although they didn't know how they would get to the sewers, Shepherd had insisted it was "need to know" information; they had rehearsed a technique to carry Russo several miles through the sewer network. First they'd trained in a dark abandoned warehouse and later across open ground at night, always naked and barefoot. "You will need well-calloused soles," Shepherd had said. Raul and Bastien had carried a net between them with one hundred pounds of rocks for up to three hours. Laurel marched point with a flashlight. Shepherd would follow with another light. They had repeated the exercise daily for two months, combining their night races with hard exercise during the day. The key to their results rested on the men's similar height and arm reach, added to their excellent physical conditioning and strength. She couldn't pair with Raul; her shorter frame meant he would carry most of the weight and hamper their mobility. Lukas would be even worse.

As if reading her mind, Raul stood, loosened his muscles, leaned over Russo, and, with a quick movement like hefting a sack of potatoes, pulled the inert form up over his shoulder.

Laurel stood. "You can't do that."

"Wanna bet?"

Raul and his trick bets, always on the weirdest of subjects. Years before, their campus had suffered an invasion of locusts.

How fast you reckon a locust can fly?

I don't know. Ten miles an hour?

Some can do sixty and more.

You're out of your mind.

Wanna bet?

Raul had grabbed a few of the insects, dropped them inside a paper bag, affixed the bag under the windshield wiper of his car, and raced around the campus.

He won the bet, but it cost him a speeding ticket. *Win some, lose some,* he'd said.

"What would you bet?" Laurel thought Raul's humor could be unnerving at times, as she began jogging down the secure sewer, her flashlight beam slashing the darkness ahead.

"I bet our lives," he said. "Yours, mine, and Woody's over there."

chapter 8

||||

18:14

From the vantage point of the platform that held the presidential table, Odelle Marino's eyes followed a pencil-size cylinder in a depression on the ceiling—an ultradirectional microphone, now scanning the crowd, its circuits overridden by the swell of applause after her introduction by Vinson Duran, the president of Hypnos. The banquet was over, tables cleared, but the army of guests wouldn't feel sated without her words. After a calculated pause, she pushed her chair back, gathered her notes, and stood.

"Thank you, Vinson." The microphone swung in her direction and locked. "As director of the Department of Homeland Security, I'm honored to join you in celebrating the tenth anniversary of Hypnos's inauguration of their first hibernation station." Odelle's gaze swept the crowd, a sea of known faces from all levels of power: the few who had it and the others who wanted it. "Today we celebrate a success story—our country's decision to abandon an obsolete correctional system for a new, more humane arrangement.

"As you will remember, the world was up in arms against our choice. Our country and its leaders suffered an unprecedented tide of criticism from both the foreign press and our own."

Odelle paused and reached for a cut crystal tumbler of water with a sliver of lime floating in it. She wet her lips, then locked eyes for the briefest of moments with Louis Hamilton from *The Washington Post*. The bastard had used the paper as his personal soapbox and harangued the do-gooder rabble into opposing the hibernation bill. Thanks to him, it had been touch and go.

"In the year 2049, we approved a bill to close down the prisons and incarcerate those already serving time and all newly convicted criminals not in cages, where they were treated—and learned to behave—like animals, but in hibernation. Truly a more humane solution.

"In that same year, Chairman Xu Wa closed China's borders and launched the Second Communist People's Republic. I hope you agree with me that Ms. Wa has made Chairman Mao seem like a moderate."

She waited until the chuckles ebbed and then gifted Louis Hamilton with another piercing glance. *So you know I've not forgotten, mister.*

"Yet instead of demonizing China's butchery and their new forced-labor rice fields, the press had a field day with us. Foreign nations recalled their ambassadors, while agitators, fueled by the filth pouring from the world's media," she darted one more quick glance at Louis Hamilton, "attacked our embassies and demanded we return to a traditional prison system—a system that never worked; a system that couldn't work because it was built on hypocrisy."

The audience interrupted with thunderous applause. Odelle lowered her reading glasses and smiled. She was giving them their pound of flesh.

"Thank you. Can I bore you with a little history?" She scanned the room, alive with nodding heads, like those bobble-headed plastic dogs a few old-fashioned cretins still carried on the rear shelf of their automobiles. "The goals of the penal institution have changed through the ages, from retribution and vengeance—the biblical eye for an eye, tooth for a tooth—to deterrence, making the inmates an example to themselves and others. Other issues, such as reform and correction, arrived much later—their goals being to repair the prisoners' character shortages and return them as productive members of society. Yet all of these approaches, however well intentioned, proved ineffective in the end. Vengeance couldn't work, as there was no real way to adapt the punishment to the offense. The example idea floundered, for how can a citizen serve as an example when he can just remove to a distant location and start a criminal career anew? Reform didn't work either. Our prisons became true universities of crime, where seasoned felons had their own fiefdoms and petty criminals graduated, often with honors."

Again, she reached for her glass. Not only was delivering a tirade cloaked as a speech thirsty work, but the audience needed time to register half-forgotten facts.

"As I said before, the old prison setup was built on hypocrisy: not just from the government but from its citizens. We wanted an effective penal system to remove those individuals unable to conform to the laws of society and to do so in a way that would deter others, but we were too entrenched in a quagmire of moral half-truths to get the job done properly. Those with money or good lawyers could hamstring the system with countless appeals and other such tricks until we were left with a system containing obscenely revolving doors.

"We were at a crossroads and chose to safeguard our fellow citizens from repeat offenders by locking them up for extended periods, often for life. This idea almost brought our nation to its knees. Long-term prison sentences and other obsolescent methods of warehousing criminals became so expensive that they threatened to bankrupt our nation."

Odelle removed her glasses and rested them on the table with her now-useless notes: She knew the rest of her speech by heart.

"Our government was desperate. Twelve years ago, with a prison population of more than six million and the national debt skyrocketing, the only solution was to reduce prison sentences, to put hardened criminals back on the streets. Criminals who, statistics showed, would only kill, murder, steal, or rape again.

"Then Hypnos proposed a groundbreaking new approach

to prisons, Congress approved it, and we built the first hibernation station and tested it over two years. The rest is history." She held a hand over her head, her thumb outstretched, like Caesar granting life to a fallen gladiator, and hiked her voice a semitone. "We have reduced the prison network's costs to ten percent of 2050 levels." Her index finger joined her thumb. "We have shrunk criminal offenses by seventy-five percent." Another finger. "We have doubled the time felons are removed from our society." A fourth finger joined the other three. "In ten years we've had no breakouts, no mutinies, and no disturbances, with a fraction of the workforce the old setup needed." Finally, she offered her hand, all fingers splayed to the audience, but her words were for Hamilton. *Soon I'll get my pound of your flesh.* "Eventually the media had to eat humble pie, when the foreign governments recanted. In only ten years, eighty-six nations—the same that tore at their vestments and recalled their diplomats when we passed the change—have adopted the Hypnos system of humane hibernation."

Close to five hundred guests at the convention hall stood to drown her last words in a thunderous ovation.

Odelle darted a glance toward the central exit door, where George Wilson, her personal assistant, had appeared next to Genia Warren, the inept bitch overseeing the Federal Bureau of Hibernation. George removed his shades and stared. Odelle nodded.

When the applause dwindled and feet started to shuffle, she looked toward the microphone.

"Thank you, my friends, but I don't deserve your applause; the man who made this miracle possible does." Odelle turned to Vinson Duran and clapped her hands.

Those who had returned to their seats sprang upright again to applaud.

She reached for Vinson's arm and dug her nails into his biceps to draw his attention. "Got to go. Back as soon as I can."

Careful to keep a blinding smile pasted to her face, Odelle strode past tables full of well-heeled men in tuxedos and high-maintenance women toward the doors where George stood, deadpan.

"What's the matter?"

George leaned over and whispered in her ear. She listened, clenching her hands until her long nails bit into her palms. Then her fingers relaxed as a powerful eddy swirled in the pit of her stomach. Odelle closed her eyes when George finished his report. The fourth point in her closing gimmick wasn't true anymore, and that small distinction could mean her promotion for life to a posting four inches below the surface of a tank.

She blinked and locked eyes with Genia. The FBH director could have set the manhunt in motion, sealed the city, and deployed the muscle; it fell within her authority. Instead, she had deferred any decision to Odelle. *Too hot for you to handle, dear? Are you learning, at last, who is in charge?* Odelle turned to face George.

"Call Nikola Masek."

chapter 9

||||

18:21

After the first tentative strides, it became obvious that running barefoot along the smooth tunnel would be much more difficult than Shepherd had expected. In the painstaking analysis of every step of the plan, several issues had remained unresolved—one of them their ability to run naked and barefoot through a stainless steel tube. Every proposal—galoshes, flip-flops, or even socks—had crashed against Lukas's capacity to carry them past scanning X-ray machines and into the hibernation station. Lukas had stolen the pads and syrettes with minimal risk from a low-security store on the same day of the breakout, but there was nothing remotely suitable to improve the grip of their "well-calloused soles."

They halted, and Lukas had to give up his canvas trousers and shirt. With teeth and powerful tugs, they tore the garments into strips. Laurel and Raul—sitting against the curved wall and keeping the cocooned Russo between them—wrapped their feet as best they could.

Laurel ran a hand over the surface of the six-foot stainless steel tube, polished to a faint brushed finish. A few inches to her right, Laurel spotted a seam, welded flush and brushed with the same pattern of tiny scratches as the rest of the tube. She couldn't put her finger on it, but there was something odd in the homogeneous finish. Laurel leaned over the inert shape of Russo, pressed her fingers into his neck, and held her breath. "Still there. Let's go."

Raul once more hefted the jelly net with Russo inside.

Laurel stepped forward, plodding awkwardly until she got the hang of the wraps. Then she lengthened her stride. Behind her, his head hunched over, Raul sounded like a charging elephant. Laurel marched point for a while, her tiny flashlight casting a ring of light around the tube, the void before her dark as a pocket. *If there's an obstacle or a valve in our path, there will be no time to avoid it. I'll run straight into it.* Then she spotted a dark shape overhead.

"Utility holes?" She stopped underneath the four-foot opening of a vertical shaft, one side bristling with the rungs of a ladder.

Raul drew near and straightened, obviously enjoying the respite allowed by the extra headroom. "Looks like it," he said.

"How far apart?" Laurel asked.

Lukas joined them and ran a finger on the edge of the vertical tube. "The sewer authorities class this spur as a secure mainline. There's an exit like this every four hundred yards." A pause. "These are the only means of access to this section."

"How many more to go?"

"Five."

Laurel trained her flashlight into the thick darkness ahead and started jogging. Her feet weighed a ton. The oily fluid at the bottom of the tube had soaked the rags, and her legs were beginning to ache. They traveled through a barrage of sounds—wet thuds mixing with labored huffs and the weird squelching noise of Lukas's shoes. The air was cool and had a slight tang of cold cream.

"What makes the fluid oily?" Laurel shouted over her shoulder without breaking stride as she cleared another utility hole.

"An emulsion of lanolin and nutrients," Lukas replied.

"How long is this tube?"

"Three miles," Lukas's voice echoed from the rear. "It runs parallel to the city sewer up to a treatment plant, where they remove lanolin and other fatty substances before it empties into the city network."

Laurel's thighs were on fire, and each stride strained her muscles painfully. She couldn't take this pounding much longer. Behind her, Raul huffed in rhythm with his feet. Then another noise, finer and stringy, joined the thuds.

"Stop!" Lukas yelled.

The splashing stopped, but the strange noise increased.

"Run! Pig!"

Pig? You bastard!

Lukas overtook them from the rear along the left-hand side, climbing halfway up the tube and sprinting ahead. Even in underpants and fancy sneakers, the bastard could run.

"Pig!" he yelled.

Laurel ground her teeth and barreled forward in pursuit.

Fifty yards ahead, Lukas's light stopped. He jumped upward and his feet thrashed in midair to disappear through the lip of the utility hole and into the vertical shaft.

"Hurry," Raul grunted, just behind her. "Climb up and I'll pass Russo to you."

When they were underneath the access hole, Laurel sprang to grab a rung with both hands. She was about to swing a leg up to get some purchase on the tube wall when a large hand smashed into her buttocks and propelled her upward.

"Grab his collar, damn it!"

The strange grinding noise filled the air like a rain of nails. In a daze, Laurel threaded her arm through an upper rung and lowered her other hand to grip Russo's neck ring. Suddenly an overpowering weight jerked Laurel's arm downward, and she was holding on to the full weight of Russo with one hand. She gritted her teeth as the ring started to slip from her fingers. Raul darted past her and over, squeezing her against the rungs. Laurel's arm trembled under the unbearable slipping weight, and then the load disappeared in a flash when Raul hoisted Russo into the crowded tube. The sound reached a crescendo as it grew into a scratching shriek. The tube vibrated. A screech like millions of fingernails on a blackboard exploded in a flurry of sparkles as something thundered by beneath their feet.

They huddled together, their combined lamps highlighting patches of reddened flesh intertwined with the green net and a large running shoe capped by a skinny ankle.

"What the fuck was that?" Laurel croaked.

"A pig." Lukas's voice had thinned. "That's what the pipeline people call them: a self-powered robot used to keep the tunnel free of excrescences. We can get down now. It's gone."

"Gone?"

"For now." Lukas's voice dropped.

After a few seconds of squirming, sliding past one another, and lugging the cocoon containing Russo, they descended from their hiding place. The scratching noise had faded in the distance, almost a memory.

Laurel blinked and panned her light over the tunnel's curved walls; they shone with a myriad of sparkles. She reached a hand to the wall. The surface had a slight bite, like a dull nail file. If a similar machine had cleaned the tank's drains, the rough surface would have skinned them alive. She glanced at the rags on her feet, already threadbare. Nobody had brushed the welds; the machine did. The void in her stomach deepened. To form the tiny furrows in the hard steel, the brushes must be powered with awesome force. The machine would have turned them to mincemeat in a heartbeat.

"Hurry up!" Lukas looked paler than ever.

Laurel was already running, her painful legs forgotten. The thumping and splashing resumed behind her.

"Whoever sent the pig down knows how far out we could

have traveled. Once they're sure we couldn't have gone any farther, they'll put the pig in reverse."

"Great," Raul grunted.

After leaving two more access holes behind, Laurel's legs lightened. Four hundred yards to go.

"Do we climb the next utility shaft?" She couldn't wait to get out of the damn tube.

"You've got to be kidding," Lukas said. "These shafts are capped by covers. You can see them at intervals in the aisle between the lanes, when driving on the ring road around the cube. The covers are high security and computer-controlled. By now there will be hundreds of DHS Special Forces out there. In fewer than ten minutes, operators will overrule the computer program, the hatches will pop open, and the heat will pour down."

"Cut the crap," Raul growled. "How do we get out?"

"Through a side door."

"I thought you said the utility holes were the only means of access." Laurel strained her ears. It could be tinnitus or her imagination, but she could have sworn the tunnel was filling with the grating sound again.

"I did."

They reached the final access hole and the sound increased. It wasn't in her mind; it was coming toward them.

"Run!"

"Where to?" she screamed. "It's coming at us!"

"Ahead!"

"Ahead? Where? We'll never make the next one!"

Twenty yards farther down the tube, a powerful yellowish light flared through a square opening.

The grinding sound filled the tube. Blindly, the rags propelling her legs at odd angles, Laurel reached the opening and dove in.

In quick succession, like late commuters piling into a speeding bus, Raul, with Russo over his shoulder, and Lukas flew after her, landing in a mushy quagmire. The roar grew, expanded by the void of a huge concrete tunnel.

Laurel opened her eyes in time to see a blur of sparks flash by the entrance, and her nose filled with a waft of rabid stench.

"Shit!"

A rueful chuckle issued from the entrance, half drowned by the receding sound of the brushing machine. "Precisely."

Laurel turned toward the voice. At either side of the opening, an old man in yellow oil clothes and tall waders hefted a curved section of steel into place. A third man fired a high-powered gas lance to weld it back.

Before sliding black goggles over his eyes, the welder gave her a quick once-over.

"Nice color."

chapter 10

||||

18:33

Senator Jerome Palmer darted a quick glance over his reading glasses toward the door of his study. He remembered leaving it ajar a while ago when he went to the kitchen for a drink, but now the gap was widening by inches. Hiking his glasses up the bridge of his nose, Palmer turned a page of the thick, legal-bound document he had been reading and lowered his head, keeping tabs on the door out of the corner of his eye.

When the gap was a foot wide, the prowler scurried in, wielding a large revolver. He flattened his back to the far corner of the bookcases lining the room and closed in, moving with measured steps.

Palmer waited until the intruder was almost upon him before letting go of the document and raising both hands above his head.

"I surrender."

Choking with delighted giggles, his grandson, Timmy, returned his plastic .45 to a holster that almost reached the floor and rushed to wrap tiny arms around Palmer's legs.

"Yup, you got me this time, Timmy. I didn't have a chance. You're getting good." Palmer ruffled the child's hair. "What are you today?"

"The law." Timmy pointed to a shiny plastic star clipped to his T-shirt.

"I see. But only yesterday you were a Comanche warrior."

"Yesterday was Sunday."

Palmer frowned. "And?"

"Men don't come see you on Sunday."

"Go on." Palmer stood. "Tell me about it."

"It's a secret."

"You can trust me. I won't tell a soul."

"When you talk with men, I keep you covered."

"In case someone pulls a gun on me?"

Timmy nodded.

"Well, I'm relieved; I feel much safer now."

"I saw the man with the uniform open his case. But it had no gun inside, or I would have shot him."

Palmer smiled. General Weston would have been mighty upset had he known a gun was trained on him. He ruffled Timmy's hair again and froze.

"Say, how could you see what was inside his case?"

"My rifle has a tube that makes things bigger."

Palmer turned his head and looked over the back of his seat and out the sliding doors to the lawn outside. "And where were you?"

"In my house."

At the far end of the garden, a clump of large trees offered a degree of privacy to the property that was valuable here in Georgetown. Palmer narrowed his eyes, but he couldn't see a thing. Then he recalled his son building a tree house a few months before.

On his desk, a red light on the phone started flashing.

"I have a very important call now, but when I finish, will you show me your house?"

Timmy nodded.

Lifting the boy, Palmer kissed his forehead. Then he lowered him onto the carpet and patted his butt. "Off you go; inspect the grounds and make sure there are no bandits about, Sheriff."

"Right, partner." The sheriff tried a salute and bolted.

"Palmer."

Silence, followed by what sounded like a burst of static. He knew the sizzling noise wasn't static but a two-way stream of encoding data to synchronize the scrambler in his secure phone with the caller's. After a few seconds, the screen on the terminal flashed *HORUS*.

"A partial success so far."

Palmer was familiar with the unrecognizable voice, without accent or syllabic stresses: a voice digitized, expropriated of everything but meaning, and recomposed by a speech synthesizer.

"You can't have partial success. Success or failure?"

"A little of each. A member of your team, the black man, didn't make it."

Palmer drew a hand to his forehead and sidestepped to flop down into his chair. *Bastien, the lawyer who would change the world. The dear boy . . .* He blinked, his eyes suddenly blurred. Horus's time was precious. "What happened?"

"Heart failure."

"And the others?"

"Too early to say, but they will have to move fast. Seth has sent for Onuris."

Another burst of static, and then the screen went blank.

Palmer replaced the telephone in its cradle, his heart heavy. He pinched the bridge of his nose as images of what Laurel and Raul must be going through—having to deal with the tragic loss of their friend as they carted an inert Russo through dark, putrid pipes—flashed through his mind. Their chances had thinned almost to nothing.

Russo had burned to death in 2051, one late October Friday after the car he drove hit a tree and caught flames on a country road, somewhere between Culpeper and Charlottesville—at least according to the death certificate issued by a Dr. James Child after perusing the results of DNA tests. Russo's charred remains had prevented any other sort of identification.

Five years would pass before a costly misunderstanding revealed that Dr. Child had been duped, or forced to lie.

From the hibernation system's inception, the congressional grapevine had been rife with hushed rumors—often preposterous—of irregularities in the DHS operation of the hibernation facilities. One particular piece of gossip kept cropping up at regular intervals: the existence of illegal prisoners—men and women who had never been sentenced by the courts. The concept intrigued Palmer, and one day he decided to indulge in a little investigation.

Each hibernation facility was organized into a series of tanks, each holding a number of inmates. The distribution and identity of the prisoners was housed in a secure database shared by Hypnos and the DHS and was available to the Senate committee overseeing the hibernation system. It occurred to Palmer there would be a relatively simple—though probably expensive—way to ascertain if the inmates in any given tank matched the records. Each prisoner's DNA markers were stored in the database, and the hibernation fluid was a chemical soup laced with biologic wastes. A sample of fluid from a given tank could be cross-matched with those supposed to be there. Unidentified genetic material would stand out. His mind made up, Palmer set out to obtain hibernation fluid. When Nadia Shubin, a mousy-looking laboratory technician at the Washington, D.C., hibernation facility, demanded five million for the samples, Palmer had almost fainted. But no amount of bargaining could convince Mrs. Shubin to lower her fees. Six months later, almost to the date, the wily technician delivered.

Palmer had expected a handful of jars, never a van loaded with three large polymer cases—each holding one hundred carefully labeled test tubes: one from every tank at the Washington, D.C., facility.

To cross-match every tube would have cost a fortune, and Palmer wouldn't think of it. Instead, he used a statistical-probability program to choose a reasonable sample. Forty tanks. Only one test tube from the original sampling yielded an unknown signature. It belonged to a man whose DNA wasn't registered in any American database. After the find, Palmer couldn't stop. He made the owners of a small Mexican testing lab very happy when he ordered tests on the remaining tubes, only to find another eight abnormalities. Seven tubes produced eleven unknown markers. The eighth contained the DNA of a man who had haunted Palmer's dreams since his youth, a man who had been dead five years: Eliot Russo.

Mercenaries, even good ones, could be had for a fraction of what he'd already spent on tests. But, in the feverish months that followed his discovery, Palmer discarded adventurers. Instead, he reached for two people for whom Russo held a meaning that transcended money or ideals: Laurel and Shepherd.

When their plan started to take shape, Shepherd had insisted on three men of similar build to attempt springing Russo, and he drew up a list of candidates. But Laurel had her own ideas. She drafted Raul and Bastien and announced she would complete the team.

Naturally, Shepherd went ballistic and threatened to quit. Over the secure phone, Palmer pleaded and tried every trick he knew to change Laurel's mind. Later—when Russo returned to the land of the living—she would be irreplaceable, but the breakout needed muscle. Still, Laurel wouldn't budge. She proved obstinate as a mule, and Palmer, after soberly reviewing her ancestry, surrendered.

A staccato of taps, like a bird pecking seeds from a dish, brought Palmer out of his reverie. He looked toward the sliding patio door where Timmy waited, his eyes expectant.

In a daze, he followed his trotting grandson across the lawn and into the clump of old oaks.

"We're almost there, Grandpa."

Palmer bowed his head to avoid a large branch. *Onuris.*

Timmy climbed a stout wooden ladder with commendable speed for his short legs, and Palmer followed, maneuvering his bulk with difficulty to a fenced platform, perhaps ten feet from the ground, one of its corners occupied by a square construction with a small door and a window.

"I don't think I'll fit through there."

"You can try on your knees."

Palmer obliged and crawled inside the small house, leaving his rump sticking outside the door. On a miniature table, he spotted several jars with water—one of them murky and with something alive inside—bottle corks, a pot full of glass marbles, and a forbidden item: a box of matches.

"Timmy, you shouldn't play with matches. They're dangerous. Please, give them to me."

The boy, far from looking chastised, smiled and handed him the box.

This time Palmer didn't fall for Timmy's mischief. Suspicious, he drew the box close to his ear and shook it. A scratching noise issued from within. "What's inside?"

"Jiminy."

Palmer reached to his top pocket for his reading glasses and opened the box a fraction. A glossy, cockroach-looking insect peeked its feelers out. "I see. But you shouldn't keep Jiminy in a dark box. Would you like to be in a dark box?"

Timmy shook his head emphatically.

"I tell you what: You come with me to the garage, bring your cricket, and we'll make a little home with wire. Then you can hang its cage up here, feed it, and hear it chirp. Would you like that?"

The boy nodded. "What does Jiminy eat?"

Palmer scratched his head and frowned. *One of the eldest serving senators in the country and I don't know a damn thing about what crickets eat.*

"Mmmm, I'll look it up." He glanced to a corner where a sizable toy rifle stood, half hidden beneath bulky feathered headgear. His knees were killing him, but he inched forward to peer out the window. Through a gap in the tree's foliage, he could see inside his study.

"So you keep me covered from here?"

"Yup. I protect you."

"Thank you. Here." He handed the child his box. "Bring Jiminy along and we'll fix him a home." Then he glanced once more toward his study. "Er, let me have a look at your weapon, please."

Timmy reached for his rifle and passed it over.

Sitting on his haunches on the platform outside the little house, Palmer held the toy and inspected it. Made of a sturdy plastic, it was a faithful reproduction of a real weapon, except for its size. He checked the barrel, the sights, and the scope, nodded, and handed it back to the expectant boy. "Excellent weapon, partner. Make sure you keep it in good condition. I depend on you."

Timmy giggled, pride in his eyes.

As Palmer descended the ladder, Bastien's face flashed across his mind, and grief welled in his chest. He reached firm ground and looked upward to watch his grandson's expert descent. Bastien's face blurred, replaced by that of a spear-wielding man, one of his arms upraised, decked in an embroidered robe and a crown with four high plumes. Onuris, the ancient Egyptian "bringer of fear," the god of war and the hunt. A most fitting moniker for Nikola Masek.

chapter 11

||||

18:42

In the thirty minutes since the alarm tripped, Sandra Garcia had done nothing but sit at her station while Kosmerl shouted orders and paced the room. She hated the phony half-Slav. She hated his starched blue fatigues, his tall lace-up boots with thick soles that added another two inches to his already towering stature, and his eye. His milky eye was sickening, especially when he closed his good one and play-stared with the white one. Why he didn't have his cataract, or whatever it was, removed was beyond her. And then there was his phony accent. The idiot would use *ze* for *the* whenever he could. But above all she hated his joke. *Der ver zwei peanuts valking down der strasse and von vas . . . assaulted! Peanut.* Sandra wrinkled her nose in distaste. She'd heard the stupid joke ten times, at least. Once, Sandra had caught a glimpse of his personnel file, and many other goodies, when programmers were rescheduling files to another memory stack. The imbecile was from Massachusetts. His parents were from Slovenia, not Germany, and he'd never traveled abroad.

She still couldn't believe Lukas Hurley had entered the restricted area to help hibernators escape. Sandra darted a glance toward Kosmerl. He looked back and closed his good eye.

Probably Lukas, running with the shits, had mistaken the doors. No, wishful thinking. The door to the restricted area needed a high-security card and the toilet door only a push.

"Is the pig back?" Kosmerl yelled to a couple of security guards entering the control room.

"Yes, but no luck."

"No luck?"

"We may have turned it around too soon, sir."

"Too soon? They could go no farther in twenty minutes. They must have hidden up one of the utility shafts."

Sandra typed the intro code in her keyboard, but the screen remained frozen.

"You check the pig? Any blood?" Kosmerl asked.

One of the officers, overweight and with a cherub's face, mopped his forehead and nodded. "We check. No blood."

Good for you, Sandra thought, and then recanted. The young man probably wasn't making fun of Kosmerl; he was only nervous.

"Should we send it out again?" the officer asked.

"For what porpoise?"

Sandra gritted her teeth. He could probably speak better English than she could. Why the affectation?

Kosmerl turned on his heel and his boots squeaked on the polymer floor. "When can we get the doors unlocked?"

At least he'd not tried *ze doors* this time.

Pete, one of her shift mates, nodded to a telephone hooked into a landline. "I'm waiting for clearance codes."

"You can do nothing?"

Pete shrugged.

Sandra narrowed her eyes and glanced at the clock: 18:48. Processing should have been back online ages ago. For an instant, she thought of the unprocessed prisoners cooking inside the truck, still waiting. Then her mind turned to practicalities. She would probably be home late, today of all days, when Pedro would drop by and with any luck spend the night. The home-cooked meal she'd planned was out. By the time she managed to get out of the station and back to the apartment with Chinese takeout, Pedro would be snoring or gone. *Shit!*

Kosmerl reached to his belt, which was bristling with all sorts of objects dangling from carabiners, and unhooked a shortwave two-way radio. Cellular phones didn't work in the station for an area of two hundred yards around the building, to thwart camera phones beaming pictures to friend or foe.

"Any heat signatures?" Kosmerl barked.

A screech issued from the contraption. Kosmerl adjusted the device and turned the volume down.

"No signatures," replied a tinny voice Sandra recognized as belonging to Rafael Sosa, a good-looking man from Aguascalientes. Just her luck he was happily married with two kids.

A loud snap at the main door to the control room startled everyone. Two large men who looked like linebackers stood at the entrance, casting quick, menacing glances in all directions.

Sandra straightened and pulled at the hem of her skirt, eyeing the newcomers with caution. Dark suits, turtleneck pullovers, and close-shaven heads seamlessly fused to beefy necks. *The cavalry?*

Kosmerl stepped forward. "You from HQ? About time! I need processing back online at once."

The two men didn't even look at him but went to stand at opposite ends of the room, seemingly relaxed but for their eyes, which were busy darting glances.

"Hey!" Kosmerl shouted to the man who had taken the station close to Pete. "I spoke to you!"

The man didn't move or even acknowledge Kosmerl in any way.

"Identify yourself!" Kosmerl reached to his belt.

The man was insane. The newcomers must have cleared four security checks before reaching the control room. Sandra detected movement by the door. Another man had entered the room. Slight, about five one or five two, and thin, with prominent cheekbones; his piercing blue eyes were rimmed with luxurious black eyelashes and magnified by thick bifocals. Obviously the man didn't believe in corrective eye surgery. From where Sandra sat, the newcomer looked like a caricature of a British professor she once saw in a book when she was little. He stood by the door, rubbing bony fingers as if preparing to roll a set of dice. The man could have been any age between forty and sixty and wore a light tweed jacket with elbow patches, corduroy trousers, and a plaid shirt. Far too hot for the weather outside.

Kosmerl jerked his head toward the door. "And who are you?"

The man put a rigid index finger to his lips. "Too loud."

Like a beast searching for an exit, Kosmerl looked in turn at the three men. "What's going on here? I demand to see IDs."

Sandra followed the exchange as if viewing a slow-motion game of tennis on a plasma screen.

"Please, remain calm."

Kosmerl froze and Sandra narrowed her gaze. The stranger's choice of words was unsettling.

"My name is Masek, Nikola Masek." The man stepped closer to Kosmerl. Suddenly a small cellular phone appeared in his hand, as if he'd conjured it out of his sleeve. Thin lips pressed a smile of sorts on his face as he flicked the phone open.

"That won't work here," Kosmerl said.

"This one does." Masek offered the open device to Kosmerl, who reached for it, a dubious look on his face.

Whoever was at the other end of the line must have been shouting, because tiny scratching noises issued from the area around Kosmerl's ear. The giant paled, continued listening, then paled some more. "Yes, ma'am." He closed the cell and handed it back.

"Well, Mr. Kosmerl, now that we're enlightened, why don't you tell me what you have bungled so far?"

In a monotone punctuated with frequent contractions and none of his pseudo-German accent, Kosmerl rattled out a full account of the security measures.

"The black man is still at tank 913?" Nikola asked.

Kosmerl nodded once.

"His neck snapped, you said?"

Kosmerl nodded again.

Nikola pondered the information. "And this pig of yours has no cameras?"

Silence.

"Sloppy. Very sloppy," Nikola said.

A loud beep issued from the central console area.

"We're back online," Pete announced. Then he swiveled his chair toward Nikola. "Your instructions, sir?"

Sandra had to suppress a smile. Pete knew how to survive.

"Thank you." Nikola smiled. Then he turned to Kosmerl. "Let me have the location codes of the fugitives. How many?"

Kosmerl's face sagged and he looked around once more as if seeking help. "Besides the controller, there are four inmates involved but as I told you, sir, one didn't make it. And there are no codes."

"Fugitives without codes?"

"Yes, sir."

"But if there are inmates with no code, how do you know how many have escaped?"

"The wires, sir. Over tank 913 there are four pairs of empty wires."

"I see."

Perhaps this could be her opportunity to be noticed. "I—I may be able to help," Sandra supplied.

Masek stepped over and laid a gentle hand on her shoulder. "You must be Sandra, Sandra Garcia."

"Yes, sir."

"And how could you help me?"

Sandra glanced at Pete, who avoided locking eyes. He swiveled his chair back and stared into his center screen. "I—"

Masek ran his hand softly over her hair. "Please, calm down. I don't bite."

She was committed, and his touch felt oddly soothing. "I know where the restricted center codes are," she whispered.

Masek leaned forward. "I'm sorry. I didn't catch that. Restricted center codes, you said?"

"Yes."

He drew closer, his lips almost brushing her ear. He smelled of cinnamon. "You have accessed restricted files?"

She shook her head, but her lips moved. "Yes."

"And Kosmerl? And the others? Have they accessed Hurley's files?"

Sandra shook her head automatically, as understanding bloomed in her mind. How could he know the center codes were in the supervisor's restricted files? He'd only wanted to find out who, if anyone, knew the center inmates' identities, and she'd fallen for it.

Masek stood and patted her shoulder. "Thank you, Sandra."

With slow steps, Masek walked over to the door, where several security officers had appeared out of nowhere. He neared one wearing sergeant stripes and stopped to whisper in his ear. "There are temporary vacancies in tank 913. Process the Mexican bitch."

chapter 12

||||

19:17

In the last two centuries, only a portion of the Washington sewers had been upgraded to concrete. The section the group now crossed was formed of brick, crumbling in places. "At the next junction we bear left," Laurel said, after checking her GPS.

Lukas nodded and trained his flashlight along the left side

of the tunnel until the jutting fork of a Y junction came into view. Behind her, Raul plodded like a workhorse. He hadn't spoken a word since they entered the city sewers. The anonymous workers had welded the curved panel back with remarkable speed after gesturing to several oversize carryalls loaded with treasure: four sets of waders, two-piece suits of stout reinforced polymer in sewer-regulation yellow, flashlights, waterproof plastic watches, a gold-foil thermal blanket, and a waterproof, military-issue Metapad carefully programmed with a map provided by Shepherd.

While they dressed, Laurel watched the closemouthed workers. Each of the three must have been close to seventy—far too old to be in active service and probably brought out of retirement for this one job. As soon as they finished the last piece of welding, they gathered their tackle, nodded, and splashed away down a side corridor.

Dumping the bags, weighed down with loose bricks—one of them containing a now-unnecessary suit and waders—had been the hardest part. Raul had picked up the now-spare flashlight and nodded when Laurel pocketed Bastien's watch. Then he gazed for a long time as the lump sunk in a pit of slime, until Laurel kissed his cheek and squeezed his shoulder to pull him out of the dark lair where he'd sought refuge.

Panning their powerful new flashlights, Laurel and Lukas waded to their midriffs through streams of foul water, followed by Raul with the unconscious Russo wrapped in gold foil and draped over his shoulder. They had been shuffling and treading for the best part of an hour through a rat-plagued and endless subuniverse of alleys, pipes, tunnels, and side tunnels.

Laurel checked the Metapad, where she'd tapped the coordinates she now knew by heart. *Two miles left.*

The darkness of the sewers enhanced noises. Ears needed to work as hard as eyes to aid navigation through the maze of tunnels. *Down in the sewer, your ears and sense of smell could save your life.* Their trainer had been thorough. Her feet squelching inside flooded waders. Laurel wondered how Shepherd had gathered his knowledge.

"Now what?" Lukas kept his flashlight trained on a dark wall one hundred feet ahead, seemingly blocking the tunnel.

As they drew near, it became clear the tunnel continued, although the roof dropped down to half its previous height.

"We carry on straight ahead," Laurel said.

Inside the confined vault, they couldn't walk upright but had to crouch down, their noses scant inches over a whitish fluid dusted with a flotsam of condoms, plastic bags, Q-tips, shit, tampons, and fat. After one hundred yards, they entered a wider tunnel, with a dry four-foot-wide walkway on one of its sides.

"Let's rest a few minutes," Laurel suggested.

Lukas jerked his head. "Rest? Are you kidding?"

"No." She doubled back past Lukas and gave Raul a hand lying Russo on the dry ledge. In their mad rush through the station's drainpipe, she'd worried that Raul couldn't carry Russo for much longer. He'd been huffing like he was out of breath, but Laurel must have misinterpreted. He didn't look tired, let alone winded.

She drew aside the gold-foil wrapper and checked Russo's pulse by touching his neck on both sides of his throat: thready but regular.

"He's hanging on to life tooth and nail." Laurel glanced down at Raul, propped her back against the curved wall next to him, and ran an eye along the tunnel: a horrible place with thin skeins of skeletonlike roots threading their way down the roof and walls.

Lukas checked his watch and glared in their direction. Something dark and bulky sailed past, turning over and dropping below the surface to bob a little farther on, bloated and shiny under a film of fat. Raul turned his head to follow its passage.

"A friend told me about these giant hairballs clogging the sewers under the city streets."

Laurel raised an eyebrow. "Hairballs?"

"It seems that over the decades, strands of hair molted by millions of citizens have built up."

Lukas checked his watch again and stepped closer.

"You're joking," Laurel said.

"I'm not. Coated in grease and dirt, tons of hair have been shaped into huge knotted boulders that swell as they trundle through the sewers."

"That's a lie," Lukas muttered.

"Wanna bet?"

Lukas bit his lower lip, shook his head, and checked his watch again. "We should get going."

After a curt nod, Raul stood up and offered his palm to Laurel. "You've lazed enough."

"Me? I thought you needed a rest."

"A shower is what I need." He squatted, checked Russo's pulse, adjusted the thermal blanket, hefted his cocoon over his shoulder with an easy swing, and straightened. Then he froze and turned slowly to peer at the darkened end of the tunnel.

Laurel lowered her head to hide a smile.

"Hear that?"

"What?" Lukas croaked, his flashlight slashing in all directions.

"I bet it's one of those giant hairballs."

Lukas's face sagged an instant, only to rearrange into a weak smile of relief. "Very funny."

They set off again and headed along a narrow ledge stretching through a winding tunnel. The atmosphere changed; unbelievably, it became darker and stuffier. After a tight bend, Laurel rechecked the Metapad and pushed forward, listening to a muted rush of distant waterfalls punctuated by their squelching waders, the rolling fetid water, and the squeak of rats. "We're almost there."

The light from her flashlight bounced off greasy streams. At another junction, they stopped an instant, enough so that Laurel could make out the leg scratching of angry red cockroaches. Startled by the light, the insects on the curved roof swarmed, collided with one another, and rained down on mounds of brownish matter that glistened in places. She cringed.

In the last tunnel leading to the station, you'll come across roaches and big rats feeding on the fat fields: thousands of tons of fat solidified into huge iceberglike formations. Millions of gallons from cafés, leftover breakfast dishes, frying pans, and fast-food joints.

"Holy shit," she heard Lukas mutter somewhere behind her.

"Fat: the effluence of affluence," Raul muttered.

Laurel stepped forward to stare at a vast tunnel, its surface seemingly solid and swarming with insects. The stench was indescribable.

"Well, he certainly didn't make it." Lukas trained his flashlight on a figure wedged between two solid-looking mountains of brownish matter.

Laurel's eyes widened as she took in a skull and a mass of bones sprinkled with a few buttons and pieces of shoes: the remains of a man, probably a vagrant, his flesh and dress devoured piecemeal by the rats.

"Through there?" Lukas asked.

Laurel noted that the beam from Lukas's flashlight fought to remain fixed in one place without much success.

"That's right. A few hundred yards."

Lukas coughed, then leaned to the side to dry-retch a couple of times before drawing a hand across his lips. "I'll take his fucking hairy balls anytime."

Raul stopped dead in his tracks. "My hairy balls?" He turned around, pouted his lips, and blew a kiss in Lukas's direction. "Can't fault you for your taste."

Lukas huffed and stepped forward into the greasy quagmire.

Laurel likewise ventured through solidified slabs of fat, careful to plant the soles of her waders with care before taking another step; a fall would be nasty, and probably fatal. Fat roaches darted in all directions before the powerful beams. Dark shapes scurried, filling the air with curious chirps. They waded through the fat for what seemed an eternity. The ground felt strange—at once brittle and squishy, like rotting cereal. Brown and white and gray—a pigeon-shit stew scattered with a top layer of tampons, disposable diapers, and condoms.

Leaving behind the fat fields, they entered a wide tunnel, mostly clear and with narrow sidewalks at either side, its air thick with the rancid stench. After ten minutes of marching single file, their oilskins rubbing against the brickwork, they reached a narrow side tunnel. Laurel's eyes watered and her throat felt raw from repeated retching. Runny fat had invaded her waders, and her toes squelched in warm slime.

Suddenly, six feet ahead of her, a torrent of light spilled into the passage after a protracted groan of rusty hinges. A blond man in a blinding white lab coat over a blue shirt and tie leaned into the tunnel, wrinkled his nose, and grinned as if greeting a favorite aunt.

"Hello! I'm Dr. Carpenter. What took you so long?"

chapter 13

||||

20:26

It had to happen one day. Reaching into his jacket pocket, Nikola Masek drew out a crumpled bag, rummaged inside, and popped a candy in his mouth. He'd asked his assistant to park outside the hibernation facility instead of in the underground parking lots. Although his specially shielded cell phone would work inside the dead zone, the sophisticated equipment in the van Nikola used as a mobile ops center wouldn't. After climbing on foot from the parking lot's upper section, he ambled across a wide belt of paved lots surrounding the station toward an unmarked dark-green van waiting at the curb of an access road circling the hibernation facility. When local authorities redesigned the northern section of Washington, D.C., the intersection of three highways had left a triangular plot of land—an ideal place for the hibernation station. Its location had eased traffic congestion. Everybody knew the snow-white monoliths were secure and harmless to people outside, but millions of commuters passed through the area as swiftly as possible or found another route.

Nikola sucked on the candy. And yet total security existed only in the minds of politicians and other amateurs. Any castle could be breached, any safe busted, any network hacked. Only fools assumed security was a synonym for safety. Security bought time. But time, like any other commodity, could be purchased by others. In security, it usually meant enlisting someone inside to supply a shortcut. Someone had bought some expensive time.

A middle-aged Japanese couple stepped out of an idling cab on the access road and strolled toward the building. Nikola stopped and brushed the sole of his loafer over the dense grass growing in the interstices between the flagstones. He turned slowly around to face the vast white bulk of the sugar cube—the nickname common folk used for the hibernation stations. The same common folk who would assume that whoever planted the grass, probably at great expense, had intended to beautify an otherwise stark landscape. Nothing could be further from the truth. The grass was needed.

The sugar cube was surrounded by two hundred yards of square paving stones measuring thirty by thirty inches each, with a four-inch strip between them where the lush grass grew. The flagstones rested on a bed of fine-grained sand, compacted without mortar or any other binding. Below the sand, a network of polymer fiber optics detected the slightest change in the weight of each flagstone. Nikola recalled a showy experiment by the suppliers of the network. A technician had dropped a Ping-Pong ball onto a slab and grinned when a loudspeaker wired to a sensor blared: *tap . . . tap . . . tap, tap-tap-tap-tap* as the ball bounced.

The Japanese couple neared the sugar cube and stopped a few feet away, perhaps afraid to draw any closer in case the white expanse sucked them in. They looked around. *Now you're wondering if someone is watching you.* No cameras in sight. *They're not; there's no need.* A computer had determined their number, weight, and direction of movement from the moment they stepped on the flagstones. If, instead of individuals, a car or truck had tried to cross over, every other slab would have sunk twelve inches. The vehicle would be stuck within a few feet. And within a couple of minutes, a DHS Fast Deployment Unit would have surrounded the intruders.

The woman fiddled with a tiny video camera, perhaps wanting to capture a souvenir. No chance. Beneath the polymer epidermis of the cube lay two feet of hardened concrete and, sandwiched between inner and outer surfaces, protective copper shielding to make the building an information black hole. In addition, strong electromagnetic pulses would prevent the gadget's operation. Only specially shielded equipment would work within five hundred yards of the station.

When Hypnos designed the first hibernation complex, there was a discussion about building a perimeter protection fence. A stupid discussion, since all access was through underground roads and there was nothing to protect on the surface. So why build stations close to city centers? Why not in the wilds or underground? Elementary, my dear idiot: People forgot networks like sewers and other utilities that lay hidden beneath the city streets. Also, people needed reminders of reality and permission to see and touch—like the Japanese couple—to gather fodder for nightmares. Masek eyed the tourists. The woman drew closer to the wall and ran a hand over the white surface—a six-inch hardened polymer without openings, joints, or cracks. He could almost read her thoughts. *You're thinking of the difference a few inches can make. Yes, my dear, a few critical inches is the difference between being in or out. Out or dead.*

Enjoying the blush of a sinking sun, Nikola dug his hands in his trouser pockets, sucked the sweet, and strolled toward his mobile control center.

"These are the fugitives' numbers." Nikola Masek drew a thin memory card from his top pocket and deposited it in Dennis Nolan's outstretched hand.

He squeezed between the back of Dennis's swivel chair and the wall of the van to a bucket seat in the corner, wedged between two racks of equipment, and flopped down to massage his knees. Vlad Kosmerl, the Washington station head of security, had been most helpful; not that he could have done otherwise without risking a long dip in a tank. After supplying the files Nikola needed, he'd agreed to seal the Washington sugar cube. Fear worked wonders. Until he recaptured the fugitives, all personnel would remain in the building. Relatives had been informed of confidential security exercises with a generous compensation in overtime pay. He doubted anyone would have had the chutzpah to gossip about the breakout, but it was safer to remove the temptation.

The call from the DHS requesting that he drop everything to await instructions had arrived shortly before six-thirty. He'd planned on a light supper followed by a spell of bliss at the tiny Temple Theater. Claus Holtermann's rendition of Sophocles' *Antigone* promised to be a treat, in particular Walter Lindt's interpretation of Tiresias, the blind prophet. *Holtermann's work doesn't look for empathy from its audience; its demand is actually greater, to completely surrender to its power and to experience it not as a sophisticated theatergoer but as a wholly immersed witness,* had raved Susan Lamarck, the *Washington Times*'s critic.

When Odelle Marino's call came through, Nikola had stifled a smile at the uncanny coincidence. Her cry for help involved a wholly immersed witness who had suddenly surfaced. He'd demanded total authority over the DHS's awesome resources and she'd agreed. Perhaps a tad too quickly.

When his eyes adjusted to the van's dim interior, he peered at Dennis's computer screen. The freckled young man's fingers flew over the keyboard, interrogating wireless networks and scouring through millions of signatures bouncing off cellular repeaters. Fear was a powerful motivator and an excellent tool of persuasion, but it didn't breed loyalty. That feeling needed to be fostered by admiration, gratitude, or a combination of both.

A few years back Dennis had landed in a tight spot when he'd hacked into one of the hardest networks in the land. He'd slipped a program into his chosen server farm like a lover seducing a virgin—a little at a time. Spaced every few hours, over days or even weeks, Dennis dripped lines of code, innocently disguised inside standard forms or routine queries. The lines would assemble in the uncharted space between memory sectors until triggered. Then the program would run, take over the network, and flash *Gotcha!* on hundreds or thousands of screens before disappearing without a trace. The NSA classed those messing about with systems as white hats or black hats: hackers or crackers. Both used similar tools, but their goals were as different as the color of their virtual headgear. Hackers never caused damage or tried to retrieve data, restricted or not. Rather, they would highlight the weaknesses of a system. On the other hand, crackers sought mayhem by crashing systems or releasing viruses. The experts agreed on this one: white hat, a prankster.

Eventually people make mistakes, usually triggered by overconfidence or sloppiness. In Dennis's case, his nemesis had been fatigue: The boy had fallen asleep while running one of his programs, only to be rudely awakened by a security squad. Nikola agreed the hacker had caused no real harm, but he was dangerous and in need of a lesson. After a couple of days in a suitable environment, cunningly prepared to scare his pants off, Dennis had repented and moved in as Nikola's assistant. Within a short time, mentor and apprentice had fused brains and talents into a formidable tracking machine. Ten years had passed, but it seemed like only yesterday that Masek had descended into the police dungeons cloaked as a redeeming angel to spirit Dennis toward the light.

"Weak signals."

Masek snapped from his reverie. "You got them?"

"Of course."

Years before, cajoling the folks at Hypnos had taken deft footwork, but Nikola had managed to have them hide a microchip in the neck sensors of the inmates, broadcasting a unique signature. *Afraid the inmates will thaw and take a powder? When pigs fly.* That had been what Vinson Duran, Hypnos's head honcho, had said. Well, pigs were definitely airborne, but not for long.

"Where?" Nikola slouched forward and examined the map spreading over Dennis's plasma screen.

"Almost four miles away. Here." He pointed to a tiny group of flashing dots. He touched the spot and the image zoomed.

"What's there?" Nikola asked.

"Commercial tanks. Nyx Corporation."

Nikola nodded. It made sense. Nyx had the equipment and knowledge to revive Russo. His respect for whoever had planned the escape increased a notch.

"Stationary?"

Dennis poked at the screen again. Three dots flashed intermittently over the same spot. "Yup."

So, the three pigs were holed up at Nyx. Lukas Hurley, the controller, would be trying to flee the country. Nikola had no way of tracking him. He carried no sensor, but Dennis had wired Lukas's holograph and biometric data to every police station and border crossing. Good luck.

"They got there through the sewers?"

The image on the screen zoomed back, and a network of colored lines superimposed themselves. "There's a main line running under their building. The folks from Nyx manage their own effluents. No need for their own spur." There was a hint of criticism in Dennis's tone, and Nikola had to agree. Hypnos's design to manage their sewage in a remote treatment plant was a weak link. A flaw that someone had used with remarkable success.

Nikola sighed. *When it is obvious the goals cannot be reached, don't adjust the goals, adjust the action steps.* Regardless of the millennia, Confucius's words held true. Worrying didn't return bolted horses, or pigs, back to the stables. Action did.

"Close shop and let's drive over to Nyx. Call the DHS and have them send muscle to meet us there in fifteen minutes."

||||

chapter 14

21:45

Her skin felt defiled beyond recovery, and no amount of scrubbing altered the feeling. After a long time under the shower's high-pressure jets, rubbing handfuls of bactericidal gel into every inch of her body Laurel could reach, it still felt the same. She reamed her ears, blew her nose, inserted soapy fingers into her anus and vagina, and rubbed between her toes, but the sensation persisted. The surface muck had run away in gushes of brown liquid, eddying around the shower's drain, but the tank's fluid had leached into her skin, clogging her pores. Lanolin and nutrients should have felt like body lotion, but they didn't. Laurel took a deep breath. At least the steam had the gel's piney tang. In her nose and ears, membranes clung to memories of cold jelly. And to think she'd been in the fluid only a few minutes. . . . How would skin feel after marinating for years? She leaned a hand on the polymer wall of the shower cubicle, doubled over, and retched for the umpteenth time. Then she wrapped her arms around her waist, turned her face to the full blast of the shower, and rocked.

Dr. Carpenter—Floyd—seemed nice. No, he was gorgeous; tanned and with unruly blond hair that screamed for a woman's fingers to comb through it. Despite her queasy stomach, she felt giddy. *It must be all that rocking.* After they dropped Russo at the surgical theater, he'd herded them into the showers, making a face as they discarded waders and oilskins. She'd glanced across at him, and her eyes locked on his raw gaze. He was ogling her, the soft weight of his smile pressing against her breasts, belly, and thighs.

A loud bang outside jolted Laurel from her reverie, hands flying to clear her eyes of the running water.

"Get out, now!" The male voice was tinged with hysteria.

Laurel slammed both hands on the enclosure door and jumped outside, to collide with a bewildered-looking Lukas and Raul. Floyd Carpenter was showing a different face from the man who had greeted them at the sewer entrance. Gone was the calm demeanor, replaced by panic.

"Your implants are broadcasting!" he yelled.

She reached to the lump in her neck. "Broadcasting? What are you talking about?"

"Come with me, fast." He turned on his heel in a whirl of lab whites.

Raul jerked his head toward Lukas. "You know anything about that?"

The little man darted a drizzle of nervous glances between Laurel and Raul. "I-I swear, I had no idea—"

"Well, you do now." Raul dashed to a pile of towels on a metal rack, grabbed one, threw another to Laurel, then bolted out the door, leaving a trail of wet footprints and water drops in his wake.

Twenty yards down an impersonal corridor, they piled through a set of double doors into a surgery room crammed with equipment, screens, and blinking lights.

"Look!" Floyd pointed to a large screen where, superimposed on a heartbeat track, another complex line spiked and fell in a fast sequence. "These implants are emitting high-frequency signals."

Laurel narrowed her eyes. Someone with enough insight must have demanded that the designers include a transmitter. It made sense. The cunning addition gave Hypnos an ace up their sleeve. A card they had kept secret, even from Congress and the committee that approved the hardware. *Damn!* She stared at the trace on the screen, her mind churning with the implications. *Another detail we didn't know. How many more are we yet to discover?*

"Do you have X-ray machines here?" she asked.

"Well, yes, but—"

"Then get an apron."

Floyd opened his mouth a couple of times like a floundering fish. Then his eyes froze as the penny dropped. In two strides, he hurtled through the doors, his footsteps echoing down the corridor.

"I swear—" Lukas started.

"Don't waste your breath." Raul slapped Lukas between the shoulder blades. The small man winced as his towel dropped off. "Hypnos has probably been discreet about whatever extras they have packed in their sensors."

Even from the government, Laurel thought. The air was thick with bactericides and the penetrating smell of lanolin wafting from Russo's body. "I wonder what else they forgot to publicize."

Laurel stepped over to a gleaming table. Under the harsh light of an overhead LAD array, Russo's emaciated and unnaturally pale body—bare of hair or nails—resembled a cross between a model of a giant fetus in its early stages of development and the larvae of a stick insect. She gaped, aghast, at the wasted shape. His pruned skin, with an unnatural sheen, twitched at intervals as if subject to electric shocks. Laurel neared the head of the table and reached to pry open one of Russo's eyelids. In slow motion, his pupil contracted. She glanced at the steady rhythm of his heartbeat on the screen. So far, so good. A peppering of wireless pads dotted his chest and head, while two lines snaked from IV ports in his hands to unlabeled bottles dangling from a frame. From his penis, a catheter drew whitish fluid into a transparent bag. She spotted tiny perfusion marks on Russo's neck and several discarded ultrasonic syrettes on a rectangular tray atop a wheeled cart. Dr. Carpenter had probably been working to stabilize Russo and scrub the sedatives from his blood.

A series of sharp beeps issued from a bank of automatic analyzers.

She scanned the printout scrolling from the printer. "Holy—"

"That man has not had his blood scrubbed in ages. No maintenance, nothing. Nobody told me. He needs a total transfusion." Floyd stood just beyond the swinging doors, a buff sheet folded in his hand. "Right now he's a toxic dump. His blood is laced with complex chemicals and heavy metals."

Laurel nodded. Another detail they hadn't known. According to Shepherd, Russo would be unconscious and weak but not a living corpse.

"Total transfusion? More like a new body. You have large scissors?"

Floyd nodded to a door set flush on the wall to a side of the theater. Laurel opened it and selected the largest shears she could find. "Bring the apron over."

Cursing under her breath at the toughness of the lead and polymer-fabric sandwich of the radiation protector, she managed to cut three-inch strips. When she finished, Laurel hurled one to Raul, another to Floyd for Russo, and wrapped the last around her neck. Then she stepped back to the wall cupboard to retrieve the adhesive bandages she'd spotted earlier.

When they finished, Russo and Raul looked like accident victims after having their necks immobilized. Laurel didn't hold any illusions of looking better. On the screen, the spiky trace had disappeared, leaving only Russo's heartbeat sailing across.

"Now what?" Lukas croaked.

Laurel darted a glance at Raul; it was her decision, but her legs had started to quiver again. After hearing an incredible tale from a man she'd never seen or met, judiciously doled out in several telephone conversations, she'd volunteered to help in springing Russo from the DHS's clutches. Shepherd's original plan contemplated enlisting three ex-professional soldiers to make up the team, but it was clear from the onset that it wouldn't work. Men with proven military records would stick out like sore thumbs when they went through the sham trial. She had recruited Raul and Bastien, in the process becoming the team leader.

"Now we get the hell out of here." Raul made a show of looking at an overhead digital clock. "The DHS's legions must be massing outside."

"Get out? Beam out is more likely." Floyd seemed to have recovered his wits.

Raul wrinkled his nose and Laurel felt her stomach heave. "We go the same way we came in." It was their only chance. To seal the sewers, the DHS needed an army they didn't have. To enlist the police, they would need to broadcast the breakout, and they wouldn't do that. Not yet.

"You've got to be joking." Lukas held on to his towel and jerked his head around like a caged animal.

"Be my guest." Raul shrugged. "You can try the front door if you like."

"Better get him ready to travel." Floyd had moved to the table and was drawing the catheter from Russo.

Laurel stared at Floyd. "You can't stay here," she said.

"A brilliant conclusion."

"Look—"

"Plan to hit the sewers decked in towels?" Floyd sounded amused.

Laurel turned to Raul and froze as the image of waders with an inch of fatty sewage inside flashed through her mind. Unconsciously, she bunched her toes. "Shit."

From the far side of the theater, Floyd unfolded a thermal sack to place Russo in and nodded to Raul for help. He then reached for the sack's fastener and ripped. "Another brilliant conclusion."

chapter 15

||||

22:01

Their script gone, Laurel fought the waves of terror radiating from her belly, blanking reason with images of dark corners where she could curl up and cry. Their carefully researched plan called for a precise set of steps. Once Russo had been stabilized and housed at Nyx, Dr. Carpenter would have driven them to a prearranged meeting point on the

northern fringes of the city to rendezvous with Shepherd.
Then they would have laid low for as long as necessary until
Russo recovered. Not long, according to Shepherd. Now, like
cornered animals, they could only run. But where? She was
racing toward the showers to throw the filthy gear back on
when Floyd grabbed her arm and pointed to a storeroom where
the cleaning detail kept clean wet suits, waders, and tools.
Laurel could have hugged him, hard. A minute later, when
Lukas, Raul, and Laurel rushed back into the surgical theater, Floyd had already cocooned Russo in a bag, probably
one of those used to move cadavers to incineration. She recalled Shepherd mentioning that, even with the lavish care
bestowed by Nyx, often the bodies were so badly damaged
after protracted commercial hibernation—by whatever sick-
ness had gotten them there in the first place—that the only
thing the family ever got back was condolences.

Floyd threw loaded syrettes, an instrument case, and handfuls of drugs from a shelf into a duffel bag and nodded for
Raul to carry Russo. Then he bolted down the corridor to return almost at once with a lightweight folded stretcher,
which he handed to Lukas. "Two floors down. Same way you
came." Floyd pointed to a door at the end of the corridor. "I'll
catch up with you." He turned on his heel and pushed the
door to the cleaner's storeroom shut.

In the basement, they recovered their discarded flashlights
and stood by the metal door leading to the sewers.

"Good stuff." Raul pinched the dark-gray material of his
suit and rubbed it between his fingers.

"Steam disinfecting gear," Lukas said.

Raul nodded. "But they have no tanks."

Suddenly Laurel jerked, pivoted, and ran toward the stairs.
"The computer!"

She almost collided with Floyd, who was barreling down
the steps.

"Where're you going?" he yelled.

"Forgot the Metapad. We're fucked without it."

"We're fucked anyway, but hurry up!" He squeezed past
her and crashed through the basement door.

When Laurel returned, wheezing from the effort—the

computer dangling from her neck—the men had already strapped Russo onto the stretcher with stout woven belts.

"Here." Floyd handed his bag to Lukas, nodded to Raul, then bent over to grab one end of the stretcher.

Sixteen minutes and thirty seconds after discovering the broadcasting implants, they were back in the sewers.

Nikola stood, his back to the security air locks joining the reception area with the underground accesses. Whoever had designed the complex didn't believe in feng shui but understood human nature. Nyx's reception area was a hangarlike monstrosity—a domed void rising one hundred feet into the air and spanning a circle of perhaps three hundred feet, with a doughnut-shaped counter in its center. The rest was empty but for clusters of plush seats arranged at the edge of the circle. Like an ancient temple builder, the architect had designed the brutal empty volume to awe visitors into insignificance.

As he waited outside for the arrival of the DHS Fast Deployment Units, Dennis's voice had crackled in his earpiece. "Signatures gone." A short sentence that altered the rules of the game.

"All of them?"

No hesitation on Dennis's reply. "Yes."

"At the same time?"

"Within seconds of one another, anyhow."

To destroy the locators required surgical removal, and the fugitives hadn't had enough time. Besides, if someone had surgically excised the sensors and left them lying around, they would still be live. Yet all three sensors had stopped broadcasting nearly in unison, and unless the fugitives had a large team of surgeons, it was an impossible feat. No. They had neutralized the sensors, and that could only mean the bastards had learned of their dual role as beacons. Nikola sighed and ran a hand over the sleeve of his wool jacket—one of his affectations. Real wool—not the smart synthetic fiber that would change color and texture at its owner's whim. The wool felt warm to the touch, as if it still remembered the heat of the animal it had come from.

The waning signal left him blind and offered the fugitives

two alternatives. They could have holed up in the research building and hoped to remain undetected—but this was a naive assumption, and whoever had planned the operation was anything but naive. On the other hand, they could be in the sewers, ready to surface almost anywhere. And he didn't have the personnel to scour hundreds of miles of city bowels *and* seal the city exits. But he could seal the city, and the fugitives would have to come up sooner or later. He stepped forward to a dozen security guards lined up by the FDU lieutenant and eyed a row of frightened faces. "Who's in charge?"

A young security officer, almost a boy, straightened. "I am."

Nikola peered into the young man's eyes, ready to deliver a rebuke that died before it left his tongue. Interrogation was an art where one posed questions and the other delivered answers. Problem was, if the questions were stupid, the answers would be even more so. He had wanted to know who the highest executive in the building was, but he hadn't been clear. And the boy replied accordingly; he was in charge of the security detail.

"Where are the medical personnel?"

"In their offices or labs, sir."

A door opened on the far end of the room, and a short, overweight man in lab whites trotted toward them. "I'm Dr. Henkel," he offered with a bland smile. "Director of—" He clamped his mouth shut at Nikola's raised hand.

"Give your name to the lieutenant over there." Nikola glanced over his shoulder. "I have no need of you." He'd decided the security boy would be easier to deal with. "What's your name, son?"

"Jeremy, sir. Jeremy Clark."

Nikola pointed to a hologram model of the buildings floating over a wider section of the reception counter. "Let's start again, Jeremy. This complex has five buildings laid out like disks on the vertices of a pentagram. We are in this one." He nodded to the pentagram. "I suppose this is admission and administration, correct?"

"Yes, sir."

"And these are the hibernation wards?" His hand waved through the ghosts of four orange-colored iridescent blocks.

"Yes, sir."

He eyed the young man but found no sparkle in his eye. "And this?" He pointed to the remaining building—a blue cylinder, the precise location where the coordinates from the broadcasting sensors had crossed.

"Laboratories and research."

"How many ways in or out?"

"One. Through here, sir."

Jeremy's voice would have been pleasant if fear had not ratcheted it tight. Nikola glanced around the cavernous reception space. As at Hypnos, hibernation stations, whether penitentiary or private, had only underground accesses.

"And vehicles?"

"Below us, but there's only a single access." Jeremy pointed to a glazed wall to one side that opened onto a wide ramp blocked by a squat black armored truck.

"Who's at the labs now?" Nikola asked.

"Nobody, sir. Employees leave at six and the janitors don't start until midnight."

"Could you check?"

"Well, yes, but—"

"Please?" Nikola was aware of how unnerving his full scrutiny could be on whoever was with him and that it had often proved more than some could tolerate. He smiled and watched the boy darting a nervous glance to the men spreading through the reception area—large men clad in black uniforms with shiny body armor, hard hats, and serious-looking hardware cradled in their arms. Jeremy turned on his heel and marched to the reception counter. Nikola cocked his head to speak into his lapel mic. "Get the police, the National Guard, and the army. Ring the city with roadblocks and flash images and descriptions to airports and public transport stations." He listened to Dennis's question and shook his head. "No escaped convicts. Terrorists. Four: a woman and three—" He paused. "There could be four or five terrorists: a woman and three or four men, one of them sick or unconscious, possibly on a stretcher or in a wheelchair. Armed, dangerous, no contact, kill on sight."

It couldn't be helped. Nikola would have dearly loved to

interview the doctor, the lawyers, or the controller if they traveled together, but he couldn't risk anyone listening to them before he got there. He leaned onto the counter, his eyes never leaving the young man's face. Not a bad face—a predatory nose, almost patrician, above firm lips and jutting over a delicate jaw. High and intelligent forehead—an illusion. Most people with high foreheads seemed bright until they opened their mouths. He glanced at the young man's fingers and flinched at the rough and ragged cuticles, the nails bitten to the quick. Nails, not the eyes, were the mirror of the soul. Abused nails belonged to throwaway people.

"I—I'm sorry, sir." Jeremy blanched, and whatever appeal he had deserted his face.

"Yes?"

"Dr. Carpenter."

"What about Dr. Carpenter?"

"He's not checked out; he's still in the research block."

"See, I knew we would get somewhere. Lead the way." He nodded to the lieutenant in charge of the FDU team and followed the young security officer. His earpiece blipped.

"Floyd Carpenter, Caucasian, forty-one, five-eleven, medical graduate, Maryland, class of forty-four, AMM doctorate, Houston, class of forty-sev—"

"What's that?"

"Advanced Mammalian Metabolism."

"Family?"

"Divorced, no children. His mother is the only surviving relative."

"Pick her up."

Silence.

"Confirm," Nikola insisted irritably.

"That may be difficult. Cecilia Carpenter, née Hailey, is the high priestess of Twilight's Children, last heard of in Pidakkesh."

"Where's that?"

"Northern Pakistan, a stone's throw from Afghanistan and China's Xinjiang Uygur Autonomous Region. She's running an enlightenment mission there."

"Try to find her, anyway."
"Will do."

In the garden outside, intermittent gusts of wind blew the leaves up and down. But Senator Palmer wasn't watching their movements; his unfocused gaze was lost in the distance. He jolted, pivoted around, and dashed to his desk in two strides to reach for the secure phone a fraction of a second after the first blip.

"Palmer."

For an instant he thought he'd been rash and messed up the link, but after a short delay, the scrambler kicked in its sizzling stream of exchange data before *HORUS* flashed on the terminal's screen.

A metallic cackle. "That was quick. Are we nervous, Senator?"

Palmer waited.

"Your boys are having a spot of trouble. Onuris tracked them to Nyx Corporation a few minutes ago."

An eddy started to swirl in his stomach. "How?"

"That's the beauty of technology. It appears the sensors carried by the inmates are also location transmitters."

"That's impossible." But after he said it, Palmer closed his eyes.

"Is it? One must agree it's a logical feature."

"Kept secret?"

"Well, that's not exactly true. The DHS knew."

"And so did Hypnos," Palmer said.

"Precisely."

Palmer's mind raced. *Your boys* meant Horus didn't know the names of those involved. The voice had sounded even, almost nonchalant. They had not been caught. There had to be hope.

"They lost them," the voice said.

Dragging words from Horus was like getting credit from a hooker.

"A few minutes before the troops arrived, they lost the signal."

"Meaning?" Palmer asked.

"Either they removed the transmitters or found a way to interfere with the signal."

"And now?"

"Onuris has lost their scent."

Silence.

"Senator, your boys are running, probably frightened, and frightened folks are unpredictable."

After a burst of static, the screen went blank. Palmer stood from his desk, neared a credenza, and poured a shot of malt whiskey from a decanter into a cognac glass. As he was about to drink, he frowned, peered into the liquid, and sniffed. Right glass, wrong stuff—or the other way around. He downed it in one gulp and returned to his desk. He had to warn Shepherd.

The tunnel passing under the bowels of the Nyx station was a dead end; they could only retrace their steps. Laurel trotted ahead toward the main sewer, as the men huffed behind her in single file and kept to the dry sidewalk flanking a trough filled with a lazy whitish fluid. With a flashlight in one hand slashing wildly over the crumbling brick surfaces, she reached by feel to the side of her computer to bring it online. Laurel glanced at a bunch of fluffy-looking stalactites dangling from the curved roof. Above their heads, the DHS would be positioning their awesome assets. A Machiavellian paradox, but the DHS involvement and the identity of the man on the stretcher worked to their advantage, affording them a slim chance of escape.

Had Russo been a common criminal, the DHS would have mustered every agency and corps in the land: police, National Guard, the army, and even the fire brigades. Within minutes, the sewers would have been swarming with soldiers. They wouldn't have had a chance. But Russo was a secret, a genie the DHS couldn't afford to let out of the bottle. If they involved other agencies, the DHS would have to offer explanations and someone might recognize Russo—although after seeing his emaciated face, Laurel doubted even his mother would. No. The DHS would go solo. They might use forces from other agencies, but only to secure a perimeter of roadblocks and mass transport exit points. Their crack Fast Deployment Units, the dreaded FDUs, numbered a scant three hundred men scattered all over the nation. At short notice, the DHS could muster fewer than a third of their elite forces. Those had been Shepherd's precise words.

"Now what?" Dr. Floyd Carpenter's voice echoed behind her as they piled out into the main sewer.

A warm waft of rancid, fatty air enveloped her like a shroud. She moved forward to a wider section of the ledge so the others could move into the tunnel. On GPS mode, the Metapad displayed a digitized map of the sewers, courtesy of WASA's Documents and Permits Section and exchanged for a large wad of cash from a supervisor at the Blue Plains sewage-treatment plant. Red lines identified sanitary sewers, blue lines storm sewers, and an overwhelming layer of brown lines identified combined sewers—a gargantuan network with almost two thousand miles of pipes and tunnels. Laurel peered at an alien universe of colored dots: flow-metering stations, storm-water-pumping stations, and thousands of catch basins, infalls, and utility holes.

Hampered by the wrap around her neck, Laurel gazed into the impenetrable darkness to her left and the fat fields. The stench grew and, with it, the uncanny sensation of fat dribbling down her throat. Floyd stepped away from the stretcher resting on the floor, bent in two, and spewed forth a thick gush of vomit. Lukas joined him with a Morse code of dry heaves. Laurel swallowed, intent on the Metapad screen.

Please, not west. The main sewer ran east to west. The roaches and the slabs of clotted, festering fat lay a few hundred yards due west. She propped the flashlight on the floor, pointing upward, and glanced at Raul, who stood like a statue, with his stiff neck encased in a white band. From a depression on the computer's rubber housing, Laurel fished a stylus and tapped the screen to transmitter mode. When a keyboard scrolled at the bottom of the display, she tapped with her stylus.

>*Help*.

Laurel jerked to a loud snort on her right. The edge of the band around her neck rubbed her chafed skin.

Floyd leaned over her shoulder. "Calling for Mom?"

"Look, Doc—"

"Drop the title. I'm Floyd." His breath had a tang of hydrochloric acid.

The screen remained blank, a tiny prompt flashing white.

"The goons above will thank you for the beacon," Floyd noted.

"No, they won't. This uses a military-issue Squirt transmitter. It alters outgoing signals. After scrambling, it packs any transmission into a burst lasting a few microseconds."

Where are you? She was using the emergency procedure Shepherd swore they would never need. If this failed, she had nothing else to try. Once more, she tapped her stylus on the screen.

>Help.

"Mom must be out of earshot." Floyd sounded amused.

The Metapad's screen flashed.

>Coordinates?

She addressed the GPS and clicked a window.

Lukas had finished retching and now squatted, his back to the curved wall of the tunnel. For a paper pusher, he was behaving with commendable restraint. The tunnel echoed with wet, slurpy sounds. She screwed her eyes to focus on a round opening on the opposite bank, a pipe hiccuping gushes of liquid. It didn't sound like water but something thicker, like bile.

Laurel blinked and a single letter flashed on the computer's screen: *>E.* She smiled.

"That way." She pointed east.

Raul and Lukas let out breaths of relief.

"Am I missing something?" Floyd asked.

"Yes, the fat." She grabbed her flashlight, stepped past the group and into the trough of the branch line, and crossed over to the walkway running along the opposite wall of the main sewer. Behind her, the men huffed, lifting the stretcher with Russo.

After a couple of hundred yards, the walkway disappeared and they had to wade through twelve inches of slowly moving fluid, its surface broken by bobbing lumps. Laurel kept glancing at the pipe openings on the walls, which spewed gushes of milky fluid, and the wider holes piercing the curved roof, half-expecting a blinding light and armor-clad men to drop through at any moment. She checked the computer. Nothing. In the main sewer tunnel, they were sitting ducks. As any cretin could see by checking a sewer map, the only way out of Nyx was through the spur line and into the main tunnel. Two small groups, one at each end, could hem them in like rats. As they reached the first intersection, the screen went crazy, with coordinates scrolling down it and then stopping at a flashing prompt, the numbers dissolving under a colored diagram, a red line snaking through a maze of brown lanes of different widths.

"Right," she announced, and swung her flashlight into the opening.

The smaller tunnel looked newer; it had smooth concrete walls, weeping as if suffering from ineffable sadness. They climbed onto a narrow sidewalk and slogged one hundred yards before reaching a domed vault with four smaller openings. Laurel pointed to the one on their far left and tramped across, giving wide berth to large clothed lumps arranged in the center. She shivered to think what lay inside.

Obviously, Shepherd had planned a circular route to thwart any attempt to track them through the sewers. After changing course at each new intersection at least a dozen times, she guessed it would take a large force to find them. Infrared sensors wouldn't work: too many hot spots of decaying matter. Motion detectors wouldn't be of much use either; large objects moved continually through the sewers, particularly in the wider tunnels. That left sound, but their splashing noises were swallowed by cascading water and the intermittent thumps when larger objects fell from side pipes or when rats, some as large as cats, dove into the filth.

"It seems you were right; there's nobody here," Nikola said.

Jeremy had the sense to press his lips together instead of offering an excuse.

Nikola panned the shower room, wrinkling his nose at a pile of discarded oilskins and filthy rubber boots. He nodded

to an FDU soldier blocking the door. "Get hold of your sci-
entific officer."

Nikola peered at the torn remains of a lead apron. *So this is
how you did it. Most enterprising.* He sniffed. Under a strong
smell of disinfectant, he caught the sweet odor of lanolin.
Again, he turned to the FDU officer, who shadowed him like a
ghost. "Seal this floor and the ones below. Have a forensics
team run over it." He nodded to the machines. "I want the data
from those." After a last look around, he turned to the young
man in charge of the Nyx security detail. "Is there access to
the sewers, Jeremy?"

"You mean our waste-treatment plant?"

"No, Jeremy. I mean the city sewers."

"Two floors down, sir."

"Lead the way."

Nikola followed Jeremy down emergency stairs to a service floor crammed with machinery, then down more steps to
an unkempt cellar of bare concrete pillars and crates piled
high everywhere: a storage area. "How do you move these
about?"

Jeremy pointed to large steel doors at the end of the room.
"Through the cargo lift, sir."

After a cursory look around, Nikola strode to a sizable
door on solid hinges, its security lock pried open. A crowbar
was leaning against one wall.

"The sewers?"

Jeremy nodded, his face pale as an alabaster statue. With a
little more character, his face would have been perfect. But
perfection, as the old Greek proverb warned, was incompati-
ble with good and truth.

"Open it up."

"Jeremy Clark, twenty-five," Nikola's ear set droned.
"Five-ten, college dropout, at Nyx for five years. One year in
charge of the night shift. Married, three kids."

"Oh?"

"Yes. They were fined heavily for the third child." Nikola
pictured Dennis accessing court records. After the 56th Constitutional Amendment, producing more than two children

was a serious offense. "He explained to the judge it was an accident; *condom interruptus.*"

"See to him," Nikola said in a low voice.

"How long?"

"Until this is over."

"Will do."

Jeremy yanked the door open, letting in a waft of almost tangible stench. "You said something, sir?"

Nikola reached to Jeremy's face and drew the tip of his finger lightly across his fine jaw before clapping a friendly arm around his shoulder.

"Nothing, son. Nothing that should concern you."

day two

||||

Inferno, Canto VI: 10–12
Gross hailstones, water gray with filth,
and snow come streaking down across the shadowed air;
the earth, as it receives that shower, stinks.

The Divine Comedy, DANTE ALIGHIERI

chapter 16

01:15

"Pet. No calls." When a thin bar atop her communications console flickered from green to red, Odelle stood, laid a hand on her desk, and reached down to remove her shoes. She eyed the door of her office. "Pet. No visitors." There was a dry metallic snap as the lock released its bolts.

A few steps from the center of the room, Odelle glanced through the vast panoramic window of her office at the DHS headquarters to a forest of skyscrapers dotting the night like the fruit of strangely prolific vines. "Pet. Privacy." The glazed surfaces flickered and frosted over.

Splaying her toes like a cat's to grip the carpet's luscious pile, she stood on the balls of her feet and stretched both arms toward the ceiling, an almost forgotten memory pushing to the forefront of her mind. *Nothing is impossible if you keep trying,* her mother had once scolded Sonia, Odelle's kid sister. The little girl wanted to give up after trying to place a piece in a puzzle for two full minutes. Sonia had looked up at her mother, her three-year-old face set in the patronizing expression one uses to address the dim-witted. "Can you shape water?"

After that, Odelle's memory was hazy. She couldn't recall Mother's reaction or her likely retort, but Sonia's question had remained forever etched in Odelle's mind. She relaxed her feet and pushed to stand again on tiptoe, her calves bunching with a welcome ache.

Through a door flanked by floor-to-ceiling bookcases crowded with legal texts, she padded into the bathroom. After unbuckling her belt, Odelle sat on the toilet, trousers pooling over her feet. *Pet.*

They had been impossibly young, students at a godforsaken college in the middle of nowhere, hemmed by fields of wheat stretching for miles around: wheat the color of Araceli's hair. Between classes, they would run back to their room and hold hands, and hug, and kiss, and splash water on their faces to hide telltale redness.

Odelle sidestepped over to the washbasin. The faucet detected her nearness and released warm water.

After graduation, they'd moved to a dingy apartment, transformed into heaven with eggshell-colored wall paint, posters, and love. *The writing is always on the wall,* Felipe Ho, her Sino–Spanish professor of criminal law, would insist as he tugged at a few sparse hairs dangling from his chin. Odelle agreed, but only to a point. Sometimes it wasn't writing but posters. She should have understood that the placards with caricatures of a brutal government on their apartment walls weren't idealistic delusions of the impossibly young but a testimony of commitment. Could she have altered destiny? Would van Gogh's cornfields and Turner's fogs have made any difference? Probably not, but she wouldn't have felt so foolish at Araceli's betrayal, given that the evidence had stared into her face for years.

Like a thief, Araceli had left before dawn to join a coterie of activists, the dangerous ones, old enough to be beyond puny idealism. When Odelle finally found her, there was only a husk left of the Araceli she had known—a meek pregnant creature who made calf eyes at Eliot Russo, the Lord of Dreamers. The scene was etched in her mind, as painful as a brand: Russo's expression of pure contempt as Odelle foolishly wondered if Araceli molded to his body as she had molded to hers.

Three days later, the riot police charged a group of demonstrators. In the confusion, Araceli's man, the mighty Lord of Dreamers, scuttled away like a startled crab, leaving Araceli sprawled on the tarmac after she'd tripped—at the mercy of storming shields, truncheons, and rubber bullets. Odelle had studied a film of the demonstration, painstakingly recorded by NBC cameras, a thousand times; she'd frozen three frames to store in the darkest repository of her memory. In one, a fallen Araceli stretched an arm, fingers splayed, toward her fleeing hero, confusion and betrayal pasted in eyes grown too large for her face. In another, Eliot Russo, after stopping mid-stride to look back at Araceli, ran to the safety of a waiting car, his features rutted with terror.

Odelle splashed warm water on her face and peered in the mirror. Her perfectly lined eyes were rimmed with eyelashes dewed with tiny water drops, and she caught a glimpse of something written in her face that she had not seen before. Her features bore a new familiarity, as though a mask had been removed, revealing the face of another woman—the woman she used to be, though when and where she couldn't tell. She put her face closer to the mirror to inspect the sparkling blue shine on her eyelids and the strong carmine of her lips, then reached to a stand and rubbed her face dry with a fluffy cotton towel, the third frame flashing against her closed eyelids.

The third frame captured the instant when a huge, steel-capped boot crashed into Araceli's elfin face.

Odelle dropped the spotless towel into a basket and glanced again at her undisturbed makeup—the wonders of intradermal pigmentation. Now the Lord of Dreamers had fled again, not carried off by his treacherous feet but by those of another generation of world-changers. Lukas, the mercenary, and the lawyers: Bastien, Raul, and Laurel. *Laurel . . . Was Bastien your man? Did you snap his neck yourself?*

On her way to her desk, she detoured to stand between two bookcases and fumbled behind a molding to press a button. A wooden panel slid upward to reveal a small, old-fashioned safe. Odelle keyed a code on an alphanumeric pad and reached for a walnut-size wooden box sitting between a leather-bound notebook and a wad of Japanese currency.

She settled on her leather chair and rubbed the soles of her feet before feeling blindly for her pumps. Yes, there was a way of shaping water. After freezing it, you attacked it with hammer and chisel.

Often, objects earned different names as a function of their use. An ice pick could become a murder weapon if found jutting from the ear of a person seemingly asleep, and a ringlet of hair metamorphosed from trash—if swept from the floor of a barbershop—into a treasure if clipped from a lover's head. Odelle examined the tiny box she'd taken from her safe. It was cylindrical, a little over an inch in diameter, its lid intricately carved by a laser in Indonesia and sold as genuine Native American artistry. A gift from Araceli, bought during a trip through Baja California and Mexico. A trip spent in a continuous state of drunkenness from sun, laughter, and wine. *This is a dream box,* a salesclerk decked in shaman garb had assured them. *Place an object inside or a scrap of paper with a wish, hold the box against your heart, and your dream will come true.* Incredibly young and foolish, Odelle had treasured the little box and hidden a tuft of Araceli's hair inside. When Araceli eloped with her dreamer, Odelle cried herself to sleep with the box pressed between her breasts, and when she woke up it had left an angry mark.

Much later, she rechristened the object "my FY box."

Sometimes people—in particular women with a trace of common sense—stashed away a "fuck you" fund: the means to disappear and start anew rather than suffer blows and sex laced with stale beer breath. Other women would put up with that and more—like being marooned in a house full of echoing rooms, with sore nipples, while somewhere an infant screamed to be fed. *Idiots.* Odelle had not one but several funds salted away in sunny islands—the largest in Antigua—but her FY box was unique and priceless. Brushing her dark mane out of the way, Odelle removed her diamond stud earrings and set them aside. Then she twisted the lid of the box, and from a cushion of wavy hair she removed two studs: two tiny dark-red spheres mounted in gold, which she fixed on her earlobes. She dropped her diamond earrings in the box and replaced its lid.

As she drew figure eights with the tip of her finger on her glazed desktop, Odelle pondered that Russo's resilience went beyond her wildest imagination. *Without regular maintenance, he'll be dead within a year.* Those had been Vinson Duran's exact words. But the years went by, and the Lord of Dreamers had refused to die. An omen? His breakout had been a blow, but it was nothing compared to the sober realization that someone powerful, resourceful, and clever was after her ass. Not many people could pull off such a stunt, and she would flush him or her out eventually. But there was a possibility, however remote, that Russo would get away. That's why she'd resolved to use her FY box. At her direction, a Chinese artisan had covered two minuscule gelatin balls with coats of red lacquer until they shone like small pearls. Lacquer was hard but brittle; a sharp blow or a determined bite would shatter it and release the gelatin pouch in its core: two milligrams of ricin, enough to kill a horse in ten seconds.

She sighed and fingered one of her new studs absently, her mind racing, weighing alternatives and courses of action. Then her concentration wavered, and she closed her eyes as her thoughts dissolved to coalesce in an image—the same face that haunted her dreams. *Pet.*

When the technicians had installed the voice-activated system, they asked for a word to precede any command. It had to be a special word. A word she would never utter other than within the walls of her office in any context. It had been easy. She had never called Araceli by her name, even when angry.

chapter 17

||||

01:23

Three hours after their descent into the sewers, Laurel stopped on a dry platform before another main branch, larger and older than the first. She peered at the Metapad screen and gauged the width of the brown lane depicted on the map. Where a red line—the path they were supposed to follow—crossed the brown, there should have been a narrow opening. She glanced up, but she could barely make it out on the opposite wall. Eyeing the volume of effluent moving through the center of the tunnel and its speed, Laurel guessed this was the main trunk line. She suppressed a shudder. Engorged by rain, flash floods would roar down the tunnel.

"Let's take a short break." She wedged her back against the curved wall and slid to sit down on the concrete, thinking that someone on the surface would be dancing for the gods of rain to deliver. A flash flood would carry their bodies all the way to the Potomac.

Floyd squatted. After checking Russo's pulse, he reached into his bag, pushed the pad of a pressure sensor into Russo's neck, and shook his head. "I don't know how, but he's hanging in there. His resilience is incredible." After digging in his bag again, Floyd produced a syrette, ripped a section of the bag open, and rammed it onto Russo's thigh.

Laurel blinked. An intramuscular shot would spread through Russo's metabolism at a much slower rate. That meant Russo was stable. For months she had pored over the scant literature Shepherd could find dealing with hibernation and its aftereffects, but nothing in the books she'd read could account for Russo's ravaged state.

His ministrations complete, Floyd stood and looked around. He stepped over to sit close to her. "Do we have much farther to go?"

She cocked her head, wincing at the strain of her neck wrap. "Half a mile."

"And then?"

"Your guess is as good as mine. We wait, I suppose."

"That man won't take much more of this. He needs blood."

"You mentioned blood back at Nyx, and I saw scores of red lines on the machine's printout. What do you people poison them with that they need a change of blood?"

"Ask Hypnos."

"I'm asking you."

"That man," he pointed his chin toward the stretcher, "has had no maintenance. I've examined people who'd served a few years in Hypnos's tanks. With a little fine-tuning, they were as good as new. Most of them walked away from sugar cubes after a week of convalescence, but I've never seen anybody like him. He shouldn't be alive with what is coursing through his veins."

She bit her chapped lower lip. "I'm sorry. I know you didn't do anything to him, but you are an expert and use a similar setup."

"We constantly monitor our patients and regularly flush their systems free of toxins. Besides, our setup, as you call it, may be similar, but it is much more sophisticated and expensive."

"How so?"

"The fluid temperature is critical for keeping a subject in ideal condition throughout hibernation. At commercial stations like Nyx, we use individual tanks to suspend the patients. Clearly, in a communal tank, with scores of individuals, the temperature is a compromise, an average. Shortages can be overcome only by altering the blood's chemistry with drugs. Don't forget renal functions are also down. Over time, impurities build up. At Nyx, we survey hematology, electrolytes, liver enzymes, nitrogen elements, protein, lipids, ratios, differentials, you name it. When counts reach a critical level, we dialyze the patients. You know, scrub their blood."

"I know a little about dialysis."

"How come? I thought you were a lawyer."

"My aunt suffered a kidney failure. She went to a clinic three times a week to be hooked for hours to a machine. Sometimes I would keep her company."

"Okay, then. Electrolytes build up and osmotic pressure goes wild, with off-the-chart levels of basophilic activity."

"What's that?"

"A white cell, which in turn triggers releases of histamine, heparin, and serotonin—the markers of allergic reactions."

"You mean people in hibernation develop allergies?"

"Right. Let's face it, the body rebels against any unnatural state, and hibernation is the most unnatural of them all for a human." He paused and his eyes twinkled. "I couldn't help but notice you didn't expect your charge to be in such bad shape. You didn't know?"

"None of us did."

Floyd pursed his lips.

Laurel glanced toward Raul. He was staring at them and had obviously been following their exchange. His mind would be reeling with the realization that, had Shepherd and his master known that Russo was a barely living corpse, they would have never entertained such a complex operation. And Bastien would be alive. She ran a finger under the ragged edge of the lead collar.

Floyd nodded. "I'll remove the transmitters as soon as we have a thirty-minute window."

"Thank you." She closed her eyes and leaned back until her head rested against the damp concrete.

After a few minutes, they got to their feet and followed the red line on the computer screen. Crossing the main sewage tunnel, they entered the narrow passage. Laurel, marching point, could hear the men's shoulders scraping against the smooth concrete walls. The air changed. Hot wafts beat down the tube at intervals. After slow progress through a brick corridor strung crazily with obsolete electric wires and plodding through a foot-deep sour-smelling mud, they stumbled across a threshold and the passage opened into a circular chamber pierced by several openings. Laurel stood aside while the rest of the group trooped in. She glanced toward Raul and froze. "Your neck!"

Raul lowered the stretcher, his face a mask of confusion. Then his hand flew to his bare neck. He swore, pivoted on his heel, and charged out of the chamber into the corridor they had just left.

Lukas's lips moved as if in prayer. Laurel bunched her fists as heavy thumps echoed from the passageway at their back. She glanced around at walls covered with fungi like misshapen tumors. The stone looked diseased in the stale atmosphere. Then Raul burst into the chamber, his hand holding the piece of lead apron, now dripping gunk, around his neck.

"How long?" Lukas asked.

Floyd rummaged in his bag, drew out a roll of adhesive tape, and secured Raul's strip with a couple of extra turns. "A couple of minutes at most. He had it on when we entered that narrow passage."

Laurel glanced at her watch—almost one-thirty—and turned to Lukas. "Can they locate us?"

He shrugged. "I doubt it. We're deep underground, but I don't know how these fucking things work."

"We better get going." Laurel pointed to one of the openings—an entrance that had formerly been closed by a grating of which nothing but the hinges remained.

Ten minutes later, the passage opened into a set of steps descending into a flooded chamber, the only exits three brick arches on the opposite wall. The foul water was capped by thin fog that left only a twelve-inch clearance at the top.

She surveyed the shocked expressions of the three men, heard a splash, and saw several spots moving across the water, like the snorkels of miniature submarines.

"Through there?" Raul's voice had lost color.

"Middle one," Laurel said.

"How far?" Lukas asked.

Laurel checked her computer. The red line ran straight to the top of the screen and ended in a flashing dot. They were approaching the point of the final coordinate lodged in the Metapad. After that, they would have to wait for further input. She tapped the screen, but with her nails trimmed back, the computer couldn't identify the instruction. Swearing under her breath, she fished out the stylus and pecked at the red line, aghast at the result. "Two hundred feet."

"Through there?" Raul sounded like a faulty recording.

"And with company." Floyd nodded at the wakes crisscrossing the water.

The men's faces were ghostly in the light bouncing off the milky water. A lump bobbed lazily across, and the dots in the water veered to explore. Laurel looked at Raul. "There goes one of your hairy balls."

Nobody laughed.

"Zip Russo all the way up. We don't want his face scraping the roof. Lukas, douse your flashlight and carry that bag above the water. Let's go," Laurel said.

With a resolve she didn't feel, she locked her gaze on the opening at the other side of the chamber and stepped forward, placing each foot with care. The water level rose until it licked the fringe of her neck wrap. On the edge of her consciousness, she fought an image of hungry rodents swimming toward her, sharp teeth laced with rabies and scores of other plagues. Another step; a splash. Something soft brushed past her thigh, the sensation sharp through the cold fabric of her suit. Another step; more splashes. Behind her, huffs, curses, and the sound of moving water. Her vision blurred. She saw a majestic oak in bright sunshine and underneath it a swing with a little girl in a white dress, giggling at each push of her father's brawny arms. Laurel had reached the opening when she heard Lukas's quivering voice launch into the first verses of "The Star-Spangled Banner." Thicker voices joined in, and she knew they would make it to the other side of the corridor.

Senator Palmer waited for the second set of beeps before answering, as *DAPHNIS* flashed on the screen of his secure set.

"Palmer."

"I sent them off to the moles." A carillon of code beeps, a snap, and then silence.

Palmer removed his reading glasses, a tribute to a bygone era; he'd refused intraocular surgery, preferring the old-fashioned lenses.

When he'd entered codes in his secure scrambler, Palmer had hesitated to assign *Daphnis* to Shepherd. Yes, Daphnis, the son of Hermes and a Sicilian nymph, was a shepherd, but his name originated from the Greek *daphne*. He'd looked up the word's etymology, to discover *daphne* meant laurel or bay tree. And now Laurel would place her life and that of her companions in the hands of strangers. *Laurel, my brave dear girl.* There had to be a hidden meaning in the coincidence.

Palmer closed his eyes. His only hope now lay in people who had lost hope in society. The mole people.

Progress through the flooded tunnel was painstakingly slow. Twice Laurel stopped when her boot caught on an immersed obstacle, soft and squishy. Keeping the flashlight above water to light the way for her companions, she sidestepped, calling out, "Lump!" The air wafted hot over the water. Halfway through, she had to wave the flashlight ahead to clear her way through a tangle of brown spaghettilike excrescences issuing through cracks in the brickwork.

"Someone had a busy weekend." Floyd moved two paces behind her, followed by Raul. He had rested the poles on his shoulders and draped one of the belts across his forehead. At his back, Raul held the opposite end of the poles against the roof, keeping the end of the bag with Russo's head clear of the water. Lukas closed the ranks.

Laurel saw a large clump of condoms floating past and cast a thin smile back at Floyd.

After another ten minutes of slow progress, something new crept into the fetid atmosphere. A flurry of soft noises traveled over the surface of the water. Laurel froze and switched her flashlight off. "Quiet!" Darkness crashed down on them. Tiny yellow lights scuttled across her eyes. She blinked and the lights faded.

"What is it?" Floyd whispered, almost on top of her.

"I don't know. I thought I heard something."

She toggled the flashlight to its minimum setting before switching it on again. They continued in silence for twenty or thirty feet, finally landing in a vast rotunda, its domed ceiling curving a good twenty feet overhead. The walls were jagged, the bricks splintered and fissured, with tufts of brown moss growing in the cracks.

"An exchange," Lukas said.

"What?" Raul asked.

"Minor branches empty here to flood into the main line." He pointed to a tunnel mouth gaping to their left. They waded to the edge of the rotunda and climbed a set of slippery concrete steps onto a dry sidewalk.

"So this is it?" Floyd asked.

Laurel checked the computer, glanced at the flooded tunnel they had just left, and switched the flashlight back on full beam. "No. Now we climb." She held the light's beam on rusty ladder rungs to an opening ten feet off the ground.

"Now you climb and we do the Sherpa routine," Raul said.

Laurel edged along the sidewalk to the rungs and tried

them. Although covered in a thick layer of crunchy rust, the metal looked sound enough to hold their weight. When Laurel reached the opening at the top, she shone the flashlight down as the men struggled to maneuver the stretcher up the steps and parallel to the wall, Russo's shape firmly secured with straps.

The narrow passage they entered was set on a slight incline and was dry, without watermarks. After a couple of minutes, they found themselves in a vast tunnel, the air warm and thankfully lacking the stench of sewage, although they carried plenty of the gunk dripping from their suits. A glint flashed a few feet ahead and she killed the flashlight.

"Now what? You saw something?" The rich timbre of Floyd's voice was laced with irony.

In darkness, Laurel advanced one foot in front of the other to a point where she squatted and reached with her hand. "A fucking rail." Again she ratcheted down the light setting and pressed the flashlight's power switch. A dim glow highlighted two sets of standard railway tracks: an abandoned subway tunnel.

As she straightened, a distinct snap sounded a few yards ahead. Not the soft scurrying sound of an animal, but a heavy step. Once more, she switched the light off and retreated toward the men. They must have heard the noise. She bumped into a shape.

"Shhhhhh." A whisper.

Long fingers sought hers. She gripped them like a castaway would driftwood.

Another crack, closer this time. She gripped the anonymous fingers tighter.

Ahead of them something moved, followed by a cackling laugh. "Plan to hold hands all night?"

||||

chapter 18

01:32

"Resourceful." Dennis Nolan fingered a sample of the lead apron used to shield the transmitters.

"How would you have done it?" Nikola asked.

Dennis leaned over and dropped the sample on Nikola's lap.

"Ouch!"

"Yes, lead is a good electromagnetic shield, great density, but they could have wrapped foil around their necks or wound up a copper wire a few times. I suppose the radiation apron is more elegant and foolproof, though."

Nikola glanced at one of the overhead clocks and turned to peer through the van's tinted window at the imposing Nyx building. The DHS scientific team would be sifting through the crime scene, and their silence could only mean there was little, if anything, of importance in the reanimation rooms or the basements. He sniffed and ran his hands over the remains of the lead apron. Not that he expected a trail of crumbs, but often frightened people behaved in the dumbest of ways.

Without a clue to their whereabouts or their sensors acting as homing beacons, the fugitives were as good as gone. The Fast Deployment Units he'd dotted through the city were mostly for show. He closed his eyes. Over a century earlier, during the Warsaw uprising in WWII, thousands of people had moved across the city through the sewers despite having masses of German troops over their heads. The Germans hated the sewers and were scared to enter them. And, after a short incursion a couple of years earlier to inspect a clandestine laboratory, Nikola understood their reluctance. Instead of keeping company with the rats, the Germans would lower listening devices and wait patiently for any noise that didn't belong. Then they would hurl stick grenades down the utility holes. But the groups moving about through the sewers were anything but stupid. They shunned flashlights, and talking was forbidden. Anytime Nikola met any reference to sewers in his daily work, a bizarre image flashed in his mind—a macabre procession of silent shadows in the choking darkness of a sewer.

"You have a theory how they found out about the transmitters?" Nikola asked.

"It was an oversight. I should have known."

"Go on." Nikola knew what Dennis was about to say, but he wanted to hear it anyway.

"When their signature flared over at Nyx, it should have been obvious they would try to reanimate Russo or, at least, stabilize him. That would mean sophisticated equipment, and nowadays they use wireless sensors. As soon as another transmitter entered the monitor's radius of detection, it would show."

"Yes, that was my guess." When he spotted the machine in the surgery room, Nikola had come to a similar conclusion.

Dennis flicked his fingers over a pad and the screens refreshed with data. "There's one thing I can't figure out, though."

Nikola reached by feel to a small fridge built in by his seat for a water pack—a flat, soft polymer container with a nipple to one side—and tore its seal. "Go on."

"If these things broadcast all the time, why don't they interfere with the equipment in the tanks?"

Dennis's best and most useful feature was a beautiful mind, Nikola thought. "That was an obstacle when I oversaw the design, and a dead end until someone found the answer. As you know, the inmates have their sensors precisely implanted, so the transducer choker circling their necks will never be farther than a quarter inch from its receiving surface. The sensors need little power to relay signals to a receptor so close, but to be effective as tracking devices they need to broadcast with more power."

"And that would mess with other equipment nearby," Dennis mused. "I suppose that scores of separate signals radiating in the close quarters of a tank must have played hell with the other receivers."

"Precisely. The answer was to have them switched off as locators when immersed."

"How did you manage that? A signal tripping a relay?"

"Much simpler. A junior engineer at Hypnos, almost a kid, figured it out. He wired a microscopic bimetallic strip switch to the casing."

"A temperature switch?"

"Correct. When the inmates sink into the tank and their body temperature drops, the transmitter switches off."

"How long can the implants broadcast?"

"Indefinitely. The erbium accumulators inside recharge from the natural current in living bodies."

"And outside a body?"

"Almost a year. So, if they remove the implants, they'd better smash them to bits instead of keeping them as a souvenir. They are pretty things, you know?"

Dennis nodded. "You reckon they're still wearing them?"

"Well, they didn't have the time to take them off at Nyx. Now"—Nikola shrugged—"they have a doctor with them." He cocked his head again to look toward the Nyx building and sighed. "I don't think the brainiacs gathering bits of fluff down there will find anything else. Let's go home." He stood and stepped over to the front of the van.

Dennis's hands flew over one of his keyboards to set the equipment on standby, then he unplugged a flat screen, perhaps six inches by eight, moved over to the driver's seat, and clipped the pad into a docking station. A red throbbing light flashed on the device. Dennis stared into the flickering light and blinked several times. The screen flared green before dissolving into a maze of superimposing lines. Now, from the front seat, Dennis could control the sophisticated equipment in the back of the van. Nikola stared ahead. Driving with an interactive video device in the cockpit would cost anyone his or her driver's license, but Nikola doubted that anyone, after checking the registration, would have the nerve to try it in his van.

"How good are these sewer maps you have?" Nikola asked.

"As good as they come. These are the working layouts of WASA, the D.C. Water and Sewage Authority."

"Accurate?"

"To a point, but these cover only the upper levels."

"How many levels are there?"

"No idea, but at least a dozen." Dennis slowed down, then turned at an intersection.

"No maps?"

"Not even records. Sewers are the weakest spot in most old cities. An army could move through the many forgotten and unexplored levels. The authorities have tried to separate the sanitary and storm systems and have even installed sensors in some new lines—in particular those near strategic areas—but it's a useless exercise."

"Why?"

"As I said, only the upper levels are covered. One can install detectors on the ground floor of a house and feel protected. Problem is the many uncharted basements under the property."

"Yes, but they still have to come up to the ground floor to get to you."

"True," Dennis conceded, "but they would be inside the property already. Combined systems is another problem; a nightmare."

Nikola stared ahead as Dennis maneuvered to overtake a lumbering truck.

"Like many older cities, most of the D.C. sewers were built at the end of the nineteenth century as combined systems to carry, in the same pipe, both sanitary sewage and storm water to the treatment plant."

"Here in Washington, D.C., I suppose that means the Blue Plains plant."

"Right. The ideal separate system would channel sewage through one set of pipes, while storm water would flow through a separate set of pipes to the rivers. But old cities rarely have an ideal prototype of anything. Washington evolved as a combined system, with newer, separated networks only in the more recently constructed areas."

Nikola frowned. "What's up with a combined system?"

"The system works reasonably well in dry weather, but the main lines can't hold both wastewater and storm water during heavy rainfall, so they divert the lot into the Potomac and Anacostia Rivers, Rock Creek, and other tributaries."

"You're implying the fugitives can make it to the Potomac without ever having to surface?"

"I'm certain there are scores of abandoned tunnels and pipes heading in that direction."

Nikola nodded absently. Dennis's details backed his decision not to commit any forces to the sewers. It would have been a pointless exercise. "But the system must have been maintained and renewed, no?" He hoped the network of sensors and security measures had been extended.

"It has. But enlarging a tunnel or pipe is a nightmare. Instead, the engineers have sunk new ones at different levels, often using parts of the old ones. There have been tunnels, private railway lines, shelters, deep stores, you name it, piled on top or below one another."

As they neared his property, a house isolated in a cul-de-sac, Nikola reached to unfasten his seat belt and paused when the dashboard screen changed color, followed by an insistent beep behind them.

Dennis stopped the van a few feet away from the already-opening wrought-iron gate, then maneuvered the vehicle to the driveway fronting the house. He killed the engine, swiveled his seat, and moved over to his console. After switching off the wireless link to his pad on the dashboard, Dennis brought the equipment online and started scrolling screens, interrogating scores of subsystems. "We had a signal and lost it."

"Location?"

"Nope. It was a weak signal captured only by a single direction finder. Without a longer broadcast, pinpointing the signal is impossible."

"General direction, then?"

Dennis hunched his shoulders as he started the routine of transferring links to the equipment in the house. "East."

The river lay due east, but so did highways, towns, and scores of residential areas. Three lawyers—one of them

dead—a doctor, and a shift supervisor: an unlikely com-
mando unit with a maverick plan and a mystery prisoner.
Rather than the thrill of the hunt, Nikola's mind thickened
with foreboding.

chapter 19

||||

01:42

The man waiting for them by the tracks had not volunteered
anything beyond a curt "Follow me." He cast an imposing figure in a long drab coat that almost brushed the floor, a yellow
electrical cord tied around his waist as a belt. In another incarnation, the coat must have belonged to a giant. Salt-and-pepper
hair, unkempt and matted, fused with a bushy beard and mustache, and a greasy stench preceded him by a good six feet.

"Friend or foe?" Floyd whispered in her ear.

Laurel eyed him warily. "He doesn't look like the DHS to
me, so let's find out. Besides, what choice do we have?"

After filing through a two-hundred-yard stretch of tunnel,
they entered a dimly lit scene worthy of Francis Bacon. Laurel had heard of homeless people living with rats in dark cav-
erns underneath the city: nightmarish tales of pain, filth,
violence, and romance. But nothing could have prepared her
for this. Scores of people, scattered along the rail bed and the
platforms, moved along an abandoned passenger station.
They huddled around open fires or scurried into cardboard-
box burrows. Flames cast dancing shadows on the curved
walls, and voices mingled with grunts and the crackle of whatever burned in the fires.

The man walking ahead stopped before a figure squatting
by a huge samovarlike contraption, which rested on a tripod
over a camping stove. He turned to the fugitives. "Refresh-
ments," he said. "I'm Henry Mayer. Henry will do."

The group stood rooted to the spot. Laurel looked around the station. It was a long structure, three or four hundred feet, split into two levels: the track bed—perhaps twenty feet wide—from which the rails had been long removed, flanked by ample passenger platforms a few feet higher up. The walls, covered in grimy tiles that once must have been white, curved to form a vaulted surface overhead.

"Over there." Henry pointed up to a yellowish glimmer issuing from an entrance roughly in the center of the right platform wall. "We have prepared a flat surface for . . ." He scratched his beard. "Your colleague."

Floyd nodded to Raul. They stepped back to climb a wooden ramp between the rail bed and the higher platform— a few planks with battens nailed at intervals to afford a grip. Once on the raised area, they carried Russo over to the side entrance.

Henry remained impassive. Then his eyes darted a quick glance toward Lukas before staring back at Laurel.

She cleared her throat and said to Lucas, "Er . . . Floyd will need a hand with Russo, and I need Raul down here. Could you?"

Lukas nodded once and dashed over toward the ramp, as if eager to hide somewhere out of the open.

The man looking after the huge kettle reached into a cardboard box for a mug and, with a hand wrapped in something that once was a woolen mitten, grabbed the spout and pulled. The contraption, obviously set on gimbals, pivoted to spew a gush of dark liquid into the mug. Then the man held it in midair and waited.

Henry huffed and reached into his pocket.

Laurel blinked when Henry's arm continued to sink past its natural stopping place, almost to his elbow, only to surface clenching a grimy ten-dollar bill.

The man at the kettle reached for the bill with one hand and advanced the mug with the other. Beyond Henry, Laurel spotted Raul returning, leaping down from the platform to the rail bed.

"Here." Henry grabbed the mug and turned toward Raul.

Raul reached over. After a sharp intake of breath, he

cursed, lowered the mug onto the floor, and blew on his hands.

"Tender, are we? Next you'll ask for cream and sugar."

When another mug was pointed in her direction, Laurel hid her hands inside her suit sleeves and reached over. Henry beamed.

"Can I have two more?" Raul asked, and glanced up toward the side entrance where Floyd and Lukas tended to Russo. Then he bent down to pick up a flat piece of wood and held it before him, arms outstretched.

Henry chuckled. "My, but we're quick learners."

Laurel and Raul settled with their grimy mugs of something hot and wet away from the groups around the fires or the sleeping shapes on cardboard mattresses, while Henry dragged a crate over and settled down in a flurry of alarming creaks.

"How did you know where to meet us?" Laurel asked.

"I gave the coordinates to your boss."

"How?"

"Phone."

"Where—"

Henry waved a hand. "We have a portable repeater, now a mile away from here. Our contact lasted thirty seconds, not long enough for trackers. We can't use it again, not until we reprogram a different handle."

"Handle?"

"Address," Raul clarified.

"Where can I use this?" Laurel drew from her pocket the sturdy Metapad computer.

"Squirt?"

Laurel nodded.

"Be my guest."

Laurel didn't move.

"Over there." Henry pointed to an empty area on the far end of the platform.

Laurel stopped by the side entrance where she'd seen the men take Russo. They had propped the stretcher on top of two wooden crates and opened the bag. Now, with the black material skirting the boxes, Russo's white body reminded Laurel of a photograph she'd once seen of an Indian cremation. Floyd was moving a pad over Russo's chest, peering at a handheld device with a bright blue screen.

"How is he?"

Floyd opened his mouth, but no sound came out. Then he shook his head. "Stable."

"What does that mean?" On the fringe of her vision, Laurel noted the still figure of Lukas holding Floyd's bag.

Floyd breathed deep. "It means he's holding on. As for how long . . . your guess is as good as mine."

She was about to remind him that he was a doctor and an expert in hibernation side effects, before the surrealism of their predicament stilled her tongue. "Thank you. I'm trying to work us out of here. I'll be back."

Floyd held her gaze an instant and nodded.

Laurel continued along the platform to a secluded corner, behind a pile of junk, bundles of copper wiring, and sacks of rags. After booting her Metapad—a rugged military-issue combination of GPS Squirt messenger and computer—she opened the instant-message program and pinged Shepherd. He replied instantly, as if he'd had the text ready to beam: >*Explain your circumstance, in detail.*

Over the next few minutes she exchanged messages—first to bring Shepherd up to date about their desperate plight and later to figure a way out. There was none. The police had effectively sealed the city with checkpoints at major and most minor roads. In addition, patrol cars were conducting spot checks on suspect vehicles and, according to Shepherd, almost anything on wheels qualified. The river was also out; it was teeming with police speedboats. As their conversation progressed, Laurel's feeling of dejection deepened. Their carefully built plan had vanished. Shepherd could drive a van to a point four miles away on the city's south side, hide the van in a disused warehouse, and wait to pick them up there, but he couldn't get any closer. Besides the police, several DHS Fast Deployment Units had spread downtown and at cardinal points around Washington, D.C., ten minutes away from almost any spot within the city limits. They were hemmed in the sewers with a dying man.

>*Problem is,* Shepherd wrote, *anything that distracts the police away wouldn't necessarily bother the DHS, and conversely.*

>*Is there anything that would distract them both or cause the DHS to call off the police?*

>*No, but perhaps we can distract them separately.*

>*How?* Laurel clutched at straws.

A long pause.

>*A major accident, a fire.*

In other words, Shepherd had no idea.

>*Still have the sensors?* Shepherd asked.

>*Yes.*

>*Henry should be able to use them to draw the DHS away from you.*

>*And the police?*

For more than a minute, the prompt flashed on the screen without any new input. Then three words scrolled across the top of the display.

>*Bring Henry in.*

>*How far?*

>*All the way.*

>*Repeat.*

There was a pause, then: >*I trust that man with my life.*

And our lives, Laurel thought, before switching the Metapad off.

When Laurel returned to the lower rail area, Henry and Raul hadn't moved. They sat in the same spot and seemed frozen in time but for their empty mugs. She reached for her now-tepid drink and made a face, but she was thirsty.

"Shepherd says you're our only hope."

"Shepherd?"

"Your friend, our . . . boss." She darted a glance to Raul.

"I see." Henry's beard contorted, and Laurel supposed he was smiling. "Shoot."

Laurel briefed him about their scheme and replayed her exchange with Shepherd.

Henry nodded when she finished. "He's right. Drawing the DHS away, if those things you have on your necks work as locators, is simple enough. But what about them?" Henry glanced toward the side entrance.

"What do you mean?"

Henry rubbed the sole of a scuffed boot on the floor. "You said they were hired help."

"That's right, but after the fiasco they share our boat. Out there they're dead, and they know it."

"To clear the police roadblocks would require a major incident," Henry said.

"Those were Shepherd's words. A fire?"

"I doubt it. Fire brigades and a few police perhaps, but even a plane crash wouldn't clear the roads unless it was in a highly populated area, and that's out of the question."

Henry closed his eyes and seemed to doze for a couple of endless minutes. "There could be a way, but we would need more people and equipment. I can volunteer my services and contacts but can't speak for the others. I don't have any money. Mercenaries and gear can be expensive."

"Can you get us out?"

"I can try."

Laurel had already booted her Metapad and was frantically pecking at its screen. After a few seconds, the first reply flashed across the screen.

>Done. What do you need?

She tilted the screen so Henry could see and waited.

"Twenty," he deadpanned.

"Million?"

Henry nodded once.

She hesitated, then typed: >20.

A second later: >Done.

And then: >Where? When? How?

Henry glanced at the screen and must have pursed his lips, because the mass of hair on his face swelled. "Where can he pick you up?"

She told him the location Shepherd had described in a disused warehouse. "He can't get any closer." Then she held her breath.

Henry reached out his pawlike hand and held her wrist in a delicate grip, as if wary of breaking it. Laurel did a quick double take to discover he was peering at her watch—02:16— before closing his eyes once more. "His pickup point is good, in eight hours. Split the money into three bags: two with five and one with ten. Make that garbage bags. It has a poetic ring to it."

chapter 20

||||

02:26

A white dash flashed twice on his screen and faded to black. Once the link was severed, Harper Tyler peered down the lines of text on the screen, the trail of a carefully planned exercise gone wrong. To one side, the racks of sophisticated equipment he'd used to eavesdrop on the DHS and police movements blinked in a slow cadence. Traffic was low and the wolf pack on standby, ready to pounce at the slightest move of their prey. The idea of a carefully planned exercise was a euphemism. The success or failure of any action depended on strategy, which in turn hinged on sound intelligence. It was now obvious that the senator's intelligence and his own sucked. Russo hadn't been in true hibernation; he had been condemned to a slow death. His status, according to Laurel, could only be described as comatose. It was painfully obvious that the enemy had kept a card up its sleeve—an ace that Tyler didn't factor into the delicate equation of springing Russo from the Washington sugar cube. That he couldn't have known the inmate's neck sensors doubled as homing beacons was no excuse. Had he designed the sensors, he would have insisted on such a simple and inexpensive circuit addition.

Tyler blinked at the double digit on the screen. Twenty million was a hefty chunk of cash—its worth plummeting rapidly but still a lot of money. Tyler sighed, rubbed his knee, and panned along a row of cramped bookcases to a wall facing the curtained bay window and a stout safe flanked by maps. He had the money and more, in used and untraceable thousand-dollar bills embedded with a passive chip that so far had thwarted the efforts of forgers to reproduce them. Nanotechnology developed and produced in the weightlessness of the U.S. space facility had its advantages. The cash was earmarked for the doctor and the supervisor, but they would have to wait their turn.

He stood, grimaced, and shifted his weight to his good leg, before limping over to a map of Washington, D.C., with the network of active sewers superimposed in clear acetate. He peered at the maze of colored lines, sadly aware that the graphic represented only a fraction of the subterranean realm, with countless levels, forgotten tunnels, and flooded galleries. On the opposite side of the safe, pinned to a board, was a laminated wall map of the world. Like countless times before, his gaze drifted along the Tropic of Cancer to the Gulf of Oman and then north into Iran and South Khorasan and its mountains—home to goats and a race of people that clung to their land like lichen to rock. Tyler narrowed his eyes. He knew better than most about botched operations and homing beacons. *Shepherd?* Rather than guiding his flock, Tyler had driven them into a blind alley.

During the last Iranian war, Major Scott Marino—the young scion of a wealthy warrior's dynasty, eager to show his worth—had recklessly scrambled three choppers on a dubious piece of intelligence. The ambivalent and choppy signal hinted at having spotted, at long last, the elusive mujahideen's headquarters at the bottom of a gorge. The location didn't make any sense and went against everything—admittedly little—they knew about their fabled chieftain, Mullah Akim.

There were several reasons why the information should have been filed instead of acted on. Theirs was just an outpost commissioned to gather intelligence and relay it to U.S. headquarters at Kabul, in friendly neighboring Afghanistan. Out of the five able chopper pilots on duty at the post, one had been shipped home in a black bag the previous day after taking a stroll in the countryside and meeting one of their own mines, stealthily sown months before by a passing aircraft and unrecorded. Another awaited extraction at their makeshift infirmary with large chunks missing from a leg, courtesy of an explosive shell that had almost downed his craft on an ill-fated inspection flight. But none of these petty details swayed Major Marino, already starry-eyed at the thought of a commendation-worthy action.

To the north of the camp, ink-black rivers cut plunging gorges toward Chah-e Mezrab. To the south, eleven-thousand-foot peaks rose in a ring above the valley, itself more than a mile high, with the town of Khvoshab and the Mahesh gorge roughly in the middle. Off went the crafts into the gorge and into a barrage of anything that could fly, from small-caliber artillery shells and rifle fire to the silly Chinese TIP missiles—little more than firecrackers but deadly when released in droves.

All three crafts took hits. Two exploded in midair. The third managed to wobble for a few miles before crashing into the barren russet ridges that folded one on the other in the wastes to the side of the gorge.

Miracles sometimes happened, and the pilot had already punched his harness release when the craft hit the rocks. The explosion hurled him a good thirty yards away from the wreck, where he landed in a heap of mangled flesh, a shattered leg, and a half dozen cracked ribs. The badly damaged pilot had the presence of mind to crawl into a cleft between rocks but passed out before he was able to activate his radio beacon.

When he regained consciousness, he could hear the cheering cries of local fighters picking over the wreck of his aircraft. He managed to crawl even deeper into the crevice. He was delirious, his torn body screaming for repairs, but he reached to a side pocket in his trousers and activated his radio beacon. The glorious Russian army had in the distant past rained explosive devices on the area—devices designed to look like toys, shaped like butterflies, kites, or brightly colored plastic, to attract the curiosity of unsuspecting children. Clearly the purpose of whoever had dreamed up the devices was to murder and maim children before they could mature into fighters. The downed pilot knew the mujahideen held a dim view of the policy; they simply handed over anyone with a shred of foreign uniform to their women. Many Iranian mountain women had lost their young to the brightly colored presents dropped from the sky. The pilot also knew that these women were adept at skinning sheep and kept remarkably sharp knives for the purpose. He crept still further into the cleft, pulled out his sidearm, and shoved its barrel in his mouth, ready to pull the trigger.

But the chopper wreckage was too hot to rummage inside, and the fighters must have been in a hurry to leave the area. After a while, before he passed out again, the pilot stopped hearing their elated chatter.

Back at the post, Major Marino was already writing his report to justify having lost his flying detail when the beacon signal tripped a receiver at the comms shack. An excited sergeant brought the news and the hope of someone still alive after the fiasco, but Marino put on a face of deep regret and cited the lack of pilots. Then the sergeant meekly quoted from memory the seven Army Core Values, stressing the fourth, Selfless Service: *Put the welfare of the nation, the Army, and your subordinates before your own.*

When the sergeant's eloquence failed to elicit any reaction, he further pointed out that Marino was a certified chopper pilot. Naturally, Marino didn't plan on piloting a chopper into the growing dusk, with the light swiftly waning beyond the mountains, and into hot mujahideen territory. He wouldn't have changed his mind but for the regulation sidearm the sergeant pushed against Marino's temple as he started a slow yet firm countdown.

That evening, as Major Marino basked in the glory of rescuing the downed pilot, he ordered the sergeant's arrest.

When the pilot was finally discharged from the military hospital where they had tried to rebuild his leg, the sergeant had already been court-martialed and dishonorably dismissed. With an almost useless leg, the pilot accepted a generous pension deal, resigned his commission, and went looking for the ex-sergeant.

Tyler shook his head. He gripped his left knee, and all the bitterness it had come to represent receded into the misty background of his mind. Then he keyed a string of numbers into the safe's keyboard, leaned over a dark oval window, and inserted his index finger into a slot. With the biometric check complete, something snapped within the bowels of the steel monolith and its door swung on silent hinges. The lower shelf held a stack of data disks, slim computer hard drives, and a bunch of inexpensive cell phones in a plastic bag. The top shelf was crammed with neat bundles, four deep, each holding $100,000. The cash was the second payment provided by the senator for the doctor and the controller, and it would also serve as the slush fund to cover other operational expenses. Altogether enough to bankroll a new life. Or several new lives.

Leaving the safe door open, Tyler turned to the window overlooking a corner of his farm.

Finding the sergeant had been a bitch. Almost a decade later, the pilot, ex–Chief Warrant Officer Harper Tyler, tracked Henry Mayer, the sergeant, to the Washington, D.C., sewers.

"Time is too slow for those who wait, too swift for those who fear, too long for those who grieve, too short for those who rejoice, but for those who love, time is eternity." Senator Palmer whispered Van Dyke's poem to silent bookshelves. Locked in his study, he was surrounded by books on ancient literature, history, and political philosophy. He hoped for, and at the same time dreaded, the ring of the secure phone. He felt powerless, reduced to the role of a mere observer to the drama unfolding before his eyes.

Bastien's death had been a blow, later expanded tenfold by the discovery of the sensors' hidden role, as was Russo's appalling condition. Palmer felt outraged by the transmitters' deception and overwhelmed by the young lawyer's death. He would mourn Bastien, the dear boy, for the rest of his life. In his grief, Palmer would reach for an end to justify the means he'd used. But if he didn't succeed, if Russo's deterioration or the sensors were their undoing, Bastien's death would serve no purpose. It would be put down to the deranged idealism of an old man, and Palmer wouldn't be able to live with that.

Laurel, Raul, and Russo, with Dr. Carpenter and Lukas Hurley tagging along, were still in the sewers, perhaps a little more comfortable thanks to Shepherd's agencies but still holed up. Springing them through the formidable gauntlet the DHS had thrown around the city while keeping Russo alive would require a regrettably scarce commodity: a miracle.

He stepped over to the sliding doors that opened to the garden and pushed them aside. The sky was the color of peat. Overhead, clouds marched quickly through thick air and against an increasingly angry sky.

At intervals during the previous hours, Palmer had heard muted thumps. He panned over the lawn, rosebushes, trimmed paths, and across the clump of trees until he spotted the culprit. Someone, probably Timmy, had left the door to the garden shed ajar. Not that it mattered, but it was an unkempt detail in an otherwise spotless garden, and a playful wind had nothing better to do than to bang it against its frame at intervals.

The gravel crunched underfoot as he walked to the shed. The pronouncement from Shepherd replayed in his mind. *Police patrols have sealed all roads and Russo is dying, tied to a stretcher in an abandoned subway tunnel. My contact there will try to spring them.*

At the shed, he peeked inside to check for Bum, Timmy's dog, just in case he had resolved to spend the night among the tools and his archenemies: two squat robotic lawn mowers that drove the nervous beast mad as they entered and left the shed from a trapdoor on one side. But everything looked fine. The lawn mowers were suckling their power from outlets on one wall, and Bum was nowhere in sight. As Palmer was about to latch the wooden door, he spotted a basket of bulbs on a shelf, packages of dormant life, and an image of Hypnos's tanks intruded in his thoughts. He leaned on the open door and made up his mind.

On his way back to the study, Palmer glanced up. The night was heavy, blanketed by featureless clouds. He glanced at his reflection on the windowpane. Sometimes he didn't recognize the face looking back at him from mirrored surfaces. "I can stand the thought of someone dying, but not for nothing," he whispered to the gods of the stars, if there were any. Then, with a conscious effort, he fought to marshal his thoughts.

One of the finest cures for a headache was a hammer blow to a finger, or so the joke went. Fresh agonizing pain soon replaced a dull head throb. Palmer stepped inside, closed the doors, and drew the curtains, shutting out the night.

chapter 21

||||

08:46

Laurel awoke to the smell of frying bacon. Scent sometimes triggered half-forgotten scenes in her mind. Details became fresh, moments she'd never paid attention to as they slipped by remembered. When walking through a department store past the men's section, a whiff of an ex-lover's cologne could bring a flash of memory, how he looked and felt. Now the smell of Washington sewers had so overwhelmed her pituitary that she wondered if she would ever smell anything without the tang of lanolin or shit again.

Her neck ached—a dull throb in the spot where Floyd had removed the sensor earlier. "Just a nick," he'd said, but it had hurt like hell. Nursing a neat sterile pad over adhesive stitches, she'd wedged her back into a corner to rest for five minutes, but the anesthetic must have knocked her out. She didn't remember falling asleep.

Laurel flicked her eyes open for a heartbeat, two, three, before closing them again to coax her senses into alertness. When the heavenly smell of bacon once more displaced the rancid stench of poverty and unwashed bodies, she opened her eyes. Before falling asleep, she'd climbed to the platform and settled on a spot next to the archway where Floyd tended to Russo. Now she leaned over and peered into the opening. A few feet away, Floyd dozed, curled up by a pile of flattened cardboard boxes. Lukas sat in a corner, his head lolling. Raul was nowhere in sight.

"Well, if it's not Sleeping Beauty returning to the land of the living!" Raul emerged from the gloom between two fires farther down the platform, followed by Henry, another man, and a scrawny kid carrying a box. She could have retorted there had been no kiss from a handsome prince, but she felt too weary and drowsy. Rather than the land of the living, the abandoned tunnel felt like someone's deep, dark thoughts buried and repressed in an empty room of the brain, accessible only by nightmares and shrinks.

"This is Metronome," Henry said.

She nodded and focused on the boy; he was perhaps ten to twelve years old, although his age was difficult to guess under a coat of grime. His head swung nonstop from side to side, a thin dribble of spit dangling from wet lips. Regardless of the motion, his intelligent eyes remained riveted on hers.

Laurel sat upright. Henry reached for two small empty crates and kicked a third one ahead of him.

"How long have I been asleep?" Laurel asked.

"Almost four hours, but don't worry, you haven't missed anything," Raul answered.

"And him?" She glanced toward Russo.

Raul paused before answering. "As the doctor says, stable."

Dying, she thought. The men moved the boxes to form a semicircle around her. Metronome lowered his box—a polymer container with a wire mesh stretched over its top. The other man remained erect, as if standing at attention, close to the curved platform wall and away from the light. He was almost as tall as Henry, and gaunt. Decked head to toe in a long black overcoat, he looked like an old photograph she had once seen of Grigory Rasputin, the mad monk of czarist Russia, complete with lank hair plastered down the sides of his face and a matted beard reaching to his chest. Laurel swallowed.

"I'll get some light." Henry turned on his heel and entered the opening in the curved wall, reappearing a few seconds later with a rusty stand, like those used in hospital wards to hang IV drips on half a century before. He reached under Russo's stretcher to pick up one of their LAD flashlights, turned it on, and hooked it to the contraption. Its last user must have set it on low, but it cast a pleasant white circle on the floor.

Henry settled on his crate, clearly disturbing whatever festered underneath the greatcoat and sending forth a sharp waft of stench. Laurel peered toward the fires, wishing someone would resume cooking, then glanced once more toward the unnerving figure standing straight in the gloom.

Henry followed her gaze and swiveled toward the silent man. "Barandus."

"Pardon?"

"My friend Barandus. He's offered to help. Good man." With that, he turned away, and Laurel suspected no further information would be forthcoming.

Floyd had roused. He stretched, looked around the area he'd commandeered as his domain, squatted somewhere beyond Russo, and returned with a self-heating unlabeled bag. He offered it to Laurel. "You must be starving. Here. Henry gave me a few. It's only rice, but your stomach can't take much more than this anyway. How long since your last meal? Thirty-six hours? Forty-eight?"

"Something like that." She inspected the bag; it looked intact but old and grimy. With a sigh, she pulled a red tab that would cause two chemicals to mix in its base and produce heat. When she felt it warming, she settled it against the wall to cook.

Henry followed her motions. "It's good rice, organic; none of that cloned stuff. My wife hoarded tons of it."

"You live here with your wife?" Laurel asked, aghast.

A cloud passed across his eyes. "I had a mate, a wonderful woman, fat and homely. Before descending to live in this hell, she worked at a natural-foods cooking school. Even after that, she would surface to go to a feminist vegetarian restaurant owned by anarchistic lesbians, and she'd return with loads of rice bags. She died last winter." He darted a glance to the box. "Rats. Mighty fine woman."

"Rats . . . ?" Laurel turned to Floyd.

"Weil's disease?" he asked.

Henry nodded.

Floyd settled down on his haunches. "It's a much-named horror, transmitted through contact with urine from infected animals. It's biphasic. First, flulike symptoms, which soon disappear. The second phase may involve renal and liver failure and often meningitis. It's a complicated disease to cure even with ample resources." Floyd looked around, then lowered his eyes. "Here, she wouldn't have a chance."

Metronome's head continued its slow sway.

Unconsciously, Laurel drew her legs tight to her body when a frantic scratching issued from the box at the boy's feet. "What's that?"

Henry rubbed his hands. "Our friend here has agreed to help us. She'll get the heat off our backs by carrying the locators away."

Laurel focused on a noise to her left. Floyd had stepped over to Russo's stretcher and picked up something from the floor. Then he returned with a crumpled lump she recognized as the wraps they had worn around their necks.

"Don't worry. I tucked the locators into the lead strips," Floyd said.

With his foot, Metronome pushed the box into the circle of light. Something huge moved inside.

"Shit, is that a rat?" Laurel asked.

Henry's beard parted to reveal a dark hole she supposed was his mouth. "Not just a rat. A very rare specimen."

She reached for her bag of rice, tore its top, and fished inside for the plastic fork.

Henry nudged the box with his foot. "Beautiful, isn't she?"

The rat shifted, its pointed nose trembling, and let out a tiny cry. Laurel cringed. "She's enormous."

"Yes, she is. They seldom grow larger than twelve inches or weigh over a pound. She's an exception—heavy, almost two pounds, and pregnant. You know anything about *Rattus norvegicus*?"

Silence but for the muted whisper of voices echoing from the station dwellers.

"They live for about twelve months, and females reach sexual maturity in ten weeks. That leaves them four-fifths of their lives to reproduce. Since their gestation period is twenty-two days, they can have four to seven litters in a year. At eight to ten offspring a litter, a pair of rats can produce forty or fifty descendants."

"That's horrible."

"Not really." Henry nudged the box again. "That's the mechanism of an advanced survival machine. The horrible bit, as you put it, is their yearly waste: fifty pounds of pellets, a gallon of urine, and a million hairs—all of it laced with rare germs. They are territorial, you know? They seldom move out of an area of one hundred feet around their lair."

"I don't understand," Laurel muttered, her mouth full of hot rice. "Does that mean the thing can carry the sensors only a hundred feet away?"

"I told you, she's special. Not from this area but from a maze of crumbling old sewers a mile away, unconnected by foot to these tunnels. Since she's pregnant, she will do her damnedest to get back home; it will take her an hour. There's a shortcut, but she can't take it. *Rattus norvegicus* are poor climbers."

"*Norvegicus?* Does it mean these horrors are from Norway?" Laurel asked.

"No, it doesn't. Someone christened the species and the name stuck." Henry shifted to produce a set of rusty wires from his pocket and started pulling and adjusting them into a large hollow bracelet.

Floyd leaned over. "How's your neck?"

"Sore."

"I kept the cut to the same size the machine made to insert it. Half an inch. It should heal well, and any cosmetic clinic will remove the scar for next to nothing."

Laurel nodded and dug back into her rice—warm, firm, and with a nutty flavor.

"Let's get this beauty loaded," Henry said.

Raul drew near and offered Henry the bundle of lead apron strips.

Metronome's hands, encased in a butcher's mesh gloves,

moved into the light. With uncanny dexterity, he flicked the lid open and pounced on the animal inside.

Raul recoiled, and Laurel pressed her back harder against the curved wall.

Henry unwrapped the strips and produced three hazelnut-shaped forms, like tiny Easter eggs, their surfaces rippling under the light, and slotted them inside the wire contraption.

Metronome grabbed the rat by its neck with one hand and gripped its hind legs with the other.

"Here." Henry fastened the wires around the rat's midriff, then draped one of the lead-fabric strips over it and secured it with another length of wire. Then he nodded to Metronome. "Hurry up, boy, let her loose by the waterfall after you remove this piece of cloth. She'll find a way to her lair."

Laurel eyed Metronome's retreating figure. "Will she be able to get the wires off?"

"I doubt it." Henry's voice didn't show concern for the rat's welfare.

"Won't this get you in trouble?" Raul asked.

Henry's eyes twinkled and he panned the tunnel. "More trouble?" The hole in his beard lengthened sideways.

"I meant—"

"I doubt the goons will do anything. They'll guess some mole—that's what they call us—has helped you out, but there are over twenty settlements. Besides, we may soil their neat tanks. Nah. They'll be pissed as hell but can't do shit about it. They'll know you've fled and they'll look elsewhere. As soon as Metronome returns—say, thirty minutes—we'll be on our way."

"You like it here?" Raul was ripping the tab from a bag of rice.

Henry cocked his head, as if he were taking Raul's measure. "We have almost everything. Hooking up wires for electricity is easy, and discards from the city provide all the material comforts we need. Only running water is lacking, but, in a way, it's an advantage; dirt and grime help us blend in with the darkness. To answer your question: No, I don't like it, but it's home, and crowded with extraordinary people."

Laurel nodded. She understood about home and extraordinary people. *Bastien.* A lump formed in her throat, and the light dangling from the IV stand seemed to break into myriad sparkles.

"You move a lot?"

"Used to. We've been left undisturbed here for close to six years. A couple of years ago, there was activity farther west by the power station. The police crashed into a community and the brothers had to scamper. Some moved in with us and a few stayed. The Marchesi clan had set up a drug laboratory in an underground cave connected by a network of escape tunnels and passageways to their headquarters."

Raul's eyes flickered. "The heat found it?"

"Eventually. They pumped in concrcte to seal all the exits."

Laurel was about to ask if the mobsters were in or out when the concrete poured down, but a gleam in Henry's eyes answered her question. *In.* "So now you stay put. I mean . . ."

"We visit other settlements to trade information or something they may have in excess. Sometimes we even have visitors, other than brothers from other tunnels—journalists and artists, principally."

"Artists?"

"Yes. It seems a floor dusted with soda straws, condoms, tampons, and diapers nurtures creativity and artistic imagination. Go figure."

Floyd darted a glance toward the opening at the end of the station. "You travel through the active subway tunnels?"

"That's dangerous. We keep to the sewers as much as we can. Some have risked shortcuts between settlements through live tunnels, but it's crazy. They may be run over by a train or touch the electric third rail—a shortcut's not worth having your head, feet, and hands explode."

chapter 22

9:11

After Metronome bolted down the tunnel, burdened with his rat cage, Henry Mayer finished his short exchange with Laurel and Raul, then moved to one end of the station, tailed by Barandus. There they sat for a while, Henry obviously talking, his hands dancing in midair, and Barandus leaning forward as if eager not to miss a word. After a few minutes, Barandus stood, strolled to a group gathered around a fire on the lower rail bed, and returned in the company of two men. Then he left again, this time to the opposite end of the station, where he shifted cardboard boxes aside. A little later he marched once more toward Henry, trailed by a plump woman swathed in a grimy military-issue raincoat.

Laurel couldn't work out what was going on from where she sat on the platform, but she felt too weary to walk over and find out. Most likely Henry was marshaling his troops. Until he made a move, they could do nothing but wait.

Floyd loomed over her. "How are you feeling?"

"Rough," Laurel said. Her throat was clogged again with all the emotions boiling up from inside. *Bastien.*

"Here, take this." He offered a decrepit-looking water pack and, from his top pocket, a piece of metal foil with two dimples on its surface.

"What is it?" Laurel was already pushing the tablets, oval with a shiny silver coating, onto the palm of her hand.

"Vitamins and a dose of caffeine. Not too strong—you've eaten only rice—but it will perk you up."

"And the hangover?" She offered a weak smile and swallowed the pills with a sip of the tepid water.

"When the effect wears off, you'll need to sleep around the

clock." He squatted by her side and, wedging his back against the slightly curved wall, sat down.

Laurel glanced at Raul, dozing next to Russo's stretcher, and Lukas, slumped in a corner, his eyes vacant.

Floyd followed her glance. "Of course, the issue may be academic. When the effect wears off, we may all be dead."

"There's a third alternative," Laurel offered.

"Yes?"

"Something in between. We may be on our way to sleep around the clock, in a tank."

Floyd didn't answer. He must have relaxed, because his arm pressed against hers. She arrested an unconscious reflex to give him more room by moving aside. Instead, she leaned her head on his shoulder. He tensed, but only for a moment. After a long sigh, Floyd shifted to free his arm and wrapped it around her shoulders. The polymer material of Laurel's stiff jacket creaked, but his hug felt good.

"I won't let it get that far," Floyd muttered.

"You came prepared?"

He shrugged. "I grabbed some syrettes we use to put down patients too far gone."

"Like dogs at the pound?"

"Mmmm, how long?"

The sudden change of topic caught Laurel unaware. "How long what?"

"Until we get out of here."

"I don't know."

Floyd turned his head toward Russo and nodded. "He's wasting away. He won't last much longer. Hours, maybe."

Laurel opened her eyes a fraction to look through her eyelashes at Russo's prone shape. "Shep—the man who planned the breakout—knows his condition. He's organized our extraction with Henry's help."

"And the blood?"

"And the blood." A while ago Floyd had given her a list of the materials he needed to revive Russo—a long list she'd keyed into her Metapad and flashed to Shepherd.

"Floyd?"

"Yes."

"You said you have more than one syrette?"

"I did."

"Then save one for me."

On the opposite end of the tunnel, something flashed, followed by tiny flames that soon grew into a roaring fire. Around it, dark figures hovered like tormented souls in a Goya etching.

"Why him? Is he a big gun? An experiment gone wrong? A mobster?" Floyd had a nice voice.

Shepherd's instructions had been clear: *Don't volunteer any information about Russo to the doctor or the controller.* But that was before. Now secrecy was moot; they were in the same boat. "Russo is a lawyer, like Raul—" She was going to add, *and Bastien,* but swallowed instead. "And me."

"And what else?" he insisted.

"What do you mean?"

"You don't spend eight years slowly dying in a tank for being a lawyer unless you're a rapist–lawyer, or murderer–lawyer, or—"

"I see what you mean. No, Russo is just a lawyer, an activist. A blue-assed fly who rattled someone in power."

"What was he convicted of?"

"He was never tried."

"You must be joking." But his voice quivered.

She moved closer, until her head touched his cheek. The sensation of warmth on her scalp was almost too delicious to bear. "I wouldn't describe this circumstance as a joke, but I always knew you quacks had a weird sense of humor."

"Quack? How dare you?" But he tightened his arm, as if dreading she would pull away. "I only use leeches when strictly necessary."

A silence followed, as satisfying as any violin concerto.

"So, our government's betters have been using the tanks to salt away troublesome folks and kill them," he said.

"Something like that."

"I see."

"What do you see?"

"The streets teeming with police, DHS FDU squads, and troops. I bet even the Boy Scouts and the Salvation Army are looking for us. They can't allow the worms to get out of town."

"Mmmm?" Laurel felt sleepy. His pep pills must have outlived their shelf life.

"I'm losing my touch. Here I am, oozing witty remarks, and all I get is snores."

"Your touch is fine." For the first time in many hours, she felt a smile tug at the corners of her lips. Floyd Carpenter, forty-one, doctor of medicine, broke after a recent traumatic divorce, no children or live-in pets. At least, these were the scant details Shepherd had rattled from his notes while they ran over the operation. It seemed years ago instead of weeks.

Yes, Floyd was damaged but cuddly and comfortable, like a worn teddy bear. She drifted in and out of dreamless sleep until his hand pressed her arm with insistence.

"Mmmm?"

"My, but you are verbose. Henry is moving."

She roused instantly, her mind clear as a foggy road after a strong wind. Maybe his pep pills worked after all. Laurel leaned over and pecked his cheek. "Thank you."

"Er, I didn't catch that. Could you repeat it?"

She stood and ran a hand over the seat of her trousers in an unconscious gesture to shake off the dirt. Her fingers caught on something slimy. She refused to look. "No."

At the end of the tunnel, Henry stood with the other men, waving for them to approach. Laurel neared Raul and leaned over to run a hand over his head. "Something is happening."

Raul made a wry movement with his mouth, reached for her hand, and held it an instant. "Latte, large, scrambled eggs on toast, and juice."

"Served by odalisques from a nearby seraglio?"

"Perfect. No veils, please; they only get in the way."

She squeezed his hand and moved over to Lukas. Out of the corner of her eye, she detected Floyd squatting next to Russo and listening to his chest before shaking his head.

"Come on, let's go see Henry." She peered into Lukas's eyes. All the adrenaline-triggered resolve was gone, leaving only fear in its wake. "Come," she repeated, offering her hand. "We're going to be all right." There was no reason for the encouragement, but, like someone hopelessly in love, his eyes begged for a charitable lie.

As Laurel neared the group, Henry slapped one of the men on the shoulder. "Let's get this show on the road."

Henry fingered his matted beard, then nodded to Laurel. She eyed the grimy faces of men and a woman, dressed in a bewildering assortment of rags, their sunken eyes ablaze with a strange inner light. Hope or drugs? She couldn't make up her mind. Like a quarterback calling the play, Henry stepped slightly inside the circle.

"You know Barandus," Henry said, gesturing to the tall, morose man on his right. Then he raised a hand to encompass the other three. "Jim, Susan, and Charlie. Good friends, and knowledgeable."

The nature of their knowledge filled Laurel with dread, but she managed a smile. "What are we doing?"

"With luck, the DHS will be busy for a while—not for too long, though. We need to arrange a small diversion to draw all the city forces away from your extraction point. To do that, we need some goods. I propose we go get them."

Laurel returned Henry's stare. He hadn't named the place they were supposed to meet Shepherd, but he hadn't explained anything about his plan either. "But we have no money."

Henry nodded. "My word is good enough where we're going."

"Who's going with you?" Raul asked.

"La crème de la crème—Laurel, you, and the five of us. That should be enough. The doctor can look after his charge, and Lukas can help him."

Henry seemed to have sorted out in his mind who belonged where.

Raul edged forward and cleared his throat. Obviously something was bothering him. "Enough for what?"

"My friend . . . does it matter?" Henry raised a hand before Raul had a chance to reply. "You're fucked. I mean, really fucked. You need to get your pal out there to a safe place. We can try to help you achieve your goal, but you do it our way. Or . . . you're welcome to try it on your own."

Raul stood very straight, his lips pressed tightly together.

"Let me get something straight. Down here we operate as a group, and I lead. You will do as I say. No questions. If something happens to me, Barandus takes over."

"Are we in the army now?"

"I wish we were, son. This is a tad harsher, with fewer rules and no safeguards. Of course, if you have a problem, you can stay here." Henry squared his shoulders and waited.

Raul pursed his lips and nodded once. "Understood."

"That's not enough. Here we depend on one another. You will do as I say."

"Cut it out, guys. Of course we'll go along. You're the expert," Laurel said in exasperation.

Still Henry waited, his eyes never leaving Raul.

"I'll do as you say," Raul agreed.

Laurel darted a glance toward Russo. "Are we going far?"

"About three miles in a straight line. Problem is, we have to go deep first. Say an eight-mile round trip."

"How long?"

Something flickered across Henry's eyes and Laurel braced herself for a sharp rebuke, but it never came. "Five hours, perhaps six, if we don't run into problems." He raised a hand to forestall the next question. "As to the possibility and nature of the problems, your guess is as good as mine." He turned to the woman he'd introduced as Susan and muttered something.

She trotted to a far corner of the station to rummage in a large cardboard box propped against a pile of others in a corner—their stores, Laurel guessed.

Laurel neared Floyd and Lukas. "You heard the man—five or six hours. Try to catch some shut-eye."

Floyd nodded. "And you take care." He reached over and brushed his fingers across her cheek.

Lukas hadn't recovered his color and looked positively sick. She neared and gripped his arm. He blinked and nodded once. Laurel guessed that a tank full of an oily mixture was on the supervisor's mind. "Be prepared. As soon as we get back, we can go home." She hoped her voice would carry conviction, but it failed.

Raul hadn't moved, probably smarting from Henry's tug at

the leash. She stepped over and draped an arm around his waist. "Angry?"

"No. He's right. This is terra incognita for us, and they've been here for years. It's just that I hate being blindsided."

"We'll figure it out sooner or later."

He threw an arm around her shoulder and drew her closer. "What do you reckon?"

"About what?"

"Those two. The doctor and Woody boy."

"They'll behave, at least for the time being. They have nowhere to go. We are their only chance."

Raul lowered his head as if to check something on the floor. "And the derelicts?"

"I don't know about the rest, but Shepherd trusts Henry with his life. His words, not mine."

"And heavy words at that."

"You bet. In another incarnation, they must have been close. Shepherd mentioned that it wouldn't be the first time."

"That he trusted Henry with his life? Probably the army, then."

"Why do you say that?"

"Shepherd's ways, and his attention to detail and discipline. He's ex–armed forces, and so is Henry, and probably that other man, Barandus. I would bet on that."

"What would you bet?"

"Get lost."

Susan returned with what seemed like a brace of ribbons. As she neared the group, she dug into the shapeless mass and shook a handful of dark tapes free.

Henry grabbed some and passed them on to Raul and her. "Here, harnesses. Strap 'em on."

The two-inch strips of webbing were stoutly stitched together in places and peppered with buckles. Laurel reached for the contraption and untangled its folds, trying to work out what went where.

"That's it." Henry blinked. "Your legs go through those hoops and your arms through there. Then you clasp it shut and tighten it by pulling this end."

"Where are we going, then?"

Henry's contortions to work the webbing around his colossal anatomy released a thick waft of stench. "Sewers. Dangerous places."

"I know about sewers and fat fields . . . and roaches." As she spoke, it dawned on Laurel that the word *sewers* had issued darkly from Henry's lips.

"I mean deep sewers. Sewer workers seldom go below levels four or five, and they always wear a harness and rubber waders that come up to the crotch like yours. We don't have waders."

Her mind clouded with foreboding. "Deep?"

Henry nodded to her Metapad resting atop an upturned gallon can. "The map you carry covers only three levels and sections of another two deeper down. Those are the systems in service. A cross-section of central Washington has fifteen levels in places, plunging as deep as three thousand feet, and mostly uncharted."

Questions jostled for priority in Laurel's mind, but she chose the bliss of ignorance for what lay ahead and didn't ask anything else.

Henry switched on his LAD flashlight. A bright circle of light appeared at his enormous rubber-boot-encased feet. "So, you know your roaches, yes?" He tilted his body and the light caught a glossy insect, almost black. "Here we have an illegal immigrant, *Blatta orientalis,* the oriental cockroach; this one must be lost, because they favor moist and warm places." He stepped over it and a faint crunch followed a high-pitched hiss. "But there we have the locals." His flashlight panned the floor and shapes scurried in all directions. "These are *Periplaneta americana,* our very own, and above all survivors, like all of us. Wonderfully designed scavengers. They need only warmth, water, and a little decaying matter to survive." With the light coming from underneath, Henry's face had gained a disturbing chiaroscuro of shifting shadows. "They're excellent climbers, as people on the surface know too well. They climb up drains to kitchen sinks and counters with leftover food, where they feed, leaving in their wake hard, cylindrical droppings that resemble fragments of pencil lead."

The bastard was doing it on purpose and enjoying himself.

Henry straightened and switched off his flashlight. "The males have wings and occasionally fly. But the best is . . . they can swim."

Barandus neared with an armload of what seemed like folded cloth, but on closer inspection Laurel determined they were new backpacks. "A factory closed down," he explained, "and we grabbed a few boxes. Have one."

She darted a glance to Lukas, who had followed the roach lecture, his face tinged with an unhealthy green hue.

"I don't understand why we should wear these." She jerked the webbing tight around her waist with what she hoped would seem fearless certainty. "Surely we don't have to be roped together like climbers."

Henry cocked his head. "No, but it's easier to drag a body out when there's a harness to grab hold of."

chapter 23

||||

09:45

Bastien Compton. Born July 8, 2026, in Lancaster, Pennsylvania. Harvard Law School. Honors thesis. Graduated cum laude, class of 2050. Admitted to the bar in 2052. Two arrests for public disturbance, demonstrations. Militant League for a Transparent Government (LTG). Sentenced to two years for trying to steal explosives.

Nikola glanced at the tiny infrared laser tracking his eye movement from the screen's frame and flicked his eyelids. LTG? What a waste of a talented young man. He scanned the résumés under the photographs of Laurel and Raul on separate screens. Same university, same years. No honors. With another blink of his eyelids, Nikola scrolled down Bastien's file. Solid Presbyterian family. A large one, predating the two-child law. Two younger brothers, one studying business administration, the other medicine. An elder sister, Laura, doctorate in AI. Father a circuit judge. Clean. What a waste.

After a final sip of his already cold coffee, he scanned the other files. All three had been sentenced for the same crime, obviously staged to get them into the tank. Raul Osborne had one brother, also a lawyer. His father was a local government official; his mother, an ophthalmic surgeon. Clean. Laurel Cole. No brothers or sisters, father a gardener—He stopped reading, drew the cup to his lips, tipped it back, and, unrewarded, placed it on the tabletop, his eyes never moving from the screen. Mother, waitress. A gardener and a minion? Harvard? Laurel had preyed on his mind from the onset: the odd piece. Why team a young woman with two linebackers to spring an inmate, a task needing notable muscle? There could be many reasons, but they were not obvious ones, and he loathed forcing the pieces of a puzzle to match.

Nikola stood, stretched his legs, and crossed the open office he shared with Dennis. The young man had napped for a few hours. Nikola hadn't slept a wink.

"Anything?" Nikola asked. It was a silly question delivered instead of a greeting. Any signal from the police, the DHS, or the NSA's listening networks would have beeped loud enough to awaken a mummy.

Dennis scanned his screens. "No reports. The usual fuck-ups at checkpoints. A group of kids tried to turn around, stoned out of their minds and without a driver's license. Another incident involving a member of Congress and a minor; that sort of thing."

Nikola nodded. Dennis hadn't said the kids would be returned to their parents inside black bags, but a measure of collateral damage was to be expected in any large-scale operation.

On a box trailing a bunch of wires atop an equipment rack, a yellow light started to throb, keeping rhythm with a high-pitched beep. Dennis pecked at his keyboard, and a single line of text scrolled on the center screen. He glanced at it and moved to leave.

Nikola reached for his arm. "Stay." Then he stood, leaned over the box, and placed his index finger on a small window by the flashing light. The drilling tone of high-speed synchronizing data poured from overhead speakers.

"Where are you?" a colorless metallic voice asked.

"At my house."

"Is the boy with you?"

"He is."

"Send him out to play with himself."

Once more, he arrested Dennis's move. Odelle was untrustworthy. Nikola reached for a book and let it drop on the floor. "Go on." Nikola settled into a comfortable slouch in an easy chair, signaled Dennis to be quiet, and closed his eyes.

"News?" the voice asked.

"No news."

"Is that supposed to be good news?"

"No news is the absence of news."

"Suggestions?"

"We wait."

"For a miracle?"

Nikola opened one eye. Definitely squirrelly. "The way I see it, unforeseen developments have complicated whatever plan they had. Originally there were three and Russo. Now they may be four, and I surmise two of them weren't supposed to be on the run. My take is they were hired hands, like the people who cut through the supposedly secure tunnel and welded the panel back on."

"Continue."

"If there are five people, one of them on a stretcher or in a wheelchair, and if Russo is still alive, they can't move about very easily."

"They must have had an escape planned for four. What's the difference with five?"

"The difference is not in the numbers but the nature of the people," Nikola explained. "Whatever plan they had is now useless. Nyx was their repair shop. The woods is a wonderful place to hide a tree. Dr. Carpenter would have booked Russo as one of their rich customers. I don't think he would have had any problem palming a subject into their network. He knows the ropes. Once Russo was conditioned, Carpenter would have lowered him into torpor once more, slipped him into one of their plush capsules, and started the slow-arousal sequence. After eight years, Russo has to be weak. Carpenter would need a few days to stabilize him."

"Would the others shack up at Nyx for the duration?"

"I don't think so. Most of the arousal sequence is automatic. Carpenter would have rigged his timers and driven them out in his car before midnight."

"Why midnight?"

"That's when the janitorial crew starts working on the research block."

"And then?"

"They would have gone their separate ways—our daring lawyers into safe houses to watch TV and wait for the dust to settle, and Carpenter back to his work routine."

"And the controller?"

"It depends. He could retire to a sunny place or end in a shallow grave if his masters worried about loose ends. Either way, he would disappear."

Silence.

"Naturally, that would only be Act One." Nikola was becoming weary of the conversation. Perhaps Odelle needed a pick-me-up. "Act Two's script would depend on what shape Russo was in. Carpenter would deliver a revived Russo to whoever has orchestrated his escape, either as a vegetable or a very pissed-off man."

Still silence.

"As for the grand finale, your guess is as good as mine." Nikola frowned at the box with bunches of wires in front of Dennis.

"That's theory. Where are they now?"

Time for disinformation padded with lies and half-truths. "Somewhere in the sewers, running out of time. They can't keep Russo alive down there indefinitely, so they have to come out. They can't go home or to relatives or known friends. They have to try to get out of the city. And they can't; I've sealed it." Though he thought it unlikely, he wasn't about to tell Odelle that the fugitives could be miles away by now, ensconced on a plush yacht and toasting with Dom Perignon.

"What if they have a safe house in D.C.?"

"In the city? No way. Too crowded. Two to four people and a stretcher? Their safe house, if they have one, must be remote. I doubt they've considered medical equipment. With their original plan, they wouldn't have needed it. Now they do. If Russo pulls through, he will need medical attention for some time." Nikola paused. *Let's analyze your reaction.* "By the way, I've had a cursory look at Russo's file. I feel that a key to this complex—and, I must add, daring—operation must rest with Russo's identity. Who is Russo?"

"What do you mean?" The voice had flickered.

"His dossier reads like a manual for teenage idealists, but he has done nothing to threaten the establishment or upset the status quo. At least, there's no mention of anything in his file. Eight years is a tough sentence and, to my knowledge, there's nothing to hint he would ever be released."

"Need to know."

But I do *need to know, my dear.* "I see. Does that mean Russo is the victim of someone's personal vendetta?"

The voice thickened. "Russo is anything but a victim."

Nikola frowned, his resolve strengthened. Rule number one for a criminal investigator was to pose the question of questions: *Quo bono?* Who benefits from the crime? The issues involved were far too delicate, and dangerous, to fumble about in the darkness. He would make it his priority to unearth Russo's real history, and that of whoever wanted him rotting in a tank.

Out of the corner of his eye, Nikola spotted a flurry of activity on the screens. Dennis's right hand came alive, his fingers dancing over the smooth surface of a control pad. Maps superimposed on the central screen, zooming over sections of the city to freeze on a maze of multicolored lines and three throbbing white dots.

"You have them?" Nikola asked.

"What?" the metallic voice croaked overhead.

Nikola shrugged and leaned over to grip Dennis's arm.

After a moment's hesitation, Dennis nodded, tapped his earpiece, darted a cursory glance at the overhead speakers, and returned his attention to the console. "Yes, moving south toward Bethesda." He panned the image.

"Speed?"

"Walking pace."

"Send squads to Old Georgetown Road, Wisconsin with Montgomery, and Cedar Lane with Rockville Pike. Hem them in."

On the left screen, a line of text grew as Dennis's fingers moved over his pad.

"You've work to do." The speaker crackled. "I'll leave you to it. Keep me posted."

"Will do." Nikola waited for the red light to fade, but the line remained open. *Now what?*

"Just a thought, kid."

Nikola tensed. Odelle was addressing Dennis.

"You must be proud. Your master has trusted you to eavesdrop on our conversation. Do you play chess? I'm sure you do. I'm also sure you know the Najdorf Variation of the Sicilian Defense: the Poisoned Pawn, a present with a sting on its tail. Your master has gifted you with his trust and, in doing so, ensured you'll share our tank if this incident is ever made public."

A wall of foul stench followed the thud of a manhole cover on the asphalt. Sergeant Theresa Corvin looked over the eight figures standing by the open access hole, their faces anonymous behind gas masks and image intensifiers. "Let's go over it once more. The marks are four hundred yards due south. Number-eight squad will drop three hundred yards behind the marks. There are no spur tunnels along the way, only drainpipes too small to access. Number-four squad has finished welding all access holes along this line. We'll hem them in. Watch out for cross fire. No warnings. No cautions. No prisoners. Shoot to kill. Go!"

One by one the DHS troops dropped through the utility hole. Corvin adjusted the HEPA mask over her mouth and nose and breathed deeply before following the last of her men.

After clearing the bottom metal rung on the tube, she dropped six feet to land in fetid water up to her knees. She sprang forward, chasing the platoon in a cacophony of thuds, splashes, and shouts. The tunnel, alive in her goggles with a ghostly greenish light, stretched ahead in a straight line. "Eight-one, you copy?" she spoke into her mouthpiece.

"Affirmative."

"Any contact?"

"Negative."

Corvin hated sewers. Nothing personal; she didn't give a damn about stench or filth. But having to clean the stuff off was another matter. She had an assistant who would endure most of it, but the guys would swear for hours, swabbing at gear dripping with gunk. Besides, she had a bad feeling about this one. Too easy. "Eight-one, you copy?"

"A—ffirmative."

Had he tripped or spotted something? "Any contact?"

"Well, that's it. I have eye contact with ground zero. No marks and nowhere to hide."

"Are you sure?" She screwed her eyes shut in frustration. Of course he was sure.

"I'm at the spot now."

Ahead, shapes started to slow down and the noise gradually subsided.

When she reached the group, a few officers stood aside so she could approach a twelve-inch pipe jutting from the wall at waist height and spewing a trickle of cloudy water. Corvin looked at a man standing next to the drain and took in the three narrow stripes on his arm. Eight-one. She moved her mask aside and took a deep breath of fetid air. Might as well get used to the stink they'd carry all the way back to their vehicles, their mess, and probably to their beds.

"No lights." She doubted anyone would ever forget when a joker, long gone from the force, had struck a lighter and blinded a full platoon on a night exercise. "What's up?"

"See for yourself." Eight-one nodded toward the pipe.

She leaned over, her head level with the drain to direct her infrared beam into the tube. Four feet farther in, behind a clump of brambles twisted with tampons and ripped condoms, two dots gleamed like the eyes of the very devil, unblinking. Corvin narrowed her eyes to peer past the rat's beady irises onto the rippling colors of the tracking devices strapped onto the animal.

"Shit."

"Now," Eight-one snorted, "why didn't I think of that?"

"Neat," Dennis offered, deadpan.

Nikola sighed. "I had to send in the troops, but it reeked of a red herring."

"For no reason? Would they plan such a ruse without an objective?"

"You mean besides getting rid of the sensors?"

"No. It doesn't make sense. They have lead cloth. They could have wrapped the lot and stuffed it down a hole where the sensors would never broadcast. These sensors were deployed for our benefit."

"You have a point there. Let me see a map."

"You mean the opposite side?"

"No, the quarter where the troops have found the sensors: north."

Dennis tapped his fingers and the central screen dissolved into a map.

Nikola's eyes darted between the railway station and the roads stretching toward the airports and the bus depots. "Keep everything we have on this sector." He waited for a question from Dennis that never came. "On the south side of town, there's the police headquarters, the power station, and the army barracks. To the north, the sugar cube. The Potomac is southwest and Chesapeake Bay is to the east. You're on the run and send us on a wild-goose chase north. Why?"

"The report says the sensors were strapped onto a rat. Unless they can remote-control the animal, my guess is the rodent could go anywhere once freed."

"I doubt it," Nikola said.

"Why?"

"The rodent could follow them or go in their same direction. I doubt they would risk it. No. The rat must have been planted."

"It says here," Dennis pointed to a screen, "that the animal was inside a narrow pipe, surrounded by what seemed like a nest."

Nikola nodded, his mind working overtime. "Are rats territorial?"

Dennis addressed a database. *"Brown rats in cities tend not to wander extensively, often staying within around sixty feet of their nest if a suitable concentrated food supply is available, but they will range more widely where food availability is lower."*

"More widely can mean anything, but my guess is the animals don't wander far from their burrows. It was planted. I still think they're moving north."

Dennis continued flicking through screens. "You mean reverse psychology. They want to move the heat south so they can move north."

"That's the idea. Keep your ear to the ground. I need a shower and a nap. Give me a shout if anything develops."

chapter 24

||||

12:03

The group made excellent progress during the better part of an hour, never leaving the disused railway tunnel. Henry marched point with Barandus, followed closely by Jim and Charlie. Susan, perhaps in her early forties—although it was difficult to guess what lay under the grime—closed the group's rear with Raul and Laurel. Raul plodded next to Laurel in silence, and Susan didn't speak much. No, Susan didn't speak at all but simply stared ahead as though preoccupied. Keeping her LAD flashlight dimmed, Laurel used their so-far-uneventful journey to peck a few lines into her Metapad, outlining their status, and sent it off to Shepherd. Although the account was far from enthusiastic, it would keep him from guessing.

"How deep does that thing work?"

Laurel started, and her Metapad would have slipped out of her hands but for the cord looped around her neck. She glanced at Henry's hulking figure, cursing inwardly. She'd not noticed his approach.

"Er—about one hundred feet, depending on the substrata."

Henry nodded. "Checking in with your Shepherd?" There was a trace of irony in his voice.

"Just an update."

He nodded again. "Tell him we're paying Santos Hernandez a visit."

Before she could ask who Mr. Hernandez was, Henry had returned to the head of the line.

Susan drew a misshapen cigarette out of a pocket, lit it up, and consumed almost half of it with the first drag. The air thickened with the pungent smell of grass.

Raul drew closer. "Know where we're going?"

Laurel cut a step short to add a little distance from Susan. "I have a general idea of what he's after, but he hasn't said anything of where or how."

"Weapons?"

"I don't think so. Explosives."

Raul was silent for a while. "I hope he knows his sewers."

"Why?"

"I bet the sewers under government buildings have security measures—sensors or whatever. It would be reckless if they didn't. Any twopenny terrorist could blow up the White House."

"I don't think he would consider something that drastic. Still—"

"Where would you find explosives in Washington, D.C.?"

"Nowhere outside military installations."

"Yup. That's my guess too, and one would think these sites are secure enough to thwart an invasion from the netherworld." Raul sniffed. "As I said before, I hope he knows his sewers."

Just ahead of them, Susan took a final drag from her joint, produced a small tin, and saved the remaining half-inch stub.

"He fucking does," she declared in a voice devoid of air as she exhaled the last of the grass from her lungs.

A short while later, the men in front of the line veered to the left and stopped.

When the group gathered, Henry nodded to Barandus. From somewhere inside his coat—the man must have had it dangling from his belt—Barandus produced a crowbar and bent down to wedge the tool into the edge of a large rectangular utility cover. Henry nodded to the other men and, when the gap was wide enough, they wrapped their fingers under the rim. The iron slab must have weighed more than two hundred pounds, and their display of faith stilled Laurel's breath. If the crowbar slipped . . .

"Leave it open," Henry said, once the chunk of metal was vertical. The men dragged the lid two feet and propped it by the opening. The cover was heavily corroded on the exposed lower side, with lumpy orange excrescences that glistened under the tight beams of the flashlights. Barandus returned the crowbar and stepped down first.

Laurel eyed Barandus's head as it disappeared below the rim of the utility hole and thought, not for the first time, that she'd barely heard the strange man utter more than single words. *What kind of name is Barandus, anyway?* One by one they followed.

The shaft, perhaps twelve to fifteen feet deep, connected with a vast rotunda, its center occupied by a derelict turbine. On the other side of the machine, they descended two metal ladders down to another level and a narrow dry tunnel. After rounding a sharp corner, the group spread out in a single line trailing through a network of pipes with obvious signs of maintenance.

"Gas and water mains," announced Henry from the front. A few tight turns later, Henry stopped at an arched side opening and stepped through. The others followed. The brick passageway opened onto a larger tunnel, but Henry stopped a few steps short. "Lights off."

One by one the bright LAD flashlights dimmed until there was nothing but thick darkness. Laurel stepped back, a hopeful hand moving toward Raul's.

"Charlie," Henry called. "See to motion and light sensors."

A rustle of steps, silence, then a curious wet twang. After a few seconds, they again heard a strange thwack, followed by a pause. "Done," a voice echoed, far ahead.

An LAD flashlight flooded the enclosure with painful intensity, then dimmed. "Lights at minimum setting," Henry said, and marched ahead to a concrete-lined structure. There, they shambled down a seemingly endless six-foot-wide tunnel lined with spaghettilike green cables. "Fiber-optic security wiring; our nation's secrets beam along these tubes." Twice more, Henry stopped and ordered the lights doused before directing Charlie to deal with the sensors. After the second time, Raul pointed to a squat box on the top of the arched roof, dripping black gunk.

Laurel peered at the device as they passed under it. "But . . . how?"

"A catapult," muttered Susan. "A pellet of tar and rat shit."

"In the dark?" There was a hint of awe in Raul's voice.

"Nah." Susan hawked and spat. "Sensors have LED lights so maintenance crews can see at a glance if they're working. Easy to see in pitch darkness."

"But won't blinding them trigger an alarm?" Raul asked.

"Alarm? These are passive detectors."

"I don't follow."

"Okay, imagine these are switches. If a light detector is blanked, it receives no light and remains switched off, or inactive, if you prefer. Same with a motion detector. They work by bouncing an infrared beam and timing its return. No return, no alarm."

Laurel smiled. "You were concerned about tunnels with security measures? There's your answer, and it didn't need rocket science." She jabbed Raul with her elbow.

Raul huffed, but in the bounce of a stray beam she could see his teeth gleam. She reached for her Metapad, selected a search engine, and typed >*Barandus*.

Ahead, the tunnel branched. Henry purposefully marched into the left fork before stopping almost at once before a small steel door, its gray paint flaking and missing in parts where reddish tracks wept.

Once more, Barandus stepped forward, fingered a padlock, and reached inside his coat to produce bolt cutters. After another descent through a round shaft, Laurel cringed at the reek of sewage. *Here we go again.* They hit a tunnel layered with viscous black goop that sucked at their boots and released a horrific stench; it opened after a hundred yards onto a sizable sewer with a walkway on one side and a whitish stream gurgling along its floor. After a prolonged bend, a large grille with two-inch bars blocked the tunnel. No bolt cutter could deal with those. She glanced at Raul, who shrugged.

"Fear not," Henry said. He walked slowly along the grille, his fingers brushing the vertical bars. He stopped at one, grabbed it, and rocked it until it broke loose from its moorings. When everybody had slid through, Henry replaced the iron bar in its slot.

"That guy knows his sewers," Raul admitted.

"I told you," Susan mumbled.

Laurel checked her watch. Over an hour and a half since they'd left Russo, and they had made good progress. *We must be getting near.* Then her Metapad issued a faint beep and its screen lit up. *>Barandus. One of the two wise men in the Acts of Xanthippe and Polyxena; Apocalypse; the Gospel According to Peter.*

I'll be damned, Laurel thought.

A few minutes later Henry stopped at another side entrance but didn't go in. "We must go through the crumbly, and that's dangerous, but there's no other alternative," he announced.

"What's that?" Raul asked.

Henry glanced at Barandus before answering. "The crumbly are the oldest sewers, narrow and lined with crumbling bricks. Cave-ins are frequent. I hear the city honchos are sinking new lines to eventually condemn these, but they are still in use."

Harper Tyler neared the old bay window in his study, nursing a squat tumbler with a splash of bourbon over a handful of ice cubes.

Suddenly a bright red tractor trailing a liquid-manure

spreader broke through the green wall of poplars separating the farm buildings and his house from the stables and fields. Tyler shielded his eyes and peered at the machine driven by Mateo Salinas—Antonio's son, decked in orange coveralls.

After Tyler's "accident," a mousy woman with colonel stripes had paid him a hospital visit to "plan your future." When a couple of medals and a promotion to a cushy desk job at a sunny location failed to elicit much enthusiasm, she offered him a sweet pension deal unreasonably fattened by a score of arcane items and payable in a lump sum with no deductions or commissions. That was the carrot. The stick was a lengthy document placing a short interval of his military career above top secret and threatening fire and brimstone should he be foolish enough to whisper a word about his time in Iran. When he requested time to study the papers, the colonel made a face and shook her head. "The wording is irrelevant," she confided. "It's the spirit that matters. The army wants you to have well-earned peace of mind. It's only fair we demand the same in exchange." She didn't say "or else," but Tyler was too weary and in pain from his shattered leg to consider rivaling Don Quixote's charge against the towering windmills of the military establishment. Major Marino was probably irrelevant. But his daughter, Odelle—the blazing star in the DHS firmament—was another matter. The army couldn't risk upsetting her. He signed on the dotted line and initialed each page before eyeing the colonel's departing derriere and upgrading his earlier rating of mousy to that of feline.

Thus ex–Chief Warrant Officer 4 Harper Tyler bankrolled a self-sufficient hog farm.

Mateo was heading to an earthed lagoon where the slurry from the pens collected before flowing slowly down a cement trench. Manure was an important element on Tyler's farm. From the trench, the waste not used on the fields was instead poured into underground pits, where an anaerobic biogas digester rotted the waste and extracted methane gas, which was then fed to his turbine. Pig manure provided all the energy the farm needed and was a source of income from the surplus-electricity feed to the grid.

The solid waste produced a valuable fertilizer. The remaining liquids would be returned to a nearby stream at the end of the process as clean water—the biodigestion having removed any pathogens or other potentially dangerous contamination from the pig waste. The water-filtration process involved a series of pools with plants that cleaned the water as they grew and made good pig feed, further reducing the need for off-site energy inputs. The system, a model of ingenuity and sound engineering, had been implemented by Antonio Salinas, the army veteran who—along with his wife, three sons, and boundless energy—ran the farm for Tyler.

Rather than heading for the slurry lagoon, the tractor stopped. Tyler frowned, watching as Antonio dashed toward the tractor, propelled by his prosthetic legs, his arms moving like the wings of a bird about to take flight. The quiet existence at the farm had given the battered Antonio a new lease on life. Still, the last time Tyler shared supper with the Salinas family, he was aghast at the tuna–noodle casserole with crumbled potato chips on top, followed by Jell-O laced with canned mandarin-orange slices and shredded carrots. A far cry from the Mexican feast Tyler had hoped for.

By the poplars, Antonio continued his gesticulation, pointing up and waving his son toward the machinery shed.

Tyler let the curtain fall and hobbled across the room to his maps, his mind shifting from pig manure to Laurel's latest signal. He remembered well the army technician Sergeant Santos Hernandez. How could he forget? One of the rare wizards of Explosive Ordnance Disposal, his team was often called upon to deal with seemingly impossible tasks, like removing the belt from a repentant suicide bomber whose charge had failed to go off. The brass had suggested clearing a wide area and letting a sniper detonate the explosives attached to the bastard. Sergeant Hernandez would have none of it. Decked in his body armor, he walked the wretch to the middle of a field and sweated for two endless hours under a merciless sun to remove fifty pounds of high explosives fiendishly attached to a much-booby-trapped harness. In the end, it was a useless gesture. Once freed of his load, the man tried to make a run for it and the sniper carved another notch into his weapon.

Explosives. Tyler's eyes roamed the Washington, D.C., map. Henry was a strangely honorable man in a dishonorable world. No blood. No innocents. How much explosive could six people carry? Thirty pounds each? Forty? He continued to scan the map. Capitol Hill, the White House, and the Pentagon were out of the question. Too many security measures. That left airports, power stations, road junctions, gasworks, trains . . . Henry would be planning a rattle. A mighty rattle. Then he froze and did a quick double take. *He wouldn't dare.* Tyler turned on his heel, and a searing pain shot from his left knee. He limped to his desk, his eye on the secure phone to warn the senator. He rested his glass, now mostly water, on a small area clear of papers—and stopped cold. The light had changed. Tyler charged toward the window and slapped the curtain aside, suddenly realizing what Antonio had been warning Mateo about. Storm clouds had quickly gathered overhead, and the poplars leaned as if pushed by unseen hands. *Sweet Lord, no!* He watched in dismay as large drops of rain threw themselves in heavy snatches on the terra-cotta tiles fronting the house.

Henry's "crumbly" was nightmarish. After going down three more shafts, they landed in an oval tunnel of bricks in all shades of gray and black. Oozing gray excrescences dangled from the ceiling like an upside-down forest.

"Holy—" Laurel gasped.

At her side, Susan hawked and spat a glob of phlegm onto the wall. "They've been called snotsicles, shitsicles, and you-name-it-sicles. By any name, bad news."

"Why?" Laurel jumped at the opportunity to get her taciturn companion to talk.

Susan withdrew a scarf from her pocket that once must have been printed with flowers but now was a confusion of grime and brown streaks. She tied it tightly around her head. "That dangling, jiggly fucking slime gets in your hair like a gel and dries into a hard, crisp coat."

Laurel lowered the dome of her head toward Susan. "I have an advantage."

"How right you are." A cackling laugh followed. "Look." Without breaking stride, Susan reached high and grabbed a handful of the spaghettilike formations. They wriggled in her hand like live worms. "Their consistency is similar to very thick come. See?" She squeezed. "The outermost layer is slippery, wet, and shiny. Just beneath this is a rubbery substance."

Henry stepped aside and stopped, waving his arms to keep the rest of the group walking. When they drew level, he grinned, his head already coated in the slimy things.

"Its exact composition is open to debate, but it's probably algae that live off the decaying materials commonly found here. Harmless, though. Let's check for fumes." He flicked a gas lighter and peered at the flame. Then he returned it to one of the cavernous pockets in his greatcoat. "Had there been a tinge of orange in the flame, it would mean trace levels of natural gas. But we're all right."

"All right?" Laurel looked around. "I mean, is there no end to the shit?"

Henry's voice took on a patronizing tone. "This is the lower world. It's a paradox that we know more about space, stars, and galaxies light-years away than about the sewers beneath our city streets. No government has ever thought of exploring, much less cleaning, these regions."

"People need to know about this and do something about it. I mean, these should be cleaned, or sealed—" Laurel bit her lip. Her thoughtless comment reeked of high school idealism.

Barandus neared and breathed deep. He panned his flashlight up and down the tunnel, painting a swath across the crumbling brick. Charlie and Jim drew near, their eyes never leaving Barandus, and Laurel could have sworn they were holding their breath. "People don't want to know what happens to their shit." Barandus spoke with a strangely measured voice, pronouncing every word with care, as if addressing a congregation. "Excrement, like everything else, has become a heritage industry. Out of sight, out of mind. For most people, shit, like death, is a private matter. Once it leaves the body, its afterlife is up to whoever collects the taxes."

He paused and his voice lowered. "Civilization has its mirror in the sewers. The filth of men falls into this pit of reality, where social class ends. Engulfed by their latrines, the rich and the powerful mingle again with their humbler brethren here." He raised a leg and brought the toe of his rubber boot to the surface of the effluent, where it created a miniature eddy. "This brew is a confession. There's no more hypocrisy, no cosmetics to disguise upbringing. Here there's nothing left but the terrible shape of our shared miseries. There, a syringe speaks of oblivion, a mop head of domesticity; there, an effigy of the Virgin Mary reverts to cheap plastic, hobo spittle meets noble puking, and, farther on, the lost engagement ring jostles the razor blade that severed a dreamer's veins. And you wonder why people deny sewers? A sewer doesn't keep secrets or keep appearances. Here we're surrounded by truth." Again he breathed deep before shifting in his rubber boot, as if testing the ground under the filth. Then he hunched his shoulders and started to plod ahead.

Laurel's head spun. She had no idea how the Paris sewers must have felt to Victor Hugo, but his source of inspiration for *Les Misérables* now seemed obvious. And Barandus had shamelessly borrowed from the French master for his impromptu speech.

Raul shook his head. "He doesn't speak much, but when he does . . ."

"What?"

"I wish he'd kept his mouth shut."

"Depressing, huh?" Laurel asked.

Henry looked around as if taking a bearing and followed Barandus. "Reality always is."

Raul rubbed his hands. "How much longer?"

"Half an hour," Henry said. "We're almost there."

As he severed the communication with Shepherd, Senator Palmer knew the meaning of fear as never before. Shepherd had sent the storm warning to Laurel but didn't get confirmation or an answer, so he'd called Palmer. It was raining hard. Through the patio doors came sounds like the percussion section of a high school band. He watched, mesmerized, as sheets of water slid down the glass expanses to the accompaniment of thunder and lightning: a classic of late-summer Washington, D.C. Then the storm ended abruptly, as though bored. Outside, the lawn steamed. Palmer slid open the patio doors to the smell of electricity in the air, his mind thick with foreboding.

They continued single file along a passage without sidewalks, trampling slimy water in their wake. Soggy clothing dripped, boots and rags squelched. The piercing beams of LAD flashlights highlighted wisps of steam rising from the hair and misshapen coats of the marchers.

"My children," Henry's voice boomed from the head of the line, "let reality shine into your dark consciences. The world is swimming in shit."

"Amen," Laurel grumbled.

"Ah, but sewers are the conscience of the city," Raul offered.

Nobody commented.

Laurel glanced down to hide a rueful smile. *How fitting,* she thought. Raul was also borrowing from Victor Hugo.

"Shhhh." Henry suddenly stopped, waving his arms to command silence.

Laurel held her breath, her ears registering dripping noises. Then, far away, a faint and low sound intruded.

Henry reached into his coat, produced his cheap lighter once more, and flicked its flame into life, an instant before bellowing, "Flash flood!" Then he swung around and started to run.

||||

chapter 25

13:30

From a small niche in the corridor between the living room and his study, Nikola selected a bottle of rum, only shreds of its faded label still clinging to the glass. He reached for a small cut-glass tumbler and carted the lot to his desk, musing that his 1959 Lemon Hart was the greatest British achievement in the West Indies.

He glanced to Dennis's vacant workstation; the young man was catching a few hours of shut-eye now that the incoming reports had trickled down to nothing. As an afterthought, he drew the sleeve of his worn housecoat to his nose and nodded. He'd warned Mrs. Sotomayor, the housekeeper, against experiments with new soaps and fabric softeners. Last time she tried, his house clothes had a smell that vividly reminded Nikola of a Turkish brothel. After a long hot shower, a couple of hours of dreamless sleep, a few minutes in the sauna until he broke a decent sweat, and a dip in a tub of water—chilled just above freezing—he certainly felt renewed.

From the beginning of the wretched breakout episode, he'd been disturbed by a strange premonitory feeling. A practical man, never burdened with spiritual or supernatural accoutrements, the overwhelming sensation of danger he felt was playing hell with his otherwise acute capacity for analysis and concentration. On one hand he had the facts: Three young people had sentenced themselves into a sugar cube. Two of them, helped by a civil servant, had sprung an obscure and seemingly inconsequential illegal inmate. Through the sewers, they had reached a commercial hibernation facility for the rich, discovered they were broadcasting their location, and fled once more into the sewers with another confederate: a medical doctor well versed in revival techniques.

On the other hand, he had an unexplained riddle: Who had sentenced Russo to a living death? Odelle herself, or was she acting on someone's behalf? Who had the means and the clout to pull off such a stunt—complex, expensive, and needing awesome intelligence and logistic resources? And the most worrisome detail: Why? No doubt the missing threads were interwoven, but the picture was blurry, as if viewed through a fogged glass.

Nikola was well acquainted with the hibernation penal system and the sordid reality of its creation, development, testing, and the internecine wars between the Department of Homeland Security and the Federal Bureau of Hibernation for control. In the end, Odelle Marino, the DHS empress, had won and trampled over the FBH.

The hibernation concept was sound; it had done away with an obsolete network of crime universities and transformed the penal system into a tool to empty the streets of criminals at an affordable cost. Yet it was fitting that perfection eluded human endeavors. The system was flawed. Hypnos, like any enterprise ruled by marketing, tried to cut corners and economize on the design, surveying, and maintenance of the facilities while maximizing their profits. Nothing wrong with trying. The DHS had enlisted Nikola and two other security consultants to supervise the design, propose improvements, and rein Hypnos in. Nikola could also understand the empty center tanks—a little extra capacity for experimentation and testing, in particular if Uncle Sam footed the bill. The crafty way in which the issue of the center spaces was palmed through both Houses—four-inmate tanks within a large tank, really—meant that not only Hypnos but also government agencies had access to an advanced meat chiller to preserve guinea pigs and the kind of subjects who couldn't or shouldn't be killed outright but kept available, just in case. The illegality of the scheme was nothing new, but issues like legality had certainly never bothered politicians before, providing the scheme was kept under the exacting constraints of the eleventh commandment: Thou shalt not be found out.

He sniffed his rum and peered with regret at the scant inch left at the bottom of the bottle. Intensely powerful nose: toffee, prunes, old marmalade, dates, overripe mango, caramel, vanilla, allspice . . . After a little sip, Nikola let the flavors develop on his tongue, swallowed, and made a wry gesture when an image of dank sewers intruded upon his bliss.

Nikola probably knew the Washington sewers better than anyone alive—not the pipes and tunnels carrying the citizenry's wastes, but the warrens of power bursting with indescribable filth. Yet, rather than becoming dulled from continuous exposure to the stench of greed and hypocrisy, his nose had remained delicately sensitive—a trait that had kept him alive after forty years of shady work. From his beginnings as a CIA operative, then later a chief of station, and eventually director of internal security at the DHS, his nose had unerringly steered him away from disaster. When he realized the value of his nose in the open market, he was a shade away from his fiftieth birthday. Nikola quit the civil service and became a security consultant—a euphemism favored by elitist mercenaries the world over.

He blinked at the sensor in his desktop screen to call up Eliot Russo's file—a fascinating document with a physical description and a few professional, educational, and personal background notes. Nikola found it fascinating not because of the scant information it contained but for the glaring voids. Someone had used the system to settle a score, of that he was certain. Another party was bent on exposing the sham, and Nikola was caught in the middle.

As a mercenary, Nikola had an unshakable code of values; he owed fidelity to the customer—in this instance the DHS. But this case was different. The customer was playing her own game by keeping critical cards close to her chest, leaving Nikola in the uncomfortable position of having to question his loyalties to avoid getting caught in the cross fire.

After more than an hour poring over the fugitives' files and preparing a list of notes—most of them questions—Nikola downloaded the lot into his hybrid data-and-communications pad. He decided against leaving a finger of the precious rum in the bottle and, with a sigh, he poured the rest into his tumbler.

Then he stood and padded over to his bedroom, carrying
the glass, to get dressed for his first visit. The legend of
Alexander the Great's expedient maneuver to untangle the
Gordian knot was a sobering lesson, its substance unimpaired by the passage of millennia. If the ends are hidden,
with no thread to pull from to resolve the tangle, hack
through the knot.

chapter 26

||||

13:34

As if powered by unseen clockwork, the group bolted forward at once, splashing madly through twelve inches of effluent. Laurel's Metapad blipped once, sharp—an incoming
message. She charged ahead into a chaos of flying whitish
water, ragged gasps, and the unnerving splash of boots
falling.

"Climb, climb!" Henry had reached a string of rusty handholds rising through the curved tunnel wall to a small opening, barely three feet across near its top.

"Climb, damn you!"

When Susan reached the spot where Henry stood yelling,
Charlie and Jim were already climbing like cats. Susan
jumped halfway up, grabbed the handhold, and hauled herself
up with one swift movement. The trio scrabbled for purchase
on the rusty treads and dove headfirst into the upper culvert.

Five feet from Henry and Barandus, who stood at either
side of the handholds, Laurel heard the roar and Raul's
shout. She looked behind at a rush of water coming toward
her and the barreling shape of Raul, his mouth wide open.

Barandus turned and was stretching a hand toward her when
the water hit.

She leaped for the handholds, missing by inches, her legs

suddenly nowhere. Water rammed her back, knocking the wind from her lungs. She screamed and saw Henry's light flash past a fraction of a second before something large and hard, probably a piece of flotsam, slammed into her back. She jerked and had drawn a big gulp of water when her harness tightened like a leash, halting her forward rush. Then an irresistible force pulled her head out of the water and smashed her against the rungs. No piece of flotsam, but Henry's hand. Eyes shut, coughing and spluttering, Laurel frantically gripped the rusty bars until a massive paw slammed against her butt and hurled her upward, where other hands dragged her sideways.

She opened her eyes in a cavern, perhaps twenty feet in diameter, with a large round opening high up one wall. No ladder went up. They were trapped. She coughed, water dripping from her nose. Raul crawled out of the hole, followed by Barandus, who looked like a wild spirit with his long black hair plastered down the side of his face. Then Henry bolted behind Barandus and pushed him roughly aside.

"The pipes. Hang on to the pipes and climb!" Henry yelled.

Opposite the high opening, a dozen rusty pipes rose to the domed ceiling. Already, bundles of rags were taking positions and scaling the tubes, grabbing at the hoops holding them in place.

Instants later, with a deep whooshing sound, water exploded from the narrow passage they had just traveled and hit the opposite side of the cavern, climbing halfway up its wall to crash down in a flurry of foam. Then the water level started to climb. Eyes stinging and stomach heaving, Laurel reached upward, feeling strangely light until she felt Raul's hand hauling on her safety harness. Then the roar ceased as swiftly as it had started, replaced by gurgling sounds as the water rose. They climbed even higher, the narrow beams of their LAD flashlights slashing across the black surface of the water below.

After a splash, a huge shape disappeared into the filthy water, which looked like a cauldron of rancid beef stew, to suddenly surface, grip the pipe, and tower above her. She turned to bury her face in Henry's chest, and his wet ripeness and his voice snapped her out of her shock.

"W-what?"

"Did you swallow?" Henry asked.

Laurel nodded.

"You should induce vomiting to empty your stomach." He showed the technique by sticking two grubby fingers down his throat. He dry-retched a few times until a yellowish gush belched out through his matted beard into the rising water. Laurel didn't need to use her fingers. Between retches, she heard Barandus's voice ring somewhere to her left. "The water is leveling off through the spill pipe. It won't rise anymore." And, after a pause, "It's over. The level is stable. It should start to drop in a minute or two."

Henry slapped a hand on the pipe. "That was close. The goddess of sewers must have taken pity on us."

"Are you kidding?" Laurel croaked. "Goddess of sewers?"

"Right, Cloacina; she was an Etruscan goddess of fucking."

"Gimme a break," she moaned. "What has fucking got to do with sewers?"

"You really want to know?" The light dangling under Henry's chin suddenly shifted to give him a definite sinister look.

"Roman logic could be twisted, but Henry is right," Raul butted in right over her. "The Romans employed Cloacina as overseer of the Roman drainage system—a very important office."

Laurel swallowed. True to character, Raul was an endless repository of scatological trivia. She reached for her Meta-pad and typed >We're still alive.

Forty-five minutes after their narrow escape, they started to climb down, leaving behind the older, flat-sided, arch-topped tunnel when it connected with an intercepting sewer. The new tunnel featured scores of adjoining branches, all spewing milky slop to engorge the two-foot-deep water running through its trough. Henry bellowed instructions down the line to walk single file, holding on to a cast-iron pipe bolted to one of the walls. Every few yards they found clumps of rags that must have caught on the pipe supports during the flood: tights, nylons, condoms, sanitary napkins, disposable diapers, dishcloths, dusters, and all the nonbiodegradable things that people flushed down the toilet. Susan followed Raul's gaze and offered what passed for a smile. "Rags don't bother the authorities. Q-tips do."

Raul drew closer, his face suddenly animated. "Why is that?"

"When shit reaches the station, they filter it to separate solids in perforated drums. Q-tips fit neatly in the holes in the drums, and they have to get rid of them with high-pressure jets."

"Cool." Raul had just picked up another snippet of his favorite trivia.

"I hear you went through fat fields."

Laurel grimaced. "Have you been there?"

"Ha, now it's not so bad. Months ago a tunnel was clogged with a fatberg. It took a team of workers a month to move it."

"How? Steam, pickaxes?"

"I don't know, but I heard a large food chain offered to buy it back for recycling to its customers."

Raul grinned. "You got to be kidding."

"I am."

Heading downstream, they came to a short passageway leading to a circular, dome-topped brick chamber, capped with a circular manhole. The chamber must have been fifteen feet high from the manhole cover at its top to the water's surface below. Down one side were the remains of ladder rungs. The pins fastening the old iron hoops into the brick looked smooth and without much rust.

Henry announced the obvious. "They've cut the rungs."

"Who are they?" Laurel asked.

"I don't know." Henry shrugged. "Workers from the Sewer Authority, I suppose."

On one side of the manhole cover, a tree root had long ago begun a hunt for moisture and had spanned the fifteen-foot fall, its many tapered and split rootlets like the tongue of a strange reptile.

They returned to the intercepting sewer and continued along, holding on to the cast-iron pipe. Soon a noise started to build up. Laurel glanced around, but nobody seemed concerned. Susan smiled. "It's coming from downstream. No flash flood. Waterfall."

The floor turned slippery and a dull roar echoed from somewhere up ahead.

Soon the tunnel vented into a vast chamber, where water roared down toward one side to overflow into a wide tunnel. Laurel cringed at a whoosh of warm air, the hiss of fast-running sewage, and an ancient, sulfurous stink. Humidity thickened the air, making it unbreathable. On the opposite side of the fall were a series of steps large enough to be called terraces. The group climbed to reach a rectangular opening leading to a second chamber, smaller and dry. Then they came to a second set of steps leading to a passageway that ended in a circular vertical shaft, this time with an intact carbonate-encrusted ladder.

Climbing up the shaft holding on to the iron handholds turned out to be a very unpleasant exercise. The drenched clothes of the climbers released a rain of fetid drops. Laurel and Raul at the rear received the worse of it.

"God is dead. Shit lives," Raul grunted, careful not to look up.

Through a utility hole, they climbed into a vast empty room that looked like a disused warehouse. Henry waved to draw everybody closer. "Lamps at minimum setting and silence from this point on." Then he strode to the other end of the room and another set of handholds, which climbed to a square opening in the ceiling.

With measured movements, they negotiated the rungs to another seemingly disused warehouse. But this one was different. Laurel turned to grip Raul's arm. A row of dirt-encrusted windowpanes lined the nearest wall. Through broken glass, she could see the outline of gorgeous clouds. Laurel stepped forward with slow steps, her blurry eyes fastened to the fragment of sky framed by shards of glass. Tears streamed down her cheeks. At the window she breathed deep—clean air, crisp, perhaps tinged with a whiff of kerosene but as sweet as French perfume. Through the opening, she saw masses of dark trees a hundred yards away. She turned to the group standing by the hole on the floor. They hadn't moved.

Then she heard a metallic noise at the far end of the warehouse an instant before lights exploded, bathing the room in blinding clarity.

Laurel stood rooted to the spot, like a rabbit pinned in the open by oncoming headlights, her hands darting up to shield her eyes. Heavy treads followed. She lowered her hands a fraction to see a mountainous shape in formal army fatigues bearing down on her, backlit by truck headlights. The figure marched past the group and stopped a few feet away from her.

Closer, the soldier looked smaller. He was a tall man but not physically imposing. She blinked to clear her eyes, squinting to make out his features against the light glare. Over his short sleeves she counted the stripes: three, but with two bars underneath. A sergeant, but not an ordinary one. His dark eyes shone, then his mouth parted and she caught a glint of white. The man was smiling. "Who are you?" He had a pleasant voice.

"Cole. Laurel Cole."

Silence.

Laurel walked a step forward. "And you are?"

"Drooling down my shirt."

"I can see that. But what do they call you if they want you to answer?"

"Santos. Santos Hernandez."

A guffaw echoed from the group as Henry strode past Barandus, his hand outstretched. "Already measuring up the talent? Have you no shame?"

Sergeant Hernandez pivoted on his heel, gripped Henry's hand, and pumped. Then he reached for his forearm and jerked his hand back. "Shit, you're soaking wet, and"—he made a face and turned toward the group—"you stink!"

"Pardon me, sir, I forgot. I'll gargle with Chanel before our next date."

Hernandez walked before the group, as if inspecting recruits. "Holy mother . . ." he muttered. When he drew abreast of Raul, he gave him a quick once-over. "And him?" he called over his shoulder.

"The other lawyer," Henry said.

He sniffed loudly and nodded once. "Get in the back of the truck." Then he marched with long strides toward the blazing headlights.

After a ten-minute drive skirting an airfield, the truck slowed down to a stop. Lying on the floor of the truck like felled timber, Laurel held her breath, but no hand parted the canvas flaps to inspect the vehicle. The muffled sound of conversation followed, then laughter, before the engine revved and the vehicle moved. Then the floor tilted and she slid against Susan, who was lying next to her. They were descending a ramp of sorts.

They exited the truck in a cavernous hangarlike room brightly lit with mercury lamps, its center occupied by a gigantic machine almost one hundred feet long and set on railway tracks. The contraption consisted of a huge tube, perhaps six or seven feet in diameter, with one rounded end. The other end was separated and set on tracks so it could push or pull a table of sorts into and out of the tube. When closed, the thing would look like a colossal double-ended sex toy.

"So that's it?" Henry asked, stepping forward and laying a hand on the separated end.

Santos joined him. "That's her. A beauty, wouldn't you say?"

Under the lights, Laurel watched her companions. With no shadows or darkness to disguise edges, colors, or textures, she couldn't think of a single word to describe the humanity beneath the layers of drab, soggy rags. Raul and she, with their plastic suits and lack of hair, could pass for filthy workers back from a day cleaning cesspits, but the others looked like a malignant species of . . . trolls, that was it. Trolls. Barandus, tall and thin and decked head to toe in a long black overcoat, looked more than ever like a filthy Rasputin. By his side, Susan, short and plump, in a horrid raincoat four sizes too large and her nondescript scarf tied around her head, added to the illusion of a scene from the aftermath of a nineteenth-century Russian pogrom. Thin-as-a-rake Jim and well-padded Charlie seemed to have dropped from a mud fight in a Stan Laurel and Oliver Hardy comedy. But Henry eclipsed his companions. Standing beside Santos—unblemished in his fatigues and shiny boots—Henry looked like a nightmare. In his drab coat tied at the waist with a length of electric wire, the towering hulk of filth embodied the bogeyman with which parents threatened insomniac children.

"How many pounds can you load her with?" Henry was asking.

"Fifty, but we never use more than thirty-five," Santos said, with something that sounded like pride in his voice.

Laurel neared, and the rest followed suit. "I'm sorry, but what is that?"

Santos slapped his hand on a vast circular piece of steel, several inches thick and probably maneuvered by the shiny hydraulic jacks around it. "She's an OZM KVG-30 horizontal detonation chamber. She weighs over one hundred fifty tons and can contain the blast from fifty pounds of high explosives."

"You detonate explosives inside?" Raul asked. "What for?"

Henry turned. "To dispose of unwanted material." He waved to Barandus to come closer. "Barandus is a friend. He was in Astaneh-e Ashrafiyyeh."

Santos turned. For an instant, Laurel thought he would stand to attention and salute, but he offered his hand and pumped away for an undue amount of time, his eyes bright. "It's an honor, sir."

No wonder, thought Laurel in awe. One hundred twelve men from the fabled Sixth Regiment of the United States Marine Corps had held a position for three days against the massed hordes of two thousand mujahideen insurgents. When relief finally arrived, there were only twelve marines alive. Having exhausted their ammunition, they had resorted to hand-to-hand combat in the city's narrow streets.

"Let's not waste any more time," Santos said. "Over here." He marched with long strides to some metal tables set against one of the walls.

The group trotted after Santos and regrouped in silence to stare at piles of puttylike tan-colored blocks. "It's a little past its shelf life, but you know good old PETN. It will last forever."

Henry leaned to peer at a label marked *Date–Plant–Shift*. "How long past?"

Santos shrugged. "A couple of years, but it's perfectly stable. Good as new."

"Okay, guys." Henry reached to his back and disentangled his arms from the straps holding his backpack. "Forty blocks in each pack." Then he turned to Laurel. "You can pack fewer."

Laurel pressed her lips together. "I may grab a handful more."

Santos smiled. Then he walked back to the truck, opened the cabin door, and returned with two small packs and a large roll of thin cable. "Detonators, wire, and timer."

Barandus reached over to the packs. "I'll take those." Then he asked something in a hushed tone and Santos nodded, pointing to one of the packs and rattling off instructions.

Their packs loaded, they stood at the back of the truck while Henry exchanged a few last words with Santos.

"Say," Laurel wriggled to adjust the straps, already digging into her shoulders, "should we be careful? I mean, banging against walls and the like?" She tried to empty her mind of the harrowing route they would have to negotiate on their return trip.

Barandus shook his head. "Nah. As the sergeant said, these are stable. You could burn them or hit them with a hammer, and nothing would happen."

"But—" She was about to persist when Henry joined them.

"Don't worry." Henry's beard shifted. "You wouldn't feel a thing."

16:16

"Would you like a cup of coffee? Tea? Please sit down; make yourself comfortable." Mrs. Cole waved a hand toward the sofa.

Nikola glanced around the living room and stepped over to it.

"Something stronger?" offered Mr. Cole.

"Tea will be fine, thank you. No milk or sugar." As Mrs. Cole nodded and shuffled on worn slippers toward the kitchen, Nikola sat on the edge of the sofa, occupying the center. "You have a beautiful garden." He turned to the rock beds crowding a small lawn, visible through sliding glass doors.

"I don't do much nowadays, besides keeping the weeds at bay and replacing sick plants." Mr. Cole sat down on one of the easy chairs and massaged a knee with a gnarled hand. "Arthritis is killing me."

There were no photographs of Sean and Jenny Cole in Laurel's dossier, but they were much as Nikola had expected: a couple aging with the graceless air of those who had scurried through life without intellectual pursuits, doomed to wither away quietly, watching TV.

Nikola took in the side wall flanking the seating area, scanning a predictable array of traditional photographs in glazed picture frames interspaced with a few modern displays that changed views every few minutes. Next to portraits of old people, probably ancestors, stood a large color photograph of a much younger Sean and Jenny in wedding garb—the smiling bride in an elaborate white dress next to a gangly young man in an ill-fitting tuxedo, probably rented for the occasion. Mixed with snapshots of flower shows and gardening events were scores of photographs of Laurel. On a far corner, flanked by two remarkable photographs of an alert tabby cat, Nikola spotted a portrait of Sean, looking terribly naive and self-conscious in his Navy uniform. His national service had been uneventful, correct, but gray; a recurrent normalcy permeated his file.

Centered on the mantelpiece over a fireplace with a basket of dried flowers stood a piece of wood with a carved motto: *Dum Spiro Spero*. While I Breathe, I Hope. Nikola pursed his lips at Cicero's quote from *Letters to Atticus* and the incorrect use of capital letters—the Latin should have been all lowercase—before realizing it was also the state motto of South Carolina, where Jenny was from. *How appropriate.* Next to the carving, a photo frame flickered and then faded. A garden scene with a group in the background too small to identify from a distance blended into a portrait of Laurel holding a furry ball.

When Mrs. Cole returned, carrying a small tray with three mugs, her eyes were reddened and shiny; she'd been crying.

Nikola pasted an innocent expression on his face and blinked twice when, probably by force of habit, she neared the sofa. She did a quick double take, assessing the seating arrangement, and made for the other easy chair after setting the tray on a coffee table.

A century earlier, B. F. Skinner had revolutionized marketing with his "radical behaviorism," but his work paled in significance before Oleg Bosky's seminal *Control*. An obscure Russian psychiatrist, Bosky had transformed motivational analysis into an awesome tool, affording his followers an unparalleled capacity to predict reactions to stimuli.

Hard-sale closing-technique number one: Never pitch to a single member of a couple. To do so will allow the punter an excuse to check with the other half before signing. Hard-sale closing-technique number two: Never allow a couple to sit next to each other. To do so will allow the punters a chance to seek the comfort of nearness and strengthen their resistance.

"Mr. Ma—sek." Mr. Cole squinted at Nikola's visiting card. "How is Laurel?"

"Please, call me Nikola. I hate formality."

Mr. Cole nodded, a glimmer of relief scuttling across tired eyes. "I'm Sean." He nodded at his wife. "She's Jenny."

"Thank you. Yes—Laurel. A dreadful episode. I checked. She's fine; asleep." No reaction from either of them. Not that he expected any, but Nikola relaxed further after analyzing their body language. So far they knew nothing of their wretched daughter's breakout.

"Is there a chance she may be set free?" Jenny Cole blurted. "I mean, before the two-year sentence is over?"

Nikola tore his eyes again from the photographic display, with the unpleasant sensation that he was missing something important, something about the photographs. *She already is free,* Nikola thought. "Indeed," he said.

"Over the phone you mentioned your department has considered reviewing her case."

Nikola noticed a brimming glint in Jenny's eyes, her fingers busy twisting a brown button on her aged cardigan, before he turned toward Sean. "All three: Laurel's, Bastien's, and Raul's. Youth. Foolish. Such a waste." Nikola reached for a mug of tea and sniffed the delicate aroma of bergamot orange rind. Earl Grey. He sipped, held the hot liquid in his mouth, and opened his lips a fraction to swallow with a little air. No. China, Indian Darjeeling, Ceylon, and a hint of lapsang souchong teas, flavored not only with bergamot rind but also with lemon and Seville oranges: Lady Grey. "Excellent."

"A Christmas present. English," Jenny said. "How can we help, Nikola?"

The scene was set to his satisfaction. Nikola rested his drink on the tray and straightened. "I have pored over the kids' files." *Kids* had a nice paternal ring. "Their behavior—breaking and entering a fireworks factory and trying to steal explosives— was stupid and unnatural."

"Unnatural?" Sean asked.

"Please, allow me." Nikola waved a hand. "Nothing in their background accounts for their foolishness. I mean, all three have fine families and have benefited from a sound upbringing and a sounder education." He paused to let the compliment sink in. "Bad company? I've explored that angle, and the more I think about it, the more I'm convinced someone tricked them into acting rashly. Perhaps they didn't even know the fireworks factory also made high explosives."

Sean wrung his hands. "Yes, but how can we help?"

"By telling me everything you know about your daughter—her friends, hobbies, her adolescence, childhood, her relationship with you and the rest of the family. The works."

The air thickened. Just a fraction, but it did. Nikola could have kicked himself for being sloppy. Any decent interrogator knows questions must be dosed one at a time, never bunched like grapes. The pair tensed, an almost imperceptible and fleeting reflex, now gone. Something in his exposition, his shopping list of requests, had triggered a defensive response.

Sean cleared his throat and opened with a lengthy piece about Laurel's lawyer friends. "We didn't agree about Laurel sharing a house with another girl and two men, mind you, but you know how stubborn young people can be."

Nikola nodded, looking at the photographs.

Jenny took over, and for thirty minutes she bared Laurel Cole's uneventful life, most of which Nikola already knew and a few precious bits he didn't, like her heartbreak with a young Latino Artificial Intelligence doctor by the name of Luis Cano. He made a mental note to pay a visit to Dr. Cano. Nikola only half listened as Jenny talked; Dennis would be recording their conversation from the van parked outside the house.

A large blackbird landed on the paved patio next to the sliding doors in a flurry of spidery clicks as its claws fought for purchase. Once landed, it strutted about, pecked at something between the paving stones, then took wing. The distraction must have triggered his lazy synapses, for Nikola panned the photograph display again as the incongruity that had troubled him suddenly rushed to the forefront of his mind. Sean and Jenny had alternated stories, details, and anecdotes covering most of the items from his list of suggestions. That was it—most but not all. Nikola nodded when Jenny offered to brew a fresh cup of tea and tried to marshal his thoughts in her absence.

Sean gripped his knees and leaned forward. "Please,

Nikola, help us." He darted a glance toward the kitchen. "She's going through hell. I know she hides it well, but our daughter's sentence has taken the life out of her. Please?"

"I will make it my priority to return your daughter." Nikola didn't lie. Sean nodded, and Jenny, approaching again with the tray, smiled for the first time.

Nikola waited until Sean and Jenny had settled down to nurse their drinks before closing his eyes to clear his mind of everything but sounds. "Tell me about Laurel's childhood."

His statement was met by silence.

Most interrogators overestimate the possibilities of detecting deceit by watching someone's behavior and underestimate the chances of catching liars by listening to what they say. They believe liars give themselves away by what they do; Nikola believed the verbal content of what people said, and the way people articulated what they said, betrayed lies.

"Er . . ." Sean opened after clearing his throat. "She was a quiet girl and . . . always conscientious. Nobody ever had to remind her to do her homework. She read a lot and—"

"She helped me with the house," Jenny piped up. "Laurel was very tidy; she would keep her room spotless and all her things in order. I know this sounds strange in this day and age, but she also helped in the kitchen and loved to help with the cooking. Baking was her favorite: cookies and cakes and gingerbread and cupcakes . . . and she would offer to help around the garden. She liked flowers. There were always freshly cut blooms in a vase by the entrance."

Nikola nodded once after listening with undivided attention to a showcase of classic lying. Long-winded explanations with many digressions, generalized by making frequent use of words like *always, ever,* and *nobody,* increased the psychological distance between people and the event they described. Of course, there were many more telling nuances in the couple's tale. Liars often resorted to disclaimers. Jenny had used *I know this sounds strange* and eventually she would have reached for *You won't believe this, but* or *Let me assure you*—disclaimers designed to acknowledge any suspicion. There had also been pauses between their words and sentences; pauses filled with *um*s and *er*s.

He composed his next question with care now that he knew its answer. *Never ask a question without knowing the reply* was the golden rule for a lawyer cross-examining a witness, and the same could be said of an interrogator. "Was Laurel a good baby?"

Another silence, longer this time. Nikola nodded again, his eyes still closed, savoring the soft rustle of nervous slippered feet.

"Er . . ." Sean started.

"She gave us no trouble," Jenny replied. "A very good baby."

The pitch of someone's voice was a good indicator of their emotional state, because when people got upset, their voices rose, and Jenny's voice had hiked noticeably.

Nikola turned toward Jenny and opened his eyes. "Did you breast-feed her?"

Jenny drew a hand to her chest and swallowed as Sean blustered, "What does that have to do with anything?"

"I—"

"Please, Jenny," Nikola raised a hand and moved to stand up. "Don't lie. I will forget what you've said, because giving false information to a government officer is a punishable offense and I don't want to cause you any harm. You've suffered enough already. But I need to know everything about Laurel to help her, and if you lie to me"—Nikola let the sentence hang in midair like a guillotine—"I won't be able to return your daughter." There, he'd done it again. *Naturally, I mean to return Laurel to a position several inches below the surface in a hibernation tank. Center.*

"She's not our daughter," Sean blurted.

"Of course she is!" Jenny sprang to her feet, looking very much like a flustered sparrow.

"I mean she's our adopted daughter. We adopted her when she was five."

Jenny glared at her husband, then her face seemed to pull inward as she flopped back in her seat, her chest heaving as she broke into sobs.

Sean walked over to his wife and ran a large hand over her hair, lowering his head to whisper cooing sounds.

Nikola closed his eyes again and bunched his toes to con-

trol his rising anger. He had figured out the explanation behind the missing baby photographs on the display, but having
it confirmed didn't give him a measure of pleasure; rather, he
felt disgust. Adopted. Outside, a reddish light announced
dusk, and Nikola felt in his bones that he would have the missing link to the daring breakout—or, at least, a finger pointing
in the right direction—before dark.

When Sean returned to his seat, he began a lengthy monologue, delivered with the lackluster tone of a penitent. After
several years of trying, a visit to a gynecologist, and a battery
of tests, they had discovered an unpalatable fact: Jenny was
barren. A gauntlet of interviews followed, along with form-
filling and more interviews to adopt a child—an almost impossible feat in a society suffering a chronic shortage of
children. Then the miracle happened.

"Ms. Cunningham from the Social Services Department
called. There was a girl at a local orphanage run by nuns. Not
a baby, mind you; she was five."

"And in five years she hadn't been offered for adoption?"

Sean turned and stared into Nikola's eyes. "She had a very
frail constitution and had needed constant attention, so the
nuns said. We raised her as our daughter and gave her as
much love as any child could have."

"And her schooling? And the university? Who paid?"

"We don't know."

"Sean, I ca—"

"I swear. We don't know. We never met him."

Nikola reached for the stone-cold dregs of his tea and wet
his lips. The bastard was telling the truth. They had never met
their benefactor but knew it was a man. "How did you keep in
touch?"

Jenny stiffened and Sean slouched his shoulders, defeated.
Nikola waited for the man to release their best-guarded secret. He could get all he wanted from the wretches after a
couple of hours downtown at a beautifully appointed cellar
with slightly inclined floors and a large drain in the middle,
but he'd already wasted enough time.

"He left us a telephone number."

Nikola put his hand out, palm up.

Sean sighed and climbed to his feet. After a slight hesitation and a glance to his wife, he neared the photograph display, reached to one of the tabby cat's portraits, and picked a yellowed card from behind it. "It won't do any good. It's an answering service."

"How did it work?"

"We would call and leave a message. Afterward— sometimes the same day, other times a few days later—a man would call. If there was no reply, we tried again a week or so later."

"And the money?"

"It was wired to an account we opened in Laurel's name to pay for her studies."

"Please let me have a bank statement with details of the account."

"Look, Mr.—I mean, Nikola. I don't think—"

"You don't think? You don't want your daughter returned?"

"Of course, but—"

"Give it to him." Jenny was now standing. She looked close to collapse.

Sean handed over the card. It was a blank business card, aged and dirtied by grubby fingers, with a string of numbers penned in blue ink. A moment later, after rummaging in the drawer of a side table, he returned with a bankbook from the local Wells Fargo, showing a balance of $6,316.82.

"That's what's left of her money. She used it to pay for her studies. We never touched a penny."

Nikola placed the card inside the bankbook and slipped both into his jacket pocket. Then he turned on his heel and walked toward the door, whispering hurried instructions to Dennis via the microphone on his collar. As he climbed into the van, he darted a glance at the group of armor-clad men spewing out of an unmarked truck, heading toward the house.

chapter 28

22:11

A motley crew lined the platform to see them off, like a
congregation of derelict souls waiting for a train.

As soon as they'd returned, burdened with the bulky backpacks full of explosives, Henry had excused himself and retreated to a quiet corner to write with a cheap ballpoint pen in
a grimy notebook, pausing often to glance away or adjust his
dangling flashlight. Laurel and Raul sat nursing fresh mugs of
the wicked brew that passed for coffee and recounted their
explosive-gathering odyssey to Floyd and Lukas, mentioning
only a warehouse—thus omitting the army base and any reference to Santos Hernandez.

Lukas seemed a little more spirited than when they'd left,
no doubt thanks to Floyd's pep pills, and Russo remained,
according to Floyd, stable. During their absence, one of
Henry's pals—a young African-American man with the
strange nickname of Pinky—had delivered a box containing
assorted IV bags of ionic solutions, new and probably stolen
minutes before. The drips had begun to rehydrate Russo and
to restore the mineral imbalances in his blood. The plasma,
blood units, and other bits and pieces Floyd had requested
would be waiting when they arrived at the safe house.

When Henry finished writing, he neared the group, then
leaned over a wizened old woman and whispered something.
The woman scampered away, returning a few seconds later
with a glassine bag housing a seemingly new cellular phone.
Henry reached into the inside pocket of his coat and drew
out a lump of crumpled banknotes. After much straightening, he selected four ten-dollar bills—the lowest denomina-
tion in circulation after the 2036 monetary change. The

woman grabbed the notes and waited. Henry huffed, picked out a tightly creased one-hundred-dollar bill, and dropped it into her waiting hand. Then he nodded to Barandus and offered both the cell phone and the notebook. "Can you read the text in those pages? I mean aloud, to make a recording in the phone's memory?"

Barandus drew out a pencil flashlight, ran it over the notebook, and nodded. He then vanished in the gloom. Instants later, his flashlight came alive thirty feet away, where he'd sat down by a thick vertical pipe.

When Barandus returned with the phone, Henry pocketed it and smiled when his second-in-command fed the handwritten note into the fire and waited until it burned before stirring the ashes with a stick.

Henry nodded to Floyd and Raul. "You better get your friend zipped up. We're going." Then he turned to Metronome, the boy who had released the rat a few hours before, and squatted beside him. "I have a favor to ask, a small service." He reached into his pocket and produced the cell phone. "I want you to go in that direction," he pointed to the mouth of the tunnel on the right, "as far as you can in one hour."

The boy blinked twice, his head ticking away.

"Then, at eleven-thirty precisely, you must press this button here, the one with a star. The phone will dial a number. When this little dot lights up red, you must press this other button with a square. After waiting one minute, get rid of the phone. Throw it down a sump or a deep hole. Then run back here."

Metronome looked troubled.

"Ah, yes." Henry scratched his head, turned to Laurel, and looked pointedly at her wrist. "You have no way of knowing when it's eleven-thirty." He made a sheepish face. "I noticed you checking out her watch a couple of times."

Laurel neared and also squatted before the boy. She reached into her vinyl jacket's top pocket, ripped open its pressure fasteners, and fished out another watch—a copy of the one she wore. "This one is precious." She cleared her throat, but emotion clogged her words. "It belonged to a dear friend, and it's only fair you should have it." Tears overflowed her eyes. "He would have wanted you to use it and help us out of here."

The boy's head didn't arrest its movement, but his eyes gleamed.

Henry reached and gently pried the timepiece from her shaking fingers. "Once you finish your mission, keep it." He waved a hand to the boy to come closer and, with delicate movements of huge fingers, fastened the watch around the piece of cord holding his trousers up. "When you are done, ask someone to make more holes in the strap so you can wear it on your wrist. Now it's too large." Henry rested a hand on Metronome's shoulder. "Please, son, don't keep the phone; very bad men will zero in on it and come after you."

Henry glanced first at Russo, then at Raul and Floyd: the stretcher bearers.

The newspaper's tiny first edition had finished rolling an hour before, and most copies would already be piling up outside the few kiosks still in operation or speeding through the city on the back of delivery vans.

Brenda Neff hated the graveyard shift. With each passing year, the number of printed copies dwindled, and there were rumors they soon would disappear altogether. *The Washington Post* was down to 250,000 copies, and lesser fish weren't faring any better. Bad news for printers, but the soaring costs of pulp and ever-changing reading habits of people didn't affect a newspaper's usefulness. The world still needed news—either wrapped in paper or computer bits. And no matter the vehicle for the news, the world still needed editors, reporters, and graveyard-shift staffers at the news desk waiting for the phone to ring.

It rang.

Brenda jerked and stared in disbelief at a squat red device she'd never heard ringing before: a secure government terminal with a direct line bypassing the newspaper's telephone exchange. General calls to the newspaper filtered through a department tasked with assessing the caller's identity and purpose before transferring the link on to the intended recipient's screen.

She touched two spots on her screen to call up Mark Cummings, the night staff editor, and Marcia Gomez from security to share in the call before reaching over to the obsolete handset on its fourth ring.

"News desk, Brenda Neff."

After a brief pause, punctuated by a soft click, a distinguished voice said, "I will not repeat or add to any part of this statement, otherwise academic since you're recording the call and can transcribe its contents at leisure. Your government's continuous meddling in the affairs of the Christian Republic of Uzbekistan has fostered untold strife and hardship among our citizens, stretching our patience to its limit."

Out of the corner of her eye, Brenda spotted Mark's lanky figure barreling toward her, a wireless terminal to his ear, chased by Marcia and other people she couldn't name.

"I, the Scourge of God, will no longer watch idly while your corporations plunder our nation with nihilistic tactics and bribes to corrupt officers. You need to be taught a lesson. In thirty minutes, my children will unleash an attack on your nuclear power station and raze it to the ground. Beware, this is only the beginning. Unless your government stops all activity in Uzbekistan, I will reduce your country to a radioactive wasteland."

Silence and a hiss of static.

Mark's hand circled in midair, urging her to keep the caller talking.

Brenda leaned forward. "Sir? Could you—"

There was a click, and the tiny red light on the secure phone faded. The call had been severed.

"Got the number and location!" someone yelled from across the room.

Brenda replaced the handset and peered at the expectant faces of the people crowding around her desk. "A prank?"

"That's a secure phone," Marcia said. "It needs a complex code besides the number. I don't know who has access, but the last time I logged a call was in 2042, from the White House after the Taiwan invasion."

Mark flicked his cell phone and dropped it in his top pocket. "Nicely done, Brenda. We'll take it from here."

"Where to?"

"I mean we'll handle it." He turned to Marcia. "Get me the police and the DHS."

As everybody scampered back to their posts, Mark reached for Brenda's box of licorice lozenges and popped one in his mouth. "You're right. This is probably a prank; a hacker must have cracked the code. I don't think the heat will take this seriously, but you never know."

Nikola had pushed his slippers away with one bare foot and was about to reach for a mug of coffee he'd just carted from the kitchen when Dennis pushed his swivel chair away from his desk. "Developments. I think you're going to like this one."

Nikola blinked to arrest Laurel Cole's file scrolling down his center screen and rubbed his eyes.

"I will not repeat or add to any part of this statement, otherwise academic since you're recording the . . ." He listened to the full recording, his mind racing. Children of Uzbekistan? "What's the DHS doing?"

Dennis fiddled with his keyboard, his screens flashing messages, flags, and other traffic between different police and paramilitary departments. "They triangulated a call to a location between Ellsmere Avenue and Forest Drive, at Lundy. Units are on their way."

"A prank?"

Dennis didn't answer at once but continued to work with his computer. "If so, it was a complex one, involving access to a restricted system and a hard code."

"How restricted?"

"Obviously not enough. White House, Congress, Pentagon, and DHS. Hundreds of people could have access." He flicked through screens. "They change the code weekly. Yesterday was the last time."

"Get me a list," Nikola said. Lundy was north, a new residential district, and Villiard power station was due south of it. The whole thing was absurd. Like every other nuclear power station, Villiard was in the center of concentric security rings, each more strict than the last. Even a tank couldn't get to within a half mile of the reactor. The rest—stores, administration buildings, and personnel quarters—had little if any strategic value. Besides, the divisional army barracks were a stone's throw down the road.

Still, the call was interesting. No kid or nomadic hillbilly behind the voice. It was refined, hectoring, its message succinctly put. He wouldn't have referred to the cloak-and-dagger intrigues of the oil industry as *nihilistic,* an adjective better reserved for revolutionaries and other pests favored by intellectuals the world over. *Raze it to the ground.* A little melodramatic, but then, the caller had a weakness for theater, obviously. Attila the Hun: the Scourge of God who left destruction in his wake, riding a horse under whose shoes the grass withered. The infamous khan would be proud of the caller's use of his moniker.

Nikola resumed poring over Laurel's dossier. "Let me know if anything develops."

Thirty minutes after leaving from the station camp, the group split up. They had divided the 280 pounds of high explosives into four heavy loads of seventy pounds each, yet Susan and Jim, the smallest-framed of the quartet, didn't seem to struggle. When they reached a fork in the tunnel, they stopped to say good-bye. After the men exchanged backslaps and good-luck wishes, Laurel sought Barandus. "Can I ask you something?"

Barandus nodded.

She lowered her voice further. "What's your name?"

He darted a sideways glance, as if priming to run away, blinked, and his eyes deepened. Then he licked his lower lip. "James . . . James Marshall."

She stood on tiptoe and pecked him on a patch of skin devoid of hair and close to his nose. "Thank you, James," she whispered.

Charlie huffed. "What has he got?"

Laurel neared Charlie and Jim. "Jeez, but you're a jealous bunch." After pecking both of them, she turned to Susan and hugged her. "You take care, hear?" Then she joined Henry to set off through the right tunnel of the fork while the group with the explosives followed along the other passageway.

Her lips tingled but not from recent activity. Laurel had

sent Shepherd another two messages since their return to warn him of their impending trek to the meeting point and to update him on Russo's status. "Stable" was all that Floyd had said, but that had been after engulfing her in a bear hug and kissing her neck, cheek, and lips. She drew her fingers to her mouth, letting her gaze stray to Floyd, just a few feet ahead and holding on to the rear end of Russo's stretcher, and felt heat creep up her neck.

They trudged along an abandoned sewer tunnel as quickly as they could. Henry led with an unerring sense of direction and urged them on without pausing to take bearings; this ghastly place obviously was familiar to him. Laurel plodded next to Lukas, closing the rear. The section of the tunnel had been excavated through schist: bedrock formed millions of years before. No tunneling machine had bored the passage. Laurel sensed ghosts filling the hollow space—the spirits of the workers who'd toiled to dig it a century and a half before, the countless homeless people who must have lived there, and the graffiti artists who had once ventured through with their spray cans.

"There's a passageway close to the surface," Henry's voice boomed from the front, "but it's terrible to negotiate. Too much yellow rain, metal gratings dogs like to pee on."

Raul huffed. "Great."

After a few hundred yards, they branched sideways into a narrower tunnel—damp, the air thick with constant sounds of dripping water. Laurel stepped around little pools of liquid collecting in hollows along the floor.

Henry stopped, motioning to Raul and Floyd to rest the stretcher on a dry patch. "We go through there." He pointed to a narrow round opening, perhaps three feet across. "It's the only way up. It narrows a little farther on and it will mean dragging the stretcher, but it can't be helped."

A few minutes later, Laurel marveled at Henry's understatement. Reaching the upper gallery involved a rugged crawl facefirst through an opening no wider than two feet and two high, but mercifully it was only thirty feet long. As Raul and Floyd belly-crawled ahead of her, pushing and pulling the stretcher over jagged rocks, Laurel waited for a birth-canal joke that never came. *Raul must be exhausted.* They finally reached the upper level—a large sewage tunnel with sidewalks and a shallow river of effluent slowly flowing across. Henry pointed to a ladder and a service hole in the ceiling. "That's it. Lights off."

With the flashlights turned off, the space became a sensory-deprivation tank but for the noises seemingly all around them.

"The FDU squad has located the phone."

Over the years, Nikola had memorized the little nuances in Dennis's voice when delivering snippets of information. He waited a moment, but only to confirm no added details would be forthcoming without a prompt. "Where?"

"The sewers."

Nikola was still, his face twitching as if recovering from an impromptu slap. His eyes darted to a clock over the antique marble mantelpiece: 23:53—twenty-three minutes since the ridiculous threat and only minutes away from its deadline. Every DHS unit was deployed on the northern side of town, leaving the south squarely in the hands of the police, their roadblocks the only way to prevent an escape. Roadblocks . . . soon to be hurriedly unmanned as all units rushed to contain a major terrorist attack.

"There's more."

This time he didn't offer a prompt.

"Bellevue Hospital has just reported a theft. An unknown person or persons have broken into their emergency supply room and made off with several pieces of equipment—and forty pints of type-O blood. The police are there with a sci-entific team. It seems one of the thieves left a set of strange footprints in the garden outside."

Nikola bunched both fists on his desktop until his knuckles whitened.

"Prosthetic legs."

chapter 29

23:58

"Carry on as usual. Imagine we're not here."

Charley Navarre swallowed hard, eyeing the three black-clad hulks weaving past the consoles at Villiard's nuclear power station control room. *How can I ignore them?* Whoever designed the shiny body armor of the DHS FDU teams must have liberally copied the bad guys' gear from a fifty-year-old film saga depicting intergalactic conflict. Heavy helmets bristling with dimples and lumps, probably housing communications gear, were mated with face masks that hid the wearer's expression except for the eyes. They were the only hint that a sentient being was actually inside the articulated Kevlar carapace. Their boots were enormous. Charley wondered if, besides protecting the bearer's feet, the monstrous contraptions doubled as some kind of storage.

He glanced at Hulk One, from which the voice originated, and at the object cradled in his arms: a rectangular box roughly the size to carry a dozen long-stemmed roses. But it was black, dotted with tiny lights and other mean-looking bits. Then Charley nodded at Sherry and Dieter, working the other two consoles, and looked down into the array of screens flanking his semicircular desk without registering the otherwise-normal diagrams sneaking across the displays. The Scourge of God? A terrorist attack? The whole thing somehow sounded too far-fetched.

His comm console flashed. "Navarre," he said.

"Everything fine with you?" The voice of Dave Vela, the night-shift plant director, sounded harried.

"Well, I have three"—Charley was about to say *gorillas,*

but checked his words—"DHS officers here, but otherwise normal."

"Let's be philosophic about this. Chalk it up to a security exercise."

"Will do."

Hulk Three changed posture and shook his leg. It suddenly occurred to Charley that inside the bulky armor, scratching an itch had to be a bitch. "I doubt they'll be here much longer. Several squads are checking—"

The room trembled. Red lights flashed over the control panels as earthquake detectors triggered a warning. The room shook again and a deafening siren, reminiscent of yester-year submarines announcing a crash dive, blared in the confined space.

"Scram!" Charley kicked back his swivel chair and bolted upright, only to be stopped by a paw slamming down on his shoulder. He jerked around to face the towering figure of Hulk One.

"Where are you going?"

"Alarm control panel." He pointed to the far right of the main-reactor control panel. "I need to shut the reactor down." Hulk One did nothing for a couple of heartbeats but stare back at him with splendid blue eyes. After tiny lights flickered to a side of his helmet, he stepped back and nodded. "Go ahead."

Charley bolted past Sherry and across the control room, skidding to a stop before a panel to press a blue + button twice, raising the installation status to emergency levels. Then he slammed a large square pad stenciled *Immediate Emergency Commence.* To his left, another, smaller panel, *Emergency Confirm,* glowed red. After a moment's hesitation, he pressed it, cutting the current to electric motors operating the control rods. Without brakes, powerful springs would ram the rods down into the reactor's core in less than four seconds, halting the nuclear reaction and shutting the plant down.

Hands trembling, Charley stepped back and glanced at Sherry's and Dieter's frightened faces. A swarm of green lights over the diagram of the reactor core slowly faded. The rules were clear about the procedure to follow after the earth-quake trembler switches tripped, but Charley understood their shock. Restarting the reactor after an emergency shutdown would take several weeks and cost millions of dollars in lost production and the replacement of parts damaged during the shutdown process. He tried a reassuring smile he didn't feel, then had to lean on the control panel to arrest a sudden weakness in his legs. The siren finally stopped, and a canned female voice announced, "Reactor shutdown successful."

The sudden silence thickened the air, disturbed only by a creak when one of the hulks changed position. Then the ground shook again and Sherry screamed. The three DHS officers stood still at their stations. Then, as if primed by hidden clockwork, they marched to the open doors and exited the room. Hulk One turned around from the corridor. "Bolt yourselves in. We're under attack."

"Now what?" Laurel asked.

Silence.

Laurel glanced around the dim interior of the van, one side occupied by Russo in his stretcher and the other by Raul, Lukas, and, next to her, Floyd. The steel floor was hard and cold. "Tyler?"

"We wait."

They had exited the sewers in a disused warehouse a scant few yards from a dark van with no windows. Shepherd—who had since introduced himself as Harper Tyler—had stood by the utility hole, helping everyone in turn and lending a hand with the stretcher before hustling them toward the vehicle. After reaching inside the cabin and lugging out black garbage bags—heavy, by the looks of them—he had turned toward Henry.

"What will you do, Sergeant?" Tyler asked in a low voice.

Henry had reached for the bags. "A quarter goes to Santos and another quarter to the old-timers helping out with this little stunt of yours; everyone involved will take a powder until things cool down a bit. With the rest, I'll move to Honduras. I have a friend there. I'll set up a chinchilla farm in the mountains."

"Chinchillas?"

"Rich bitches love their fur."

"Sounds good. What about the others?" Tyler nodded toward the gaping utility hole.

"It'll be hell for a while, moving about and hiding, but they're used to living rough. Most of them wouldn't be able to live any other way." He offered his hand.

Tyler brushed the hand aside and hugged Henry, a strong waft of decay spreading like spores from a bursting seedpod.

"Take care, my friend."

"It's been a pleasure." His eyes bright, Henry knotted the mouths of the bags together, dropped them down the utility hole, and, with a departing wave, disappeared down the shaft.

As soon as Henry left, Tyler had opened the warehouse's creaking sliding door and driven the vehicle to the end of a narrow alley, where he killed the engine. "Half a mile down that road there's a police patrol." Tyler nodded at the windshield. "As it is, we can't get through. Within the next few minutes, however, we hope the police will remove their barriers and thus grant us safe passage."

Next to Laurel, Floyd made a face of resignation. Then he unfolded his hand palm up. Laurel turned to glance into his eyes, dimly lit by a streetlight half a block down the road, and realized his extended palm held a deeper meaning. Raul and Lukas didn't miss the gesture and also stared at Floyd's hand. She glanced at the empty metallic wall above Russo's reclining shape, Floyd's palm unmoving in her peripheral vision. Of course, she'd read her share of romances in her teenage years and fantasized about princely proposals, but these belonged in fairyland. Reality was his hand, now, in a dark van reeking of sweat and sewage, with a dying man on the floor and a syrette loaded with cyanide pressing against her breast in her top pocket. She didn't surrender her hand to his straightaway. Some things were far too important to rush—such as letting him know she understood—and took precedence over the promise of warmth. Then she reached for his hand and held on to it. Raul and Lukas breathed again. Laurel closed her eyes. His grip felt like a toast to life.

"Here we go," Tyler muttered.

The inside of the van started to flicker in blue as the sound of sirens grew. Tyler ducked in the front seat to hide beyond the dashboard. "Everybody down!"

The sirens neared, reached a crescendo, then lowered in pitch and began to fade.

After a couple of minutes, Tyler straightened up and fired the engine. "At the next bend in the road, we cross the point of no return."

"What a bundle of fun," Raul muttered from the back.

"You want me to sing?" Tyler asked.

As the curve in the road unfolded before her eyes, Laurel realized she was gripping Floyd's hand so tightly that one of his finger joints popped.

The road was deserted.

After a few moments, Tyler slammed his hand over the dashboard. "Damn! We're through," he said to a chorus of relieved curses from the rear of the van.

"Let me have it back," Floyd said.

She let go of his hand. "I'm sorry."

"I meant the syrette."

day three

||||

Inferno, Canto V: 1–3
*So I descended from the first enclosure
down to the second circle,
that which girdles less space but grief more great,
that goads to weeping.*

The Divine Comedy, DANTE ALIGHIERI

chapter 30

14:53

"Let's not waste any more time." Genia Warren, director of the Federal Bureau of Hibernation, scrolled down her thin tablet computer and stabbed its corner with a stylus before pushing the pad away from her and toward the center of the table. "We know what's happened. I've read the report. Before long, the DHS will be breathing down our necks, and I need to have answers."

"Answers? What answers?" Lawrence Ritter, Genia's executive director of security, sometimes pretended to be slow-witted in a bid to gain time for his sharp mind to race ahead.

"The only kind I know: solutions to problems. Madam Director will want a scheme to guarantee, beyond reasonable doubt, that a breakout cannot happen again anywhere in the system. She'll also demand a scapegoat to take the blame for what's happened."

Ritter wasn't taking any notes, but he stared at her, his frown deepening. In his fifties and without a hair on his head, Ritter oversaw the security of all the government hibernation centers in the U.S. Since joining the FBH in 2049, he'd never once altered his dressing habits: black suits, black shoes, black turtleneck sweaters, and a beret. Once, when Ritter was required to go before a Senate select committee, a conservative senator had made a wry remark about his professional decorum. Ritter replied by rattling off, from memory, eighteen rules that specifically forbade federal personnel, in particular law, security, and intelligence officers, from wearing suits and ties. After the general dress-code relaxation imposed by the new generations of civil servants, people with suits and ties stuck out like a sore thumb. That day, the hapless senator discovered Ritter's phenomenal memory, and the then-new director of security at FBH became a minor legend.

"It had to happen, you know?"

Genia didn't answer. From the oblong meeting table occupying the far end of her office, she glanced toward her desk and the slanted patterns thrown across the carpeted floor by the light streaming in through the venetian blinds. She looked across her desk to the limp flags flanking it—one the star-spangled banner, and the other a blue ensign with stars circling three letters, *FBH,* and a motto: *To protect the public through efficient and effective management of offenders.*

The Federal Bureau of Hibernation had replaced the Federal Bureau of Prisons and the prison agencies of all fifty states and the District of Columbia, the Virgin Islands, and Puerto Rico, drawing the responsibility of running a new generation of jails and penitentiaries into a single entity. Municipal and county jails, houses of correction, juvenile detention centers, work camps, and municipal lockups—all typically holding inmates sentenced to three months or less, as well as people in various stages of the criminal-justice system—remained the responsibility of state authorities, but their number and size had been reduced to less than a quarter of 2050 levels. Although the FBH was a federal law-enforcement agency and responsible for managing the new hibernation system, it had ceased to be a subdivision of the Department of Justice. It was now part of the Department of Homeland Security. And that meant Odelle Marino.

Odelle ran the DHS as her private fiefdom. Her first deed in office had been to rewrite the original charter of the prison system: *To protect the public, protect staff, and provide safe, secure, and humane supervision of offenders.* Grudgingly, Genia had to admit the genius behind the bland words. Naturally, after hibernation went into operation, Odelle had ordered the old promise, *to provide inmates with opportunities that support successful community reintegration,* removed from every printed document and government Web site.

"The center," Ritter said, "as originally created, was ethically sustainable, though still vigilante, to punish those who had managed to evade justice through an error or a loophole and as a lab to improve the technology. Anything else is morally untenable." He raised a hand to forestall her retort. "That includes Hypnos's opacity. From the start, Congress allowed Hypnos to run the center spaces without control other than having to supply a code name and the number of subjects involved in each of their research projects. No names or location within the system. This means we don't really know what Hypnos is doing in the center spaces."

"That's besides the point. Anything concerning center operation is beyond my authority." Genia drummed the fingers of one hand on the table. "And yours. Center management is the exclusive domain of Hypnos and is supervised directly by Odelle Marino."

"You know Memok?"

Genia nodded. "Hypnos's code name for one of their long-term research projects."

"Indeed." He reached into his jacket pocket, drew out a handheld, and scribbled with a stylus before sliding the device over to her.

Neatly printed on the screen was a single word: *МЕШОК*. She stilled her fingers. "Cyrillic?"

"Bag or sack."

"Probably a coincidence," Genia said in a voice she hoped would sound even. The Memok project involved dozens of subjects at the Atlanta and other neighboring facilities. Of course, she also knew of numerous unidentified Russian aircraft takeoffs and landings—sanctioned by the DHS—at a nearby military airfield.

"You knew. And that proves my point. The existence of center spaces and unidentified guests poses a perverse security problem. There are far too many people in the know. Perhaps three or four in this building alone, a score or more at the DHS, God knows how many at Hypnos, and an unknown number at each sugar cube: supervisors, security people, technicians, and perhaps even the cleaners. All told, that makes several hundred people. In my mind, it was never a question of if but when."

"The DHS has thrown a blanket over it. Nobody knows about the breakout," Genia said, to test whether Ritter shared her fears.

"There you're wrong. The workers at the station, security personnel, and the DHS men there know. What can the DHS do? Sink the whole bunch into the tank centers? Kill them?"

"The thought must have crossed their minds."

"This is ridiculous. The team pulling off the breakout had superb, almost military backup. They rattled a nuclear power station with hundreds of pounds of high explosive, just for a diversion. The fugitives are almost irrelevant, except one." He held a hand out and counted on his fingers. "Laurel Cole and Raul Osborne must keep low, to watch over their shoulders until they die or the DHS's memory fades, whichever comes first. Lukas Hurley and Dr. Floyd Carpenter are probably lying facedown in a ditch or floating down a canal with sundry body piercings courtesy of artisans unknown; I doubt the organization behind this will risk loose ends. That leaves the wretch they sprang from the center. Who is he?"

Genia cradled her fingers and slowly shook her head. Ritter was a sucker for challenges. By fobbing him off, she was making sure his priority would be to find out about Russo before the day was over. Naturally, he already knew the wretched account of the third member of the maverick team: Bastien Compton. He hadn't mentioned his name. "I'm sorry. Need to know."

Ritter held her gaze for a couple of heartbeats. "Fine. But why would anybody stage such a complex operation to spring an unknown man? And, further, how many people in their organization know about center inmates?" Ritter shook his head. "There are too many people involved, mostly uncontrolled. This will hit the news within two weeks, mark my words."

"I've been thinking about that. Without someone who has been illegally hibernated and supporting witnesses, there wouldn't be a case."

"What about the rest? According to my data, besides the human guinea pigs in Hypnos's research projects, there are scores of men and women hibernating without trial. If a whiff of it reached the press, Congress would slap a compulsory inspection on all sugar cubes. A recount of inmates by independent parties would follow."

"And what would they find?"

Ritter drew a hand over his head and narrowed his eyes. "You mean getting rid of the evidence? They would have to be out of their minds."

"Look at it this way. The DHS and Hypnos must have anticipated such an eventuality. They have bright people—not many, but enough. If tomorrow morning the papers carried an uncorroborated rumor about people in hibernation without trial, by the time inspectors reached the nearest facility, they wouldn't find anything amiss."

"You mean the drains?"

Genia nodded. "The Washington sugar cube is the exception. Having to ship their waste to a remote location for processing stemmed from a fluke. A weird salt-dome formation prevented Hypnos from sinking more than three levels underground."

Ritter's head came up. He was like a dog on point. "I know the Washington sugar cube is the odd man out without in-house waste processing, but I don't know the history."

Genia nodded. "As I said, it was a fluke. The site chosen for the sugar cube—a triangle of land hemmed in by highways—had never been built on before. As you know, when planning a building, the first step is to check all existing drawings for things that may lie underneath."

"You mean utility lines, pipes, and the like?"

"Right. And, in a city like Washington, sewers and old tunnels."

"I doubt any drawing will show tunnels built a hundred or more years ago."

"That's why, after checking the drawings, engineers drill a pattern of holes covering the entire site to map the subsoil and find out the best foundations."

"And the depth they can go with basements. No?"

"As luck would have it, the engineers drilled into rock at every test hole, but when it came time to dig, they uncovered a void."

Ritter nodded. "I get it. Once the containment walls were in place, they started digging to find a big void somewhere in the site."

"With most of the excavation done, it was too late by the

time they found out," Genia continued. "The sugar cube could be built, with stores and parking lots, but there was no room underneath to process the waste."

"I hope they fired the geologists who did the preliminary ground studies," Ritter grumbled. Then he drummed his long fingers on the table's surface, his eyes focused somewhere on the opposite wall. "So, since all the other sugar cubes have processing plants, you're implying that someone would order the disposal of the bodies?"

"Why not? You know the system as well as I do. The processing plants are simple decanting pools, where they mix the emulsions with flocculants to separate the parts."

"And an untraceable graveyard for nonexistent people you don't want others to know about."

"Yes. In ten minutes, the computer would release the inmates from their harnesses and, as the tanks emptied, their bodies would be sucked into the system and reduced to slurry, their solids separated, packed, and shipped to the incinerator. Gone without a trace."

"I hope you're wrong."

"So do I." Genia bit her lower lip before squaring her shoulders. She had decided her next step hours before calling Ritter, but having reached the moment of truth, the queasiness in her stomach deepened. Eventually she would have to jump into the void.

Ritter shrugged. "About the answers you want for Director Marino, tightening security is easy. I've already drafted a document I'll log into the server by 18:00. It will mean installing active and passive devices in the sewage line, rigging cameras and stunners on the pigs, and reworking security routines. I don't mention anything about rounding up the fugitives, since it's out of our hands. The DHS has taken full control; you said so in your memo. As for scapegoats, you have the facility's head of security, his men, the people in my department, and me. Take your pick."

"Don't be facetious."

"I'm not. It would make more sense to fire me than anybody else."

"Why?"

"Simple. I can get a job—a better-paid job—in one of a dozen security outfits. And, since I know the score, I would keep my mouth shut. The others, in particular the Washington sugar-cube staff, may not be so knowledgeable and may think, 'What the hell! I'll blow the whistle.'"

"Would they?"

"I don't know. People do the stupidest things."

Again he ran a hand over his head before staring into her eyes. "Have you made up your mind?"

She feigned ignorance. "About what?"

"You've been debating for an hour whether to clue me in on whatever you're planning to do."

She decided to take the leap. "Have you considered security inspections without warning?"

Ritter froze, then, in slow motion, he placed both hands palms down on the table. "Go on."

"It would mean a resident computer program that could be activated to test the security readiness of any station."

"And . . . what would that program do?"

"Shut down the computer."

"How long?"

"Until the exercise ended. The inmates wouldn't be in any danger. Their life-support system is autonomous."

"The idea has merit, but—"

"I know: Drains and displacement machinery still work."

Ritter didn't move, his eyes fastened on her lips as if daring her to voice her next thought.

"Unless the main computer ordered the backup system to block instructions to these subsystems."

"As a mental exercise, your idea has merit, but it's impractical. Hypnos supervises the computer network, and they would spot such an instruction in your security exercise program."

"Not if the program doesn't stay in the station's computer."

Ritter leaned forward, a devious spark flashing across his dark irises.

"That imaginary program—how heavy?"

"Five hundred kilobytes or smaller."

"How long to download?"

"Under a second."

Ritter blinked, once. "Any instruction to release the supports of the center inmates and void the tanks would come from a satellite transponder."

Silence.

"If there was another transponder on the same satellite tuned to the same frequency, it would receive the same signal and download your program to override the instruction, block the deployment and flushing systems, and shut the computers down. Of course, your theory is useless without the transponder codes. . . ."

As a teenager, Genia had hidden money in her bra so her brothers wouldn't steal it from her pockets. Now she fumbled with two buttons on her blouse and reached inside a cup to draw out a folded paper with scores of machine-code lines typed on one side. With deliberation, she slid the paper across the table, keeping a finger over it.

"You can stand up and walk out that door without this paper."

Ritter stared at her fingernail, his face set, before turning his gaze to her unbuttoned blouse.

"My sister used to hide love letters in her bra." Then he reached for the paper.

chapter 31

||||

15:12

A continuous sound of crunching gravel shattered Ethel's concentration. She lowered her book and glanced at a bulky figure wrestling to keep his bicycle within the margins of the narrow path. The man was bent over the handlebars, his face obscured by a bandana drawn almost to his eyes. He needed the exercise, no doubt about that, considering the jiggly lumps his lightweight tracksuit strained to contain. Ethel sighed at the view of vast buttocks dwarfing the machine's tiny seat as he pedaled past. *No amount of exercise will get rid of that.* The sound decreased as the rider approached the next bend, missing a trash can by inches, to disappear into memory when the bicycle faded from view.

After cycling around the park twice more, Senator Jerome Palmer finally spotted another bicycle rider sitting on a bench next to a ratty clump of eucalyptus. Palmer was out of breath and his butt hurt. He almost fell after fumbling with the brakes, wildly twisting the front wheel to keep balance. After dismounting with a remarkable lack of grace, he rested his bike next to the other one—an old and muddy machine, brown paint flaking in sections off its steel frame.

"You look awful." Palmer eyed the black tights hugging Tyler's spindly legs—and his deformed left knee. The pants disappeared under a nondescript windbreaker with more than a passing likeness to a deflated parachute.

"Seen yourself lately?" Tyler reached for a metal bottle clipped to his bicycle frame, flicked it open, and offered it with an outstretched arm.

The brandy was rotgut, but it warmed Palmer's belly with a welcome glow.

Over the next thirty minutes Palmer listened to Tyler's monologue of recent events, interrupting to ask for clarification or to take his turn at the flask traveling back and forth between them.

"Now what?" Palmer glanced sideways at an enterprising squirrel diving into a trash can, climbing back an instant later in a flurry of scratches as its tiny claws fought for purchase over the smooth metal.

"We wait. There's not much else we can do."

"Will he make it?" Palmer asked.

"As I said—"

"I know what you said. It's the unsaid that worries me."

"Floyd Carpenter is resilient and knows his stuff. I was afraid he'd buckle under the pressure and try to bring Russo out of torpor prematurely just to get the job done and over with."

"But he hasn't."

"Right, and that takes guts. Floyd must have guessed that every minute counts. The DHS goons are turning the city upside down. Yet he's chosen a slow procedure, to build up Russo's metabolism before attempting arousal."

"Will Russo make it?" Palmer persisted.

Birds paused in their song as if glutted with sound. Tyler waited until a jogger and his companion, a panting dachshund, were out of earshot around a clump of tall grasses. "My gut feeling is that Floyd will bide his time in an attempt to give Russo a real chance and . . . yes, he'll bring Russo around. But as for the state of his mind . . . I don't know. He's been subject to calculated deterioration. Floyd had never seen anyone in such wasted condition—his own words, according to Laurel. Still, had the escape continued according to plan, we would be in the same situation."

"Hardly the same."

"We would. Everything hinges on Russo's mental capacity, or lack of it. Without a witness, we're shafted. At Nyx, Floyd would have had state-of-the-art equipment at his disposal and all the time in the world, but otherwise nothing else has changed. Our success hinges on Russo's mental state."

"How's Laurel?"

"She's fine, and Raul is too. They're young—perhaps a little older after this experience, but they're doing fine. My take is she's making eyes at the doctor, but it could be my imagination."

"What about the supervisor?"

"He's a wild card. So far he's holding up. Out there he doesn't have a chance until the dust settles, if it ever does. He's a marked man, and he knows it."

"But?"

"The kids and the doctor know the score. I saw Laurel returning a loaded syrette to Floyd, and he keeps another with him always."

"How do you know?"

"Laurel told me."

"Poison?"

Tyler nodded.

Palmer shook the flask to gauge how much was left. Suicide involved considerable resolve. He had no truck with those who glibly dismissed it as a coward's way out.

"Lukas Hurley is a civil servant," Tyler said.

"So am I. What has that got to do with it?"

"In my experience, people cling to groundless ideals: The mob looks after its pals, the army after its men, and the system—any system—after its kin."

"That's wishful thinking."

"Most people thrive on similar fantasies."

"And you reckon he may be tempted to trade?" Palmer asked.

"It will depend on the pressure. Before long, the DHS will make a move; they can't afford not to. And when they do, they will dangle a carrot in front of Floyd and Lukas. Laurel and Raul are driven by ideals, and Russo doesn't count. That leaves the hired talent, and Floyd is no fool."

"Come home and all is forgotten?"

"Something like that."

Palmer turned to face the warm buttery brightness of the sun. "Will Lukas fall for it?"

A breeze pushed past Palmer and Tyler down the path, shifting the leaves and making them whisper. Tyler squinted at the sky, as if trying to attach words to the sounds and failing. "I don't know, but I'll keep my eyes open."

Palmer nodded. "Time for the second act."

Tyler reached into his windbreaker to produce a cell phone—a plump model made obsolete by card-thin devices.

Palmer dug an oblong tube out of his jacket pocket, removed its lid, and shook it to dislodge a pair of foldable reading glasses.

"Wait." Tyler fumbled with his wristwatch—a cheap bright-yellow plastic piece. After pushing several tiny buttons on its side, he nodded.

Palmer keyed a string of numbers into the cell phone.

"Louis Hamilton," a voice answered.

Palmer followed Tyler's lips as he mouthed, "Ninety seconds," then the senator nodded.

"There's not much time, so you better listen carefully."

Palmer tried what he thought would pass for a gangster's voice. Tyler rolled his eyes.

"Who is this?"

"You don't want to know, buster."

An audible intake of breath followed and Palmer relaxed a notch. The penny had dropped at the other end of the line. It had been Hamilton's idea of a code word: *When Valerie calls me "buster," I know she doesn't want her husband, but her man. I'll know it's you.* Palmer smiled. That's what he liked about the *Washington Post* reporter. He always called things by their name, without resorting to euphemisms.

"I'm listening."

"There's been a breakout from the Washington sugar cube."

"Repeat."

"You heard me. Three inmates have escaped with the help of Lukas Hurley, the shift supervisor." A faint high-pitched noise intruded on the line. The NSA computers scanned all U.S. domestic and international communications, sampling and comparing them with a list of words. *Washington sugar cube* and the supervisor's name must have triggered the alarm. He nodded to Tyler, who adjusted his watch.

"Thirty seconds," Tyler mouthed.

"The DHS has launched a covert operation to capture the fugitives while keeping the event under wraps. Wednesday's terrorist attack on the power station was a diversion perpetrated by the fugitives to fool the security forces and effect their escape. They detonated the charges at a distance to guarantee no damage to the core."

Tyler offered both hands, fingers splayed: ten seconds. One bird chirped high up; there was a pause; another chirped lower down.

"Can you back up your claims?"

Palmer could almost sense Hamilton's smile at the other end of the line.

"That's your job." Palmer severed the communication and handed the phone back. Tyler switched it off, opened its back, and removed a wafer-thin battery before pocketing it.

"What can Hamilton do with that information? Surely he can't print it."

"Of course he can. He may drop a hint here and there, starting with *an unconfirmed rumor* . . . You know the score. But that wasn't the reason for my call. As you predicted, the NSA locked on to the call. Within seconds the DHS will know about it, and they'll know that Hamilton knows. Someone is bound to get nervous, and nervous folks make mistakes."

chapter 32

||||

16:47

"I'm sorry, but I can't help you."

"Can't or won't?"

Dr. Kyle Hulman breathed on his glasses and rubbed the lenses with a square of crimson chamois before balancing them back on the tip of his nose. He peered uncertainly around the room, as if disappointed by the result.

"Look Mr. . . . . er, Masek. Your search relates to events dating back, what, twenty-six years? Those records are long gone. Destroyed."

"I hope you're mistaken, Dr. Hulman. By law, birth and death records must be retained permanently." Nikola drew his knees together and shifted on the hard padding of the chair facing the doctor's desk—a chair admirably designed to distress visitors.

"That's correct, and those records exist at the local health authorities that serve as the registrars of vital statistics. They keep a registry of births and deaths. But if I understand the nature of your inquiry, that's not what you're after. You want the medical record of a maternal health patient, and there the law is clear. The attending doctor must keep the records five years past the last date on which service was given."

Nikola nodded. "Or until the infant's twenty-first birthday, whichever is later."

"Yes, but—"

"It means, since the subject of this inquiry has just turned twenty-six, you must have checked over the record I'm after only five years ago." In fact, Dr. Hulman had done much more than that. On Nikola's instructions, the department of criminal investigation at the DHS had served notice of his visit at exactly eleven-thirty. By then, Dennis had set up a system to monitor all traffic from Dr. Hulman's office—even that of his personal cell phone, for good measure. Within five minutes the good doctor had contacted the hospital records department to check if there was anything left on someone named Araceli Goldberg. Later, using his private phone, he'd dialed another number. A woman had answered, "Petals; how can I help you?" After ascertaining that the number belonged to a downtown flower business, Dr. Hulman had muttered an excuse and hung up. Nothing out of the ordinary; everybody makes mistakes. But Dennis was thorough. He ran through the telephone company database to discover that the florist's number had changed hands several times. Twenty-six years ago it belonged to an association of radical lawyers.

"I deal with hundreds, thousands of records every year."

"Maybe, but those would be hospital records. I'm inquiring about a document you must have drafted."

Dr. Hulman was middle-aged, in the limbo between fifty and sixty, neither young nor old, hair not dark but not white either: ordinary. Yet there was something shifty about him, an air of mendacity that Nikola found invigorating. His skin was white and spongy, almost translucent from a lifetime away from the sun—and similar to those who had spent time in the tanks, even years after their release.

"Do you recall destroying these particular records?"

"How could I? Hospital staff deals with record destruction by shredding, pulping, or burning. You'll have to ask . . . Let me check." Dr. Hulman stabbed his finger at a computer screen, scrolling down a departmental structure tree. "Here it is: Ms. Rosemary Wilder in the archives department. And, no, I don't recall anything about the document you're looking for."

After learning that Laurel was adopted, it had been relatively easy to follow the thread to her real mother. Laurel's father was still a mystery, and Nikola hoped the good Dr. Hulman would be able to shed a glimmer of light on the subject. On his way, he'd checked Bellevue Hospital's personnel records dating from a few years back to spot a familiar name. He'd known Walter Romero from his time in the DHS. That Romero was now in charge of security at a hospital didn't speak highly of the man's intelligence, but Nikola paid him a short social visit before meeting Dr. Hulman. Romero's gossip had been priceless.

"You were Araceli Goldberg's attending physician."

"Yes. As I've already explained, I was a young man then. She was a trauma casualty. When I was called in, the woman was dying, probably comatose. I delivered her child, probably by cesarean section, and that was the extent of my involvement. She wasn't my patient."

"She was when you delivered the girl."

"A girl? If you say so. Still, the record of my intervention was attached to her file." He checked his watch, although there was a large digital clock on the opposite wall. "How time flies! Now, if you'll excuse me, I must do a round of the wards."

Another lie. Dr. Hulman had chosen paper pushing over poking at abused flesh a decade earlier. "Did Araceli name the father? Did she ask you to notify anyone? Did you take notes?" Romero had remarked that Dr. Hulman had the annoying habit of taking copious notes at meetings or when attending patient reviews on small notebooks he always carried with him, to the chagrin of his secretary, who had to transcribe his spidery longhand. Whatever doubt he had about Hulman keeping notes of Araceli's delivery evaporated. As soon as Nikola mentioned notes, Dr. Hulman had darted a nervous glance to a tall safe supporting a pot with an artificial plant.

"I've told you, I don't remember. For crying out loud! It's over twenty-five years ago. What do you think I am? A computer?"

I must be getting old. He'd planned to grow calmer with the years, but his emotions only ran hotter with the extra mileage. In the past, Nikola would stoically endure uncooperative subjects and coax them into surrendering whatever information they may have had. Of late, his capacity had shrunk to a point where he bored of the game with surprising alacrity. He stifled a yawn and ran a tired glance over the impersonal office, the safe, the false plant, and the pristine medical textbooks that lined the shelves and were probably never consulted.

When Nikola was a child, his father would take him to an old bookshop in Chicago. There he would leave the boy to roam through dusty bookshelves while he disappeared to do "research" with Mrs. Gibbs, the owner, on the upper floor. About two hours later, Nikola's father would descend a spiral staircase, at times freshly showered. Nikola suspected his father's "research" might have something to do with water, but he'd never asked.

During his waiting periods, the attendant, Vito—a small old man with a florid face—would suggest a book or an illustrated tale. Vito would complain about the waning habit of reading. Customers, eager to flaunt their cultural prowess, would fill their bookcases with yards of books with correctly colored spines to match the decor. A new fashion, Vito had confided in whispers redolent of cheap booze, was to sell only the book spines pasted to a board. Lighter and more manageable. Nikola sighed and snapped back from his reverie, still wondering if the medical tracts on the gleaming wood shelves had any pages attached to their covers. "No, Dr. Hulman. I think you are a liar, and a bungling one at that."

"How dare you?" Hulman reached under his desk, his face set.

Nikola didn't move or try to stop his call for help or react when he felt the door opening at his back. He stared into Dr. Hulman's slowly widening eyes, intent on the sudden flash of fear scuttling across his irises.

The door closed.

A huge black mass clouded Nikola's peripheral vision as Sergeant Cox, clad in regulation body armor, approached the desk. At his back, another officer would be blocking the door.

"Where were we? Ah, yes: a liar, and a damn poor one."

The thud wasn't too loud, perhaps hushed by the Kevlar padding under the ceramic articulations covering Cox's fist, but blood gushed from Dr. Hulman's mouth and shattered nose as his head slammed back against the leather executive chair. For a moment, he didn't move. Then his reading glasses, miraculously dangling from one of his ears, surrendered to gravity and dropped to the floor. Blood traced rivulets to collect under his chin and bloom like poppies on his shirt and lab coat. Then he snorted or sneezed, and a spray of red droplets dewed the desktop, peppering the documents in an open folder with curious marks, as if a child had been let loose with a red marker.

Slowly, Dr. Hulman reached to his mouth with a trembling hand to retrieve a tooth, and he looked at it with the same suspicious intent one has when peering at an unidentified lump found in a meat pie. He then pursed his lips into an almost perfect bloody O and, without transition, started to cry—deep sobs racking his chest.

"Please, Sergeant, there was no need for such violence," Nikola said in a conversational tone. "So messy. . . . Restrain yourself. Let us conduct this conversation in a civilized manner." Nikola pushed his chair back, noting with distaste a tiny drop of blood marring his trousers. He sighed and nodded.

Cox grabbed Dr. Hulman's hand and slammed it on the desk.

"What a wonderful sight—friends holding hands." Nikola tried a wolfish grin. "I will pose a few questions and you will answer them truthfully. If you don't, this officer will break one finger, and then another, then another. Of course, fingers don't last as long as conversations, but you also have toes, and countless other bones. How many bones?"

Dr. Hulman made a croaking sound and opened his mouth, reddish bubbles foaming over it; the sound grew into a scream punctuated by a sickening snap when Cox folded the doctor's middle finger against the back of his hand as if turning the page of a book.

"Sergeant! Don't be so hasty; give the man time. You must excuse him, Doctor, he's young and eager. How many bones?"

"Two hun—two hundred six," Hulman moaned.

"Wonderful. Excellent. And more than half that number are in your hands and feet. Amazing, isn't it? Let's start again. I suggest you open that safe while you still have some operational fingers and give me the notebook where you wrote about the father. The father of the girl you delivered to Araceli Goldberg."

chapter 33

||||

22:38

Laurel glanced from her book to Russo's reclining figure and tried to make out, for the umpteenth time, some familiar line along his nose, jaw, ears, or mouth. After almost twenty-four hours at Tyler's farm, she'd committed every detail of Russo's anatomy to memory. He had wasted to an extent that his own mother might have had trouble recognizing him, but still Laurel searched his face for something familiar, with the same intensity that she rooted within herself for a flicker of feeling for the stranger named Eliot Russo. Before the operation, during the long months of preparation and training, she'd been consumed with loathing for the man who had left her real mother at the mercy of the riot police. She'd longed for the moment when she could confront him. Later, his pathetic condition had filled her with pity; no one, regardless of the crime committed, deserved such punishment. Now she felt nothing. Over the bed, where Russo battled to heal bruised synapses and rid his organs of toxins, an array of dated equipment monitored his vitals. Still no change after the more than fifty-two hours since he was raised from the tank. He was alive—at least, a spiky trace on an oscilloscope certified there was electrical activity in his emaciated body—but barely. Fear returned, as it had at ever shorter intervals, and fluttered in her chest like a bird caught in a net struggling for freedom. Springing Russo from the tank had been nightmarish but nothing compared to their future if he didn't recover coherent consciousness. Which was a long shot, according to Dr. Floyd Carpenter.

Russo's blood was new, thanks to the supply stolen by Antonio Salinas, Harper Tyler's farm foreman and, Laurel suspected, comrade-in-arms. Throughout the first twelve hours after they arrived in the safe house at Tyler's farm, Floyd had used over fifty bags of blood products and scores of packed red-blood-cell units in a series of transfusions to replace Russo's blood. Among the items on Floyd's shopping list that she'd beamed from the sewers was a hemodialysis machine, a special three-way valve, and supplies of bicarbonate for rinsing the machine. But regardless of the intensive blood replacement, Floyd worried that some readings remained alarmingly irregular. He had not been forthcoming, but it was obvious that extended hibernation without maintenance could cause long-term side effects. To reverse it, according to Floyd, would entail lengthy therapy.

They decided to take eight-hour shifts supervising Russo, keeping the steady drip from the IV lines flowing, noting the volume of his waste every hour, and ensuring his vitals remained within the limits prescribed by Floyd. She preferred the hollow hours between dusk and dawn and had volunteered for the night shift, seeking a little peace and quiet away from Lukas Hurley's frightened face. Everybody had carefully avoided any mention of Bastien, as if silence could somehow deny the harrowing reality of his death.

Laurel jolted after hearing a floorboard close to the door creak. She held her breath and released it slowly when Floyd's figure, clothed in jeans and a loose plaid shirt from the supply provided by Tyler, materialized. A far cry from the debonair figure he'd cast when he welcomed them from the sewers, but a sight better than the refuse-encrusted man he'd been at the subway station. Laurel could still feel the cauterizing fear she felt before the fat fields. "Damn, you scared me," she muttered.

"Sorry, I didn't mean to. Everybody is knocked out?"

She checked her watch—22:45—and nodded. "You couldn't sleep?"

He didn't answer but stepped over to Russo, checked the machine readings, drips, and lines, then neared the settee.

Laurel gathered her legs and moved aside to make room.

"That man is incredible." Floyd nodded toward the bed.

She waited.

"When I first saw him, I was shocked. I was expecting someone who had been serving a hibernation sentence for a few years, not a living corpse."

"What do you mean?"

"At the sugar cubes, the inmates are monitored constantly. Once their vitals show signs of decay, they are raised to the medical facility. There, an army of specialists backed with advanced instruments flush their organs of built-up toxins and redress most of the damage." He nodded again in Russo's direction. "I doubt that man was ever brought up from his tank."

Laurel didn't know, but Floyd was probably right.

"Back at Nyx, I would have given him a one in ten chance of recovery, maybe. If he were one of my patients, I would have recommended he be terminated."

"You'd have killed him?"

"No. I wouldn't have tried to revive him."

"Isn't that the same thing?"

"Life is not an absolute, but death is. Some patients decay to such an extent that recovery is almost impossible. Yes." He turned to look into her eyes. "You can be ninety-nine percent dead with an active brain. Before we return a patient from torpor, we must always weigh how alive the patient will be when we finish. This is an issue we have to consider daily in my line of work."

"You play God?"

"That's a spiny subject. We play at being God whenever we extend life by artificial means."

She picked up her book, placed the beer coaster she'd been using as a bookmark between the pages, and closed it, laying it down on a small side table. "And now? What are his chances?"

"I don't know. His metabolism is responding and his blood chemistry is much better. Not normal—that will take a long time—but acceptable. The problem is what will happen after I withdraw sedation."

"His mind?"

"If they'd do this to his body, what did they do to his mind? Yes. I'm familiar with standard hibernation side effects—the physiological imbalances and systemic damage—but in my work we're careful to keep mental activity monitored and vitals within tight limits. Whoever did this to him must have hated him beyond reason."

For a while they shared a silence, punctuated only by the faint beeps from the machines.

"I'm sorry about your other friend, er—Sebastian."

"Bastien. Bastien Compton."

"I'm sorry."

Her eyes filmed over. "Why did it happen?"

"What you did was a crazy stunt—much more dangerous than any of you could have guessed. Sinking into torpor only to be roused a few minutes later subjected your body to a huge systemic shock."

"You mean we all could have died?"

Floyd didn't answer at once. When he did, his voice seemed to come from somewhere farther away. "Yes. In a way, it's a small miracle Raul and you pulled through intact."

She straightened, aghast at the implication. Floyd shook his head, as if he could follow her train of thought. "Don't be harsh on Tyler and the others who planned the operation. They probably didn't know."

"How could they not?"

"I spoke with Tyler earlier; that's when he told me about Bastien. He couldn't understand what had happened to your friend either. The truth is, little has leaked from Hypnos, or any of the companies offering commercial hibernation, about the drawbacks of the technology."

"Couldn't you have warned them?"

"How could I? All I knew was that a group of people would bring an inmate over to Nyx through the sewers. I had no idea of the details."

She leaned back and shook her head. *Had I known all the*

risks, would I still have done it? It came as no surprise that the answer was yes, but their ignorance had come at a harrowing cost.

Floyd turned again toward the shape on the bed. "Who is he?"

His question traced a line in the sand; she could cross it or maintain her silence. But she'd crossed the line when she reached for his hand in the van. "His name is Eliot Russo."

Floyd stood, his brow creased. He wandered randomly around the room, his restless fingers touching a tube or a container as if looking for something to do. At the top of the bed, he paused to look at the taut skin over Russo's skull. "I remember. . . . A lawyer, a political activist, ostensibly killed in a car accident, five, six years ago?"

"Eight."

Floyd sucked air and smacked his lips. "Shit."

"You can say that."

"So it really is him and us."

"I don't follow." Laurel did, but she wanted to hear his voice.

"You do. I presume this operation is about exposing what's happened to him."

She waited.

"To do that, he must recover and keep his mental faculties, at least a little. If he dies or turns up insane, we'll never make it. Whoever did this to him will make sure." Floyd paced back to the settee and slumped at her side without much elegance. "How many more like him are there?"

She looked up to find his eyes searching her face. "I don't know. I once heard Shep—Tyler speak of many."

After removing his moccasins, Floyd coiled his long body into the settee and curled up his legs, hiking his feet onto the seat so that their toes touched. "Hopeless." His voice grew darker.

"There's always hope."

"Hope is the denial of reality."

Laurel bunched her toes over his. "Where have you pilfered that quote from?"

"No idea. How can the government tolerate such bestiality?"

"In this case, because they know nothing about it," Laurel said.

"Impossible."

"Is it? Governments have grown pyramidal—too large, complex, and fragmented. Those at the top don't know what happens at lower levels. Providing the waters remain calm and the bottom line tallies, they have no reason to dig into the bowels of any one department."

"So is this a DHS operation?" Floyd asked.

"In cahoots with other intelligence agencies."

"And Hypnos? It doesn't make any sense."

"Why?"

"Something like this couldn't be kept secret forever. Eventually someone would blow the whistle."

"That's what we're hoping to do." Under the soles of her feet, he splayed his toes like a cat.

"So you're crusaders championing the ideal of omnipotent justice." There was a hard tinge to his voice, as if people fighting a corrupt system for the sake of ideals embodied something shameful, even dangerous.

"What's troubling you?" Laurel asked.

"You are." He waved a hand toward the door, and Laurel realized he'd used the plural. "You seem like good people, but you know next to nothing about whoever is pulling the strings or their motives. Ideals have a nice ring, but this reeks of a political struggle—one of the age-old battles for power after which nothing ever changes. Chances are, the players will regroup to tally up their wins and losses after mopping up the spent pawns in the field."

"You mean that regardless of the outcome, even if it becomes public, what the DHS . . ."

"Right. *If* it ever becomes public. Perhaps the threat of blowing the lid is all our unknown master puppeteers need to achieve their ends. If so, we are nothing more than a troublesome loose end."

"Twenty years ago, a cover-up like this couldn't have happened," Laurel said.

"You mean the Internet?"

Back in the '30s, artists and writers had waged a vicious campaign to change the rules, or lack of them, governing the Internet. Naturally, film, play, book, media, and music producers had supported the initiative with enthusiasm. As a result, the last glimmer of real freedom the world had ever known disappeared almost overnight. The exercise had been a remarkably simple two-step operation under the cover of intellectual property protection. Part one of the process entailed placing government-controlled server farms in high-security buildings buttressed by a new generation of supercomputers. Once the hardware was in place, individuals and organizations were given six months in which to migrate to the new servers. Then part two came into effect: Before a private server, network, or Web site could be housed, every piece of content needed a hard-crypto electronic signature to identify its author.

Against all predictions, the public uproar faded rapidly, because authorities leveled a morally unshakable argument: The new laws didn't reduce anyone's freedom to post whatever they wanted, providing it hadn't been stolen.

Surfing remained unchanged; anybody could browse the World Wide Web and download at leisure in relative anonymity. But uploading was a different matter. To upload content, the files entered a short quarantine until the sender's identity could be certified—a procedure lasting a few minutes. Whoever published an item whose authorship was disputed became blacklisted from further postings until the matter was settled. Any content backed with a banned signature would never reach the server. Naturally, dissidents—and a few nations—had tried to fool the system, and some managed to upload "delinquent" material. But it was a short-lived victory. After a flurry of stiff prison sentences and even banning entire countries from the Web for protracted periods while the software was purged of glitches and the procedure fine-tuned, anonymity was eradicated from every scrap of data on the Web. Like its predecessor, the Wild West Web had finally been tamed.

Laurel straightened but didn't shift her feet. "I follow your line of thinking, but you're wrong. This is not only a matter of ideals." The silky feeling of his warm toes was too delicious for words.

He waited.

"He's my father."

Floyd jerked his head toward Russo as if harboring the hope she could be referring to somebody else. "I—I'm sorry."

"So am I, but parents are hard to choose."

"I meant—"

"I know."

"So puny idealism had little to do with your involvement in this operation."

"You sound relieved."

"Few ideals survive past sophomore year, and those that do owe much to delusion and wishful thinking."

"Well, I'm sorry to disappoint you, but I believe the center inmates are an obscenity. I've gambled my life to stop it."

"But you said—"

"That man is my father, but he's also a stranger. I've been told he happened to contribute his sperm, but I had never met him before." Over the next few minutes Laurel painted verbal-shorthand sketches of her upbringing by the Coles, the only parents she'd ever known, and the unknown patron of her exclusive and costly education.

"Is he the leader? Your benefactor—is he running the operation?"

She shook her head. "I don't know if they're the same person. I've never met him—either of them." Laurel narrowed her eyes. "We've spoken on several occasions; that's how I know Russo is my father. My benefactor, as you call him, outlined his plan, but it was my decision to become involved. Only Tyler has met him, and I trust both of them."

"Why did you do it?"

"Ideals is the byword, but it's more complex than that. The offer came at a difficult point in my life. I was depressed and feeling useless. This was a chance to do something important, something that could change our society a little, and . . . I wanted to confront my father. It may seem puny, but I wanted him to know I knew of his cowardice."

He reached for her hand and wrapped long fingers around it. It felt good. "What about Lukas?"

"Money. A new life."

Floyd nodded. Another puzzle piece to slot into whatever picture was forming in his mind. Laurel followed his profile, sharply delineated against the white wall. "And you?" Laurel asked. "They told me you didn't ask for much money, only enough to settle your debts and pay off your ex-wife, so I assumed you were also a puny idealist. But you seem to view idealism with distaste."

"My involvement was supposed to be slight, and I believe that hibernation has the potential to be a godsend for humanity, but the science is still in its infancy. And if the status quo continues, it will remain so. Let's face it, next to nothing has been researched since its beginning—Hypnos has made sure of that by keeping a tight rein on the snippets of technology they license. Don't get me wrong. I'm all for free enterprise and for the rights of businesses to extract profit from their patents, but this is different. Hypnos has kept the lid on a technology that could herald a new era for humankind."

"How so?"

"Reducing trauma in patients enduring long surgical interventions was the original reason behind the hibernation research. The U.S. government, however, had already thought of using hibernation to store people and ordered NASA to keep a watchful eye on the research, to be ready to pounce and seize the technology to send astronauts to far-flung destinations."

"Yes, but besides cold storage in its different guises, what else could you use hibernation for?"

"The medical applications are countless; many illnesses are lethal because of how fast they spread through the system before the body defenses can kick in. Think of cancers and all sorts of opportunistic viral attacks. A hibernating body with only a fraction of metabolic activity could have its defenses boosted to a point where an infection would be history as soon as it appeared. For vaccines, we could study the viral mechanisms in slow motion. And develop much more sophisticated surgeries."

"But I thought these avenues had been explored already."

"Only superficially; most work has been done by the military or Hypnos itself. Imagine what would happen if the technology became available to researchers: Tens of thousands of brilliant minds could study untold applications. They could open avenues we can't even imagine now. Take endangered species; once the processes responsible for damage and decay were fully understood, the species could be placed in long-term hibernation. Food preservation is another possibility. This technology is in its infancy, and the possibilities are infinite."

"Was that the carrot dangled before your nose?" she asked.

"If they could cajole Hypnos into freeing the technology, there would be untold opportunities for research."

"And there aren't many people around with your expertise."

"That's about it. Of course, I had no idea of the DHS's involvement."

"Come on. Who else? They had to be in it somehow."

"Not really. I've been aware of center occupants for a few years, and so have scores of others."

Laurel jerked back in shock. "You what?"

"This is a relatively small industry. I always thought the extra space in the center of the tanks belonged to a research operation run only by Hypnos without the DHS's knowledge. But, as with many other angles in this mess, it seems I was wrong."

Laurel frowned at Floyd's unexpected revelation. "You mean doctors and technicians were in on this?"

"In on it? No. We thought it was financial chicanery, a way of saving money."

"I don't understand. What do you mean?"

"Therapeutic hibernation is for the rich; it costs a fortune to provide for someone who may be suspended for years. Part of the deal Hypnos has with the government involves a degree of research to improve the system. There's an inexhaustible supply of willing human guinea pigs out there—disenfranchised people with incurable illnesses inclined to accept inclusion in research programs—but labs are expensive to run. To use the center spaces for in-house research was Hypnos's original idea—sort of running their everyday investigation under the noses of the DHS and having them foot the bill. When the tanks' final design was submitted to Congress, the wasteful arrangement of space became obvious and they asked for a redesign. But somewhere along the line a compromise must have been reached, because the centers remained empty. I got the gist of the story eons ago from Peter Blake, the chief scientist at Hypnos."

"Now I get it. You thought the inmate they had asked you to revive was a Hypnos research subject."

"You got it."

"How were you contacted?"

"First by phone, then at a meeting."

"But I thought you'd never seen—"

"I was blindfolded, but Tyler was there. Once we met him I recognized his voice."

"And they told you the center inmates were a Hypnos setup?"

Floyd didn't answer for a while, his thumb absently caressing the back of Laurel's hand. "No, they didn't; it was my assumption. Another wrong one, by the looks of it."

Like the Russian nested dolls, that's how Hypnos and the DHS had planned the use of the centers in their tanks; a ploy within a ploy within a ploy. She blinked, assimilating for the first time the vastness of the deceit: fifty sugar cubes in the homeland, with between fifty and three hundred tanks each; thousands of center spaces with room for tens of thousands. Worldwide, the numbers would be staggering.

"Half a million, at least."

"What?" Laurel snapped from her calculations to focus on his eyes, bright and tinged with a veil of sadness.

"That's the number you're seeking. Half a million is a fair estimate of the capacity Hypnos has to house the nameless to run its research and, at the same time, provide a limbo for whoever crosses swords with the DHS at home and God knows with how many foreign government agencies in countries where the system is in operation."

"Where's the origin of the system's flaws? Its use? The safeguards?"

"There are many flaws—some in the system, and others in the hibernation process."

Laurel nodded. Unlike most technologies, hibernation didn't appear to have been helmed by people driven by good intentions.

"When Vinson Duran, then an obscure scientist, isolated the protein mechanism governing the onset of torpor," Floyd continued, "he didn't publicize his discovery but instead founded a corporation and set out to find the most profitable way to use his technology. As it turned out, it became a commercial venture successful beyond Hypnos's wildest dreams. Once achieved, their goal has been to perpetuate their monopoly by denying others the research tools to further the science.

"And here lies the origin of the flaws. Hibernation needed ten years of open research to iron out the kinks present in every new technology. Instead, Hypnos offered the government a solution to an otherwise stubborn problem: the prison system. But there was a condition. Hypnos would run it. Our government jumped at the chance and built a dicey legal framework, because they didn't understand the technology or its implications. Only Hypnos knew some of the finer limitations of hibernation, and they weren't about to make a full disclosure. As a result, our government imposed a new system controlled by a corporation. These are the system's flaws: hasty deployment of an untried technology, and private ownership without effective government control. The rest is history and, let's face it, once the technology was available, to use it as an alternative to the old prison system was unavoidable."

"I agree; the previous setup wasn't economically feasible," Laurel said.

"Economic viability was only part of the problem. The fact is, the old system didn't fulfill any of the goals it set out to do."

"Was the old system better?"

"No, and the question has been debated to exhaustion. I'm

just saying there are still flaws in hibernation, but there will be no return to the old system."

"Why not?"

"In itself, hibernation is a strong deterrent because of fear. Prisons weren't scary enough."

"No wonder." She darted a glance toward Russo, and it suddenly dawned on her that he couldn't have changed much in eight years. "Has he aged?"

"Patients in hibernation age differently, but we all age."

"He's supposed to have aged only slightly. Isn't that right?" She looked at Russo again.

"Yes, only slightly, but you must factor disbalance in."

"I've never heard that term. Did you make it up?"

"Not at all. Disbalance is one of the paradoxes of hibernation. Slowed-down metabolisms arrest aging but not completely."

"From what I've heard of hibernation, decay progresses but at ten percent of the normal rate. A prisoner can do a century and return with a body only ten years older."

"That's the theory. But reality is different. Disbalance is the phenomenon of differently aged cells sharing the same organism. Some of the cells in a living body continue to work regardless of temperature or metabolic speed. I'm referring not only to the nervous system but also to the respiratory, digestive, circulatory, and endocrine systems. After prolonged periods of torpor, the body hosts a weird mix of free radicals and other antioxidants that serve cells with different lineages—I mean cells that have evolved at different rates. This may trigger the immune system to act unpredictably." Floyd turned toward Russo and nodded. "That's one of the problems with him."

"Will he pull through?" Laurel asked.

Floyd moved his hands to form a sphere in midair and then peered into his imaginary crystal ball. "Some contend the future can be known and anything short of accepting predictable doom is denial. Others contend the future has not yet unfolded and may harbor untold possibilities."

"How can you be witty in our situation?"

He lowered his hands. "Because I don't know what to say, except that miracles sometimes happen."

Laurel shook her head, suddenly weary beyond description. *A miracle?*

"Wa . . . ter—"

Laurel and Floyd jerked their heads toward Russo's bed, where suddenly a miracle had occurred.

chapter 34

||||

22:45

Still no word from Nikola.

Odelle Marino kicked her shoes off and closed the penthouse door with her foot without turning around. She laid her briefcase and the file she'd been reading in the back of her official car on one of the matching sideboards flanking the entrance. During the forty-minute drive from DHS headquarters to Chesapeake Bay, she'd studied Hypnos's breakdown for the next fiscal year—including a hike of more than seven percent in the fees the corporation charged the American taxpayer per inmate and day.

She darted a quick glance around and sniffed, her unconscious routine when arriving home. Right temperature, right smell, and right order. The Venezuelan couple caring for the gardening and housekeeping were inching toward their green cards. After a quick detour to the kitchen to gather a tub of raspberry mousse and a spoon, she climbed to the upper floor.

The vast bedroom walls had been decorated by Greek artisans to resemble the houses dotting the Aegean Sea islands, in rustic and rough plaster finished in blinding white with several coats of whitewash. On the ceiling, scores of triangles crafted from stout ivory canvas and held tight by ropes over-lapped to cover most of the surface. Fluffy clouds in an azure sky peeked from places where the fabric panels met at odd angles. The floor, made from uneven waxed cedar planks, was on two levels. On the raised area sat a huge antique bed, its heavy canopy supported by four dark columns intricately carved with acanthus leaves. The dark wood contrasted sharply with the Egyptian cotton bed linens, stacked pillows, and gossamer curtains.

After a slight detour to leave the mousse on a rolltop desk, Odelle padded past the bed to the other side of the room, to a wide arched opening flanked by two huge eighteenth-century Spanish chairs with dark tooled-leather seats. Through the arch and a short corridor set with floor-to-ceiling mirrors in aged wood frames, she entered her bathroom—its slanted glazed ceiling now obscured by sliding unbleached linen cur-tains. Odelle stepped over the slatted teak floor to a sunken rectangular bath of white marble with spidery green veins. She opened the faucet, and a two-foot-wide waterfall arched from a bronze panel on the marble wall. The water tempera-ture would remain constant, recirculating through a thermo-statically controlled heater set in the lower floor. When water reached its preset level, a sensor would turn the faucet off.

Odelle straightened and gazed through wafts of steam to the bath's backdrop—a jungle rising to the ceiling and cov-ering the bathroom's rear wall. Heliconias, gingers, and ba-nanas wrestled for space next to anthuriums, ficus, ti, aloes, and yuccas intertwined with passionflower vines.

She opened a small wooden door set on the wall to a side of the bath and hefted one of the six Baccarat crystal flasks: her perfume, custom-made by Maison Guerlain at their gor-geous Champs-Elysées shop, a bargain at ninety grand a quart. She poured a generous splash of the Madeira-colored liquid into the hot water, and the air thickened with aromas of musk, sandalwood, and violet. She returned the flask to the darkness of its niche, undressed, and laid her clothes on a chaise longue set to a side of the arch.

Through the passageway, she returned to the bedroom and paused to gaze at the lazily fluttering flimsy netting driven by the carefully positioned jets in the ceiling. Odelle caught her reflection in the mirror. Small breasts, untouched by the knife and still defying gravity, flat stomach, and not a hair on her body below her eyes but for a carefully manicured mound of dark curls.

When a faint peal echoed, she padded to her rolltop desk and slid back its curved slatted lid. A rectangular plasma panel folded upward and stopped at a slight angle. Odelle glanced at the numbers beside the prompt and choked a curse. Not Nikola; Vinson. For a heartbeat she was tempted to turn around and return to her bath, but running away from a confrontation wasn't her style. She sat on the leather chair facing the desk and ran her hands lightly over the armrests. She'd bought the chair over the phone at a secret auction: one of the chairs from the railway carriage where the French had surrendered in 1940. She didn't know which buttocks her seat had nursed: Pétain's, Hitler's, Keitel's, Huntziger's, or Jodl's. Not that it mattered.

Odelle stared for an instant at the tiny camera over the desk and blinked twice. The camera whirred to focus on her face, and the screen dissolved to reconfigure into an image of Vinson's face, drawn in an angry grimace.

"Any luck?" Vinson opened.

"Zilch. It's as if it never happened."

"How can that be? No way. . . . What's the NHS doing? Then there's the police. . . . We must . . ." When nervous, Vinson had the unsettling—and unrelated to syntax—habit of surrounding odd words with pauses, leaving confused listeners wondering if a hidden significance lurked beyond his comments.

"There are two million residents in Washington, D.C., three on workdays. I can neither close down the city nor do a house-to-house search."

"Have the fugitives left the city?"

Odelle raised one leg and propped her heel on the desk's edge, then repeated the movement with the other leg, adjusting her foot on the opposite edge. The camera remained focused on her face.

"Yes, they probably have by now."

Intelligent brown eyes, set in a serious-looking, heart-shaped face in its early sixties, stared back at her. His cheeks had paled, but it could be the light. Odelle scooted her butt to get more comfortable and reached down with her hand.

"What are we going to do?" Vinson asked.

"You should calm down and run your company. I will do my job."

"But the press—"

"I'm working that angle." The previous morning, Nikola had hinted at calling a press conference and disclosing the breakout. There had already been a whisper in the evening's edition of *The Post,* tucked away in Hamilton's editorial. Nikola said he'd call later. That was more than twelve hours ago, and he hadn't called. She increased the pressure of her fingers and shuddered.

"And if they talk?"

She smiled at her interrogator. "Who?"

"The fugitives."

"Talk? To whom?"

"The press. They could—the government. Not to mention . . . There's a design behind this madness." The face on the screen was a picture of growing discomfort.

Odelle narrowed her eyes and breathed in her heavenly musk. "They can't. No paper will entertain gossip or anonymous calls without clearing it with me first. It's a question of time. Relax."

"But the organization . . . They bombed the power station. . . . If it comes out—"

"Then we'll pull the plug."

He suddenly leaned forward, like a snake about to strike. "We can't do that."

"Mmmm?" Her belly glowed. "Why not?" But, of course, she knew the answer.

"We will have to pay. . . . Not only that, there could be . . . reprisals. Those people—"

She shuffled in her seat and slowed down. "You mean the mob? There, sweetheart, I fear you're on your own. I never dealt with them. I don't exist. Your sugar cubes, your tanks . . ."

Vinson raised himself, his veins swollen, cheeks flushed;

he was angry. His camera zoomed in and out a couple of times, until it locked on his face once more. "The fuck I'm on my own." His words hissed, like fat dripping from a roast onto the fire. "You took your cut. We're partners, equals."

Odelle narrowed her eyes before twisting the knife. "I don't agree. Not intellectually."

Back in the early '50s, the Krasnaya Mafiya had discovered the wonders of hibernation. Some people were troublesome enough to merit a quick bullet or worse. But permanent measures often meant a waste of talent that could be useful in the future. Russian sugar cubes weren't safe, but U.S. facilities fit the bill admirably. Thus, Vinson had hammered out a cold-storage contract with the dons and cut Odelle in on the deal.

"It's not only money. . . . These people—"

"Yes, money. I've been reading your report. You are asking for increases of almost eight percent. A little heavy, *non*?"

"Maintenance costs are soaring, and wages, and consumables."

"You mean inmates?" She silently bet he would miss the funny side of it.

"Chemicals, drugs, equipment."

He did. "I've been checking your papers. Inflation doesn't justify what you're asking."

"Will you endorse the increment?"

Odelle sensed movement. She glanced over her shoulder. The bed's netting moved with more intensity. She would leave a note for the housekeeper to have the air-conditioning flow checked. The pin camera whirred faintly. On the screen Vinson's irises gleamed. Still she waited.

"Half a percent?"

She did a quick calculation. After the increase, Hypnos's daily housing fees would peak at two hundred dollars per inmate. With a sugar cube population of a little over one million, half of one percent meant a million dollars a day. She could push Vinson for twice as much, but greed could backfire one day. "My friend, would I leave you in the cold?" She would without batting an eyelid, regardless of the money, but mobsters had long memories and she didn't want to enlarge her bodyguard retinue. "Yesterday I ordered slight rearrangements. You know? Nothing drastic. A few inmates shifted from the centers to the sides and conversely. It's numbers that count, isn't it?"

On the screen, Vinson metamorphosed. Muscles relaxed and conformed to the arrangement that made people trust him—an air of competence and self-confidence. Odelle knew Vinson's chameleonic savvy well and focused on the avalanche of sensations warming her loins.

"You're—"

"Brilliant?" she interrupted.

"Beautiful."

Although he could see only her face, subliminal tendrils must have mixed with the digital bytes streaming from her set. Her reflection was disturbed by a quiet cough. Odelle stared into Vinson's smiling eyes.

"Er—there's a problem with your camera."

Odelle arrested the motion of her fingers and checked the tiny light signaling the device's operation.

"What's up?"

"That would be of no interest to you. But your camera changed to wide angle a while ago."

Odelle sat on the bathroom's chaise longue, replaying her conversation with Vinson. *There's a design behind this madness.* She frowned and scraped up the last of her raspberry mousse. Indeed there was. And Nikola had not zeroed in on the designer. Yet. But he would. Nikola was a patient man—thorough and a loyal mercenary. Loyal, because he knew she could destroy him, drag him down in her wake if things got hairy. She stood, reached to her earlobes, and removed her glossy studs, depositing them with care on a crystal tray. Pulling the plug and pulping a few inmates so that the number tallied would leave only Russo and his helpers as loose ends. The young lawyers were no longer minor felons but murderers, after culling their comrade. The lot could go down for life, and she would make sure they did. If—she quickly corrected herself—*when* they cleaned up the mess, she would set up a different set of rules for center use, perhaps to the point of doing away with the scheme altogether, and to hell with Vinson and his freebies. Well, perhaps not completely if she could recover Russo. *Life consists of compromises and missed opportunities,* thought Odelle, as she reached for a glass of Pellegrino. Then she grinned and took a sip. She'd seized too many opportunities to be entitled to complain.

On the edge of the bathtub, she lowered a foot into the scalding water with agonizing slowness, biting her lower lip to ward off a cry. Time seemed to slow until Odelle could plant the sole of her foot on the bathtub's bottom, the muscles of her other leg bunching in a painful cramp. She repeated the movement until both her feet settled under eighteen inches of water. To sit down needed a slow ballet lasting several minutes. When she could relax her neck, water lapping her chin and her feet propped on the bathtub's edges, Odelle surrendered to the steaming water. Her submerged skin had turned an angry red, and the built-up tension in her groin screamed for release.

She slipped her hand under the water.

Eons ago, Miko—a Tayü or first-class Oiran, in Ginza— had taught her the mysteries of a hot bath and shown her a bewildering array of funny-looking things she carried in a long sandalwood case. *I must go back to Ginza. Soon.* Then Odelle started to shake and the scalding water lapped against the marble sides, darkening the teak slats as it sloshed over. She ground her teeth and shook her head from side to side. Then her mouth sagged as a low-pitched wail escaped her lips.

day four

||||

Inferno, Canto XXXI: 57–59
*For where the mind's acutest reasoning
is joined to evil will and evil power,
there human beings can't defend themselves.*

The Divine Comedy, DANTE ALIGHIERI

00:06

When Genia Warren finished poring over the thick wad of documents, it was past midnight. She'd been in and out of meetings all day with her staff, drafting security proposals, following the passage of several bills through Congress that affected FBH, and waiting for a summons from DHS Director Odelle Marino. A summons that never came. During a recess, she'd exchanged a few words with Lawrence Ritter, the Federal Bureau of Hibernation security director. He hadn't heard from Odelle either but knew that she'd been closeted in her offices after canceling or rescheduling all outstanding appointments.

Out of habit, and before turning in, Genia checked her personal e-mail in-box. She read of her mother's concerns for the pounding her flowers were taking in the fickle weather, and there was a short update from Clare, Genia's sister doing a postgraduate degree in Europe. There were also a handful of funding requests from her parish and voluntary organizations, but nothing of note. Then her secure console beeped and *RA* scrolled across the screen, followed by a succinct *Check The Post.* She read the advance headlines on the newspaper's Web site and went to bed with the foreboding that her rest would be brief.

One of Odelle Marino's most maddening idiosyncrasies was to call meetings with the same forewarning Caligula gave his senators, often gathering directors or staff from the agencies of her fiefdom in the middle of the night, in particular to deliver bad news. Genia had managed four hours of sleep when the telephone blared, announcing Odelle's ultimatum— a hairbreadth short of a subpoena.

Genia's security detail, permanently stationed outside her house, would already have been alerted by her night duty staff. By the time she managed a hasty shower and a gulped-down cup of espresso, they had gathered her routine three-car motorcade to whisk her down to the Department of Homeland Security headquarters—a thirty-minute race through half-deserted streets. Once tucked inside her car, she called Lawrence Ritter's number twice—unaccountably busy at such an early hour—before checking the screen of her communications pad to discover he was trying to reach her. Odelle had also ordered Lawrence to the conclave.

"Know what this is all about?" His voice suggested high spirits.

"No idea," she lied. "Any developments on the breakout?"

"Nope. Yesterday I requested updates from the DHS. Twice. So far unanswered. I'm limited to whatever they see fit to filter down. As you know, I was asked—no, make that ordered— to keep away from their investigation. Yesterday I also tried to raise the staff at the Washington, D.C., sugar cube. No dice. Whoever is running the show has clamped down the facility to any outside office, and that includes us."

Genia smiled in the gloom of the partitioned compartment. Lawrence's reply was unnecessarily lengthy and convoluted, strictly for the benefit of eavesdroppers. "We'll find out soon. Where are you?"

"Outside the building. I'll meet you by the elevators at the parking lot."

"Roger that." Genia severed the communication and retreated into a corner of her mind, the only place she felt safe from the increasingly obtrusive DHS surveillance, to weigh for the umpteenth time the slowly unfolding events and dangers ahead. A string of weak presidents had looked the other way as the DHS mushroomed out of congressional control, sucking power from scores of other agencies like a vortex. No, she corrected herself, more like a black hole from which not even light could escape. Genia suspected that no one, not even Odelle Marino, had planned to monopolize so much power. But, like a chain reaction, control had radiated from the DHS to permeate decision-making layers of government to a point where constitutionally elected bodies became paralyzed and a travesty of their former selves. Yes, the DHS needed powerful light shining on its bowels and a thorough flushing of its bilges.

When her car finally stopped feet away from the bank of elevators at the DHS restricted parking lot, five stories below street level, she rushed out, swinging her legs without much elegance and, judging by Lawrence's cocked eyebrow, forgoing her ingrained decorum. *Calm down, girl, you're racing.*

"Good morning," Lawrence greeted her, flashing his ID card past a long slot by the farthest elevator.

Genia eyed his signature uniform—black suit, gleaming black loafers, and cashmere black turtleneck—before glancing at his face, blinking at his faultless beret, and stopping at his sparkling brown eyes. "How you manage to look so awake is beyond me." She flicked her wrist to steal a glance at her timepiece—05:26.

"I don't sleep, that's why." He stood aside when the elevator doors opened. As she walked past him, he reached to her neck. "You don't look so bad. I say, forgot to check the mirror, did we?" He leaned over. "It's on the news," he whispered, and tugged at the otherwise perfect neck of her blouse. "There, much better."

As the elevator doors closed silently, she smiled. "Why the fake British accent? You should try French. Last I heard, you were from Manitoba."

"It gets me better tables at eateries. You should try it."

Genia nodded once. Ritter knew. He could have been forewarned as she had, not by her source but by his own staff. But the most likely origin of his knowledge would have been a quick scan through the digest prepared by his round-the-clock press department as soon as he received Odelle's summons.

After exiting the elevator at the executive floor and submitting to the routine body scan and the surrender of their weapons, George Wilson, Odelle Marino's personal assistant—a fastidious middle-aged man with a slight limp and green eyes—ushered them through a long corridor onto a small rotunda with double doors flanked by a pair of oil paintings depicting blurry seascapes. At the doors, George glanced at a small brass panel to one side and its slowly pulsing green light before sliding the panels open and stepping aside.

Genia nodded before striding in. Years before, she had studied Odelle's bodyguard's file: George Wilson, a full ex-colonel from the British SAS, untainted by the political loyalties besieging American personnel—a killing machine.

"This is unacceptable." Odelle Marino stepped into the boardroom from her inner office and hurled a folded newspaper across the table. Then she marched to the head of the large oval table, slipped into a high-backed chair, and waved a hand for them to sit.

Genia reached for the newspaper. On the front page, tucked on the right-hand side of the headline announcing a major bomb scare in Paris, was a piece by Louis Hamilton, opening with a question: *Are our prisons as secure as we've been led to believe?* It was followed by a carefully worded article based on rumors not categorically denied by the FBH.

"Do we have any idea who leaked it?" Genia asked, careful to sound outraged but without overdoing it.

"I was hoping Mr. Ritter, your director of security, would be able to enlighten us," Odelle said.

"I'm afraid not." Ritter hadn't glanced at the paper.

Odelle leaned forward. "You don't seem surprised about the news, Mr. Ritter."

"I'm not. I read the article an hour ago in the digest prepared by my press staff. It was predictable."

"What was?"

"That sooner or later the press would get a whiff of something foul, in particular after the power station's fireworks."

"You call a terrorist attack at a nuclear installation 'fireworks'?"

Ritter sighed and pursed his lips. Genia flinched; she knew his body language and guessed what was coming next.

"With all due respect, madam, although high explosives were used, other than tickling the trembler alarm switches of the station, the facility was never in any real danger. The charges were placed in the sewers a mile away, clinically arranged so the blast would travel under the station and trip the alarms. Had the so-called terrorists wanted to inflict harm, they could have easily positioned the charges right under the reactor and probably fissured it. Then we would have had a major nuclear emergency on our hands. It's my view that the explosions were part of an elaborate ruse to divert your forces so the fugitives could escape."

"Where did you get that information?"

"It's my job."

"That was a direct question."

"I'm sorry, Ms. Marino."

Odelle Marino placed both hands on the table and had started to rise when Genia felt compelled to intervene, inwardly cursing Ritter's chutzpah. "He has a right to protect his sources. If such information is classified and an offense has been committed, Mr. Ritter will answer in writing on a documented request from your office."

Odelle stood, eyes narrowed. When she spoke, her voice had dropped several decibels to slightly above a whisper. "I order you to tell me the source of that information at once."

Ritter stepped away from the table and stood erect, his eyes on the door leading to Odelle's inner office. "No, madam, I will do no such thing. Article 612, section four, paragraph two: *Executive personnel will not answer questions relating to security or classified issues but to the director of his agency, Congress, or the President,* and, to my knowledge, your office doesn't qualify as any of those things."

"How dare you?" Odelle turned slowly to face Genia. "I expect the source of that information on my desk within the hour, along with his resignation."

Before Genia could answer, Ritter continued without having moved or shifted his gaze. "Director Warren can have the information and my resignation as soon as she sees fit to demand it."

It had to happen. That it was happening so fast was further proof that Odelle was losing her cool. Her outburst was petty. Still, there were limits. "Ms. Marino, I beg you to reconsider," Genia said. "The resignation of a senior officer in federal service must be served to his agency director with a copy to the Congress's permanent committee: article 163, section six, subsections two and three of the disciplinary code. Such a resignation must include the superior officer's certification of the reason or reasons why such a resignation was tendered. No doubt Mr. Ritter will draft intent of personal reasons, but I am honor bound to add that the resignation was demanded by you because of his refusal to obey an illegal order." She didn't add that Ritter's revelation painted an appalling picture of incompetence in the handling of the affair by the DHS. But Genia could swear Odelle had caught her drift.

In a chameleonic turnabout, Odelle Marino's face relaxed and a faint smile curved her lips. "You're right, of course. But this wretched episode will soon be over. Then I'm sure we'll have a suitable opportunity to review this conversation." Her face set. "That will be all, for now."

In silence, Genia Warren and Lawrence Ritter collected their regulation weapons and communication pads from the security desk and headed for the elevator. As soon as the car doors closed, Ritter yanked off his beret and, in a movement too fast to follow, slapped the black beret over the surveillance camera, grabbed for Genia's waist, and pulled her to him, kissing her with something close to ferocious urgency. Genia tried to gasp but only managed to accept his tongue. She could have reached for her piece or rammed a knee into his groin, but she did neither. Of its own accord, her hand moved to the nape of his neck, to bask in the fact that unconsciously she'd been dying to feel his smooth skin for ages. With the same haste, Ritter released her, grabbed his beret, slapped it on his head, and regained his habitual deadpan expression. Genia blinked, her breath coming out in hurried gasps, wondering if she'd imagined the whole episode. Her lips tingled. "What was that?" she breathed.

Ritter raised an eyebrow, a gesture that gave his face a curious Mephistophelian look, and whispered, "Heroic gestures have the strangest effect on me."

At the parking lot, Ritter held the doors from closing and

leaned toward her as she squeezed past him. "She wasn't alone. Someone was listening from her office."

When Genia Warren and Lawrence Ritter left, Nikola Masek opened the connecting door between Odelle Marino's office and boardroom and stepped through, inwardly aghast at her handling of Ritter. She was clearly outmatched. The man was a walking encyclopedia of rules, laws, and legislation.

She turned to face him. "Who leaked it to *The Post*?"

"It could have been anyone."

"That's not an answer."

"I have the tape—a synthetic voice. Its identity is irrelevant, for the time being at least. But my bet is, whoever organized the escape leaked it to the press."

"Why?"

"They're losing their nerve or Russo has died or both."

"And how did Ritter get accurate details of the explosion?"

Over the past few minutes, eavesdropping on Odelle's careless display of brute force, Nikola had weighed what his answer should be to her predictable question. "Anybody could have given him that information, from within the DHS. More than two hundred operatives were involved, and he's the director of security. Only an idiot would fail to judge that the explosion was meant to be all thunder and no damage. Anyway, disclosing the breakout was a rash move, and a welcome one; it will spare me the hassle of feeding the breakout to the press myself."

Silence.

Nikola sighed. "We made a gross mistake in keeping the escape under wraps. In retrospect, it's obvious that the linchpin of their plan was our predictability. They wagered we would keep the lid down and we fell for it."

"Why do you keep using the plural? It was your call."

"No, it wasn't. You insisted the damage had to be contained."

"Would you have acted differently if I hadn't demanded discretion?"

"I wouldn't; that's why I use the plural. But it was a mistake;

it limited our resources and the scope of our response. In an all-out hunt, we would have drawn in the police and the army. After sealing the city and flushing the sewers, these bastards would have been history."

"Inside job?"

"You mean the government?"

She nodded.

"It would seem likely. At least, someone very high up."

"What would you do?"

Her choice of pronoun was telling. *You,* not *we.* Nikola sighed, his resolve strengthening. "Everything hinges on Russo. Is he alive? Is he coherent? The stakes are too high to ignore the possibility, however remote, that the answer to one or both questions could be yes. Without an insider's help, your chances of impeding eventual disclosure are almost nil." He raised a hand to forestall her comment. "I know you can probably cover your tracks as if nothing ever happened, or at least try to."

"Do you?"

"I don't know the details, but it's a matter of respect." Or the lack of it. That was the crux of the issue. "I would have made sure I could, and I have no reason to doubt you've not considered the eventuality."

"You mentioned insider's help."

That Odelle still kept part of her brain, regardless of her drowning thrashes, gave Nikola a glimmer of hope that she would remain predictable. "By elimination, your possible sources are limited to one. Forget about the idealistically committed; you can't bribe them. But there are a few mercenaries involved, and a large chunk of money may sway their loyalty. Among the hired help, there's someone with a face and name: Lukas Hurley. I doubt you can tempt him with money. If he's dead, he doesn't need it, and if not, he has too much already. But his honeypot is another matter. The fool joined the fray to bankroll a future with his Peruvian princess." He darted a glance at his timepiece, nodded once, and stepped toward the door. "I have a flight to catch. Can we meet this evening? I will have most of the information you're seeking by then."

She stared at him fixedly before pursing her lips and nodding. "Nine o'clock. Can you make it then?"

"I'll try."

chapter 36

||||

09:51

Adaptation, a trait shared by the San and Inuit alike, underlies success in otherwise harrowing environments. After a nap on his way to the Air Force base, a simple breakfast of cereal, juice, and tea while he waited for the pilot to ready his machine, a short flight from Washington to Chicago, and a pleasant drive to Kenosha—across the state border in Wisconsin—Nikola felt ready to tackle his next call.

Running the DNA of everyone involved in the Washington, D.C., sugar-cube fiasco through the federal database would have saved him many hours of painstakingly collating details and reading files, but it wouldn't have solved the riddle. It was now clear what the connection was between Laurel, Eliot Russo, and Araceli Goldberg. Yet the mystery remained, and Araceli's past was a good next place to search.

After collecting his rented car from the airport—an almost-new Kioshi Matador—Nikola drove north on Route 45 to Miner Street and then took 94 past Skokie Boulevard to the coastal road bordering Lake Michigan. Soon, the smoke of chimneys from another era, stretched and torn against a gray sky, became part of the fleecy canopy that hung over the lake and the fields.

Martha and Vance Brownell, the subjects at his next port of call, were different animals from the Coles—a similar phylum but a different class. In the ever-changing social tapestry of civilization's third millennium, class was no longer determined by birth, upbringing, or even money but by power—the age-old currency of rulers.

On the flight, eyes closed to ward off any attempt at conversation from a major sharing the cabin, he'd mulled the nature of power. Many years before, when Nikola still harbored hopes of redeeming humanity, a disenchanted political science professor and itinerant lecturer, Marcus Lassiter, had spoken to an audience of young people eager to discover the ways of the world. Power, Professor Lassiter had reflected, was about change, about forcing others to do what they would never have done of their own accord. And, like everything about our wretched species, change had its own mechanics. After reaching for his glass of water and moving it about without raising it to his lips, Lassiter had gone on to explain that the mechanics of change revolved around three tools: love, money, and fear.

The professor had carried on his monologue for almost two hours while his spellbound audience soaked in his words, at times laced with a left-wing touch carefully designed to delight his listeners. Toward the end, he'd offered a gem, one that Nikola had saved in his repository of useful data. Stability, status quo, and security—however illusory the security may be— and the possibility of losing these, floated to the uppermost layer of our fears in later years when most other dreads had been tamed into submission.

The Brownells were successful, professional, rich, and well connected. The retired couple—Martha, the ex-dean of a prestigious university, and Vance, an old-fashioned four-star general—didn't fear much. Now in their seventies, they had surrendered to the unstoppable ravages of time, had more money than they could ever spend, and their family had long since disappeared or climbed to respectable heights on the social ladder. Socially, they were untouchable, and threatening them with changes to their physical integrity or their life span was out of the question. If prodded, they could tap into the awesome power of friends and relatives.

As Nikola sped north, weighing how much Mrs. Brownell valued her peace and security, he relaxed behind the wheel. He read the names of the towns as he passed—Winnetka,

Glencoe, Ravinia—rolling the words over his tongue like wine, and he toggled the entertainment panel until he found music worth listening to. As a wistful oboe filled the car with the notes of Mikhail Kinsky's "Rhapsody for Steppes and Silences," the skies got wider and brighter, the horizon flatter and longer.

The previous day had yielded a precious puzzle piece: a corner, an anchor to which other pieces could be attached. Dr. Hulman had a prodigious memory after Sergeant Cox paved the way with a conscientious dose of the world's best oil: three broken fingers. With the help of the plentiful notes in a notebook jealously stashed away in his safe—with scores of other pads and agendas—the obliging doctor remembered calling a young man to Araceli's deathbed. He had nodded to the page in the agenda where he'd noted the man's name and address; pointing would have been difficult under the circumstances.

In retrospect, Laurel's father's identity was almost predictable, and Nikola could have kicked himself after reading the name in Dr. Hulman's spidery longhand. Laurel's adoption by the Coles and the identities of her natural parents explained the young woman's involvement—a relationship that Nikola could have learned at once had he ordered comparisons from the fugitives' DNA.

Damn! Araceli Goldberg had been Eliot Russo's woman, and heavy with his child.

Dennis had pulled the images of Araceli's last minutes from a film archive. Sobering. After the demonstration, when she fell before a trooper's well-aimed kick, Eliot, with remarkable political savvy, ran away. Afterward, when the good Dr. Hulman humored his dying patient by calling her absent lover, he refused to admit his paternity. A moot point now. The DHS had genetic material from both Russo and Laurel. Within a few hours, Nikola had a lab report confirming that Laurel was Russo's daughter.

Yet, in the family portrait forming in Nikola's mind, there were two figures in the shadows: one, whoever had stored Russo in the center of tank 913 in Washington, D.C., and, two, Laurel's still-anonymous benefactor. Number one's identity was slowly forming in Nikola's mind, and the emerging shape filled him with foreboding. Then there was number two, whose persona had to be inextricably linked to the subjects in the picture, but he couldn't figure out how or why. Nikola knew that as soon as he determined the *why,* a name would emerge.

To flesh out numbers one and two, Nikola had compiled a hand of playing cards, a list of names tied, however thinly, to Araceli, Laurel, and Russo—family, friends, relatives, and a few professionals like medical doctors and teachers who could perhaps shed a little insight into their lives. In Nikola's game, the Brownells were almost insignificant. The card they represented, if it existed, wasn't an ace but a little one in a side suit. Of course, in the endgame, when all the trumps and big guns had been laid down, the humble card they held might afford Nikola a missing trick and net him the contract.

As a student of human frailty, Nikola knew the richest depositories of treasure didn't hide in safes or vaults but in the dark recesses of wardrobes. Nikola frowned on coincidence, but the fortuitous discovery of a noisy skeleton lurking in Martha Brownell's wardrobe had given him a tool.

Before Martha's election to preside over Grimes University in 2036—an appointment she held until her retirement in 2047—she'd run the privately owned Paulson College for over twenty years. It was widely acknowledged that, under Martha's tutelage, Paulson had grown from insignificance into an elite institution for grooming young women with powerful or wealthy pedigrees.

After Martha resigned her post three years after Araceli's death—ostensibly to claim her rightful place at the top of academia—Candace Bishop, her second-in-command, had taken over as principal. Both had been Araceli Goldberg's teachers and mentors.

Seemingly intelligent people do the dumbest of things in the name of self-mortification, like writing diaries. It's well known that diaries are written for others to read, but only one degree of sublime stupidity can improve on committing compromising or even criminal events into the permanence of text: entrusting the data to the treacherous care of a computer.

Dennis Nolan had sifted through Paulson College's computer more as a pastime than to look for anything specific. Nikola had expected him to skim over Araceli's college record, perhaps noting a few peccadilloes, but Dennis was curious and loved to track archives with long roots.

Candace's diary, tucked at the end of a score of subdirectories, inside a calendar-making program but unaccountably accessed daily, was a sobering read. Martha had not left Paulson College of her own choice. Rather than meeting twice a week with the college's benefactors, Martha had been exercising Candace's husband, Edward, for the previous ten years on Mondays and Thursdays. In itself, the affair wouldn't have merited exposure but for a tiny detail: Martha and Edward loved to invite a few chosen pupils to share in the fun. To beef up her case, and before pulling the rug from under Martha's feet, Candace had secured the services of an obliging detective. The sleuth had compiled a bulky, graphic document brimming with acrobatic competence and bound to delight the vice squad. Instead of raising a stink, Candace had counseled Martha into seeking greener pastures and surrendering her post, but not before heartily recommending herself as successor—or else. A shrewd move, at odds with the recklessness of leaving the incriminating evidence on her hard disk.

After parking the car in front of the house, Nikola strolled past a well-tended lawn, breathing the tangy mid-morning air and eyeing the beds of pansies and marigolds. Pendulous figs, almost black with ripeness, hung from a generous tree. Nikola stopped to admire a small rectangular pond, its margins fashioned from old bricks. No faun with water spurting from its mouth or similar ghastly statuary but a simple rippling sheet carpeted with water lilies, broad and bright. To a side, a band of sparrows competed over a spray of bread crumbs in the grass. He paused at the door to tune his mind to the task ahead and pressed a brass button on the nose of a small lion's head.

"Good morning. Can I help you?"

Nikola appraised the starched uniform of a prim Asian woman. Outside old bondage books, he hadn't seen a maid's uniform in years. "I have an appointment with Mrs. Brownell." Nikola reached into his coat pocket and offered a card from an obscure government department but with his real name.

She stood aside to allow Nikola into the hall. "Please, wait here."

Nikola glanced around, taking in the art—a passable Mac-Tarvish oil on canvas of a stormy sea and a group of watercolors he couldn't identify. Subdued but expensive. Class. The room was a reflection of its owners—neat and with a tightly controlled atmosphere of wealth and orthodox good taste. A slight noise drew his gaze to the facing wall and a display of schiavonas, rapiers, foils, and a couple of smaller side swords. Underneath, a clepsydra—an ancient time-measuring device worked by a flow of water—whispered and clicked. Nikola stepped closer and peered at tiny cups slowly filling and emptying into larger ones. It wasn't a reproduction.

"Mr. Masek?" A tall thin man with the gait of the career soldier marched across the hall, one hand outstretched.

Nikola caught a glint of determination in his light-blue eyes and arrested a reflexive move to accept his hand.

"Let me see your credentials." Delivered in a measured tone, but an order.

Nikola produced a wallet and offered the ID he'd chosen for this particular errand without taking his eyes from the general. With a carefully combed-back mop of white hair and trim mustache, General Brownell didn't look a year older than sixty, although Nikola knew he was seventy-two. In khaki trousers, a dark-brown wool jacket, and tan loafers, he cast the imposing figure of a driver of men—an illusion, because General Brownell had never seen real fire besides the one blazing in the adjoining living room.

"What's your department's interest in my wife?"

After stowing away his wallet, Nikola squared his shoulders and straightened. "None, sir. Our inquiry concerns an alumnus of Paulson College, from the time Mrs. Brownell was the principal."

"Shouldn't you address the college authorities?"

"I would, sir, but it's a sensitive matter." He lowered his voice a fraction. "Terrorism. If possible, we want to restrict the matter to the highest levels without involving people who might not be familiar with security realities."

General Brownell stood even more erect. *There, you loved the "highest levels" bit, associating you with the patricians instead of the commoners. After the "security realities" line, I bet your ears rang with "The Star-Spangled Banner."*

"I see."

I doubt it.

"Please, keep it short. My wife is recovering from a long illness and she's not strong." General Brownell marched to a set of double doors at the end of the hall. The doors slid open, revealing paneled and tapestried walls flanking another lined with bookcases and a woman sitting in a wheelchair. Slender, with high cheekbones and silver hair held off her face with tortoiseshell pins, her sage-green shirt and matching trousers seemed to glisten and reflect the light. With a thick gold choker at her neck, she looked like an aging Egyptian princess.

"It will take only a few minutes," Nikola said.

When Nikola heard the door latching behind him, he approached Mrs. Brownell's wheelchair, which rested beside a gleaming leather Chesterfield sofa, and tendered another card.

She glanced at it and dropped it on a glass tray resting on a small side table. "Never heard of this department."

"We are attached to the DHS, dealing with sensitive matters."

"Bullshit."

"Pardon?"

"You heard me. I listened to the way you soft-soaped my husband." She glanced at a squat intercom resting on a sizable desk. "Nicely worded, but it won't do for me. What do you want?"

A change of tack was compulsory. Nikola stepped to the couch, picked the creases of his trousers between thumb and forefinger, and sat down on its edge, his eyes on Mrs.

Brownell's as he shelved his carefully prepared speech. He hated needless insults, and his sense of aesthetics cringed at addressing an intelligent woman like a dimwit. Nikola studied her face. She had a high, intelligent forehead and a predatory nose over full lips—too full to owe nothing to a surgeon's needle. An attractive face but not altogether pleasing—too sensuous, hinting at stubbornness and self-will rather than firmness or strength. This woman controlled her passions and never burned by any fires other than those of hate, worldly ambition, or anger.

"Are you done?" she asked.

"No." Nikola stared into her eyes for a few heartbeats, reached into his jacket's inner pocket, and drew out a flat device the size of a PDA. After flicking a switch, he waited for a line of red LED to flicker and slowly turn green before pressing a bar on its lower half. Satisfied, Nikola deposited the device with care on the table before the couch, where it continued to emit a faint high-pitched drone. She followed his movements and smiled but didn't offer any comment. "I propose a trade," Nikola began.

"What have you got?"

Nikola leaned forward and offered Mrs. Brownell a glassine bag with several snapshots inside.

She reached over, glanced at the first photograph through the transparent cover, turned it over, and deposited it on her lap. If the uppermost print had shocked her, she disguised her feelings with such mastery that Nikola couldn't spot any telltale sign. His respect for the old girl increased.

"And in exchange?"

"The life and miracles of Araceli Goldberg." He raised a hand to still her reply and complete the specification. "Not the college records; I have those."

She nodded, and a fine-boned hand rested over the glassine bag with the photographs before returning to the wheelchair's armrest.

Nikola stiffened when she glanced down and pressed a red button by the wheelchair's controls.

As if on cue, the double doors opened and General Brownell stepped in, turned, and slid the doors closed.

Mrs. Brownell handed over the photographs to her husband.

The general extracted the prints and examined each one until the stack played out. "The lighting is wrong, as is the choice of lens. Good resolution in the center, but a tad blurred on the edges. The composition is passable, though." After replacing the prints in the bag, he handed them back to his wife and stood still, as if at attention.

Mrs. Brownell's long fingers laced together over the photographs on her lap. "I fear this barter of yours is a little lopsided. You don't have much to offer."

"And you?"

"Oh, I have exactly what you want." She raised her face and eyed her husband, a smile, soft as candlelight, touching her lips. "Mr. Masek and I could do with a tot; would you join us, dear?"

General Brownell nodded. From a shelf between bookcases, he picked out a decanter and poured the amber liquid into three whiskey snifters.

Nikola relaxed, feeling suddenly at ease. He leaned back onto the tufted leather. The glass you drank whiskey from made a huge difference in its enjoyment. A tumbler was widely thought of as correct, and it was fine for ruining a good liqueur, in particular if one planned to desecrate it further with water and ice. He accepted the tulip-shaped glass and sniffed. Ambrosia.

A jet flew overhead, leaving in its wake a deeper sensation of quietness, broken only by the occasional creak of leather and the soft ticking of a carriage clock over the drinks shelf.

"Where did you get the prints?" she asked.

Understanding bloomed in Nikola's mind. He narrowed his eyes and sipped, letting the flavors develop over his tongue before swallowing. Life would be hugely pleasurable and so much easier with valid interlocutors. He opened his eyes and offered a small toast to Mrs. Brownell, ignoring the towering general back at his station by the door. A toast of recognition between equals. "Candace Bishop's computer."

She pursed her lips, sipped her drink, and returned the compliment with an almost imperceptible movement of her

248 carlos j. cortes

glass. Then she closed her eyes slowly, her free hand cupped over the photographs on her lap. "If you can copy her files, you can also have them erased, correct?"

Nikola nodded, enjoying the way she marshaled her thoughts along the line he'd surmised from her first question.

"And, to even matters, other files could be substituted. . . ."

Beloved, never avenge yourselves but leave room for the wrath of God; for it is written, "Vengeance is mine, I will repay, says the Lord." "I can see that would bolster my bartering position. Of course, our trade would depend on what you can offer in exchange."

For a long time nobody spoke, but they shared a silence, quietly sipping exquisite malt. The sensation of mental cogs whirring was almost physical. Over the fireplace, the portrait of a red-haired young woman in white muslin holding a basket of flowers on her lap smiled down on them. Bernice, their oldest daughter, now married to an up-and-coming senator, Frederic Maass, old money.

The general glanced in turn to Nikola and then his wife before nodding behind his glass. She turned to Nikola and cocked her head in mute interrogation, her eyes alive.

Nikola sighed. With a nod, he closed the deal and leaned farther back on his seat. To strike a civilized bargain in a civilized setting and with civilized people was almost too pleasurable to bear.

"Araceli Goldberg was a fine young woman," Martha Brownell stated, her head high and proud.

General Brownell, obviously weary of standing up, rescued the decanter and neared the sofa to attend the performance by Nikola's side.

"She was beautiful, and bright, but paled before the raw intelligence of her lover, Odelle Marino."

chapter 37

11:22

Everybody was free to take a walk, Tyler had said—keeping to the area framed by the cluster of buildings—as long as they donned blue overalls, wide-brimmed hats, and refrained from looking upward. The chances of being photographed by satellites was slim, but he didn't want to take any chances.

Floyd stepped outside the house, his feeling of uneasiness increasing. He breathed deep and dug his hands in his pockets. Lucky Laurel. She was still asleep after her night shift by Russo's side, but he hadn't managed a wink. Although Russo had recovered consciousness for only a few minutes, it was obvious his mind was in one piece. That could only mean Tyler and the others would make their move soon. The city had been sealed tight; that much he'd gathered from the stream of news blaring from the radio and frequent interruptions on TV. Whatever the plan, when they left the estate they'd run straight into the gauntlet the DHS had thrown nationwide.

He glanced around. Tyler had sworn they would be reasonably safe at the farm unless the DHS launched a house-to-house hunt. But Floyd shook his head in frustration. Going it solo would be tantamount to suicide; his biometric data would by now be lodged in the hardware of every officer's pad and squad car.

He stopped, glanced around, and tried to get his bearings by studying the different structures. A diagram set on a glazed frame by the house's entrance displayed a large property, almost two hundred fifty acres, ten times larger than when Tyler had bought it more than fifteen years before. It seemed the government had contributed a large tract a few years ago, but Tyler had not offered more explanations. Shaped roughly like an 8 and divided by a small river where the circles met, the business end was centered in the middle of the lower circle. Although most operations were automated, the farm was the livelihood of many people. But only Tyler and Antonio and his family lived within the compound enclosing the farm buildings. The workers, mostly from Chile, lived on the other side of the river, on the farthest edge of the upper part of the 8, in a row of cottages nestled by a two-story building, with labs built with subsidies from two universities. According to Tyler and Antonio, the farm was a "clean" address, widely known in farming and husbandry circles as a test bed of innovation, connected with ecological energy sources and autosufficiency—a good background to justify movements in and out of the area, and a sound alibi when stopped at roadblocks.

He took another breath and let it out, long and slow. Other than a cup of coffee, he'd had no breakfast. Dread gripping his stomach had prevented him from eating anything solid.

As Floyd breached the gap between two barns, he nodded to a man in overalls leaning against a wall with what Floyd thought was a knapsack strapped over his shoulder. Then he did a quick double take when he identified a mean-looking semiautomatic carbine attached to the strap. To defend them or keep them in? Floyd guessed it was the latter. Tyler was taking no chances and, in his shoes, Floyd wouldn't have either.

And then there was Laurel.

His marriage had been a fiasco from the outset. *So, what happened?* his mother had asked on one of his rare visits to the family home in California. *Nothing much,* Floyd had answered, but his mother had waited, hands on her hips. But there *had* been no real reason. No major drama, no yelling, just the feeling that the relationship had run its course. He could never picture Carol, his ex-wife, starting a family. The author of a syndicated column on high cuisine, she spent most of the year traveling to competitions and chasing the latest recipes from French gurus. True to form, she set memorable food on his plate when she happened to be around, but other than in her career, she didn't seem capable of taking responsibility. The loose relationship had suited him for a while, but one day he discovered he missed having children in the house and a dog in the yard. Whenever he tried to broach the subject, Carol would shrug. One day she walked away. The morning after, Floyd fielded a call from a woman with a beautiful suave voice, who introduced herself as Carol's lawyer. Between the two of them, they took him to the cleaners.

"Hello, Doc!" In jungle-green work trousers and a T-shirt that clung tightly to his padded frame, Antonio stepped over from one of the warehouses with his springy gait. At close quarters, his T-shirt was soaked, as were his trousers, and his face was shiny with perspiration.

Floyd nodded, marveling at the control Antonio had over his prosthetics. If his trouser legs weren't a tad on the short side, most people would miss the detail. They talked a bit about the weather. Then Floyd asked, "Where did you have your legs fitted?"

"At Brooke Army Medical Center's amputee-care facility in San Antonio."

"What happened?

"A rocket-propelled grenade."

"I've noticed the ease with which you move about. Those prosthetics are excellent."

Antonio nodded. "The army can be a bitch, but they pull out all the stops with amputees. These were the most sophisticated money could buy at the time. Ossur Power Knee, fused directly to bone. The limbs adjust their motion on signals from my brain and body. The feet have multiaxial rotation and anticipate movement."

"Powered?"

"Knees and ankles both. I'll race you."

"No way." Floyd grinned. "You have me at a disadvantage."

Antonio sighed and ran a huge hand across his face, his skin ravaged by years of unprotected exposure to the sun. He was about fifty years old—perhaps older, given his high forehead, which was clearly visible beneath a baseball cap. His nose was kinked halfway down and set off at a tangent; broken and badly set.

"Nice operation you have here," Floyd said.

"Yeah. These are the intensive piggeries." He pointed to the row of warehouselike buildings.

"What are our chances?" Floyd asked.

Antonio breathed deep, as if to deliver a lengthy tirade, then clamped his mouth shut as he shook his head. "Not good." Then he sniffed. "Let me show you the pigs."

Floyd nodded at the swift change of subject and followed Antonio to a twin set of doors that slid sideways when they approached, opening to a six-by-six cubicle with another set of doors ahead. Before entering; Floyd arrested his step. The floor was flooded with an inch of water.

"Well, go ahead." Antonio waved when Floyd looked back at him. "No other way in for visitors. You'll have to get your shoes wet. We don't want soil bacteria entering." He gave Floyd a gentle push.

Floyd splashed into the building. As soon as both men were in, the outer doors closed and the ones facing them opened with a gentle hiss. Obviously the setup worked like an air lock. The hangarlike building was enormous—endless concrete corridors flanked on both sides by steel pens and brightly lit with powerful lamps disappearing in a misty haze. The cacophony of grunts was deafening. Everything was wet.

"These are our guests. The pigs are constantly monitored and fed automatically. We control temperature through ventilation and water spray misting."

"You keep them wet all day?"

"At night we turn off the mist and douse the lights. They're delicate—in particular, pink-skinned animals like these. Here they don't have mud to wallow in and adjust their temperature, so we do it for them. Our systems are now replicated all over the nation, and I suppose the world."

The mist explained Antonio's soaked clothes. Floyd ran a hand over his face and eyed his moisture-laden palm; it was shaking. He pushed his hands into the overalls' pockets and fisted his fingers, the void in his stomach deepening. "What about dead animals?"

Antonio cocked an eyebrow. "What about them? Fortunately we don't have many."

"And the ones you do have?"

"We'd better get out of here," Antonio said.

Once outside, Floyd raised his face to the sun. "You didn't answer my question."

"Those other buildings over there house sow stalls and farrowing crates."

Floyd choked a sharp retort and glanced at three smaller sheds in the direction Antonio had pointed. So Antonio didn't want to talk about dead pigs. "I thought those were banned."

"Only in Florida and Arizona."

"Why the crates?" Floyd tried to remember what he'd read about the cruelty of sow stalls, where the animals couldn't move.

"Sows will often crush their piglets. In farrowing crates, we separate them in adjacent compartments. The mother can feed her young but not harm them."

"Hey, guys!"

Floyd turned to see Laurel hurrying down the lane. Dressed in similar overalls—two or three sizes too big and cinched at the waist by a piece of cord—she was far removed from the sorry figure he'd first encountered in the sewer. Even the wide-brimmed Stetson suited her.

"Having fun without me?" She drew level and threaded her arm through Floyd's, as if it belonged there. "I thought hog farms smelled." Laurel gave him a peck on the cheek. "You're all scratchy."

Antonio smiled. "Most do, but here everything is controlled. We send the manure from the piggeries into a sealed underground concrete pit. From there we pump it to those green tanks over there. That's a two-stage, low-solids digester. The smaller ones on the left are balance tanks, and the squat big guys are sequencing batch reactors."

Laurel gripped Floyd's arm harder. "Sounds complicated. How does it work?"

"It isn't, really. In anaerobic digestion, microorganisms stabilize organic matter and release methane and carbon dioxide."

The green tanks, Floyd realized, were much larger than they seemed at first—huge metal cylinders pierced by a network of large and small pipes and tubes.

Antonio continued his explanation. "The result is biogas—mostly methane and carbon dioxide, with a small amount of hydrogen and trace hydrogen sulfide."

"At Nyx we use plenty—" Floyd muttered, and then he could have kicked himself for his lack of tact at bringing hibernation into the conversation.

"Hydrogen sulfide? What on earth for?" Antonio frowned. "It's horrible stuff."

"It's one of the gases we use to lower patients into torpor."

Laurel must have sensed his discomfiture. "So you send the animals' waste to the digester and . . . ?"

"We pump pig shit and water into them, heat it, and leave it there to complete the process."

"You heat the shit?" Laurel asked.

Floyd reached for her hand.

"Right, to keep it around one hundred degrees Fahrenheit."

They walked slowly around the vast concrete area of the digester installation. Floyd reached to one of the insulated pipes and touched a valve. It was warm. "How long does the process take?"

"About two weeks."

Laurel laid her hand on the nearest tank. "So there is two weeks' worth of pig shit in those tanks?"

"That's about right."

Floyd followed Antonio's gaze. Past the tanks, in an open field, a large machine trundled, raising a cloud of dust. Whatever the beast was doing, it must have pleased Antonio, because he rubbed his hands and smiled.

"And the biogas? What do you do with that?" Laurel seemed genuinely interested to discover how the system worked.

"Once cleaned, we store it in the gasholder."

"That sphere?" Floyd eyed a huge white ball on stilts, set on its own in the middle of a grass patch.

"Right."

Through a passage between two piggery buildings, Floyd spotted Tyler limping toward them. He peered at his face, obscured by a large hat, but couldn't detect any telltale signals of alarm.

"Taking a guided tour?" Tyler nodded to Antonio. "I left a pager with Raul." He patted his shirt pocket.

"This is huge," Laurel said. "I still can't get over the lack of smell. I thought hog farms stank."

"We couldn't have gotten away with odors so close to town. The digester reduces most odors from the livestock. Antonio's spray system to keep the animals cool and clean does the rest. We contribute no odor, groundwater contamination, greenhouse-gas emissions, or pathogens into the environment."

Floyd glanced around. The void in his stomach had been deepening. He turned to Antonio. The man was staring at him, his eyes ablaze with a strange intensity.

"The doctor wanted to know what we do with our dead animals."

Tyler looked down and scoured the ground with the tip of his boot. "They're protein. We hack them to pieces and add them to the digester."

Laurel's fingers dug into Floyd's arm. The penny must have dropped.

"Prices for farm hogs are stable at $7.40 a pound, deadweight. These animals," Tyler nodded toward the piggeries, "weigh 270 pounds on average; that's about two thousand dollars a head, and a small tragedy when we lose any."

Floyd swallowed. "Look, Har—"

"In your shoes, the thought would have probably crossed my mind. After all, the DHS supposedly knows nothing about us." He glanced at Antonio. "If things got hairy, we could always throw you in the digester. Expensive meat, though." Then he looked straight into Floyd's eyes. "But it would have been a fleeting thought I would have discarded at once."

"Why?" Laurel blurted.

"I'm a better judge of character than either of you."

"I didn't—" Floyd felt heat creeping up his neck.

"Of course you did." Antonio smiled. "For months we planned how to spring Russo, knowing what the stakes were, not only for you but for the lot of us. Things have turned sour, but we're still alive and kicking, and the difference between them and us stands."

Floyd waited.

"I don't think the doctor understands," Tyler said.

"I do. Antonio is talking about honor . . . and I apologize."

Antonio's smile widened. "See, there's still hope."

"How many animals do you have here?" Laurel intervened, her voice weak.

"Four-legged, about fifty thousand." Tyler slapped Antonio and Floyd's shoulders. "And lots of the two-legged variety."

"Christ." Floyd ran a hand over his face. "I'm falling apart."

"Some call it shell shock." Tyler walked along the lane hemmed by barns and stores. "But the enemy must move soon, and until then we can only wait."

"This must have cost a fortune," Laurel said.

Antonio nodded. "It did, but most of it came from estate and federal government grants and supports. We've pioneered many renewable-energy production technologies. We also get money from universities. They run a few projects here, in a building lab on the farthest edge of the farm. Normally you would see a gaggle of guys and gals with lab coats puttering about, taking samples and the like, but we've declared the place off limits while you're here. Special cleaning and maintenance for a couple of weeks. They will leave us in peace for a while."

"So you've built this on grants?" she asked.

Tyler shrugged. "You can say that."

Over the rooftops of the farm buildings, Floyd spotted occasional flashes of heat lightning and wondered if there would be a storm. "What happens to the final wastes from your digestion?"

"There is none. The liquid can be used as a fertilizer. The

solid, fibrous part we use as a soil conditioner or sell it to make low-grade building products such as fiberboard. The final output is water."

"How autosufficient are you?"

"If you discount stationery, pharmaceuticals, and a few cleaning chemicals, totally. We have orchards and vegetable plots, chickens, rabbits, and a few cattle to feed us all. The crops in the fields are for the pigs."

"You mean all these fields are to feed the pigs?"

Tyler raised an eyebrow at Antonio, who grinned and waved to a concrete slab fifty yards away with two dark-green vehicles with four wheels on each side and without cabins.

"Not only the fields." Antonio chuckled. "Come over."

As they neared, Floyd assessed the contraptions to discover they were amphibious vehicles.

"What on earth is that?" Laurel asked.

"Transport. Argo Raptors." Tyler leaned to grip his knee and grimaced. "The weather is about to change again."

"Can't you get it fixed?" Floyd thought there had to be a good medical reason why Tyler endured so much discomfort.

Antonio had already climbed behind the wheel of the nearest Argo, and Tyler slumped on a bare wire seat by him. "Only by chopping off the whole thing and grafting on one of these." He patted Antonio's knee.

Floyd pretended to help Laurel climb onto the vehicle, his hands on her waist. She cocked her head as if she was taking a measure of his feelings and blinked to accept his ruse.

"It would mean years of surgery and rehab. So far, I'm managing," Tyler explained as Antonio maneuvered the Argo into a dirt track between fields of hay. They were headed toward a cottage nestled by the woods between the farm buildings and the fields they could see from Tyler's house.

"So far, he's going through hell," Antonio grumbled over the whine of the vehicle's electric engine.

They passed a cottage surrounded by a white fence, its windows lined with boxes filled to bursting with rows of crimson geraniums. A small woman was bent next to a row of wooden tubs fronting the porch. Red and yellow marigolds crowded the containers. She must have heard the gravel crunch, because she turned, waved a hand, smiled, and carried on.

"My house. My wife," Antonio announced.

Laurel gripped Floyd's hand harder. There was pride in Antonio's words. A vast garage with more than a passing likeness to a barn was attached to a side of the cottage, and Floyd spotted a man there—tall, preppy, and black—with a powerful athletic frame. Antonio followed his gaze and nodded. "Lester, one of my sons."

Both Antonio and his wife were Hispanic, but Floyd didn't comment, reveling in the texture of Laurel's hand. They were all silent for a while, Floyd's mind spilling out into the deep blue air as he considered that Tyler and Antonio had crafted a small miracle.

Antonio veered the Argo away from the track and into the woods, zigzagging between the trees. The light dimmed. Then the scene changed to a swamp worthy of the Everglades.

The smile faded from Laurel's face. "Holy—"

Antonio threw the Argo down an incline toward what looked like ground carpeted with grass around clumps of tall plants. Then the ground cover parted to reveal black water climbing to within inches of the vehicle's sill.

"It's a lagoon!" she said, drawing closer to Floyd and darting glances at the black water, as if she expected an alligator to raise its snout.

"A two-cell lagoon with a four-million-gallon capacity; all of five acres," Tyler explained. "This is the separated water after the digestion process. We use it for irrigation or flushing and other needs on the farm."

The Argo progressed slowly to enter a mass of vegetation. Floyd reached over to let a long leaf slide through his fingers. "And these are . . . ?"

"*Typha,* phragmites, and *Eichhornia crassipes*—water hyacinth," Antonio said.

"But where did you get all this water from?" Laurel asked.

"The river."

"You buy water?"

"On the contrary; they pay us." Tyler chuckled. "We return

most of the water we use, but much cleaner—almost drinking water."

"The plants?"

A nod from Antonio. "These absorb most of the nasty stuff from the effluent water—metals and the like. Every so often we run a floating reaper to keep the plants under control."

Floyd grinned. "Don't tell me, and you feed the plants to the pigs."

"That wouldn't be a good idea. These plants are fibrous. After drying, we shred them. A company buys the product to make insulation panels for buildings."

Tyler turned around as Antonio edged the Argo toward another incline on the pond's opposite side. "This is his baby." He patted Antonio's shoulder. "He dreamed it up and built it."

Once on dry land, Antonio maneuvered once more between tall trees to a clearing.

"Wow!" Floyd pointed to a row of huge hangarlike buildings covered in blinding white polymer.

"We pump the water from the lagoon into these greenhouses," Antonio said, glancing at Tyler and winking an eye.

Inside, the building looked like the hold of a gigantic space station but for the floor, which was carpeted in green. Overhead, a line of pipes held hundreds of arms capped with what seemed like lawn sprinklers spanning the width of the construction.

"Duckweed," Antonio said. "These plants further purify the water before pouring it back into the river, and, yes, these plants we feed to the pigs, with other proteins and feed-grain crops from the farmland."

Floyd frowned. "Proteins? I thought you only had pigs." A few yards away, the carpet of greenery rippled. Floyd looked attentively to discover that it rippled in multiple points. "What the fuck are you growing here?"

Tyler laughed. "Fish by the ton; also in the lagoons."

"And other things too," Antonio said.

"Go on." Laurel shook her head in wonder.

"When we dredge the ponds, we use the sludge, mixed with compost and some of the fibers from the water hyacinth, to raise worms. We also grow mushrooms, but those we sell."

After a sharp beep, Tyler slapped his hand to his shirt pocket and produced a pager. He toggled it, then pivoted on his heel toward the greenhouse's entrance. "Russo is awake, and he's hungry."

chapter 38

||||

17:12

After a long day punctuated by the absence of news of the breakout and an impromptu press conference convened without warning by Odelle Marino, Genia Warren left the office early and returned to her house for a sinful bath of piping hot water laced with half a jar of salts. Just before meeting the press, she'd joined Odelle outside the DHS conference room for a barrage of clipped instructions. *Make that orders,* Genia thought. After the farce, where Odelle had dangled her poisoned bait before the cameras, she'd marched past Genia, her head high as a galleon's figurehead, without so much as a glance.

On her way to the bathroom, Genia picked up a dish of crudités and a small bowl of the chocolate dip that Herminia, her resident housekeeper, had left in the fridge before adjourning to her cottage at the far edge of the backyard. Thus prepared, she abandoned herself to the caress of fragrant water up to her neck, while happily munching celery, cucumber, and carrot sticks covered in the dark sauce.

Thirty minutes later, Genia padded to her office, nursing a glass of Riesling. She tucked behind her desk and initiated her computer by staring at a dimple over its screen until its IR laser locked in and identified her iris's signature. On the rugged slate mantelpiece to one side of the room, a compact grandmother clock chimed six-fifteen. Unless something drastic developed, she should be able to clear her work backlog by nine o'clock and catch up on her sleep. She glanced at the plasma screen on the wall and decided against switching it on to watch Odelle's performance—and her own—before the cameras, scheduled for prime time.

Instead, Genia reached inside her bathrobe to a thin composite cord circling her waist and unscrewed the halves of its hazelnut-size clasp. Then she ran a hand over the smooth edge of her desktop communications pad, sliding the nail-size stick she'd pulled from the locket—an encryption and voice-synthesizer board, one of a matched pair—into a slot. The other was plugged into a similar machine atop Senator Palmer's desk. The encrypting algorithm driving the device was secure; the equivalent of a single-use pad, it changed every time both boards synchronized. Whenever she was in her house, Genia had the chip in its slot and returned it to its container around her waist when leaving.

Genia recalled vividly one evening at a Russian embassy gala dinner, almost three years before, when a stocky though distinguished Senator Palmer in an impeccable tuxedo had requested they dance. A little tipsy after two glasses of champagne and gliding over the polished timbers of the ballroom nestled in expert arms, she'd instinctively nodded when he'd whispered in her ear, "Would you change the way the DHS rules this nation?"

Two days later, after a routine appearance before a congressional select committee, she'd found a small box with a strange piece of lustrous black jewelry in her overcoat pocket. At first she took it to be a necklace, but printed on a flimsy paper folded inside the box were the instructions. Genia adjusted her bathrobe belt and smiled. She didn't believe in coincidences. Senator Palmer, besides having a brilliant mind, had an unerring sense of proportion. The waist cord fit her perfectly.

It was ironic that Odelle Marino had been responsible for their choice of code names. Years before, Odelle had boasted she had the perfect headhunter and enforcer: Onuris. It had taken Genia more than a year to put Nikola Masek's name to the moniker.

During their first communication via their ultrasecure line,

Palmer had suggested they use suitable code names. When Genia warned about Onuris, Odelle's freelance enforcer, Palmer had deadpanned, "I see. Then I'll be Ra." And, after a few seconds of silence, "And you are Horus, since Odelle is obviously Seth."

In the process of deciphering the meaning behind Palmer's words, she'd discovered his almost obsessive fascination with Egyptian mythology, and, from that instant, her respect for the aging senator's phenomenal intellect had climbed to new heights.

Seth, the Egyptian god of chaos, embodied the principle of evil. His war with Horus lasted eighty years, during which Seth tore out his rival's left eye. When Horus was pronounced the victor by a council of the gods and thus became the rightful ruler of Egypt, Seth was forced to return the eye of Horus and was killed.

On a first reading, the legend wasn't too insightful and not awe-inspiring, except for how the council of gods settled the winner.

Seth was homosexual and had tried to prove his dominance by seducing Horus. But Horus placed a hand between his thighs to catch Seth's semen before casting it stealthily into the river. Horus then spread his own seed on a lettuce leaf, Seth's favorite food. After Seth ate the lettuce, they appeared before the gods to settle their feud. The gods first listened to Seth's claim of dominance over Horus and called his semen forth, but it answered from the river. Then the gods listened to Horus's claim of dominance over Seth and called his semen forth. When it answered from inside Seth, Horus was declared the ruler of Egypt and Seth's fate was sealed.

After selecting a number residing in the tiny stick, the pad went through a flurry of beeps and pauses, until the boards synchronized when the receiver at the other end engaged the connection. Two letters, *RA,* scrolled across the pad's screen to stop on its edge, a cursor slowly blinking. Sometimes Genia would simply type a short message instead of engaging a voice link, but today they had too much to discuss. "The leak to *The Post* certainly stirred up a frenzy."

"And?"

"It's Seth's move. My guess is Onuris will lead the charge and . . ." She bit her lower lip, unsure if her emotions had altered her capacity for perception.

"Yes?"

"I may be mistaken, but I fear Seth thinks Ritter knows more than he does," she said.

"And how much is that?"

"Nothing."

"You reckon she'll send her goons after him?"

"Could be."

"Good."

Her stomach clenched. Somehow she'd guessed Palmer's reaction, a logical one.

"Can't be bad to have the enemy busy chasing illusions."

Silence.

"Unless . . ."

She closed her eyes.

"Unless the possibility disturbs you."

"He's a fine man, and an excellent professional."

Ra's metallic voice was preceded by a sound that could have been a sigh. "It does matter. I'm sorry, but if he's the professional you think he is, he'll know how to take care of himself."

Genia doubted it. If Odelle sent her shadier operatives to gauge the extent of Lawrence Ritter's knowledge, they would damage the man, perhaps irreparably. She was about to sever the connection when she remembered. "Thank you for the warning about *The Post*."

Silence.

"What warning?"

The task light over her desk seemed to flicker and dim as the atmosphere suddenly thickened. Genia stared at the tiny sliver of polymer protruding from her communications pad's edge: the foolproof security device that no hacker could bypass and no cryptologist could unravel. Their communications were secure; it was a byword in the business that paired boards could not be broken into. Only the NSA held the codes, supposedly guarded under far safer measures than nuclear weapons. Not safe enough. She drew in a long breath to calm her racing heart and had an insane urge to sever communications as the logic crashed in on her. Someone other than Ra had sent the message.

"Tell me about it."

When she finished, the line remained silent for a long time before the metallic voice echoed again. "What an interesting development."

"*Interesting* is not the adjective I would use. Forgive me, but you don't seem concerned. Your boards aren't as foolproof as we thought."

"Oh, they are. Whoever has managed to send the message is undoubtedly listening to our exchange now. Very clever. An old English aphorism is most fitting. If you can't beat 'em, join 'em."

"I don't follow."

"It's simple. Our friend has found out who we are from the government-issue signatures of these boards; otherwise, he couldn't hack into our setup to beat the system. To do that, he must have access to the highest reaches of the NSA. Yet that in itself wouldn't explain how he could be listening. I suppose he's obtained one or several of these boards and tinkered with them to slip a line of code to join in. Now our conversations are three-way."

"You mean he can listen to all government-encrypted traffic?"

"I don't think so. He must have obtained the code signatures of our boards from the NSA. These he can track, listen to traffic, and, if he chooses, join in the conversation."

"Who?"

"That's the question. Someone with resources, access to NSA software, who's a computer genius and willing to help, no doubt for his or her own agenda."

"Help us?"

"Yes."

"Are you sure?"

"As sure as I can be. Otherwise, we'd both be a foot under thick liquid, attached to a tube."

"And now?"

"A riddle. We could stop using our little setup, but I fear it would be like closing the stable door after the horse has bolted. Our friend out there knows who we are and what we're after. On the other hand, we could continue as if nothing had happened and insure that our silent partner knows exactly what we're doing."

"And dig ourselves a deeper grave?"

"Not at all. Tanks are a standard eight feet. We couldn't go any deeper."

Palmer's humor could be unnerving at times, but Genia's anxiety had subsided. It would be like walking on thin ice, but that's what they had been doing for months now.

Before the line went dead, Ra, the head god of Egyptian deities, chuckled. "Just a small point to cheer you—and our listening friend—up: Russo is conscious, coherent, and very pissed off."

chapter 39

||||

18:20

"This covers everything?" Antonio Salinas, Tyler's foreman, friend, and, Laurel suspected, associate held the sheet of paper Floyd had given him, crammed with lines penciled in neat script.

"Almost everything," Floyd said. "It's impossible to anticipate all eventualities, but I reckon these should be enough. That man," he nodded in the general direction of the corridor, "is climbing out of an unnatural state. He needs vitamins and glucose to boost his system . . . and lotion; his skin is very delicate. He will also need clothes. Loose cotton garments. You know the skin is the largest and heaviest organ in the body?"

"I know now." Tyler stepped over to them and reached for the list. "What's his status?"

Floyd's voice changed and took on a professional tone. "He's stable, drifting in and out of consciousness, which is excellent, considering his condition. As far as I can determine, he doesn't seem to be suffering irreversible brain damage, although he's understandably confused."

Lukas leaned against the living-room door frame, his face as reserved as usual. It was his turn to stand guard by Russo.

Laurel craned her neck over the sofa's back to face Lukas. "Is he awake?"

Lukas shook his head. Over the past eighteen hours, Russo had climbed back from unconsciousness several times, squinting in all directions before returning to his semicomatose state.

"Has he said anything else since last night?" Tyler asked.

"Besides asking for water and food twice, nothing," Floyd said. "Altogether he's been awake for fewer than thirty minutes, but the periods are lengthening steadily. I've told Laurel to talk to him whenever he's conscious, to explain that we've sprung him out of hibernation, that we're friends, and that we'll soon need his help."

"When?" Tyler asked in a sharper tone.

Floyd's features hardened. "I'm a medical doctor, not a soothsayer. In plain English, Russo has been more dead than alive for years. My guess is he'll recover quickly, but that doesn't mean overnight. It will take weeks of painstaking care to nurse him back to something resembling normalcy."

Tyler squared his shoulders. "Your guess?"

Laurel swallowed. The atmosphere had been tightening progressively over the past hours, and frayed nerves were starting to show. She turned and laid a hand on Floyd's arm. "We don't have weeks."

"Unless he stops fighting, *my guess* is he should be able to start communicating soon. That is, if he wants to talk."

"He will," Laurel said. "I've seen the hate in his eyes."

A vein throbbed in Floyd's temple. "Does he know who did this to him?"

"He must have a good idea."

"That's probably what has kept him alive all these years."

Antonio reached to take Floyd's shopping list back from Tyler and squeezed past Lukas. "I don't know how long it will take me to put this stuff together."

Tyler followed him, to reappear a moment later with a pack of beer cans he handed around before settling in his armchair. Like mountain cats parceling their territory, everybody had seized a favorite spot. Tyler and Antonio each had an easy chair—sort of an "I was here first" privilege. Laurel shared one of the two sofas with Floyd, while Raul and Lukas used the other. Laurel glanced at Raul's large frame stretched over the opposite couch, his head propped on one arm of the sofa and his legs on the other. He hadn't said much over the past hours and, in an unguarded moment, she'd seen him weep. *Bastien.*

On TV, a round of advertisements gave way to an old cops-and-robbers film.

"I'm sorry. We're under a lot of stress, but some things can be improved only with time. Time we don't have." Floyd licked froth from his lips and leaned forward. "My gut tells me Russo is gathering information about his surroundings and getting stronger by the minute, but we must give him time."

"I know I'm jumping the gun, but if he continues to improve, how long would it be until he can walk?" Laurel asked.

"Hard to say. He will need rehabilitation. Despite the computer-controlled muscle exercising, there's notable withering. With proper treatment, two to three months."

"Er . . ." Tyler rested his beer on a side table. "I recall you mentioning some people could walk straight out of hibernation, something to do with the squirrels' mechanism . . ."

Laurel nodded, inwardly cringing at the added difficulty. If they had to move, Russo would have to be carried.

Floyd jerked his head toward Tyler. The half-empty can crumpled in his fist. "When I asked how long the subject had been down, you mumbled, 'A few years.' No!" He stood and towered over Tyler, stilling his retort with an outstretched hand, beer trickling over his fingers and onto the floor. "I've had enough bullshit. Nobody said I would have to revive a wasted shadow while being hunted by half the country. That man," he pointed in the direction of the corridor, "is public enemy number one for someone powerful and ruthless. We're fucked. I mean, really fucked. A half-dead man, broadcasting sensors, and a bunch of amateurs. What else have you forgotten to mention?" By now Floyd was yelling.

On the TV set, the thief neared the window and reached for a black cord, intent on rappelling to salvation. Then the picture went blank, and everybody froze. After a few seconds, a field of blue filled the screen, soon fading to zoom in on a taciturn-looking newscaster holding a sheaf of papers.

The man glanced to his right before reaching a hand to his necktie. "Three days ago, on the evening of September twenty-first, several convicts escaped the Washington, D.C., suspension facility, aided by the terrorist organization responsible for the attempt on the Villiard power station. All security forces, the police, and the army have been placed on highest alert. DHS director Ms. Odelle Marino has recorded a press conference to be transmitted at eight P.M. Eastern Standard Time to update the nation and the media of the measures and progress of the investigation."

After a long discussion trying to speculate what the Department of Homeland Security mavens would have to say, they gathered before the TV set a few minutes before the scheduled press conference. The atmosphere was tense and gloomy. With the nation's full security forces gunning for them, the rules of the game had changed for the worse.

Lukas leaned on the door frame, also intent on the screen, but he turned often toward the faint beeps from Russo's cardiac monitors.

On the television screen, the scene shifted to a room crammed with reporters. After a short wait, two women entered from the right and stepped over to twin lecterns. The camera zoomed in on a tall, distinguished-looking woman in a smart gray suit. A caption scrolled underneath in bold yellow characters: *Odelle Marino, Director of the DHS.*

"As disclosed earlier," she started without preamble after adjusting a pair of gold-framed reading glasses, "several convicts have escaped the Washington, D.C., suspension facility. The breakout was contrived by a terrorist organization led by an unknown leader calling himself the Scourge of God, and it was aided by members of the facility's personnel. These terrorists were also responsible for the attack on the Villiard nuclear power station. All security forces, the police, and the army are following several leads, and we are confident the fugitives will be captured shortly." She slid her glasses toward the tip of her nose and peered at a sea of raised arms as if noticing them for the first time. After a pause, she pointed an outstretched finger to a lanky young man.

"Pete Robertson, *Washington Post*. Why was the breakout not announced earlier?"

Odelle smiled, as if the question pleased her. "Due to the breakout's extraordinary nature, it was decided to keep the matter confidential until a full assessment gave us a clearer picture of the dangers involved." She jabbed a finger toward a nerdy-looking woman fumbling with pencil and pad. Obviously, recording equipment had been banned.

"Cornelia Schaffer, *New York Times*. Are we to understand that security at federal suspension facilities is not as tight as it's claimed to be?"

Odelle turned toward the woman who had entered the stage with her, up to this moment off camera. "My colleague from the Federal Bureau of Hibernation is better equipped to answer that question."

The camera panned to a slightly shorter woman with blond hair pulled from her face by a slender circlet of matte material. Below the image a caption scrolled: *Genia Warren, Director of the FBH.*

"Security at penitentiary installations remains unimpaired." A faint smile, soft as candlelight, pulled at the edges of her lips. She turned toward Odelle and opened a hand in a small gesture, as if returning a ball.

The camera zoomed on Odelle's tense face. She seemed about to retort, but the moment passed. She scanned the crowd and pointed again.

"Maria Schmidt, *Boston Globe.* How many inmates are involved?"

"The breakout took place with the help of a federal employee," Odelle answered at once, "as well as medical personnel from a private facility."

"My question was—" the journalist protested, but Odelle silenced her with a gesture.

"I heard your question. This is a case where extraordinary security issues are at play. I will not give any details that may risk the investigation. Next." She pointed toward the rear of the room.

"Charles Douglas, *Los Angeles Times.* Can you tell us what progress has been made in your investigation?"

Again she smiled; it was obvious the question had been agreed upon earlier. "Several arrests have been made, including a family of Peruvian origin. On a raid by units of the DHS task forces, a quantity of explosives, weapons, and communications equipment hidden in the family's home was subsequently seized."

As if a bolt of lightning had suddenly energized everyone in the living room, all heads jerked toward the figure of Lukas, still leaning against the door frame, his face frozen in pain and horror.

On the screen, Odelle paused to stare fixedly into the camera. "No more questions, but I'll leave you with a statement: Extraordinary events need extraordinary measures and the use of unparalleled resources. I've been empowered by the President to offer an unprecedented deal." Once more she paused to stare into the camera lens, her stark expression softening. "The U.S. government will guarantee full protection, total immunity from prosecution—including that of the informer's family—and fifty million dollars to whoever can supply information leading to the capture of the fugitives. We believe some of the people helping the terrorists may have been coerced or brainwashed. This is a unique opportunity to step forward and serve your country." Odelle Marino's face set once more. "It's only a matter of time before all the terrorists are apprehended and brought to justice."

The image faded into a blue background with a string of numbers in white, throbbing across the center of the screen. A phone number aimed straight at Lukas.

Although Henry Mayer didn't count any gods among his friends, he believed there was a reason behind every event, even if that reason was not clear at the time. When, by two measly minutes, he missed his connecting bus to Tampa, he fumed for a while, dropped his bulky backpack on the concourse floor, and even considered kicking it with his new lizard-skin boots. But he thought better of it and slumped on a hard plastic bench to curse under his breath. There had to be a reason, a reason tied to his destiny.

Getting rid of his old persona had been much more involved than he ever thought possible. After acquiring supplies from a twenty-four-hour store, he'd unsuccessfully tried to rent a room at two small hotels, only to be turned away by the nose-twitching night staff. Eventually he'd managed to sway the attendant at a dingy hostel, suitably greased with five hundred extra bucks, into letting him in. After applying shears to his matted hair and beard, he shaved all hair from his head, except eyebrows and lashes, then soaked in an overflowing bathtub of hot water and liquid soap. It had taken three water changes before his skin lost all trace of ingrained dirt and shone pink. Then he discovered twenty nails a quarter of an inch long and hard as concrete. He swore and reached for a pair of sturdy cutters he'd sagely bought at the store. When he'd finished his toilette, he crashed on top of the bedcovers and slept most of the day.

Missing the bus wasn't a big deal, but Henry had arranged passage in exchange for work on the *Carolina*—a container carrier bound for Recife and loading cargo at San Pedro Sula, where he planned to jump ship. An otherwise costly trip for a song. After glancing around for signs threatening smokers with fire and brimstone, he fished a crumpled pack of Marlboros from his pocket and lit one, under the reproachful gaze of a lone police officer who must have kicked the habit recently and begrudged anyone who dared to light up. He puffed away contentedly and weighed his alternatives. He had money to spare and could grab a flight to Tampa and be at the docks before the *Carolina*'s appointed time to cast off. He could fly to San Pedro Sula, for that matter, and be done with it. But after years of rubbing coins together, he couldn't bring himself to be careless with money. He'd splurged on the boots, new jeans, a plaid shirt, a sage-green windbreaker, and a black Stetson hat. He'd needed new clothes. Okay, perhaps the boots qualified as a want, but he needed something on his feet, and he'd dreamed of narrow-pointed high-heeled lizard-skin boots. So he bought them. *Henry,* he thought to himself, *you've worked hard and gone through lots of shit and you deserve a superb pair of boots.*

Another alternative was to wait almost four hours until midnight to grab a night bus heading in the right direction. Eventually he would get to Tampa. There he could bum around and hope to find another ship. Fat chance. Yet as he drew a small tin box from a side pocket of the backpack and ground the butt inside—to the obvious chagrin of the police officer, who must have hoped to call him to order for tossing it on the concrete— he thought about destiny. Had missing the bus been a signal? Could it be that he wasn't destined to catch that bus or board the *Carolina*? It would be sobering to read in the next morning's paper that the bus had hurled itself from a bridge or down a ravine, coaxed by a sleepy or bungling driver. Or the ship. Damn ships disappeared all the time. Agreed, the run to Recife wasn't the Bermuda Triangle, but what if? Stranger things had happened.

Some people nurtured the most outlandish beliefs— reincarnation, homeopathy, or the flatness of the earth were only a few examples—but not him. Yet he routinely admitted to a higher office entrusted with drawing the destiny of every human being and ensuring nobody strayed from the set course. Definitely, there had to be a grand reason why he'd missed the Tampa bus.

Henry nodded, glanced toward the police officer, and produced his pack of cigarettes again. He made a mute offer

and, basking in the disgust shadowing the face of law and order, lit another cigarette.

He must have drifted or zoned out. When he jerked his
head, the shadows had shifted into dusk and the concourse
looked deserted. Then he heard a woman's voice, little more
than a whisper, and was about to reach for a small bottle of
water from his windbreaker's pocket when he caught "Washington, D.C.," then "facility" and finally "breakout." He
snapped alert, craning his neck toward the sound.

Smack in the middle of the concourse was a kiosk selling
soda, hot dogs, candy, and ice cream, staffed by a morose fat
man in a filthy apron, looking at a small TV hooked to one of
the booth's supports. Hefting his backpack, Henry neared the
stall, his eyes never leaving the screen where a woman with
something mean about her spoke to the camera.

"The U.S. government will guarantee full protection, total
immunity from prosecution—including that of the informer's
family—and fifty million dollars to whoever can supply information leading to the capture of the fugitives. We believe
some of the people helping the terrorists may have been coerced or brainwashed. This is a unique opportunity to step
forward and serve your country."

He didn't need to listen anymore. Henry turned on his heel
and walked purposefully away from the booth toward the
exit. Once on the street, he sought a secluded corner between
two buildings, lowered his backpack to the ground, and rummaged in its pocket. When he found his new cellular phone,
Henry flicked it open and keyed in the number he'd memorized. Now he knew why he'd missed the Tampa bus, and, besides, his fucking new boots hurt like hell.

20:45

"What do you think?"

Nikola glanced at the single sheet of paper with a list of Egyptian deities, the names appended after them, and the notes in red ink penned on the margins with Dennis's all-capitals print. At the bottom of the page was an underlined and circled address—a hog farm an hour away from downtown Washington, D.C.

"Fitting. The sewers and now this." Jean-Paul Sartre wrote of a category he called *the slimy*—a state with no fixed edges where existences flow into one another. *The slimy is a soft clinging, there is a sly . . . complicity of all its leach-like parts followed by a flattening out that is emptied of the individual, sucked in on all sides by the substance.* He flicked his eyes at the IR sensor atop the twin screens on his desk and searched the files. Mercenaries, misfits, cripples, and idealists, laced with indescribable doses of heroism. Then he focused on Senator Palmer's photograph. No general could hope for a finer army. "We wait."

If Dennis was surprised by Nikola's lack of enthusiasm, he didn't show it. He just sat taking measured sips from his Coke can. Finding out the fugitives' hiding place had been a feat of sleuthing worthy of Holmes. Dennis had collated all the bills, committee work, and any scrap of paper where Senator Palmer's name appeared, fused them into a database, and set to work. Eventually a strange thing emerged—a hog-farm-cum-research-station with a score of grants and land acquisitions promoted by Palmer. Running a check on the farm had yielded the names of two army veterans—one a national hero, and both crippled in action. A cursory scan of

Antonio Salinas's service file had produced nothing beyond heroism by the truckload. The other file belonged to Harper Tyler, Air Force Chief Warrant Officer 4, chopper pilot, with a damaged left leg, pensioned lump sum, and hog farm. But Dennis was thorough. He spotted a void: a full year between an entry in Tyler's service file and the date of his hospitalization.

After his return from a memorable cold lunch with the Brownells, Nikola had taken over Dennis's investigation, called in an old debt, and stopped over at the Pentagon for a brief glance at a top-secret file.

Harper Tyler had been in Iran. His commanding officer—now a retired colonel—was Major Scott Marino, Odelle's dad. Reading the top-secret file of Major Marino's exploits had been a revelation and explained Tyler's involvement. But Nikola couldn't understand why Tyler had not killed the bastard and been done with it.

Then Nikola had shuffled his painstakingly collated information and dealt hands for Odelle, Russo, Palmer—the puppeteer behind the scenes—and himself; a few cards he planned to play close to his chest. In this game, instead of concentrating on the hand held by the defense, he'd had to waste precious time and resources to figure out what cards Odelle held, to the point of openly cheating by lowering her hand and looking. Such a waste. Nikola checked the time at the base of one of the screens and sighed. He would need to get going for his meeting with her soon. He glanced at the can in Dennis's hand. "I could do with one of those."

Dennis nodded, stood, and went to the kitchen.

Nikola shook his head. He was now a part of the plot. There could be no redemption for him, and he smiled faintly when he determined that he didn't seek any. Perhaps a little fresh air, and light, and the warmth of the sun—he loved the sun licking his face—but no redemption.

He reached for the tumbler of dark liquid that Dennis handed over his desk, conceding that he really had made up his mind hours before.

"You still write to that lady in the Dominican Republic?"

Dennis nodded.

"Tell me about her."

"She grew up close to San Francisco de Macorís, in a neighborhood where they shared bones."

Nikola sipped his drink and waited.

"They passed a beef bone from one family to the other to make soup. After boiling it a few times, the water ran clear, but still they drank it. She says the liquid probably held on to the emotion of having been next to the bone."

"Is there a contract between you?"

Dennis nodded again. "I dash over whenever I can."

"And flesh her bone with a little meat, I hope." Nikola knew of Dennis's frequent trips; it was his job to know. He also knew the young woman's name and that his assistant's funds had helped her large family get on their feet with an industrial laundry operation catering to the hotels. *I didn't know about the peripatetic bone, though.* After panning the screens one last time, Nikola sighed. Contracts were important, and he was pleased to observe that Dennis understood their significance.

Allegiances, like most contracts, rested on implicit mutual trust but held a coiled device insidiously primed inside. If one of the parties failed, the other—providing it survived— was automatically freed from its oath. *Need to know* had probably been the most important words Odelle Marino had ever uttered.

After being ushered into Odelle Marino's inner sanctum, Nikola waited for her to dismiss George. "There are rules in tradecraft, and you've broken them all," Nikola said without preamble as soon as the door closed at his back.

Odelle Marino leaned forward a few inches, two white spots forming on her cheeks. "*Et tu*, Nikola?"

"Number one is trust," Nikola carried on, ignoring her outrage. "An agent must trust his handler to treat him above the rank of mushroom. By which I mean keeping him in the dark and feeding him shit."

Odelle frowned.

"Rule number two: A professional never mixes business and pleasure; it's a recipe for disaster."

She pointed her chin at him and leaned back in her chair. "Go on."

"When you sent for me, I asked you about the reason behind Russo's punishment. 'Need to know' was your reply, and a poor one at that because *I did* need to know. I needed to know this was your private vendetta against the man who seduced your girlfriend."

Odelle surprised him by relaxing further and allowing a faint smile to rise to her lips. "And, if I had told you, what would you have done?"

"Run as fast as I could."

"Precisely."

Nikola nodded. He'd surmised that much already.

"You know who is behind the breakout?" she asked.

Nothing would be gained from avoiding it, and much could be risked by lying; Odelle still commanded awesome resources. The trick when trying to rescue a drowning person was to avoid the mad thrashing that could drag you under too—a dicey maneuver in the best of cases. "Senator Jerome Palmer."

"You're sure?"

Her automatic question didn't deserve an answer.

"Why?" she demanded.

"Two reasons. Rumors about shenanigans in the FBH have been rife for ages, and Congress is weary of the ever-increasing power of the DHS. Naturally, that means you."

"Ever-increasing power? Our nation needs strong deterrents and stronger institutions. My mandate demands I protect the American people by removing criminals so our citizens can sleep soundly at night."

"That may be, but it doesn't include using the system for personal revenge. The second and weightier reason is personal."

She waited.

"Perhaps *personal* is the wrong adjective; the whole setup is almost a family affair. Jerome Palmer is Russo's father, and Laurel Cole is his daughter."

The wonder of DNA matching had paid off. In theory, a

DNA record was the data with the highest security rating, to protect the constitutional rights of citizens, and no data was more jealously guarded than that of government officials. But theories were fine for lengthy arguments and susceptible to hacking if you knew how, and Nikola—or, rather, Dennis— did.

"Palmer's daughter?"

Nikola peered into Odelle's dark irises, appalled at the hope lurking in their depths. To witness the most powerful woman in the country clutching at straws filled him with aesthetic horror. "No. Eliot Russo and Araceli Goldberg's."

For a long time neither spoke. Nikola reached for a chair and toyed with the idea of pouring a drink of water from the carafe on a tray in the center of the table, but he thought better of it after inspecting the fine bubbles festooning the liquid. Stale, probably from the morning or even the day before. Were he inclined to show off, Nikola could have written down what was to follow. Odelle would probably pick up the gauntlet and deal with Palmer herself. Blood feuds had to be squared within the family, and Nikola was an outsider. But such battles had a momentum of their own and, probably for the first time in her life, Odelle was in a defensive position. To stage a successful counterattack, a commander needed a cool head and warriors, not mercenaries. Machiavelli had argued the same point in *The Prince.* Sun Tzu, in his *Art of War*—the finest collection of strategy insights humanity had ever known—had made the same observation. Granted, mercenaries were fine soldiers, probably the best, but they couldn't be trusted to forgo their lives to defend ideals. Mercenaries demanded payment and a fair chance to enjoy their plunder. To take the next hill and face certain death so a remote commander could eventually claim his laurels needed honor, king, or country. Certainly stronger lures than money.

"You have evidence?" she asked.

A sensation of unbearable fatigue nibbled at the edge of Nikola's consciousness. "Family lines are easy to plot from the DNA database. Of Palmer's involvement, no. There isn't a scrap of evidence, and I doubt any could ever be found. He's an old fox, and a damn clever one. To flush out a wily fox, the final recourse is to torch the woods, and you can't do that. Before you attempt to grapple with a senator, you'd need the President's sanction. A sanction you will not get without hard evidence, and, again, there isn't any."

"Do I detect a certain admiration for the man?"

Overestimating an enemy meant wasted time and resources, and underestimating it could be suicidal. Nikola believed wisdom resided in correctly assessing situations or the enemy's strengths and weaknesses. The mean: the middle ground Aristotle referred to as virtue. "No. No admiration. Respect."

chapter 41

||||

22:18

"Pet. No calls." A thin bar on her communications console flickered from green to red. Odelle peered into the retinal scan atop her computer screen until it locked. Then she ran her fingers over a laser keyboard embedded in her glass desktop and called up the building's security center records, entered the date and the time span she wanted, and waited until a menu scrolled across with a list of available recent digital recordings. First she selected the garage cameras, and the screen split into four smaller rectangles: two general views, the access ramp, and the area before the elevator bank.

Once she located the section she wanted, Odelle followed Ritter's car as it entered the garage at 05:16. She noted the choreography of his security detail. The man adjusted his ridiculous beret and stood by the bank of elevators, unmoving, without fidgeting or glancing at his watch. She zoomed in on his face and caught a slight puckering of his lips, as if he was weighing a thorny issue. After a few minutes, three cars slipping down the ramp appeared on the top left quadrant of the screen. The motorcade maneuvered through a wide corridor to stop at an open area before the elevators, where Genia Warren alighted from the middle car. When Ritter leaned over to adjust the neck of her blouse, Odelle froze the image before advancing the scene in slow motion. She zoomed on his lips, moving like dragonfly wings. *Clever.* Ritter had likely warned Genia about the probable reason for the impromptu meeting. Odelle closed the views, returned to the menu, and selected the recording from the cameras in the elevators. She watched the scene, ran the audio, and once more closed the file.

After keying in a later time, she selected the recording from her executive elevator and ran it forward until the pair entered the car after their tumultuous meeting. Suddenly the screen went black. Frowning, Odelle stopped the image and backtracked to the lightning-fast gesture, to analyze the recording in slow motion. Ritter had removed his beret and draped it over the camera. *What had he passed on to Genia? What couldn't wait until they reached the garage?* No, she corrected herself: At the garage, they'd meet their respective security details and then board separate cars. *Still, what couldn't wait?* Suddenly the image returned and Ritter was adjusting his beret. Genia looked dazed. Then her lips moved. Odelle paused the recording, went back to the moment when the image returned, and hiked the volume.

What was that?

A short pause.

Heroic gestures have the strangest effect on me.

She ran the digital recording twice more, noting the short exchange as Genia exited the elevator car, far too feeble to be registered by the microphones. *It can't be.*

"Pet, security."

Two clicks and a low-frequency buzz. "Sergeant Oscar Sanchez."

"Who is in charge of recordings?"

"Pardon me, ma'am?"

"Who staffed the screens this morning?" She changed tack. "The cameras?"

"Oh. That would be Agent Cossio."

"Have you registered any incidents, camera failures, or glitches in the elevators?"

"Yes, ma'am. Er . . . this morning there was a—"

"Has anyone studied that tape?"

"Agent Cossio filed a report."

"That's not what I asked," Odelle snapped.

"Well, Agent Williams has run the tapes several times and—"

"Is he on duty?"

"Well, yes, bu—"

"Thank you, Sergeant. Send Agent Williams to my office at once."

"Yes, ma'am."

Odelle killed the line, paged floor security, and told George Wilson, her aide, to let Williams through.

In fewer than five minutes, a nervous young man stood before her desk, looking ill at ease. She kicked her chair back a foot and waved a hand to Williams. The young man swallowed and walked around the table like a lamb to the slaughter. Odelle ran an eye over Williams and fought back a smile. *You're thinking I'll order you to service me on your knees?* Just for the hell of it, she stared into his ridiculously young face. The guy was practically quaking.

Odelle nodded to the oversize screen on her desk. "Have you seen these images?"

After an audible sigh, Williams croaked, "Yes, ma'am."

She ran the recording to the point where Ritter covered the camera, then she hiked the volume as high as it would go.

"Have you examined this recording before?"

"Yes, ma'am."

"Why?"

"I . . . er, there was a report filed by the morning staff. They thought the camera was broken."

"Have you analyzed the sound? What's going on there?"

Silence.

Odelle turned to Williams, whose face had acquired a healthy reddish hue. "Out with it, son. What's happening in that elevator?"

"They're . . . They're making out. I mean—"

"I know what you mean, Mr. Williams. I wasn't born yesterday." Then she rewarded the young man with a thin smile and waved her hands at him, as if shooing chickens. "That will be all. You've been most helpful."

When Williams left her office, Odelle leaned back in her chair and stared at the black surface of her computer screen until it blurred. *Making out.* Just as she thought, but . . . couldn't it wait? Her mind flew to another elevator—at the Atlanta Marriott Hotel, a sixty-eight-story obelisk—and a memorable ride to the roof terrace, a finger firmly pressed on the door override. No matter how many times the elevator stopped, the doors refused to budge. Making out in an elevator—of course she knew what it meant.

Outside, the clouds must have parted, because a sudden beam of moonlight subdued by tinted windows caught her eye. Ritter and Genia's behavior, however unprofessional, didn't even count as a misdemeanor in an age where interdepartmental personal relationships had stopped being frowned upon, thanks to the damn Constitution. She closed her eyes and ran their earlier meeting through her mind, as her stomach knotted with mounting spasms of badly repressed fury. They had been playing her like a fool. For an instant, she entertained the idea of reaching for the phone, giving an order, and spying through a little hole as the bitch and her lover swallowed green hoses. But it was only wishful thinking. Unfortunately, the pair was too high up in the federal service, and there were limits to what she could do. For endless minutes she seethed. *What do you know about loss and longing?* Then Odelle straightened with a jerk. Perhaps she could teach Genia Warren the meaning of loss. She rubbed her hands—suddenly clammy—over her skirt and rolled her chair to the desk.

"Pet, George Wilson."

It was time for a counterattack.

chapter 42

23:20

The lights flickered once, went through a series of erratic hiccups, and faded. A choked cry echoed from the end of the corridor. "What's happened?" Laurel's voice ratcheted high.

"Damn generator!" Antonio shouted. He stood amid a rustle of paper as the screen of the cellular phone flared from its cradle on the mantelpiece, bathing the room in ghostly light before it, too, died away. "I thought you'd topped it up," Antonio complained.

"Sorry, it must have slipped my mind." Tyler's voice issued from the direction of the door. "I'll fix it." He turned toward the room where Laurel stood guard by Russo. "Don't worry. I can see lights on in the farm buildings. There's no danger."

"I'll come with you." Antonio's voice. "Where's the flashlight?"

"Right here, in the hall."

Floyd followed the sounds as they left the room, blinking to clear dancing lights before his eyes in the sudden pitch darkness. Somewhere to his left, leather creaked, followed by the rustle of rubber-soled shoes as Lukas stood. The man had not uttered a word since the TV announcement hours before. He'd sat on the edge of a sofa, his face set in a semi-catatonic expression, his eyes unfocused. At first, everyone had tried to mouth comforting words and offer a glimmer of hope: Once Russo revealed the truth, they would have to back off Lukas's woman and her family. But the promises had sounded hollow and unconvincing. Lukas didn't react, and after a while they gave up and left him alone. Faint crunchy treads sounded on the gravel outside. From inside the house, a faint high-pitched sound echoed—the power-failure alarm of Russo's cardiac monitor. It would continue recording for thirty minutes, its screen doused to conserve energy.

Floyd made his way over to the living room's door, panning an outstretched arm before him like the feeler of an insect.

"I'm checking on Russo," he said over his shoulder.

Lukas, somewhere in the living room, didn't answer. With a shrug, Floyd stepped into the corridor, dimly lit by a sliver of moonlight from the open door.

At the end of the corridor, the scant light gave way to a thick penumbra. The beep sounded louder. Floyd reached ahead of him, caught the tip of his fingers on a surface laid at an odd angle, and pushed the door ajar.

An instant before bare arms wrapped around his neck, he sensed her scent—a mix of the unimaginative strawberry shower gel they had all been using and her skin. "Are you sure everything is all right?" Her voice wavered.

"I checked; there are lights all over. It's only the house." He understood her nervousness. His first thought had been that they were under attack. Then her mouth sought his, and Floyd closed his eyes to chart the moment and store it away in all its intensity for future reference. Laurel's body adjusted to his, and Floyd marveled at the uncanny perfection with which her shape seemed almost purposely made to fit his body.

Then the lights flickered and came back on at full strength.

Laurel chuckled and drew away from Floyd. "Saved by the bell."

"But, madam, in my condition—" Then he froze. The day they arrived at the farm, he'd been out with Antonio, stretching his legs and looking around. In a shed attached to the house were stores, timber, snow gear, and a generator, a powerful twenty-horsepower Honda. He pictured the brightly painted machine hooked to a five-hundred-gallon fiberglass tank, enough to last a long winter. Topping up? The generator didn't need any topping up. The generator was a backup for emergencies. Floyd remembered Lukas and the cell phone nestled on its charger atop the mantelpiece, and something icy coursed through his veins. Tyler had arranged the blackout as a ruse, to trick Lukas into—

"Come." He tendered a hand to a frowning Laurel as the front door opened and heavy treads echoed down the corridor.

At the hall, they almost crashed into Raul as he barreled down the steps, somehow roused from his sleep.

When they reached the living room, Antonio and Tyler were already there, standing in the middle of the room and staring at Lukas, stationary by the window.

"I may be an idiot, but I'm not crazy," Lukas said in a strangely detached voice.

Tyler nodded to Antonio, who neared the fireplace, peered at the cell phone, and shook his head once.

"Odelle Marino's offer is a trap; even a child can see that. Our only chance—and that includes mine and my family's—rests with Russo's capacity to testify. Besides," Lukas glanced toward the cell phone, "I bet the fucking thing doesn't even work."

Floyd neared Antonio and Tyler without letting go of Laurel's hand and stared, dumbfounded, at the sorrowful Woody Allen look-alike by the window. Raul edged around them and slumped on a sofa, his eyes never leaving Lukas.

"But it occurred to me we could use her offer to our advantage," Lukas continued. "You don't need to disclose your plans. Just tell me what to say when I call that number."

Tyler paced over to Lukas and towered over him for an instant before slapping his shoulder, making the shorter man wince. Then he turned to the others. "I propose a war council." With that, he marched to a corner bookcase, removed a few books, tweaked something that produced a few clicks, and returned to the center of the room, a device the size of a small book in his hand. "Communications," he explained.

Antonio reached to his neck, pulled out a glossy black cord, fingered a rounded object threaded on it to recover a tiny plastic sliver, and slotted it on a side of Tyler's device.

"Who are we calling?" Laurel asked.

"That's irrelevant," Tyler answered. "What matters is who will be listening."

day five

||||

Purgatorio, Canto XXII: 30–32
Indeed, because true causes are concealed,
we often face deceptive reasoning
and things provoke perplexity in us.

The Divine Comedy, DANTE ALIGHIERI

chapter 43

||||

06:45

Although their brainstorming had lasted until late, Floyd
was already up at dawn, soon joined by everybody else. He
insisted Russo be moved from the den at the rear of the house
to the living room. "I've withdrawn the last of the sedation."
He nodded to the sofa they had moved to face a wall with the
TV panel. "Let's make him comfortable on the couch. Our
talk and the TV chatter may reassure him this is not Hypnos
or the DHS."

Once Floyd had removed the lines tethering Russo to the
IV stands—but kept the intravenous ports in place—Raul
hefted the emaciated figure with the same care he would
have a baby and carried him to the living room. At the couch,
they propped Russo on cushions while Floyd once more secured a bag to his penile catheter and reconnected the IV
lines. Then he motioned with his hand for Lukas to lower the
blinds and switch on a low-wattage lamp in a corner.

While Antonio rustled up a fresh pot of coffee, the others
dragged furniture around to compensate for the new arrangement and stopped to hear a news announcement: Congress
had launched an inquiry into the breakout. Genia Warren, the
FBH director, and Odelle Marino, the director of Homeland
Security, had been subpoenaed to appear before the congressional select committee overseeing the penitentiary system
in two days.

Laurel sat on the edge of the sofa at Russo's feet, absently
rubbing her hand over his alien-looking toes, bone-thin and
sans nails.

"They won't grow back, you know," Floyd said.

"Why not?"

"Prolonged immersion in the fluids softens keratin. Nails continue to grow at a good clip, perhaps an eighth of an inch a month. With the subject's spasmodic movements within the protective net, nails catch and tear from their bed. Although the nails continue to grow for a time, they can't anchor to a softened bed. The new stumps catch and rip. After a few years, those in suspension lose the capacity to regenerate nails."

"And their hair?" She unconsciously reached to her head. It felt funny, the stubble catching on the palm of her hand.

"That's a different issue. Some people retain follicular activity and others lose it."

Tyler neared the peninsula on the kitchen side and grabbed a mug of coffee. "Antonio and I will leave shortly. I suggest you take it easy for the rest of the day and try to sleep." He turned to Raul. "You were up all night."

Raul stifled a yawn and nodded.

They had agreed that phone calls or any other means of communication from the house were an unnecessary security risk. It seemed Tyler had considered all eventualities. After using the Squirt transmitter of his Metapad twice the night before, he had decided to stop using it at the farm. It was supposedly safe, but he didn't discount the possibility that repeated use could be detected. Every day, Tyler and Antonio had gone on errands, using the travel as their excuse to send and receive expensive messages: expensive because no two consecutive texts could be beamed anonymously from a single m-phone.

It made sense the DHS would pay special attention to traffic from m-phones. Specially designed for teenagers, m-phones were available at vending machines—cheap at two hundred bucks each—and were sealed disposable units with no other feature than about a month's worth of local messaging; they were useless for long distance or international. Once used for a single message, Tyler ran each phone through an industrial bone-meal processor and dusted the resulting powder in a septic tank to join the house effluent and the pigs' waste. Laurel followed Tyler as he pocketed the Metapad he'd taken from the bookcase the night before and thought that, in this instance, the communications Tyler had to make would involve more than short messaging.

After Antonio and Tyler left, Lukas and Raul went outside to stretch their legs. Laurel nestled by Floyd, their couch angled between Russo's and the TV, which was showing two human mountains crashing together in a sumo-wrestling championship.

Floyd draped his arm around Laurel's shoulders and drew her to his chest. "What's next?"

"I suppose Tyler will come up with a plan to move Russo in the next few days to a place where he can make some sort of declaration."

"But he can't speak."

"Can't or won't?" Laurel asked.

"What do you mean?"

"I've caught him awake once or twice, his half-closed eyes following me around the den as I checked his vitals. I think he could have said something but chose not to."

"And Lukas?" Floyd asked.

"What about him?"

"How can we use his offer?"

"My take is that Tyler will make his contacts and structure his plan today. When he's ready to go for broke, he'll ask Lukas to contact the DHS, probably this evening or tomorrow, and give details to send our enemies like a pack of wolves in the opposite direction. That's what I would do, anyway."

"Makes sense. Ever thought about the identity of whoever planned the breakout?"

"Many times. It has to be someone high up in government. Probably a group."

For a while neither spoke. Floyd took one of her hands and kissed the tip of each finger in turn. She peered into Russo's placid face. He was awake and sentient, easy to determine after the previous days.

Unlike the common pattern of average sleepers, Russo thrashed and moaned constantly in his sleep, his brain probably racked by nightmares. He reverted to immobility only in wakefulness. Floyd had suggested they prepare a quart of watered-down broth, and Laurel had pushed a straw down the side of Russo's mouth from time to time when his breath and heartbeat steadied. Then, although Russo didn't seem to move, the level in the glass did. His body wouldn't hold anything solid, not even soft foods, but Russo's ability to process salty broth was a giant leap to jump-start his digestive system—a critical step toward his recovery.

Sucking required a conscious effort, however feeble. Floyd had also removed all traces of sedatives and the IV lines but kept the pulse monitor clipped to one of Russo's fingers, its volume turned down to a weak blip, its tempo now steadily accelerating as Russo probably sank back into his dreams of cold horror. At intervals, Floyd had drawn a few drops of blood from a port on Russo's hand to monitor his SATs—the oxygen levels in his blood. After such a protracted time relying on mechanical respiration, Floyd was worried about Russo's lungs' ability to provide enough oxygen to his body.

"Will he remember?" Laurel asked now.

Floyd didn't answer straightaway but drew her closer. When he spoke, his voice sounded strangely muffled. "We have different types of memory. Procedural memory is where we store functions, like walking, laughing, how to use a knife and fork, or how to perform mechanical tasks. A singer doesn't think about singing when he sings, or a driver how to adjust to different flows of traffic when he drives. If he had to, his responses would be too slow and would cause an accident. Then we have semantic memory to store facts: What is a book? What are garters? What is a keyboard?"

"So, in semantic memory, you have the clue about what a keyboard is, but the ability to use it resides in your procedural memory?"

"More or less. Then there's episodic memory, the most volatile, residing principally in the frontal lobes of the brain. Picture episodic memory like flypaper—a strip of material with two critical properties: area and stickiness. Over time, the flypaper surface crowds with flies. As its coating becomes less sticky, some flies drop and make room for others, but the new ones don't adhere as strongly."

"But I thought the capacity of our brain was almost unlimited."

"Almost, but like any other system, the brain deteriorates with age. Our brain shrinks at a rate of one percent a year after the age of thirty. Granted, there are one hundred billion neurons packed into our three-pound brain, constantly sending and receiving signals, but over time the signals weaken."

"And we lose our capacity to remember?"

"It isn't as simple as that. Fortunately for Russo, the frontal lobes are the ones that shrink earlier and faster. There's where our capacity to recall events lies."

"You mean he will eventually forget his ordeal?"

"Not totally, but it will become hazy and, I hope, bearable."

"I remember."

They both turned to Russo, and to a voice so ragged it seemed like an old recording. His face was serene and his eyes were closed, though his heartbeat raced, but the words had come from him. Laurel shifted her legs to sit straighter.

"Who are you?" Russo's lips moved but he didn't open his eyes.

"He's Floyd Carpenter, a medical doctor and hibernation specialist from Nyx, a corporation offering commercial hibernation services. I am . . ." The surreal nature of her relationship with Russo suddenly crashed down on Laurel. "I am a lawyer."

"Have I been released?"

Laurel glanced at Floyd. He nodded once. "No. We sprung you out."

Russo's head lolled in their direction, and the line where his eyelids met widened a fraction of an inch. After so much darkness, even the dim light of a floor lamp on the other end of the living room and the TV panel's luminance must have seemed painfully bright.

Floyd stood to step out of the room and returned moments later with a pair of sunglasses. "I noticed Tyler kept a pair in the hall drawer." He leaned over Russo and slipped the sunglasses on.

"Who is 'we'?" Russo asked. In dark wraparound shades, Russo's alien appearance deepened. His hand reached to his crotch and seemed to scratch, although Laurel wasn't sure if his fingers were attempting to relieve an itch from the catheter or trying to ascertain if other parts of his anatomy remained unimpaired.

Over the next thirty minutes, Laurel recounted in broad strokes their scheme and some of the events that occurred after they broke him out of the Washington sugar cube. Throughout the monologue, Russo didn't move much and she couldn't be sure if his eyes were open or shut, but the beep of his cardiac monitor remained strong and steady.

"Why?"

"To prevent the DHS from doing what's been done to you again."

"Who are you?"

"I told you: a lawyer."

Russo made a wry movement with his mouth, as if trying to erase an unpleasant taste. Laurel stepped over and slipped the straw from the mug of broth between his lips. He made a face. "Water . . . please?"

After fixing a glass of water so Russo could suck an inch worth through the straw, Floyd withdrew it and patted his parched lips with a moist towel. "Too much and it won't stay down," he admonished.

Russo's response was directed to Laurel. "I've asked twice who you are, and all I get out of you is your profession. You are indeed a lawyer."

"Well, thank you."

"Should I ask again?"

"I'm your daughter."

Russo's face tensed and the beeps from the monitor increased in pace. "I have no daughter."

"I agree, but you impregnated Araceli Goldberg, and she gave birth to me."

"She died." His weak voice came out as dry as a wasteland.

"Not before giving birth." Laurel clenched her fists. "You denied paternity to the doctor, but that's a moot point. Things have changed, but not the infallibility of DNA matching."

"Do you recall awakening at intervals?" Floyd interrupted, obviously to change the drift the conversation was taking.

For a while Russo didn't answer. "After the first time, I decided it must be a dream, a recurring dream. I refused to accept that it could be real."

"An unconscious decision that shielded your mind from disintegrating," Floyd observed.

"Taking notes for a paper, Doctor?"

"Now that you mention it . . ."

"And you say you've never met the person who planned the breakout?" Russo asked, his voice gathering color.

Laurel shook her head. "No, we never met."

"I suppose the old bastard can be persuasive."

Laurel exchanged a quick glance with Floyd. "Do you know his identity?"

"If, as you say, you are my daughter, he's got to be my father: Senator Jerome Palmer."

"Senator Palmer? Your father?" *My grandfather?*

"It runs in the family. Jerome Palmer was earmarked for political greatness." Russo paused. "When in his sophomore year he *impregnated,* as you said, his high school sweetheart, his father tried to force an abortion. My mother was young and silly but high on ethics, and she refused." He stopped and breathed deeply. "So your grandfather arranged an adoption. I found out only in my late twenties, by a stupid coincidence." He paused, obviously exhausted by the effort of speaking. Floyd was moving to his side when Russo continued, his voice barely above a whisper. "I met him once, to spit in his face and tell him what a bastard he was, but it was ironic. I'm no better."

chapter 44

||||

11:10

A harried woman straining to untangle two leashes—one holding a vociferous toddler and the other a playful puppy—blocked the entrance to the bank. Nikola paused, sighed, and stood aside while the mother got her act together. *I can't be all bad. Wasn't it W. C. Fields who said, 'Anyone who hates children and animals can't be all bad'?*

Nikola eyed the pretty brunette and even stole a quick look at her pert, freckled breasts when she bent over the dog. But he had to concede he didn't qualify, hate being a burning passion better spent on worthy enemies. No, Nikola was indifferent to brats, although he found the mechanics of producing new ones a challenging exercise if addressed with curiosity and a zest for innovation. With a last assaying glance at her departing derriere, he mulled that, innovative or not, someone must have had a hell of a time, perhaps someone yearning for that woman at this precise moment.

He sighed and reflected, not for the first time, that he was alone not because he had chosen to be but because every turn his life had taken had ensured it. His was a different order of mind. Nikola had never tried to hide his intelligence but had attempted never to show it off or point it directly at anyone. Lesser intellects immediately felt threatened, and his equals didn't need the advertising; they recognized it at once. Nursing a great intellect was like owning a precious watch, he'd often thought. When Elisabeth Schwarzkopf, probably the twentieth-century's grandest coloratura soprano, was arraigned before a court of victors at the end of World War II to answer charges of collaboration, she had been heard to state that she performed only for the elite. "For whom else could I sing?" she answered to the panel of judges. Indeed. Only the elite could understand the breathtaking beauty of her voice as she caressed Mozart's lieders.

An avid reader since the age of two, according to his long-deceased mother, Nikola had never understood the habit of hoarding books, except dictionaries and perhaps an encyclopedia. Books were made to be read and stored in the vast repository of a mind, to be revisited at leisure when attending a boring lecture, waiting, or traveling through uninteresting scenery. The few visitors he'd ever entertained in any of his sundry homes through the years must have assumed he didn't read, judging by the lack of books on display. Only one person ever remarked, "Your books gather no dust in the library of your mind": the late Eve Morse, a Supreme Court judge who could accurately quote Cicero, Wittgenstein, and the *three* books of the major religions.

"Well, hello, Mr. Masek! It must have been . . . what, two, three years?"

William Stearns, the branch director, rolled from behind his desk and maneuvered his vast anatomy toward Nikola, propelled by short legs. With a shiny dome capping a rotund face, he suffered more than a passing resemblance to Humpty Dumpty.

Nikola faked a smile, shook the blubbery hand once, and nodded, fighting the urge to reach for a handkerchief to mop his palm after.

"Please, make yourself comfortable." Stearns nodded to a leather sofa. "Can I offer you coffee? Something stronger?"

"No, thank you." Nikola detoured to occupy an easy chair.

Stearns turned to his secretary, who stood by the door. "That will be all, Mrs. Chapman." With that, he turned, edged to the sofa, and collapsed on the leather, the cushions groaning as air sighed through the seams. "Well." He opened his hands as if to part the waters, cradled them over his distended belly, and composed a beatific smile. "What can the bank do for you?"

Nikola considered how to play the forthcoming scene. He had met Stearns a few times over the years, always on issues of little relevance but complex enough to preclude using the Internet. Although he had mentally rehearsed several approaches, Nikola didn't know if Stearns would be accompanied by other bank officials. The man could have been sick or chosen to conduct their business in one of the open offices outside. Now that his choice had been settled, Nikola decided to lose no time with niceties.

"Mr. Stea—"

"Please, call me William. We've known each other . . . what, twenty years?"

Like most people marshaling their thoughts, Stearns repeated formulas to keep a section of his brain on automatic pilot while the analytic part did its bit. Now he must be debating the reason behind the visit. His porcine eyes darted, trying to evaluate Nikola's body language. Regardless of his ludicrous physique, Mr. Stearns owned a first-class brain—one that was, according to Nikola's file, in perfect working order.

"I need a small service."

Stearns jiggled his triple chins. "That's what the bank is for."

"I didn't mean the bank. I need a personal service from *you.*"

Whatever doubt Nikola harbored about Stearns's intellect evaporated before his neutral reaction. He didn't move a muscle, and his cupid smile didn't falter.

"If it's within my power, consider it done."

More formulas. Nikola reached into his jacket pocket and withdrew two dulled brass keys that he deposited neatly side by side on the polished surface of the low table. Then he fished out a slim device the size of a pocket calculator, punched a few buttons, and rested it by the keys.

"Your audio- and video-recording equipment has suffered a glitch. Nothing permanent, I assure you."

The beam in Stearns's eye dulled.

"I have two safe-deposit boxes in your vault—large boxes, the ones to store quarto files." Nikola adjusted one of the keys a fraction of an inch to align them. "Inside each of them are four smaller containers the size of a shoe box—locked, naturally. I call them my armless boxes."

"Harmless?"

"I had a lisp when I was a little boy; luckily, it's long gone. No. I meant *armless,* no *h.*"

Silence.

"You see, Will—I can call you Will, can't I?"

More chin jiggling.

"The locks on my boxes are sophisticated and wired to capsules holding an ounce of high explosive—not much, but sufficient to blow the arms off whoever attempts to open them without the correct key and combination. I could have nicknamed them Faceless, since one would probably lose his head also, but I didn't like the sound of it."

"That's illegal," Stearns blurted.

"Perhaps, but let it be our little secret." Nikola slid back on the leather and closed his eyes for a few seconds to bask in the definite alteration of the tempo of Stearns's breathing.

"This bank has offices dotted all over, including one in Santo Domingo, Dominican Republic. I need my boxes removed from this branch and transported there, intact. I happen to have an account in the Avenida Las Americas office, including two safe-deposit boxes exactly like the ones you have here."

Stearns was shifting his bulk to stand erect when Nikola halted him with a wave of his hand. "Like a magician's trick. Here are the keys. You only have to make my boxes disappear from here and materialize in the Caribbean."

"That's illegal."

He was repeating himself, although now it wasn't a formula but a feeble attempt to win time in which to stand, return to his desk, and summon help.

"Will . . . tsk, tsk, you're concerned?" Nikola chuckled. "Our souls brim with illegal thoughts from unspeakable deeds. Isn't that so?"

Stearns's brain must have been particularly honed, because he froze and lifted his face a fraction, his nose twitching as if sampling remote pheromones.

"We keep our thoughts safe, in the shadiest corner of our dark minds. Deeds are another matter. They happen, perhaps in a flash, but time is a fickle subject—once gone, there's nothing you can do to recover it."

And still Stearns didn't move.

"Unless you can freeze it." Nikola reached once more into

the inner pocket of his jacket and retrieved a small folded envelope. Shunning theatrics that could afford him no advantage, he flicked it onto Stearns's belly, where it rested.

One hand with stubby fingers reached for the envelope, Stearns's tiny eyes never leaving Nikola's. His other hand joined the first to maneuver the flap and withdraw a few glossy photographs. Stearns lowered his eyes, then his color changed to ashen, as if the sun had suddenly disappeared beyond a cloud.

Nikola held the theory that the human brain stored certain events in a section dealing with dreams. It was a survival mechanism. In time, its owner could pretend the sickest debauchery had never happened—unless an image asserted reality. Like an image of a corpse in a roadside motel. Rubber and leather games sometimes got out of hand. With a sleight of hand while he checked the crime scene, Nikola had palmed the bag containing three hairs that could have sent Stearns to a tank. One of the things Nikola hoarded for a rainy day. "As I said, William, a magician's trick. Don't let these disturb your sleep. They don't tie you to the crime, and the bits of biological stuff that do are still safe with me. Cross my heart. Shall we say a week from now?"

Stearns's chin jiggled once.

"Dear me . . . You don't look too chirpy. Tummy upset? You should have someone look at it." Nikola leaned back in his chair, getting into a more comfortable posture. "I'm an incorrigible romantic, you know? I take a liking to people, and that will be my undoing. Still, it can't be helped; one is what one is. I'll tell you what: You have expensive tastes, haven't you? Yes, I'm aware of the cost of meat nowadays. And your health is iffy. . . . Your bank is a member of SWIFT? You know what I mean? Society for Worldwide Interbank Financial Telecommunication?"

Stearns nodded his head a fraction.

"Wonderful! I happen to know of a little nest egg, a trifle over three hundred million, nicely tucked away in a sunny island's private bank that also happens to be a member of SWIFT." Nikola reached to his other inside pocket and drew out a fresh envelope. "Here are the codes and all the details you could possibly need. Twenty-five percent is yours."

A little color returned to Stearns's cheeks.

Nikola smiled. "See? That's what friends are for. You look better already." He pushed the envelope across the low table and stood. "Here you'll find precise instructions for what to do with the rest of the money. You have offices in Antigua?" It was an unnecessary question, because Nikola already knew, but some questions helped to maintain a fluid conversation.

Stearns nodded again, his cheeks definitely rosier, as Nikola stood.

One hand on the door handle, Nikola turned. "It just occurred to me that a cretin might entertain keeping the lot and taking a powder, but you're not one of those." He inspected the tips of his loafers as if pondering a thorny issue. "No, you want to live a long and quiet life." Then he stared for an instant into Stearns's porcine eyes before his face broke into a wide smile. "You're too intelligent."

chapter 45

||||

16:22

"Where do we stand?" Odelle Marino drummed her fingernails on the polished wood of the boardroom table.

"Where? I'll tell you. In shit up to our eyeballs."

She glanced at Vinson Duran, Hypnos's president, and Nikola, at the opposite side of the table. Vinson might be one of the wealthiest men in the world, but no one ever forgot he was raised on the streets. "Go on," she said.

"The situation at the Washington facility is untenable. The place has been sealed for several days—"

"Three."

Vinson turned toward Nikola, jaw clenched. Odelle waited for a retort that never materialized and was pleasantly surprised at Vinson's wisdom. Although they both were men, mature and probably attractive, the similarities stopped there. Vinson's patrician countenance and Savile Row suit contrasted with Nikola's comfortable tweed jacket trimmed in leather at the cuffs and elbows—a throwback to British fashion a century old. The real difference between the men ran deeper and had to do with intellect. Regardless of Vinson's scientific brilliance, he was outclassed before Nikola's awesome brain. Patrician, yes—the tag brought to mind an image of Vinson in toga addressing a senate—but Nikola was a centurion.

"Three days," Nikola insisted.

"Fine. You've had the place clamped down for three days. Today is the fourth, and the people are edgy. There are too many people involved."

Odelle skewered Nikola with a silent plea.

"You should have thought of that," Nikola offered.

"Look, mister . . ." Vinson's face darkened.

"Yes?" When Vinson clamped his mouth shut, a vein throbbing merrily on his temple, Nikola continued. "The probability of a system failure is directly proportional to the number of its components. In this instance, yes, there have always been too many people involved. I don't think it was ever a question of if but when."

"The facilities were designed with a concept of total security," Vinson argued. "This was an inside job, the result of one facility's sloppy design. I warned about the risks of the sewage line."

A wry smile stretched Nikola's lips. His gaze wandered over the paneled walls and came to rest on his empty cup of tea. "Total security has always been a myth, used by governments and corporations like yours to demand extortionate rates from their citizens or customers or to ensure the sacrifice of rights and personal freedoms in pursuit of even more illusory security. Absolute security is no more attainable or desirable than is absolute freedom. The point is never to sacrifice the reality of freedom or security for the ideal absolute of either."

Odelle blinked once. *Bravo!*

Nikola continued. "To pretend that, out of hundreds of men and women with knowledge of the shenanigans going on at the stations, no one would ever blab to his or her drinking buddy is unreasonable. It had to happen, and now it has."

"Let's pull the plug."

Odelle turned, livid, toward Vinson, aghast at his slip. Nikola knew nothing about any plug. Out of the corner of her eye, she saw that Nikola's expression didn't waver.

"Pull the plug?" Nikola asked.

"A figure of speech. I meant getting rid of anyone who's not supposed to be there." Vinson reached to adjust his cuff, his eyes alive.

"That would take time, weeks perhaps, and the involvement of more people," Nikola said, and Odelle breathed a sigh of relief. "I don't think that's an option."

She waited. Nikola was an introverted intellectual, a social maladroit, and detached from the outside world. But she didn't underestimate him. Nikola had a plan; he must have had one when he suggested a meeting.

"Lukas Hurley, the station's controller, is alive. At least, he was with them after they left the sewers. I have reason to believe he will get in touch soon."

"How do you know this?" Vinson said.

Silence.

Odelle checked Nikola's lips. "Don't waste your time. He won't reveal his sources or methods."

"I hear Congress has rushed an ad hoc committee to look into the station's security and, in particular, the series of events resulting in the escape of three prisoners," Nikola said.

Vinson frowned. "Three? They don't know about Russo?" His voice wavered. "You mean the woman, Russo, and the other lawyer? The black man didn't escape."

"Congress doesn't know about Russo," Nikola pointed out. "What they know is the stations are not as secure as promised, and they will want answers."

"What kind of answers?"

"I should have said reassurances. An undertaking to prevent breakouts from ever happening again."

"But you said total security was a myth."

"That's correct, but some of your facilities are more secure than others—in particular the few you have in remote places. Deserts and the like."

Vinson frowned, as if he didn't like Nikola's voice. "Are you suggesting . . . ?"

"I am. Inmates come in two categories: common criminals, and those with the clout or the association with institutions capable of breaking them out. Those are your security risks; the others are just meat. And of course there are the illegals—in my opinion, the most dangerous of the lot."

"But shifting people around would cost millions!"

"So? A radical change in the way people are held will please Congress. Let's face it, in the old system, high-security prisons served exactly that role: pens as impregnable as possible to hold the inmates most likely to attempt escape."

"The breakout from Washington was made possible by a faulty design of the sewer system," Vinson said.

"I don't agree."

"You don't?"

"No. The Washington breakout was the result of someone wanting to have an illegal prisoner close by."

Odelle felt the blood rush to her face. "How dare you?" She moved to stand, but Nikola continued in the same sedate tone.

"Had this inmate been elsewhere—in the Nevada facility, for example—the escape attempt would have failed. Russo was in Washington so you could look him up from time to time. I checked the log. Sloppy."

"What about Hurley?" Vinson asked.

Odelle breathed deeply and slid back on her seat, inwardly cursing her outburst and thankful for Vinson's attempt to defuse the situation.

"I expect contact within the next twenty-four hours."

"And then?" Odelle asked.

Nikola shrugged. "Then you can offer Congress your plan to beef up security by sorting prisoners into categories and presenting them with the runaways safely back in custody."

"What about Hurley and the doctor? What do you suggest we do with them?"

Nikola arched the fingers of one hand and inspected his fingernails before turning toward Vinson.

"You really want to know?"

chapter 46

||||

18:04

"My name is Lukas Hurley . . ."

Enrique Castillo jerked upright and blinked repeatedly at his screen laser tracker to shift input onto the keyboard, then routed the call to the speaker system and slammed a pad to his left. Overhead, a small mirror dropped to reflect the intense light of a powerful xenon projector, highlighting his booth like a beacon.

Bill Anderson was in charge of the scores of people fielding the telephones. Having commandeered a full floor of SINTA, a corporation providing telephone support for government services, the operators sifted, around the clock, through thousands of calls reporting sightings of suspicious-looking people or vehicles. So far, and however well-intentioned the calls, none amounted to anything beyond wishful thinking.

Enrique craned his neck and spotted Bill barreling down the corridor to crash-stop before his booth, the side panels rattling with the impact.

". . . shift supervisor of the Washington, D.C., hibernation facility." A short pause. "ID number 17395878 XCJ."

Bill made a rolling motion with one hand, the other busy with a cellular pad. "Could you repeat, please?"

"No."

"Pardon?"

"If you missed something, listen to the recording. Testimony is slated for day after tomorrow at ten-thirty A.M. at the ABC TV studios down Rhode Island Avenue Northeast. We'll be there an hour before."

The line went dead.

"Twenty-two seconds," Enrique announced. Not enough.

"Prepaid SIM," someone yelled.

"Radio mast at Meridian Hill Park," another voice shouted. "Sander transmitter."

"Switched off," a third voice rattled.

Enrique exchanged glances with Bill. The caller knew the system. Had he kept his cell phone switched on, the direction finder could have zeroed in on it, given another minute or so.

Text started scrolling against his screen. The SIM had been bought three days before in a pack of five from a machine dispenser at Union Station.

Bill Anderson nodded. "Log the recording into the system; I'll download it into my station."

Enrique followed Bill's retreating figure as it marched along the corridor to his glass-walled office, where he closed the door and reached for a secure phone.

chapter 47

||||

20:30

After bridging its alarm circuit, George Wilson picked the lock and pushed open the heavy steel door. Hefting a long polymer guitar case, he stepped onto the rooftop and closed the door. A knee to the floor, he fished in his coat pocket for two slim neodymium wedges and rammed them between door and casing.

The sun had set minutes before, and its feeble residual

light was drenched in red. Wilson peered around the Paige Building's deserted roof—a vast esplanade capping a hundred-story skyscraper, with a huge water tank and a room housing the air-conditioning machinery. Carrying his case, he strolled to the southernmost edge of the building and the foot-high parapet that topped the roof. From his vantage point, Wilson spotted long chains of streetlights coming alive. Eight hundred feet below, the already heavy evening traffic snaked down New York Avenue toward John Hanson Highway and the suburbs. A mile ahead in a bend of the road stood Mason Tower, his target.

A four-foot-wide puddle, left by rain the day before and stretching almost the length of the roof, rippled in the breeze. The construction workers must have been sloppy, probably eager to head for a beer at ground level. It was a ridiculous puddle, no deeper than an inch, but he would have to lie in it, perhaps for hours on end. Wilson hawked a wad of phlegm and spat it to the side. Sloppy. In time, the puddle would cause dampness on the lower floors. Not that the workers cared, and that was the problem: no pride in workmanship—a trait Wilson possessed in spades.

With a final look around in the rapidly waning light, Wilson rested the case on the ground, squatted, and threw its catches open.

Based on the venerable CheyTac M100 rifle, the CT-16XBO had evolved into a wonder of precision engineering and electronics, delivering stunning accuracy at two thousand yards in the hands of a rookie. With thousands of hours clocked at ranges and a bunch of soft target interdiction scores—the euphemism for sniper kills—Wilson was anything but a rookie.

After assembling the rifle's collapsible stock, IR laser, and scope, Wilson linked the weapon's Kestrel—a squat box housing temperature, wind, and atmospheric-pressure sensors—to his computer pad and set the weapon down on its squat tripod in the water. Then he assessed the puddle. He could try to lie partially on top of the case, but that would hamper his hold on the rifle. With a huff, he laid the case open on the water and next to the weapon, removed his jacket, folded it with care, and lowered himself into the puddle, stretching prone in the water. After turning and twisting to get as comfortable as possible, he reached to a side pocket in the rifle case and picked out a plastic box by feel.

Although designed almost five decades earlier, the precision-machined .408 cartridge remained state of the art: supersonic at over two thousand yards and with more punch than a .50 at shorter ranges. Out of habit, Wilson selected each gleaming projectile and rubbed it over the crook between his chin and lower lip for a film of body oil that wouldn't affect the bullet's performance but would give good luck. When the six-projectile clip was full, he rammed it in its housing, turned his cap around, leaned on the stock, and adjusted his eye to the scope, a finger slowly rotating the focusing piece until the view leaped into crisp detail. Slowly, Wilson panned vertically until he found the windows he sought: the upper story of a penthouse in a building a mile away.

Although his bodyguards had not turned around when he got into the car, Lawrence Ritter recognized their necks and the mounds of solid flesh curling like doughnuts over stiff white collars: Demorizi and Bancroft, good ex-army muscle, loyal and unhampered by high IQs. His personal assistant, Bernard Gluck, traveled in a car behind with another security officer, although at times they would maneuver ahead or to the sides, in particular when slowing down at intersections or at traffic lights.

Ritter patted his case and was about to unclasp it when he thought better of it. The documents weren't that important, and he had to think about the piece of flimsy paper with machine-code lines burning in his jacket's inner pocket, re-turned to him—after the program was lodged in the satellite—by a friend from infancy who happened to have risen to the higher echelons of the NSA.

Genia Warren's moxie the day before had taken him by surprise. Her codes to lodge what amounted to a dead-man's handle in the satellite routing at Hypnos's traffic, and the program printed on the paper, had needed deft footwork and time. Genia had an army of computer specialists and could have cashed in a quiet favor for the program, but the codes were another matter and hinted at someone high up. Yet Ritter found the details irrelevant before the real issue: time. Such a devious plan to cancel the disposal of center inmates needed not only intimate knowledge of the system but the time to mull over its chinks, gather the data, and shape the package. Since such a scheme would be useful only if the disclosure of Hypnos's shenanigans was imminent, either Genia had developed the ploy since the breakout or she knew earlier that it would happen. Ritter had thought of little else since the day before, arriving at the unshakable conclusion that Genia hadn't had the time to work out the intricate details since the prisoners escaped.

So, you're planning a coup. Genia had been in Odelle Marino's sights for a long time. He'd watched from the sidelines as Genia bowed to Odelle's whims with a meekness he'd found maddening and at odds with Genia's character and intellect. Now the pesky pieces slotted nicely into the puzzle, but Ritter viewed the evolving picture with foreboding. Odelle was a formidable opponent and wielded enormous power. He patted his jacket and felt the soft crunch of paper. For an instant, he pictured Genia's fingers slipping into her bra, closed his eyes, and enjoyed the warm feeling. That he would never allow her to go solo—however harebrained her scheme—had little to do with loyalty, honor, or a sense of duty, but she didn't know that.

The deed was done and the program in place. Now what?

A rapid series of sharp beeps pulled him from his reverie. From a holder clipped to his belt, Ritter drew his secure phone. *CALL WHEN YOU ARRIVE AT YOUR APARTMENT,* read the message in its bright orange screen. No greeting. No name. No need.

Back in the '20s, the forty-sixth U.S. president, Edwina Locke, had blown a fuse when a delicate private conversation with her teenage daughter was posted word for word on the Web, years before the Internet rules changed. With the virtual disappearance of landlines and increased sophistication of electronic eavesdropping, it had become impossible to guarantee privacy with portable devices working on the cellular network. President Locke had scoured MIT and Caltech for unorthodox brains and shanghaied them into a think tank accountable only to the White House. Soon dubbed EBD, or Edwina's Boffin Department, by security directors, she tasked her group to develop a system of secure communications for high-ranking government officers. The group discovered that such a system existed, developed and run by the army. When the military stonewalled the EBD, Locke tore a broad strip from a four-star general's hide and forced him to release the technology. Thus the SSC1, or Secure Squirt Communication equipment, became an essential accessory for high-ranking civil servants.

Shaped like a thin cellular phone, the SSC11X7 in Ritter's hand was the latest model of a pager—useless as a regular phone, and devoid of popular gadgets such as a 3-D screen or theta-wave relax, but so secure that after thirty years it remained hacker-proof to anyone but the NSA, who kept the keys.

When the user spoke, the device identified, compressed, and encrypted each word, to squirt it as a pulse lasting nanoseconds in the pauses between sounds. The receiver could read remarkably crisp plain text on a screen barely larger than a wristwatch and in the top left-hand corner a three-digit number identified the caller. An iris scan and a devilish DNA comparer prevented unauthorized use.

Ritter glanced through the darkened side windows as they crossed Florida Avenue, five minutes from his apartment at Mason Tower. On the corner of Brentwood Road, he caught sight of Enzo Semprini, closing his fruit shop for the day.

After the 2026 building act allowing construction higher than the Capitol in Washington, D.C., scores of high-rise buildings had forever changed the capital's image. Washington boasted several buildings with high-security ratings, but none like Mason Tower. The condominium had been privately built back in the '30s and all its residents were government employees. In a bid to guarantee protection at reasonable costs, federal agencies encouraged their more sensitive personnel to move into a secure property. Those who couldn't be convinced to take up an address at a secure condominium required expensive twenty-four-hour protection by a rotating team of bodyguards, which put an incredible strain on the system. Genia Warren was one of those who had refused to leave her family home in Galesville, Maryland, on the Chesapeake Bay.

Soon Ritter's motorcade reached the approaches to the building—a vast rotunda with synthetic lawn and a flagstaff at its center. Instead of approaching the main door at street level, they continued down a circular ramp sinking under the building. Two floors underground, the ramp leveled and straightened into a clear three-hundred-foot stretch, ending in a burnished steel wall, which blocked further progress.

The two-car motorcade had slowed to a standstill, the front car only a few yards from the gleaming wall, when a low-frequency thump echoed from behind.

Ritter ignored the noise, adjusted his beret, and reached for the suitcase as the windows lowered. He knew that another wall of three-inch-thick steel had dropped behind them, to isolate them from the rest of the world while sensors ran inside and outside the vehicles.

When a small yellow light flickered on a plate in the near wall, he stared fixedly at it until it dimmed. It required concentration; even a glance at the sensors deployed at either side of the plate would have triggered a silent alarm to draw the security troops down into the basement like flies to rotten meat. Then the wall ahead started to disappear into a slot in the ceiling.

At the elevator bank, Ritter stepped out of the car and gave cursory nods to his assistant and the driver before entering the waiting elevator. As the doors closed, he noted the delighted looks passing between his retinue. Since he'd not given them any special instructions, they were free to go home for the night.

In the loneliness of the elevator, Genia's words wouldn't leave his mind. She was going all the way along a road with no possibility of turning back. He felt apprehension, elation, and no little curiosity. Who was backing her? Obviously, it was someone with clout. And clout meant someone high in the government.

After dropping his briefcase on a sofa, Ritter approached the kitchen counter, opened a bottle of scotch, and poured a finger of it into a tumbler. He downed it in one gulp and repeated the procedure before heading for the stairs, his skin tingling at the prospect of a long shower. The liquor sloshed in the glass as Ritter climbed the steps. He couldn't recall when he'd taken to splitting his homecoming drink into two, but it wouldn't feel natural anymore if he didn't. Some habits grew ingrained, like woodworm, and once settled, they were almost impossible to excise without killing the host.

As he padded into his suite, the lights grew brighter and the strains of Grieg's "Anitra's Dance" rose, to complete the homecoming Ritter had programmed into the system years before. He shrugged off the holster with his regulation weapon and laid it at the foot of the bed. Then his pager buzzed.

Ritter stopped, exchanged the hand holding the tumbler, and reached to his belt, as the curtains on the curved panorama window overlooking the cityscape opened noiselessly, having detected his nearness.

He frowned at the string of zeros flashing on the device's tiny screen, a number not included on his list and one he'd never seen before. Then a message scrolled in flashing bold capitals: *MOVE AWAY FROM THE WINDOW.* The air thickened.

Another second ticked before Ritter, as if trying to swim through molasses, released his grip on the tumbler and dove onto the bed just as the curved plate glass imploded with a deafening roar. Over the next two or three seconds, Ritter experienced the weird sensation of inhabiting an alien body with its own agenda. After blinking when tiny glass shards peppered his face, his body rolled away from the middle of the bed, with Ritter a simple observer being taken for a ride. Then he dropped over the far edge as the bedcovers swelled and burst into a shower of snowlike mattress fragments.

"Lights off," he yelled. A stupid command, because the sniper would probably have infrared sights and, besides, the system wouldn't understand. When Ritter programmed the houselights, he'd kept his prompts to single words, like *Television* or *Sleep*. In a rare display of wishful thinking, he'd also logged *Fun,* but he hadn't used that one in a long time.

On all fours, covered by the bulk of the bed, he scuttled to the door and dove out of the line of fire headlong into the corridor as the door frame also exploded, scant inches over where his head had been a split second before. Then his body sagged, as if its hayride driver had abandoned the vehicle. One hand on the banister and the other still clutching his pager, Ritter barreled down the stairs. On the lower floor, Ritter caromed off the newel post and slammed to a stop against the sanctity of a side wall, his breath coming in ragged gasps; the contraption in his fist purred again. *NICE.* Ritter swore. His head felt wet. Eyeing the blood-smeared palm he'd just swiped over the top of his head and face, he swore again, breathed deep once, twice, and neared the kitchen sink. After dropping the pager on the counter, Ritter rubbed his hands under the faucet and splashed tepid water on his face and head.

Two blocks away, on a side street, Nikola flicked his pager closed and handed it over to Dennis. "Hold on to it, just in case." He peered once more at the crisp satellite images on the plasma screens flanking Dennis's workstation in the van.

Dennis accepted the device, an eyebrow raised.

"I logged your statistics in the pager. You have access." Then Nikola nodded once and made up his mind. "Retain the satellite link and drive over to the Paige Building's underground parking lot."

As Dennis busied himself to move onto the driver's seat, Nikola reached to a side. Lodged against the van's bodywork was an old Malacca cane, a walking stick he used at times when strolling through the park. He had too much work to do to waste any more time playing babysitter and worrying about Wilson's repeat performances.

Ritter knew the layout and security measures of the building intimately. The alarm wouldn't have gone off. Perhaps bits of glass had rained down below, but it would take time

314 carlos j. cortes

before someone noticed and pinpointed his window. The shooter would be gone, but not the contract. It would mean endless hours or days spent inside a flak jacket, cringing each time he was in the open, until the shooter was caught or his aim improved. He knew who was after his guts, and the building's security detail was formed entirely of DHS personnel. The men were professionals, and probably clean, but they obeyed orders from the top. And that might include driving him to a point where the killer couldn't miss his car. He had to get out of the building. Alone.

The fire stairs were out of the question. As soon as he pushed the panic bar, alarms would trigger and pandemonium would follow; security personnel would flock to the exit on the ground floor and shut down the building. He would be trapped. That left the elevator—not much better. There were four security men in the garages and two staffing the room with the recording equipment on the ground floor. He paused to picture the small door opening from the recording room to the rear of the building.

On the ground floor, there would be four armed men: two by the door, one at the desk, and another by the elevator. Regardless of how much weight he tried to pull, they wouldn't allow him out of the building without a phalanx of bodyguards. He needed to draw all available personnel away from the entrance hall and get into the recording room.

Ritter shut off the tap, reached for a thick roll of paper towels, and dried his hands and face. Then he opened the oven door, shoved the roll inside, and turned the broiler on full before marching toward the door. At the penthouse lobby, he reached under a wall shelf with drawers, ripped off the weapon he had taped underneath, and slipped it inside his trouser band. Then Ritter opened the door and sprinted along the corridor for the benefit of the video cameras. His beret must be somewhere in his bedroom with his other weapon, but he wasn't about to go looking for it.

The landing was predictably deserted, as his apartment was the only one on that level. The four floors below housed as many agency directors and their families, all ensconced in their own private fiefdoms.

The iris scan by the elevator doors took an unreasonable time to lock on, its red beam flickering on and off until Ritter's eyes were awash in tears. Once inside the car, he swept a glossy black card in a slot to override the machine's instructions. Instead of the parking lot programmed into the machine, he keyed in the main lobby. He doubted the sniper would have backup but, if he did, the most likely point to watch would be the underground garage and his car.

As the elevator plummeted, Ritter stole a glance at a smoked mirror covering half of the wall facing the sliding door. He choked back a curse. His face and head glistened with innumerable cuts, giving him the vague appearance of raw hamburger. He patted his trouser pocket for a handkerchief and froze when his fingers caught his now-silent pager. He pushed back an overwhelming sensation of foreboding as he returned the device to his belt holster and turned around to the slowly opening elevator doors and a sea of wide-eyed faces. To try wiping his face now would only make things worse. Ritter straightened, tried a painful smile, and stepped forward, the men parting as if to present honors or make him run a gauntlet.

Lionel Beckerman, the security chief, frowned. "What the—"

"A sniper shot out my bedroom window," Ritter muttered, wringing his hands to bolster his performance. "I saw ropes, and at least two men, perhaps more." The security man exchanged a quick glance with his colleagues when Ritter stepped over to him. "You have to do something."

Something flashed across the dark irises of the security man: contempt or understanding, Ritter couldn't be sure, but his powerful shoulders relaxed. Then the fire alarm tripped.

Beckerman drew his weapon as the security detail sprang alive. "You two, grab an elevator to the top floor." He turned to a giant by his side. "We'll take the stairs." Then he reached to his belt for a flat pad and tapped in a sequence. Light spilling from the outdoor floodlights dimmed when a series of sharp snaps sounded by the entrance doors and steel shutters dropped, effectively sealing the building. "You still carry your locator?"

Ritter lowered the neck of his pullover and showed Beckerman the capsule.

He nodded. "Stay here."

Here we go. "Could I go into the security room?" Ritter wrung his hands some more for effect.

Beckerman made a feeble attempt to hide a sneer, but it proved too much for him. He nodded and dashed toward the stairs, speaking into the tiny microphone of his earpiece.

Ritter waited until the emergency doors leading to the fire stairs had closed before marching to a wooden door behind the reception desk and standing before it as the overhead camera moved and panned.

The agent who opened the door was in his early twenties and looked sheepish, but Ritter knew it had nothing to do with respect. Instead, it was embarrassment at seeing the mighty security director of the FBH running scared. As Ritter entered a room crammed with screens and recording equipment, his nose twitched at the biting smell; the men had been smoking a joint. In a secure building, that could mean dismissal or, at least, a stiff disciplinary warning.

"Take a seat, sir. You'll be safe here."

Ritter eyed the speaker over the youngster's shoulder—a saturnine man in shirtsleeves toggling a stick to follow two shapes sprinting up the stairs—and, beyond him on the far wall, a steel emergency door. "Thank you." Then he turned to the agent who had ushered him in. "What's your name?"

"Sean, sir. Sean Clancy."

The other agent's eyes didn't shift from the screen. Ritter drew his gun, rammed it in the young agent's belly, reached over, and yanked the weapon from his shoulder holster. In a swift movement he released the clip, threw the pistol into a corner, and shoved the startled man aside. Then he turned to the seated agent. "Don't do anything silly. We're on the same side, remember?"

The security officer's hand hovered in midair as Ritter's weapon dug into his beefy neck. "Your name?"

"Bob—Robert Fowler."

After slapping his hand aside, Ritter removed Bob's

weapon, repeated the clip-releasing routine, and sent the gun clacking over the linoleum floor to join the other. Then he nodded to the door on the far wall. "The card."

Bob didn't move.

"You're doing your duty, and I'm proud. But you're in a bind. I can make your pension vanish in an instant, just by asking." He lessened the gun's pressure and leaned over, his lips almost touching Bob's ear. "On the other hand, I never forget a favor. Someone is gunning for me and I'm not about to stay here or drive around like a sitting duck. Open the fucking door and forget about Beckerman." He nodded to the screen. "He'll be mad, but I'll look after you."

Bob took a deep breath. "Florida?"

Ritter nodded.

"The boy too?"

"Deal."

"In my top pocket."

Ritter fished the plastic between two fingers and flicked it at the young man on the other side of the room. "Open it."

When he could see a patch of synthetic grass out the open doorway, Ritter straightened and turned to Bob. "Now walk over to the other side and stay there."

"Take care, boss."

Ritter pocketed his weapon and gave Bob's shoulder a gentle squeeze before bolting for the door and sprinting toward New York Avenue, a smile tugging at the edges of his lips. Bob wasn't overly concerned for his safety, but a posting to sunny places was riding on Ritter's capacity to stay away from a sniper's sights.

chapter 48

20:54

Instead of waiting for the lights to change, Ritter descended the steps to the underpass, crossed over, and exited at Montana Avenue, taking the steps two at a time rather than the escalator. He glanced around, reached to his neck, and removed the locator. Once on the other side of the six-lane thoroughfare, by now almost empty of traffic, he walked at a brisk pace past Mt. Olivet Cemetery, careful to mingle with a group of young people moving in the same direction toward a theater. At a narrow alley cutting toward Bladensburg Road, he squeezed past people already maneuvering supermarket carts brimming with the detritus of their lives and vying for the best spots to spend the night.

He dropped his locator into one of the carts. Then he spotted a small puddle of water on the upturned lid of a garbage bin. He dipped his handkerchief and ran it several times over his face and head. He was more afraid of alerting a policeman with his bleeding face than of whatever infection he might contract from the water.

He could have gone in the opposite direction, to the Rhode Island Avenue–Brentwood Metro station, and boarded an underground train to get out of the area as quickly as possible, but the system was rife with surveillance cameras, on both the trains and the platforms. If whoever was after him accessed the right feeds, he could be hemmed inside the underground network—not a pleasant proposition. When he was almost at the other end of the alley—the sporadic traffic of Bladensburg Road visible between garbage bins lining the passage—his pager warbled. Ritter stopped and squeezed between two large steel containers brimming with fast-food remains. His lungs filled with the stench of congealed fat.

GET OFF THE STREETS

Ritter swore. Although also unknown, this sender was different from the previous one. *Is the NSA giving secure pagers away in cereal boxes?* He darted a quick look overhead and clipped the pager back on his trouser waistband. Whoever called the shots was guessing. Good guesses so far, but they couldn't have tracked him. Then he froze and glanced up to the rectangle of clear sky between the buildings. They could, and they were. *Satellite.* He retreated further into the gap between the containers until his back rested against the brickwork, and he took a few deep breaths. He could shack up at a hotel, but his ID would flash like a beacon through the system. Within walking distance of his present position, he knew some finer establishments where a few hundred-dollar bills might replace his ID, but it was risky. Friends were a no-no; he couldn't think of even one unconnected with the administration, at least within Washington, D.C., and the closest family he could think of languished in an Oklahoma dust bowl.

Before leaving Mason Tower, Ritter knew the sniper had to be almost a mile away; there was no clear line of fire anywhere closer. He also guessed the contract on his life had something to do with whatever Genia Warren was attempting to do, and that could only mean Odelle. He reached to pat his shirt pocket and the flimsy piece of paper with Genia's code. Could they have spotted Genia giving him the paper? Was her office bugged? Ritter shook his head once. Executive offices were swept twice a day. But that didn't mean much. Security measures were in the hands of DHS personnel. He checked his watch. Thirty minutes since his window exploded and twenty-nine since the sniper realized he'd missed. Now what? The security detail from Mason Tower would have reported his disappearance, and whoever fielded the report would have sent it higher up; the sniper and his or her handlers knew he was on the run.

Ritter darted another glance to the sky and sighed. "If you can't beat them . . ." He needed a place to spend the night, something to eat, a secure computer, and a few answers, and only one address came to mind where he might be able to fill his shopping list.

Faced with the choice of trundling one hundred floors down the fire stairs or taking to the elevators, George Wilson chose a combination to reach the parking lot and his vehicle. From the rooftop, he walked four floors down, bridged the alarm circuit on the fire door, picked its lock, and exited to a corridor by the elevator bank. The express car looked tempting, but it would stop at the lobby, and there was a chance an alert security guard would spot the wet stain spreading on his tightly wrapped coat. Instead, he descended to the tenth floor and the shopping center, exited, and stood next to two women to wait for another elevator, his guitar case propped in front of him.

"Coming to the party?"

One of the women rubbed the sole of a cheap shoe on the linoleum and hiked a slowly sliding shoulder bag. "I haven't been invited."

"Of course you have. We all have. Mr. Morris said everybody."

"He's a creep."

"He's the boss."

"A creepy boss."

The woman with the sloppy shoulder bag glanced at George, did an almost seamless double take over the wet edges of his coat, and sniffed.

More people gathered before the elevator doors, eyes following the changing numbers overhead. Only one car went straight to the parking lots; the others would stop at the lobby. Out of the corner of his eye, George spotted two security guards approaching with the bored nonchalance of mercenaries. A high-pitched single bell, and the sliding doors to one of the cars opened, quickly followed by another. The woman with the keen eye filed past, not without darting an-

other look at his coat. When the security pair was almost
abreast, the far elevator pinged and slid open. George picked
up his guitar case, glanced at a two-inch wet spot where he'd
been standing, and filed into the car, his free hand reaching
inside his coat. Once inside, George turned around. One of
the security men stared at the puddle, then his lips moved
and his companion burst out laughing as the sliding doors
silently closed.

At the parking lot, George waited for his traveling companions to scatter in different directions before taking his bearings. There were three elevator banks, and he'd used the
farthest to the right. He checked the overhead signs: 3W—right
level, wrong letter. His car was at M. After checking the lay of
the letters, he hefted his guitar case once more and walked
purposefully down a wide aisle, reaching into his jacket pocket
for the remote.

"Mister . . ."

George glanced sideways to see a man with a walking
stick, wearing thick old-fashioned glasses, set on an inter-
ception course. How beggars managed to bypass security
was beyond him. *Damn vermin.* He glanced around and
lengthened his stride, the rear lights of his rented four-wheel
drive flashing twenty yards ahead.

"Mister . . ."

The voice sounded farther away; the gimpy bastard couldn't
keep up.

He opened the vehicle's hatchback, dumped the guitar
case inside, and reached for a tire iron he'd spotted earlier.
He would give the beggar some alms. He turned around, covering the iron with his body, and froze. Overhead, a fluores-
cent lamp flickered. George remained immobile, his eyes
slowly panning the parked vehicles, the concrete pillars supporting the structure, and the aisles. The beggar was nowhere
in sight. In a shoulder holster, George carried a squat Glock,
safety off and a round up the spout. It would take a second to
dive to the floor and roll over while his free hand flashed to his
armpit. Then he heard a tiny metallic sound, like a chime, and
out of the corner of his eye he spotted the slightest of movements and a glimmer. Through narrowed eyes, he followed a

single silver coin—probably a dollar, no longer in circulation—as it rolled lazily toward him, and he realized that a second might be an inordinate length of time. It was the oldest trick in the arsenal of an illusionist, to divert attention to one hand while the other did the business, and he knew the beggar would be at his back.

"Mister . . ."

The first bullet tore through his neck even as he turned toward the voice, followed by a mighty kick to his chest. The hatchback's bumper raced to crash against his head, but he didn't feel a thing.

In another few minutes, Ritter crossed Bladensburg Road and took a left turn to head down 22nd Street to the sanctity of Letters—a curious mix of bookstore and coffee shop frequented by literary buffs.

As he entered, Ritter darted a quick glance through the room, his gaze stopping at a table where a tall man with an impressive leonine mop of white hair was extolling Thomas Wolfe's stream-of-consciousness virtuosity. He stepped over to a tiny bar counter.

"What can I tempt you with?"

"A smile?"

Lucia Fosse blinked, the skin around her mouth crackling under countless coats of thickly applied makeup. "Trying to seduce a working girl?"

"One day I might get lucky."

She poured a mug of coffee from a carafe and slid it before him. "Perhaps one day."

Ritter sipped the coffee and made a face. "Yesterday's?"

"Almost closing time, but for you I'll brew a fresh pot."

"Forget it." Ritter darted another glance around. "I need to get out the back."

Lucia raised an eyebrow and her face cracked even more. Then she frowned, reached to the side for a pair of tiny reading glasses, and held them before her eyes, inspecting the myriad cuts on his face and head. "A husband?"

"A father."

"I see. Messing about with the preacher's daughter?"

Ritter pushed the mug away. "The father I'm talking about wields convincing arguments. A sawed-off shotgun."

"I told you to keep clear of the mob's goods." She glanced at a ridiculously small wristwatch. "I'll give you a lift in forty-five minutes."

"I don't have that long. Could you get me a cab?"

Lucia looked over his shoulder toward the sidewalk before searching his face again. "Go sit at the back. I'll call a cousin."

He held her gaze for a heartbeat and moved to reach for his billfold. She laid fingers with inch-long nails on his sleeve and squeezed. "On the house."

Lucia's cousin pulled around the back of the shop within ten minutes, driving a nondescript black sedan sorely begging for a merciful last trip to the scrap yard. Yet Ritter had to concede the engine sounded remarkably younger than the thing looked. A quiet man with hands much too large for the steering wheel, the driver kept his eyes on the windshield and didn't utter a word when Ritter slid onto the rear seat. He shifted the vehicle into gear and stopped at the end of the alley.

"Galesville," Ritter said.

Even though the directions were impossibly vague, the driver didn't comment. He kept the engine idling inside the alley, waiting. When the lights changed at the nearest intersection, he slipped smoothly into the incoming traffic, eyes constantly darting between an oversize overhead mirror and smaller ones on the doors. Ritter suppressed a smile and made a mental note to send Lucia flowers, chocolates, and the works. Then he relaxed a notch, slid down onto the backrest, and reached for his pager.

HEAVEN? he typed. He reread the single word, entered the recipient, and pressed send.

On Atlantic Avenue, the driver kept his speed within legal limits, frequently changing lanes and adjusting to traffic conditions.

In his hand, the pager beeped: *653 LOWERSIDE RD.*

Ritter stared at the unknown address for several heartbeats before the ploy registered. He leaned forward and read the address aloud. The driver nodded, reached to the dashboard, flicked a switch, and a GPS panel came alive. After entering the details, he resumed his careful maneuvering between the lanes. Fifteen minutes later, the car slipped onto Pennsylvania Avenue, then followed Southern Maryland Boulevard to the Greenock Road junction, where it detoured toward the coast.

"Five minutes to go," the driver said. "You want me to wait?"

"No, thank you." Ritter wasn't sure of the procedure once they got to the supplied address, but having a car waiting wouldn't enter into the equation.

When the driver pointed the car down Lowerside Road, Ritter noticed they drove past the address registered on the GPS at a sedate pace, then turned around a hundred yards farther on for another run. Lucia's cousin had definitely not acquired his savvy driving a cab, and Ritter wasn't going to ask about his training.

The car slowed to a stop before 653—a single-story ranch-style property with a red tiled driveway down one side and a broad expanse of manicured lawn. Ritter leaned over to the driver, a hand outstretched with two thousand dollars hidden in its palm. The man gripped the hand and was about to complain when Ritter shook his head. "We all need to eat, pal. It's been a pleasure." Still unsure about what came next, Ritter stepped out of the car and walked over to the main door.

As soon as Ritter pressed the bell, the door opened to reveal a very tall black man outlined under the door frame with a white clerical collar on a gray shirt. "Here you are. Come in, come in." The priest reached for his hand and dragged him in with a swift movement. Outside, Ritter heard the noise of the engine revving away.

One hand firmly on his arm, the priest propelled Ritter along a short corridor, past a kitchen with obvious signs of recent cooking, and through a dining room with a large table and five or six people sitting around what looked like a large fowl, perhaps a turkey, with good-looking trimmings. A plump woman carving the bird paused an instant, smiled, and continued slicing. Ritter half hoped they would offer him a chair, but the priest moved to a set of sliding doors leading to the yard, opened them, and stood aside. "You'll have to climb over." He nodded to a freshly painted white fence and smiled. "The Lord be with you." Then he slid the doors closed and drew the blinds.

chapter 49

||||

21:16

Although she'd had only half a tuna sandwich for lunch, she couldn't face the prospect of supper. Genia Warren's stomach had been queasy for days—nothing to do with bugs, just nerves. After flicking the pages of a document she'd been trying to concentrate on for the last hour, she sighed, rested it on a side table, and straightened to consider a foray into the kitchen to raid the fridge for yogurt. Anything else probably wouldn't stay down.

As she leaned on the kitchen counter to fix a slipper that kept coming off, her pager buzzed. She reached to her bathrobe pocket and drew the device to the light to stare at the single word: *HEAVEN?* The sender was Ritter.

"I'll be . . ." Her mind went into overdrive. She checked the kitchen clock. Whatever had driven Ritter into seeking her help must have taken place in the past two hours and probably involved the department. She thought of calling Mason Tower's security but discarded the idea at once. If something had happened there, her call would be flagged. After dousing the living-room lights, she stepped to the bow window to peek through a gap in the curtains. The car with her bodyguards inside was stationed, as usual, up her drive.

As a high-level executive, she merited twenty-four-hour protection, and her house was under constant surveillance by a security team whenever she happened to be in. Like now.

The house brimmed with extra security systems and panic buttons in the most unexpected places, including bathrooms and bedrooms; her neighbors had been security-vetted, and she had to carry a small capsule with a geolocator around her neck. That in itself had been a small victory, still hotly debated at intervals by the NHS honchos who insisted that all sensitive government personnel should carry the capsule *in* their necks.

Most people subject to high surveillance wrongly assumed the security measures sought to protect them. But Genia, having developed many of the procedures, knew better. The security schedules were meant to protect the system by making it almost impossible to abduct or otherwise take advantage of the knowledge such high-echelon individuals possessed. It should be much more difficult to capture rather than kill a high government executive.

With the goons outside, Ritter couldn't walk through the front door without being recorded by at least five or six departments. But, providing he'd gotten rid of his own locator, nothing prevented him from sneaking through the back door—barring the local parish priest. With a sigh, Genia keyed her neighbor's address on her pager, pressed the button to send, and moved over to her study, rehearsing the tall story she was about to deliver to Father Damien over the phone.

After switching off the lights, Genia padded barefoot into her backyard, skirting the pool and sitting at a bench under the large grapefruit trees she kept threatening to chop down. She hated grapefruit, and, as revenge, the trees exhibited an obscene fertility.

After a while she spotted movement by the plum tree's branches, which sat almost on top of the fence. Ritter was trying the easy approach. Then she saw him swinging from a branch, followed by the sounds of a loud curse, the sickening rip of tearing cloth, and a thud. She stood and walked over to the fence, choking with ill-contained laughter.

"Boy, you make a lousy thief."

Ritter also made a lousy patient. Between gasps, hisses, and countless sharp intakes of breath, Genia thoroughly cleaned the literally hundreds of tiny cuts on his face and scalp, most of them little more than pimple size. After swabbing the nicks with peroxide, she applied dabs of a spray-on dressing, then stood back to examine her handiwork. He looked like someone with a bad dose of chicken pox.

"Have you eaten?" Ritter stood from the kitchen stool where he'd endured her maintenance work, removed his jacket, made a face at the ripped pocket, and hung it from a wall hook next to the kitchen towels.

She was about to explain about her queasiness, then realized she was miraculously hungry and shook her head.

"I'll make supper," he said, and moved to the fridge. Genia climbed onto his vacated stool, tightened her robe, and settled in for the performance. He rummaged through the freezer to unearth a tray of leathery-looking chicken legs and a few odd vegetable lumps. Over the next hour, with pasta, eggs, sour cream, and other bits and pieces he'd scrounged from the kitchen, Ritter produced a huge bowl of luscious fettuccini. And throughout the culinary exhibition, he related his version of the sniper attack, his exit from Mason Tower, and the drive to her house, without omitting the providential coaching by his anonymous caller. She wasn't overly surprised. Whoever was listening to her exchanges with Palmer was doing an excellent job as guardian angel. Except by now she had narrowed her list of possible candidates to one: Nikola Masek. War was indeed a strange scenario, and mercenaries fickle in their allegiances.

After supper, they moved into the living room, dimly lit by whatever spilled over from the kitchen, with a coffee tray, snifters, and a bottle of cognac that had once belonged to Genia's father.

"That was my bit. Now, care to tell me what's going on?" Ritter asked.

Genia sipped her cognac and shelved devious thoughts. Her stomach hadn't begrudged the five-star treatment. She had eaten more at one sitting than in the previous week. "The DHS has been keeping illegal prisoners in the tanks."

"We've already been through this. I take it 'illegal' means people who weren't supposed to be there in the first place. You mean innocent people?"

"People who have not been sentenced by the courts."

"That means nothing. Innocent?"

She stalled.

He waited.

"People sent into cold storage by the Russian Mafiya." There, she'd said it.

"How many?"

"Many."

Ritter swirled his liqueur, sniffed it, and swirled some more. He was a cool customer, but his reaction had been too tame.

"You knew?"

"Since the unveiling of the first sugar cube there have been rumors of illegal inmates, but I would have never guessed that someone was using the tanks as storage. It makes sense, though."

"Unsubstantiated rumors?"

"Persistent, as befits the inevitable. Once humanity had firecrackers, nothing could stop the advent of the cannon. Throughout history, we've used prisons to house not only the delinquent but also the troublesome. Now you tell me someone is renting stays in our sugar cubes. Someone getting filthy rich in the process." He paused and sniffed his liqueur. "The first weird tale I heard about the hibernation system was in connection with the Bova brothers."

Genia nodded. Nine years before, two young men had been acquitted on a technicality, although they were guilty of murdering six children aged two to six in nasty satanic séances. A year later, they both disappeared. "I remember."

"I recall hearing at the time that if the Bovas weren't in a tank, they should be. It stands to reason. If there's a system with a possible function, someone will use it eventually. Unless you render it impossible."

"How?"

"Transparency. As it is, the system is opaque, and that can only mean some of its uses wouldn't stand up to scrutiny." At last Ritter took a sip, and, judging by the time he kept his eyes closed, it must have met his expectations. When he spoke, his voice dropped a semitone. "I take it Odelle is in this up to her neck."

"Why do you say that?"

"I thought the idea was to fill me in, not practice sounding-board techniques."

She waited.

"Odelle Marino is desperate and becoming more so by the day. What happened this evening confirms it. If the operation involved other departments in the government, she would be resigned to take her fall with the rest of the agencies or people involved. But to me it reads as if she would be taking the rap alone, and that can only mean it's been her setup all along. Who's pulling the rug out from under her?"

Genia rested her warm snifter on a side table, shocked at the speed with which the moment had presented itself. But to bring Ritter in meant revealing the identities of the others involved. She bit her lower lip. Yet Ritter had committed himself by accepting the codes. "Jerome Palmer."

Ritter paused his swirling. "I should have known." He chuckled. Then he turned, his profile in darkness, highlighted by a buttery moon filtering through the sheer drapes. "Who got out?"

"Two young lawyers and—"

"I've read the report; three went in and only two got out. But those people just got in. What I meant is, who did they spring out?"

"Eliot Russo."

Ritter whistled without actually producing any note. "Not bad. Because of his political activism?"

"No. Strictly personal." She sketched a spurned woman's vendetta.

"No wonder Odelle Marino is rattled. What surprises me is that she hasn't cleaned the stables already."

"She can't. The men of the Mafiya can't be trifled with.

330 carlos j. cortes

They command armies and billions of dollars. Also, Russo is sufficiently important to be a credible witness, not to mention the other two. She will attempt to cover her tracks as soon as they're captured, not before."

"Why not? It would be a preemptive safeguard."

"I don't think it's that easy. We know that Eliot Russo has been her personal prisoner, but she needs time to deal with the others."

"I still don't follow."

"If the fugitives are captured, my take is that she will ensure the dons remove their property from her tanks as soon as possible. After the hints *The Post* has been dropping, there's bound to be an investigation. The inspectors would find nothing amiss, and that would be that."

Ritter nodded slowly. "And if they manage to fob off the manhunt?"

"She will probably switch the Russians about and make the numbers tally. To physically check the identities of every inmate in the system would take months, perhaps years. At least that's Palmer's take."

"And the hearing?" Ritter asked.

"Day after tomorrow, in the morning." She finished her drink and outlined the overall strategy.

"Where's your computer?"

Genia grabbed the bottle and headed toward her study.

day six

||||

Paradiso, Canto VII: 54–56
*But I now see your understanding tangled
by thought on thought into a knot,
from which, with much desire,
your mind awaits release.*

The Divine Comedy, DANTE ALIGHIERI

chapter 50

09:36

"My uncle Hector used to pick me up from boarding school on Fridays and drive me to his cabin in the mountains. . . ." Russo's voice trailed off, to pick up an instant later in a lower tone. "He lived there with a quiet woman, Beth. I never called her anything else. I don't think they were married, but they shared the kind of relationship I've sought all my life. I remember their faces and shapes, even their smell, but the image that keeps coming to mind is of moving lips. They spoke to each other often, in low voices, almost whispers, so that I couldn't overhear their conversations. But she frequently blushed and lowered her eyes with a smile.

"In the evenings, Beth would sit by the fire, hum, and rock her chair until I settled at her feet. Then, without taking her eyes from the fire, she would reach to a shelf by her side and pick up a book. She had many books, and I think the random selections added to her pleasure. Sometimes it was Kipling, other times Virginia Woolf, or Pasternak, or Capote. She would read in the same tone of voice that she spoke—low and throaty, as if she kissed the words. My uncle would join us, having lit a huge briar pipe, much stained by age. He would close his eyes and seem to doze but for the glow of his tobacco and the wisps of smoke escaping his lips. Some evenings I fell asleep at Beth's feet; on other nights, she would glance at the clock and close the book. Then my uncle would stand, pocket his pipe, and walk me to my room while Beth closed the house for the night. They never went to bed together—I mean, not at the same time. From my door left ajar, I could look down the corridor and peek at Beth entering their bedroom. A little later, freshly shaven, my uncle would tiptoe in like a thief. A smiling thief."

Floyd Carpenter reached for a glass of juice and placed the straw between Eliot's parched lips.

"I got lost in the snow when I was eleven. We weren't far from the house, just checking a few traps my uncle had laid for rabbits. I still don't know what happened, but the wind hurled powdered snow into the air and I was blinded. I shouted his name, but I couldn't beat the wind. I had seen a clump of pines a few hundred yards to my left and headed there. My uncle had taught me well. When I reached the tree line, I dug out a hole, tore a few low branches to cover it up, and slipped underneath with a long stick to keep poking open an air vent. It was cold and pitch-dark and I couldn't stop shivering. I knew I was going to die. In that endless night, I learned the pliable nature of time. All that I could remember afterward was blackness and cold stretching into eternity and Beth's voice as she narrated Marco Polo's splendid travels.

"When I saw light at the end of the hole, I dug myself out. No." Russo made a wry movement with his mouth and shook his head a fraction. "My hands were numb and I couldn't move my arms well, so I gathered impetus and stood up, banging my head on the roof of twigs. It took a few tries but I managed it. Beth was only twenty yards away, with eyes grown too large for her face. Then she started screaming. I had never heard her do that before."

"Is that what sustained you?" Laurel's question sounded redundant, but she voiced it anyway.

"I must have denied the tank."

"What do you mean?" Lukas asked.

"Things exist only if you acknowledge them. An insult is only sound; it needs your collaboration to have impact."

Lukas nodded. "So you refused to accept the tank's existence and shrank instead into the cold and darkness of your childhood snow hole."

Laurel reached for Floyd's hand and breathed deeply, awed before the capacity of the human mind to clutch at selected memories to survive and feeling sorry for the lonely being imprisoned in Russo's skin and skull. Most men would be raving mad after what Russo had gone through, and that would have played heavily in Tyler's mind when planning the breakout. Had Russo been insane, their endeavor was doomed to start with.

For a while nobody spoke. Raul and Antonio sat together, their eyes never leaving Russo's face, now placid and seemingly dozing. Tyler leaned against the living room's door frame, a can of beer in his hand, probably warm; he hadn't sipped from it since Russo started to speak. Each seemed lost in their own thoughts, perhaps wondering how they would survive a tank—a frightening possibility considering their circumstances.

Then Russo's eyelids fluttered and again he moved his mouth as if to dislodge a bad taste. "Cold, darkness, and Beth's voice."

"Marco Polo?"

Laurel glanced at the Woody Allen look-alike, surprised to notice that Lukas fixed Russo with an intense stare as if he was sending or waiting for a vital secret.

"Yes. And *The Jungle Book*, and *Kim*, and . . . 'Gunga Din.' "

"Did they wake you often?" Floyd stretched his arm again to slip the straw between Russo's lips.

"I suppose so. It was numbing cold and dark. Then, after a long time, I would drift back to sleep and the darkness of my nightmares."

Behind her, Laurel heard ice cracking and chinking against the sides of a glass as Tyler trickled a drink over the cubes.

"How long?" Russo asked.

Laurel jerked upright and dug her fingers into Floyd's hand. She had been dreading the question. Probably they all had, but nobody voiced it. The air seemed to pulse and flow like water running under ice.

A faint smile tugged at Russo's lips. "That long?"

She realized all eyes were on Floyd.

"Eight years, two months, and six days." Floyd's voice rang with the brutality of truth.

"Thank you." The smile never left Russo's lips.

"You knew . . ." Laurel blurted.

"A rough guess only."

"But, how . . . ?

"You. Difficult without hair, but mid-twenties is my guess. And you," he turned his face toward Raul, "also helped to fish me out?"

Raul nodded.

"Thank you," Russo repeated. Then the dark sunglasses Russo had permanently stolen from Tyler rotated, and Laurel could sense his eyes settling on her. "Why?"

It was a personal question voiced in public—a question she couldn't answer yet. "First we need to win this war."

Russo nodded once.

"How did they do it?" Lukas asked.

Russo turned his head a fraction in his direction. "I don't follow."

"I mean, they said you died in a car crash."

"Ah, that. I don't remember much. It was done in a tunnel. As I neared the exit, I spotted two cars blocking it; behind me was another car. A police car. As I reached for my driver's license, an officer hit me with an electric prod. When I woke up it was cold and dark."

"But why?" Lukas insisted.

"I can answer that," Laurel intervened. "The vendetta of a spurned woman." She highlighted the salient details from the story her anonymous recruiter had hinted at in their telephone conversations and from the dossier Tyler had let her read when she knew him only as Shepherd. Laurel detailed the tragic relationship between Odelle Marino and Araceli Goldberg, stopping the narration after Russo's abandonment of the pregnant young woman before the police's charge.

"I was twenty-three," Russo whispered. "And a coward." He paused. "I still am."

"Well, she extracted her pound of flesh," Floyd said.

Russo moved an almost translucent arm to his emaciated thigh and squeezed. "Rather more, I fear."

"Still." Floyd pinched his lower lip. "I can't figure something, though. Why did she wait so long? There were almost twenty years between Araceli's death and his abduction."

"Clout," Russo said. "Up until ten years ago, Odelle Marino wasn't powerful enough to get away with it."

"And means," Laurel echoed. "Hibernation is not that old a technology."

After a thick silence lasting a few seconds, Russo's head lolled, and the sound of his breathing deepened.

—

Russo slept until well past dusk. When they switched on the TV screen to watch the evening news, he stirred and waved his hand to hike up the volume.

Laurel neared the sofa to help lift him higher on his pillows so he could watch. As she reached under his emaciated arms, she felt Russo's hand grip hers with a fierceness she didn't believe was possible in his condition. She froze and peered into his wraparound sunglasses, unable to see beyond the dark lenses. Then he let go and his fingers traced the outline of her cheekbones, her nose, her chin, as if he was committing her features to memory. A drop of liquid peeked from under the frame of his shades, then rolled swiftly down his gaunt cheek.

chapter 51

||||

10:30

Jerome Palmer glanced at a battered ormolu clock sitting above the fireplace when it produced a ratchet noise ending in a hollow clunk: ten-thirty. Eons ago, he'd helped his father castrate the clock by excising its bells. He'd been impossibly young, on short reprieve between sophomore semesters at Harvard. After polishing off a decanter of port—a vintage Sandeman, from which Mother accepted only a sip—Senator Leon Palmer had led a foraging party of two to a seldom-visited corner in the house's cellar. Later, after much arguing over the respective merits of grape and grain, they had adjourned to the library, clutching a dusty bottle of cognac and two snifters.

After listening to his father's preposterous tale of a de-frocked bishop turned pimp—to cash in on his proselytizing savvy—and with the contents of the venerable bottle a memory, they had suffered in hazy stupor the racket of the clock as it chimed away at midnight. With the sudden enlightenment of the very drunk, they carried the clock to the garage and proceeded to strip its back and remove the bells to thwart future interruptions. Mother would never let anyone forget and would mutter, "That poor castrated clock," every time the machine struggled to accomplish the task conceived by its creators.

The house had been silent for a long time.

Chelsea, his daughter, had left for work before seven with her husband. Regardless of their efforts at stealth, he'd heard the swift rush of their sedan's motor and the crunch of gravel as they left. When by seven-thirty Mrs. Timmons, the house-keeper, failed to make an appearance—for the first time in ten years—he roused Timmy, supervised his toilette, and rustled up a breakfast of cereal and juice. Brad Hawkins, a lame ex-marine who refused to take a pension at forty-five, and who doubled as his driver and handyman, hadn't turned up at the appointed time either to take Timmy to school. The situation abundantly clear, Palmer climbed the steps and marched to Timmy's room.

"What are you reading, son?"

The little boy held up his large book.

"Let me see." Palmer donned his reading glasses and leaned over Timmy's shoulder. He scanned the picture of a lone officer in impeccable blue atop a small knoll, surrounded by a sea of feathered warriors. A caption underneath read: *General Custer's Last Stand*.

"I don't understand, Grandpa."

"What is it you don't understand?"

"Instead of stand, why didn't General Custard attack?"

Palmer thought it over. "Beats me, but I'll look into it." Then he gently squeezed Timmy's shoulder. "No school today. I have an assignment for you, soldier. Will you accept it?"

Timmy nodded his head enthusiastically.

"Good, here is what you must do. I am waiting for some

people. Bad people. Probably there will be a woman. She's a spy, a wicked spy. You'd better go to your tree house and keep me covered at all times. Now, soldier, this is important: Don't come down, no matter what you see. Don't come down until I call you. Promise?"

Timmy seemed to weigh his orders and then sprang to his feet, drawing a hand to his chest. "Cross my heart, sir!"

That had been over an hour ago.

The wide screen flashed an artificially colored thermal image showing a large red spot, another of smaller size, and a few tiny ones.

"The large blob is the senator, this is the boy, and the others are a few squirrels, a rabbit, and rats in the senator's basement. There's nothing else within a mile radius; no other heat signatures."

Odelle peered at the screen. "And these?"

"One car with our men and the housekeeper at the intersection with the E 311, and another with the senator's driver at the track leading to the house. Er . . ."

"Yes, Sergeant?"

"The crippled driver—he tackled the men . . ." A predictable description of stupidity under the guise of heroism followed.

Silence.

"Where's the boy?"

"In a tree house. Should we grab him?"

Applying force was an art. Often a threat was more effective than an action, and Senator Palmer was unpredictable. "No, leave him there."

With a final glance to the dim van's interior and the four men hunched before surveillance and communications stations, she turned to the sergeant by the side door. "Get my car and let's pay a visit to our friend."

Palmer snapped from his reverie at the buzzing sound of the main entrance gate opening. Besides his daughter and her husband, only Mrs. Timmons and Hawkins had access cards, but he doubted any of them had opened the gate.

340 carlos j. cortes

At the kitchen, he glanced at a split screen offering different views of the estate. A dark sedan was progressing along the graveled road to the house.

He sighed, his mind replaying Seth's trial before the gods. *I have the lettuce leaf loaded for you.* He walked toward the main door, opened it, and stepped onto the porch in time to see Odelle Marino alighting from her car, chaperoned by two young men with lively eyes. Another woman, the driver, remained behind the wheel. *Let's see if you wolf it down.*

"Madam Director, what a pleasant surprise."

"Thank you, Senator, I was passing by and I thought I'd pay you a visit." She climbed the steps and offered her hand for a dry, warm, strong handshake.

"Please, come in." Palmer pointed to the open door and led the way into the house and his study. "We'll be more comfortable here."

She told her bodyguards to wait by the car.

As they entered Palmer's den, the clock whirred to follow with twelve evenly spaced thwacks. Odelle spied the contraption, one inquisitive eyebrow flexing upward.

"Ah, the clock . . ." Palmer chuckled. "A long story. Coffee, tea, something stronger?"

"Thank you, Senator, nothing. I will be leaving shortly." From her handbag, she drew a flat frequency analyzer. "May I?"

"Be my guest."

After a while, apparently satisfied, she made as if to sit on an easy chair but seemed to think better of it. She glanced through the twin glazed doors leading to the back garden and smiled. "You have a wonderful garden. Could we take a stroll?"

"Of course. Here, let me." Palmer gripped the handle and slid one of the doors aside.

"Senator, this is truly magnificent."

Palmer offered her a dazzling smile. "Madam, I'd rather you cut the bullshit, deliver your pitch, and get the hell out of my house."

Her composure never cracked. "I admire your profession-alism. Business first."

"Only, in this instance, the pleasure is all yours."

She drew closer and gripped his arm. "Charming as usual." Then her voice altered and dropped—low, throaty. "You've been a naughty boy, Senator, stealing something of mine. I suppose that, as he is your son, you have a claim of sorts on Russo, but I find your sudden discovery of earth-shattering pa-ternal love gratuitous. You could have acted like a real father, given him an education, and taught him to be a man, whatever that means. Instead, you sired a despicable bastard and got rid of him. But let bygones be bygones."

They continued strolling arm in arm toward the center of the lawn. "Your driver was killed on his way to work."

Palmer whirled and grabbed her wrist. "You bitch!"

Instead of backing off, Odelle drew near until her breasts brushed Palmer's chest. Her mouth twisted. "It was an acci-dent. The man tackled four DHS officers from the Special Forces, bare-handed. Epic, but a waste. Don't worry. His car will explode somewhere. Accidents happen every day."

"Have you finished?" Palmer fought to control his mount-ing rage.

"Here is my deal. I want Russo back. As soon as you deliver him, I will have him disappear with the rest of the center in-mates without a trace; they would have never existed. Then I will tender my resignation. You'll be able to clean the stables and bring Hypnos to heel. That's what you've wanted all along, isn't it?"

Odelle Marino was much more intelligent than he'd given her credit for, Palmer conceded. Rather than fighting a battle she couldn't possibly win, she was willing to step down, as long as she could keep the spoils. It wasn't surrender but a negotiated armistice.

"And if I don't?"

"I spotted your grandson earlier. Timmy, isn't it? Hiding in his tree house, adorable."

Palmer knew what was coming next. Predictable. "You have no shame. . . ."

"None. We're talking survival, Senator. As a student of history, you should take Sun Tzu's counsel and leave a gap for your enemy to flee. A cornered foe is as formidable as its desperation."

She'd shown her ace, and she wasn't bluffing.

"When I get back downtown, I plan to announce the imminent recapture of the fugitives. Twenty-four hours, Palmer. That's how long you have to hand over Russo."

"What about the others?" he asked grimly.

"They're irrelevant in the scheme of things. Keep your granddaughter and the young lawyer as a consolation prize. The doctor won't ever be able to practice again, but he's young. The turncoat can elope to Peru and sire dozens of cinnamon-skinned bastards; I couldn't care less. Get them new identities and make sure they keep their noses clean. I'll send photos to the press showing a few prisoners returned to justice, and that will be that."

Palmer backed up a pace to recover his personal space. She stared—not at him, but through him.

"You can hide him in a vault, Palmer, in Switzerland or Tierra del Fuego, but I will find your Timmy. And, when I do, so help me God, you'll never see him again. So don't fuck with me, and don't push me any further. I can use the full resources of the DHS to get that boy, and his mother, and his father, and his father's father, and all of your wretched kin. You'll get me, eventually, but it will cost you."

"Are you done?"

She smiled. "I am, but . . . I would love to hear you accept my reasonable offer."

Palmer pasted a suitably shaken grimace on his face.

"Will you deliver Russo within twenty-four hours?"

I will, indeed. Palmer stared at her, then nodded.

She swiveled toward the copse of trees and waved a hand. "Don't be a fool, Senator. I could have snatched your grandson an hour ago." She paused, raised an arm, and snapped her fingers. "Just like that."

chapter 52

23:36
"What will you do after?" Floyd asked.

"After what?"

"After tomorrow."

"What tomorrow?" Laurel reached into her trousers pocket for a nonexistent piece of gum—a shameful ruse to give her hands something to do. The house was quiet. After a marathon of brainstorming and Tyler's continuous trips carrying his communications pad, he had laid out the plan. Some details were still hazy. He'd kept the means of transport close to his chest, as well as who would be going and where, but the gist of the plan was deceptively simple. The group would split into two. While one team would ostensibly drive toward the ABC TV studios on Rhode Island Avenue, the other, with Russo, would head for the Capitol and Congress, where Senator Palmer and his confederates would be waiting. Somewhere along the way, the first team would detour and head for Congress also.

Harebrained would be a merciful adjective to describe the ploy, but Tyler seemed very much in control and everybody agreed they were alive thanks to his, so far, passable scheming. But tomorrow held too many unknowns. Hypnos and the DHS would not stand on the sidelines while a bunch of fugitives apparently headed toward one of the most prominent TV facilities in the country. And the Capitol, after the White House, was the most secure building in the world. How the police or DHS forces would play their hand was anybody's guess, but the consensus was they would shoot first and answer questions later. Yet Tyler had disclosed that there was another force at play—someone helping them from the shadows—and that his or her intervention could make the difference. Who? He didn't know. The highlight came when Lukas asked directly what their chances were. Tyler had drawn from his already extinguished pipe, producing a strange sound between crackling and gurgling, before deadpanning, "Ten percent." And even that sounded unreasonably optimistic.

Russo looked good—still as helpless as a newborn, but with a seething resolve to speak. Halfway through one of their long conversations, Floyd had mashed the tip of a banana and given him a tiny morsel on the tip of a spoon. Russo had kept the mush in his mouth for an inordinately long time, shifting it from right to left, his eyes narrowed as if in a trance. Later he offered a weak smile before mouthing a single word: "Ambrosia."

Laurel reached for Floyd's hand. "We can live only one day at a time, and a day is all we have."

"I meant—"

"I know. You meant us, and that requires time—time we don't have. Yet. We're strangers. How long have we known each other? Four days? Five?"

"Six." Floyd put a hand around her shoulder and drew her closer. "I know all about the acceleration of emotional processes in the presence of impending doom."

"I know you do, and I've done my best to exorcise any thoughts of continuity from my mind. I don't want to engage in pyrrhic dreaming exercises about what might be, when chances are we'll be dead tomorrow."

"But dreaming marks the difference between us and other creatures in the cosmos."

"You got it," Russo said.

They both turned toward the couch where Russo lay. He'd removed his dark glasses and was looking at them with remarkably bright eyes.

"Why does a blade of grass push its way through scorched earth in the middle of a battlefield? Chances are it will be obliterated by the next blast, but it will still try. We're not that different from any other creature except we can imagine, dream, and hope. Emotions are what keep us alive."

Laurel stood up and padded to Russo to fluff up a cushion under his head and offer him a drink of juice. "It's very bad manners to eavesdrop on other people's conversations."

"Then you should keep the volume down." He sucked on the straw and attempted a smile. "But you're right inasmuch as it makes little sense to plan certain things around the unknown. You're nice people, and the species is rare, probably heading for extinction. Later, if there's time to be had, you should spend it learning about each other."

"What would you do if there were time?"

Russo smiled. "Here we go again, daydreaming."

"That's one of the things we do best as a species," Floyd said. "Please don't tell me you've not given a second's consideration to the possibility of winning."

"*Touché.* If by the fickle hand of fate we pulled through, I would attempt to set up the machinery to oversee the hibernation system."

"Revenge?" Floyd asked.

"Not at all. The past is gone and the future has not happened yet, hence we cannot travel to either, or undo it, or recover any part of it save through dreaming. To seek redress would serve no purpose. Laurel spoke about pyrrhic dreaming, and vengeance would be indeed a pyrrhic exercise."

Laurel caught the odd glimmer in Russo's eye and turned to Floyd in time to spot his frown.

"By pyrrhic you mean pointless?"

"I'm sorry." Russo chuckled. "This is the problem of our era—to append imaginary meanings to the things we don't understand instead of simply asking for an explanation. Pyrrhus was a Spartan king who won a battle against the Greeks at the cost of losing his entire army. *Pyrrhic* means a bitter victory: a victory won at such great cost to the victor that it is tantamount to a defeat."

Floyd nodded. "You have a point. We find it difficult to simply ask for an explanation of something we don't grasp. In my job, I know from the halfhearted nods I get from patients or their families that they don't understand anything of what I'm saying, yet they seldom ask me to clarify."

"Do you like your job?" Russo asked.

Laurel turned to Floyd. It was a question she'd often thought of asking him and never had.

"I can help people."

"You're sidestepping the question," Russo said.

"I keep forgetting you're a lawyer. Yes, I like my job. I only hope that more resources will be allocated to basic research on the mechanics of hibernation."

"Independent research?" Russo insisted.

"Nothing else can be true research. Corporate research is necessarily biased to match their goals. If these goals coincide with the public good, everybody wins, but that's wishful thinking."

"I agree. Hibernation in itself is the solution to an age-old problem of civilization: what to do with those who represent a danger to society. But to place the responsibility in corporate hands is madness."

Laurel straightened, suddenly aware that Russo was outlining something to which he must have given much conscious thought. "You mean the hibernation system should be government run?"

"No, I don't. If governments ran the system, it would soon become bogged down in bureaucracy, departments would fight over allocations, and eventually it would mushroom into a quagmire of complexity and expense, defeating its original purpose. This new prison system is inherently sound. It's well suited to be run by a corporate concern, but only with the right safeguards in the hands of government and independent bodies. But no corporation should be allowed to own the technology and conduct its own research."

"Talk about dreaming." Floyd chuckled.

Russo grimaced. "Well, as Tyler said, we have a one in ten chance."

"I fear Harper Tyler is an inveterate optimist," Laurel said.

"Still, *dum spiro spero*," Russo whispered.

Floyd frowned.

Laurel smiled. She'd seen the quote on her parents' home mantelpiece every day since childhood. "While I breathe, I hope."

"Amen," Floyd said.

"And you? What would you do if there's a tomorrow?" Russo asked.

For a while Floyd didn't answer, then he drew a hand over the incipient stubble on Laurel's head, as if caressing a newborn. "I would go for broke and ask her out for coffee."

As his hand warmed her scalp, Laurel suddenly felt as if tomorrow was real.

day seven

||||

Paradiso, Canto XVII: 12–14
Not that we need to know what you'd reveal,
but that you learn the way
that would disclose your thirst,
and you be quenched by what we pour.

The Divine Comedy, DANTE ALIGHIERI

chapter 53

08:10

The noise of an approaching engine drew a flurry of glances and nervous gestures from Raul and Lukas. Laurel turned to Tyler, who sat on a stool by the kitchen peninsula, seemingly unconcerned. She leaned over Russo and ran a hand over his brow. "Don't worry; they're friends." She hoped.

Russo nodded once.

Lukas stepped over to the window overlooking the front porch, slid his fingers to widen a gap between the blinds' horizontal slats, and peered outside. "Shit," Laurel heard him mumble.

"Indeed." Tyler smiled and strode past them toward the front door, Antonio at his heel.

Laurel squeezed Russo's shoulder for reassurance. The previous days had been emotionally draining. Gradually she'd stopped seeing Russo as the father who abandoned her and let her mother die and started to see just a frightened human being in need of help. She trooped from the living room with Raul and Lukas. Once outside, she gasped. Parked parallel to the house's front porch, a huge tanker truck—of the type rigged to empty cesspits—revved its engine. The driver looked vaguely familiar.

A door clunked shut, and the towering anatomy of a vastly different Henry Mayer materialized around the front of the truck, a wide-brimmed Stetson on his head—probably shaved by the looks of the smooth skin down the sides. The gravel crunched noisily under the soles of gleaming lizard-skin boots. Laurel peered at the naked skin of his face, awed at the change. But for his bulk and voice, she would have never recognized the sewer chieftain. He had an interesting face, almost handsome.

"Hey! Fancy seeing you again." He ran an eye over the congregation and raised a hand to the brim of his hat. Then he slapped the truck's fender. "Isn't she a beauty?"

Tyler stepped forward and indicated the rear of the truck. "Let's see her guts."

At a nod from Henry, the driver killed the engine and climbed down from the cabin. Laurel exchanged a quick glance with Floyd. The man driving the truck smiled. She eyed the jeans and a drab coat that had seen better days that were hanging loosely from his meager frame. *Can't be.* She stepped forward to peer at the tall, cadaverous-looking man with sunken eyes and thin lips. His freshly shaved head gleamed under the still-weak sun.

"Jame—Barandus?"

He smiled. "The one and only."

They shuffled toward the rear of the truck to face a vast circular door with a hinge on one side, secured around its perimeter with a score of sturdy bolts fitted with handles.

"Cleaning trucks," Tyler explained, "cannot be pumped empty. The contents of a septic pit decants to a thick slurry. When the trucks reach the treatment plants, operators free the bolts at the rear and tilt the tank to slide the contents out."

Laurel backed up a step when Henry and Barandus worked the bolts to open the tank—a sudden premonition too horrible to contemplate forming at the edge of her mind.

When the ponderous door rotated on its hinges, a waft of dank moisture billowed out, bringing with it barely forgotten memories. Laurel cringed. Light spilled into the bowels of the tank to reveal a cavernous cylindrical space and three two-hundred-gallon drums lying on their sides in line, bolted to the bottom of the tank and spaced three feet apart. To the side, wedged between the drums and the inner curved wall of the tank, rested several panels of quarter-inch plate peppered with two-inch holes. Laurel dug her fingers into Floyd's arm.

"You must be out of your mind." Laurel intended to sound outraged, but her voice came out as a croak.

Lukas blanched. "In those?"

"Wonderful stuff." Henry climbed up to the gaping tank, bent over the first drum, and yanked its quick-release rim fastener. The interior of the drum was padded with two-inch foam. On its floor, like fat wasps, were two seventy-two-cubic-foot scuba cylinders. "We tested it last night after fixing the drums. After a two-hour runaround with the tank filled to the brim with water, not a drop seeped into the drums."

"Then why the scuba tanks?"

"The air inside the drums wouldn't last five minutes."

"You're going to drive around with us inside the drums?"

"That's about it."

"In a tank full of water?"

"Nah, shit. We'll fill her halfway up with shit."

Tyler neared the open tank. "Washington is sealed. Vehicles entering or leaving the city are being searched. A tank will certainly be stopped and checked."

"But what about the company?"

"Company?"

Laurel pointed to the block capitals stretched over the tank's side—O'MALLEY CLEANING SERVICES, 24/7— and a phone number.

"It's a real setup—a small family business with six vehicles like this and twenty employees, established almost forty years ago. We bought it yesterday."

"We?" Laurel asked.

"Antonio, Barandus, and me," Tyler answered. "Could be a good business."

"If a patrol checks who owns it, won't it look suspicious that the company just changed hands?" Lukas asked.

"Good point, but it hasn't," Tyler said. "This is a small, unlisted firm. Although the sale was executed yesterday, it won't be filed until tomorrow. By then there shouldn't be any heat."

Laurel shivered at Tyler's choice of words. Hibernation tanks were a hairbreadth above freezing. She scanned the others. Behind their somber faces, she could almost see the thoughts—the chances of an accident and death by suffocation in sewage.

"How long will they have to be locked up there?" Floyd asked.

Tyler's left eyebrow shot up. "They? No way. Russo, his attending physician, and Antonio will go in the tanks. That will do nicely. You're his doctor, and Antonio can help you carry him when we get there."

"But—" Floyd had paled.

"I will ride up front with him," he said, glancing toward Henry. "Raul, Lukas, Laurel, and Barandus will make the sham run toward the TV studios in the van. Barandus will lie on the stretcher with Laurel attending him. Raul will drive, with Lukas up front. The DHS will snatch photographs along the way to identify not just Russo but you. In fact, they can't identify Russo; they'll just assume it's him when they identify the rest."

Something didn't add up in Tyler's plan. "Why is it so important they identify us?" Laurel asked.

"I don't know. But whoever is helping us insisted the DHS must make positive identification for the plan to work at all."

She'd been balking at the thought of being under tons of sewage, but suddenly the prospect didn't seem as harrowing as facing the DHS agents, who would undoubtedly shoot on sight. "Where are we going?" *I know where we are going: to our deaths.*

"The Senate."

A few inches over her head, a sharp intake of breath exploded. "Hang on a minute. We'll never get within a mile of the Capitol in that," Floyd blurted, his eyes on the truck.

"Oh, but we will." Henry jumped down from the tank, landing with a sonorous thump. "We've got a job to do: a major sewage-pipe blockage needing our expert attention. The urgent request came a while ago, with a job number and the head of maintenance's signature."

"But you said the tank would be full of shit," Floyd said.

"No, I didn't. Half full, just enough to cover the drums."

"Sloshing every time you brake?"

"Nope. These panels will go back in place across the tank once everyone is cocooned. No sloshing."

Floyd's eyes continued to dart all over the truck. "Forgive

me, but I can't figure out how you can justify going to a job with a tank already full."

"Only half full, remember. We've made an earlier call."

Antonio smiled. "We were drowning in pig shit—" He bit his lip and seemed to wither under Henry's caustic stare.

"But to open the drums, you have to empty the tank . . ." Floyd insisted.

Henry opened his arms wide, an expression of fatalism on his face. "Well, shit is shoveled around Congress all the time. Another cartload won't make any difference."

chapter 54

||||

08:45

"I hope you know what you're doing."

Senator Palmer bit his lower lip before reaching for his snifter. "Is this a condemned man's last wish?" He swilled the liqueur.

Bernard Robilliard, the senator from Maine and secretary of the Senate, shook his head once and waited.

"I have covered every possible angle, every eventuality, trying to predict anything Vinson or Odelle might have up their sleeves. Nothing, I hope, but there's a chance my scheme will collapse," he conceded. "Too many unknowns."

"Your witnesses?"

Palmer nodded. "Their fate rests elsewhere, in seemingly puny details and in the hands of a man who seems to have switched sides but who is, in the end, playing for himself, and that makes for a dangerous ally. You know about illumination; it strikes at the unlikeliest of moments. He might back out yet."

"And then you will have?" Robilliard asked.

"Nothing."

"And I will be forced to stand aside while Odelle Marino flushes the bilges," Robilliard said.

"Nice analogy. And one I've heard recently."

"Problem is, she would be reborn with awesome power. She would have this nation by the balls."

"She already has."

"But she's not squeezing," Robilliard pointed out.

"Yet." *If I fail, I, my family, and everybody else will be fucked.*

Robilliard nodded and wet his lips on the liqueur. "Now it all hinges on your ability to convince Caesar to do something unthinkable. In my opinion, he won't. You're asking too much."

"To save one's country from dictatorship is asking too much?" Palmer asked.

"No. But to ask someone to wager his or her hide on the strength of your word is. For the best part of two hundred years, we've never been a democracy, at least not a real one. Too many powerful cartels: oil, weapons, and, above all, the security agencies. They, not the current White House resident, have dictated this country's policies. Why do you think I know that paper is a fake?" He nodded to the single page with the presidential crest and seal resting on his desk. "Because no president would have the balls to tackle this country's rulers and survive. They learned their lesson from Kennedy."

"So the answer is to do nothing? Fiddle while Rome burns?"

Robilliard shook his head. "The eternal romantic. Within the past couple of centuries, no fewer than four empires have disappeared: the Nazis, the British, the Japanese, and the Soviet Union. They flared like shooting stars and burned out, some sooner than others. Now it's our turn. You know the common denominator of their downfall?"

"I do. Implosion. They collapsed when their core rotted."

"Exactly." Robilliard nodded. "Now you're planning to ask Caesar to cross the Rubicon and lay his head on the block of your dreams of justice. Can't you see the difference? Caesar did it to overthrow the status quo and become emperor. You're asking a man to do it so you can take the mantle."

"I'm not. One way or another, I'm out. This will be my last public deed. I retire."

"Oh?" Robilliard frowned. "And have you named a successor?"

Palmer shook his head. "You still don't get it. I want to challenge the system because it's the only chance left for my country, but I'm too old to carry on righting wrongs. I only hope others will have it easier."

"I see. So President Hurst *knows* about your coup."

"I didn't say that."

"Yet if you manage to pull off this stunt, with Odelle Marino disgraced, the President will have the floor clear to step in and really flush the bilges. Neat."

"You and your imaginings."

"Hardly. Common sense only, of the kind that has kept me in office twenty years." Robilliard stood from the easy chair, holding on to his glass, and walked to stand beyond his desk, as if suddenly needing the physical protection of office. "He won't do it, you know. And yet there's something you're not telling me."

Palmer swirled his cognac in its glass, peering into the liquid amber whorls, but the answer he sought wasn't there. Then, as he returned the snifter to the table, the thought hit him with such clarity that he had to blink repeatedly to clear his vision, as in the aftermath of sudden lighting. "Have you ever wondered why Caesar crossed the Rubicon?"

"To become emperor."

"No, that was the outcome, perhaps the thought behind his action, but not the reason why." Palmer leaned back and narrowed his eyes. "Let's find out. Would you call Caesar in?"

It wasn't the gait of the career soldier, or the field of medals covering most of his chest, or the close-cropped hair, or even the chiseled face. The authority and might that surrounded four-star general James Erlenmeyer like a halo had other roots—ancient roots, honed in the same forges that had cast generations of warriors before him. The same fire that had forged Patton.

"The issue is clear," he said after listening to Palmer. "I

would hear the request from the President herself. Then I would give it my consideration and, since the proposal entails high treason, I would refuse. That paper," he looked with disdain at the single sheet of White House stationery, "is as false as the Roswell cover-up. Now, if you don't have anything else to say, I will forget what I've just heard and be gone."

Palmer waited, but General Erlenmeyer didn't turn on his heel. "General. I have shown you proof of the DHS and Hypnos's debauchery. Such depravity has become commonplace to a point where our prison system has become the private fiefdom of agencies and corporations to use at their own volition. Everything is in here." He tapped his portfolio, more for effect than for any real reason, since the hard data was branded in his memory.

"Senator." It was obvious the general was making an effort to keep his voice level. "You're asking me to bring in the army and take over the Capitol. That's a coup, rebellion, sedition, high treason, the works."

"I won't march the army into Rome," Robilliard muttered.

General Erlenmeyer jerked around to face the senator. "You're damn right I won't!"

"You're wrong about one thing, General. That paper is not a fake. President Hurst signed it less than an hour ago, but you would have to take my word for it."

"Like everything else," General Erlenmeyer retorted.

"Right. But whatever I might be, I've never reneged on my word. On the other hand, President Leona Hurst will not give you the order herself. It's all a matter of deniability. She's a political animal, like Robilliard and myself. But for once I'm determined to do something honorable, even if it costs my life. I have the data, the proof, the witnesses, and the floor of the House, but I'm on my own. Others, like him," Palmer nodded at Robilliard, "have agreed to do nothing, to stand on the sidelines—a phenomenal display of courage, if I might say so. But they leave a path for their escape: their own deniability if things go wrong. They have given me access to the stage, but the performance is mine alone. Yet, even though

I've laid my life and that of many others on the line, I can't expose the rot that will eventually destroy our nation unless I'm granted security. This building is held by DHS personnel, and Odelle Marino will not be a party to her own destruction. All I need is a neutral zone secure for my witnesses and the select committee in which to present my case. Ms. Marino and Vinson Duran will be arriving shortly, unaware that their efforts to destroy the proof of their infamy have been ineffective. As soon as they learn of it, she will order my arrest."

The general's brow creased. "She can't do that."

"This building is totally controlled by the DHS. She can and she will, and she'll answer questions later. If there's anyone to pose them, that is."

The general shook his head again when Palmer stood and squared off with the warrior.

"General, there's a reason why President Hurst refused to give you a direct order. You see, she's also sorely aware of her limitations. She knows power has been leaching slowly from the constitutional seats for a long time and that a showdown like today's would tip the balance. She further realizes that, even as Commander in Chief, this is an order she can't issue. In fact, sadly, nobody in this nation can voice such an order." Palmer changed the weight of his body to the other leg, hoping to forestall the unconscious shaking that threatened to become obvious. "I will go on the floor with the building secured or not, because I'm the only one who can do it. Call it a last-ditch effort. And you know the most surreal aspect of the whole sorry affair? The thing that singles out you and me? Even though nobody can legally issue the order, only one citizen can give it: me. And only one can obey it: you."

For a long time, General Erlenmeyer stood rooted to the spot, two white circles slowly forming on his cheeks. "So help me God . . ." He lunged forward and, for an instant, Palmer flinched before the blow that never materialized. "Damn you to hell, Palmer." The general pounced on the table with fury and swiped the sheet of paper from its surface. He turned on his heel and strode to the door. One hand on the handle, he looked back. "You have until noon." Then he yanked the door open and slammed it shut in his wake.

"Well, I'll be damned . . ." Robilliard leaned over, both hands flat on his desk. "He'll do it. But instead of the Rubicon, he'll march his legions across the Potomac!"

"I never doubted he would." Palmer reached for his glass, covering his shaking hand with the bulk of his body so Robilliard couldn't see through his lie.

"Good luck." Robilliard raised his glass, took a sip, and then straightened. "Go on, spare me the misery. Why did Caesar do it?"

Palmer reached for his briefcase. "Because he *was* Caesar."

chapter 55

||||

09:30

"Stop the engine and step down, hands on your head."

"What's going on, Officer?" Henry Mayer leaned out the window, pasting a silly smile on his face.

"Stop the engine and step down, hands on your head. I will not repeat myself. Step down or I'll open fire."

Henry shrugged, nodded to Harper Tyler, and opened the truck's door. Once on the ground, he obliged by placing both hands on his head, turning around to face the truck's bodywork, and spreading his legs. To one side, two DHS FDU officers in full body armor took station ten yards away, helmets bristling with communications gear mated with shiny face masks. Their boxy assault weapons were trained on him. A couple of seconds later, Tyler walked around the front of the vehicle, shadowed by another hulk in carapace.

The police officer who had ordered them to stop in the first place stepped forward, kicked Henry's legs another foot apart, and ran his hands over Henry's body in a much-rehearsed pattern. Henry flinched and tittered. The hands paused. "It tickles." A huff and more hand-running. Then the heavy boots moved toward Tyler and repeated the frisking.

"Turn around. No sudden movements."

Henry didn't alter his splay but turned around with mincing steps, hands planted on his head.

The officer frowned, arms akimbo. "What are you, a joker?"

"You said to turn around, not to change position."

"Cut out the crap. Where do you think you're going?"

"That building ahead; their toilets are blocked solid. Or so they say."

"Who says?"

"How would I know? I only drive the fucker; he's the boss."

The officer turned to Tyler.

"We're answering an emergency call. I have the papers here." Tyler nodded to folded sheets stuffed in his shirt's top pocket.

The police officer stepped over and slapped a hand over the papers as if they were poisoned. He held them at arm's length and, looking a little crestfallen, reached for his reading glasses.

On the opposite side of the street, three more cars had been stopped and their occupants underwent a similar routine. Henry counted six DHS FDU trucks, at least fifty officers, and, a couple of hundred yards farther off, a blue van. He froze, then did a quick double take. The van across the street was the same color and model as the one carrying Laurel and the others. Across Capitol Avenue, different teams had laid chains bristling with spikes on the tarmac, creating a zigzagging path any vehicle attempting to reach the Capitol would have to negotiate—although by the look of things most vehicles were being turned back. Other accesses to Capitol Hill shared similar checkpoints, or so the radio announcer had said.

"You can't pass." After much peering at the papers and turning them in all directions, the police officer handed them back. "Get inside your vehicle, turn around, and come back tomorrow."

Tyler smiled but didn't reach for the papers. "That's great with me, but I need a signature."

"A signature?"

"Yup. As you can see, the order came this morning at nine o'clock, flashed through the head of the Capitol's maintenance services with top priority. They must be swimming in it down there. It's no skin off my teeth, pal, but I need the signature of someone in charge to attest that we came and weren't allowed in." He leaned forward and winked. "That way we can charge extra for this call . . . and again tomorrow."

The officer looked back at the papers, stopping at the scrawled signature and stamp at the bottom of the forms.

"These are copies."

"We received them on the fly." Tyler nodded toward the driver's cabin. "A printer in the cab."

After a frown and a step back, the officer's lips moved close to his shirt collar.

A flurry of shouts drifted across the tarmac as a plump woman in a flower-printed dress spoke angrily to a towering FDU officer. Then she whirled around, slipped into her car, and continued to deliver a steady stream of invective over the racing whine of her engine as she threw her vehicle in reverse.

Farther on, the side door of the blue van slid open, and a man in an old-fashioned hat and thick glasses alighted. As the door closed at his back, he raised his face to the sun for an instant, dug his hands into the pockets of a tweed coat, and strolled unhurriedly in their direction.

Tyler exchanged a quick glance with Henry, who had suddenly found the tips of his lizard boots irresistible.

The man with the tweed coat made a beeline for the officer holding the papers and put out his hand, palm up, his eyes running the length of the truck and stopping at the rear door and its bolts.

"What's in there?" His voice was refined, with a slight lilt to it.

"Er . . ." Henry turned around and eyed the truck as if the vehicle had just materialized behind him. "Shit."

"Pardon?"

Henry wrung his hands. "Refuse, sewage . . ."

"But it says here you are supposed to unblock drains, you always go to a job already loaded with the stuff?"

The police officer leaned over to the man and whispered, nodding toward Tyler.

The plainclothesman lowered the papers and turned to Tyler, his head slightly cocked to one side. He blinked startling china-blue eyes beyond his old-fashioned bifocals.

"We had an earlier call at a Lebanese takeout down on Mulberry Lane," Tyler said. "I have the papers in the cabin. When we flagged this call, we drove straight here. Plenty of room in the tank." For once, Tyler delivered his lines without gesticulating with his hands.

"Open it," the man said.

Tyler gaped. "Here?"

"I didn't say empty it. That thing at the top opens, doesn't it?" The man nodded to a circular lid on top of the tank.

"Yes, but . . ." The two FDU men had already shouldered their weapons and climbed the truck, negotiating the front and rear handholds. When they reached the top, one grabbed the wheel of a screw fastener and twisted with energy. Then he lifted the lid and jerked his head out of the way.

The man in charge raised an eyebrow.

"Shit," the DHS officer blurted.

The man in the hat nodded and turned to the police officer. "May I borrow your flashlight?" Then he rammed the offered device in his coat pocket, neared the truck, and climbed. He leaned over the opening, pointing the flashlight downward and flicking his wrist. Then he nodded and retraced his steps. "It's shit, all right."

Once on the tarmac, he returned the flashlight to the police officer and dug his hands once more into his coat's pockets. "You may go through." Then he turned on his heel, walked a few steps, and stopped, only to turn around slowly, drawing a finger to his lips. "Say, you mentioned a greasy spoon—er . . . a Lebanese takeout—didn't you?"

Henry tensed and glanced at Tyler, following his slow nod.

"It smells like pig shit to me, but then, I'm not an expert." With that, he once again raised his face to the sun and strolled toward the van on the opposite side of the road.

chapter 56

09:56

At the intersection of South Dakota and Rhode Island Avenues, something strange happened. When the traffic light changed, they turned onto Rhode Island, but the light must have changed again, because no other car followed. Someone had to be controlling the lights from a remote location. Before them opened a vast stretch of road, also empty of traffic.

"This is it, then?" Lukas gripped his seat belt, as if ready to withstand impact.

"Looks likely," Raul said, steering closer to the dividing line down the center of the road.

Laurel leaned forward, peering into the distance as a dark line of trucks converged from both sides of the next intersection, like sliding doors. She narrowed her eyes, imagining that a similar scene would be unfolding at their back. Her fingers tightened around the syrette Floyd had slipped in her pocket.

Barandus rustled on the stretcher and wrapped the drab blanket tighter around him, before breaking into the chorus of "We Shall Overcome" in a deep voice.

Raul reduced their speed even further and slammed an open hand on the steering wheel. "For crissake, shut up!"

Lukas lowered his head, his lips moving, and Laurel thought there couldn't be a much better reason to pray.

"Stop the vehicle and switch off the engine," boomed a voice with a Hispanic accent coming out of nowhere and everywhere at once. Raul jerked and slammed on the brakes. Barandus resumed his singing in a low voice.

"Stay in the vehicle. Don't attempt to leave it," the same voice echoed once more.

Raul yanked out the van's ignition card. The chunky piece of plastic swung from a thin chain attached to the steering wheel, clicking against the dash. Otherwise, there was silence.

"Now what?" Laurel asked.

Raul placed both hands on the steering wheel at ten and two. "Now they blow us to kingdom come."

Lukas sat straighter.

Ahead, the trucks disgorged never-ending lines of armor-clad DHS FDU teams, who deployed in an advancing semicircle. Through the driver's-side mirror, Laurel eyed a dark wave approaching from the rear. She thought the ancient Roman legions must have looked like that. Not like individuals but one unit: an army. Then the ranks ahead parted to allow a squat tracked vehicle—like a miniature tank—through, with what looked like a cannon mounted on top.

"They're going to fire." Laurel closed her eyes when Lukas joined with Barandus in singing, "We shall overcome, one day . . ." in a trembling voice.

"Someone is coming." Raul glanced at his mirror, almost filled by a dark van approaching from behind at a sedate pace.

The tiny tanklike vehicle slowed to a standstill thirty feet ahead, then it swerved to the right and continued moving at an angle to take up station ten feet to their side, the cannon rotating on top as if preparing for a broadside.

"It's a camera," Laurel said.

"What is?" Raul asked.

"The cannon. It's a camera."

The contraption drew closer, motors whirring. Three feet from their van, it stopped, and the tube rose on concertina arms like the eye of an alien cyclops. Then powerful projectors fired, bathing the interior of the van in bluish light. Laurel flinched and her knees started to shake. After endless seconds, the lights doused and the contraption whirred away, its rubber tracks producing curious flapping noises.

On their left side, some fifty feet away, the dark-blue van stopped and its side door slid back to disgorge a slight man in an old-fashioned hat, smart tweed overcoat, and thick glasses. The man raised his face to the sun, then turned toward a single DHS officer standing to one side and nodded. When the officer drew near, the man in the hat reached into his jacket pocket and handed him a piece of paper. He waited until the officer finished reading and recovered the paper. Then, hands deep in his coat's pockets, he strolled in their direction, lazily glancing right and left.

Around them, scores of DHS FDU officers, their black armor gleaming under the strong sun, deployed in a circle perhaps one hundred feet in diameter containing both vans. Their weapons were trained steadily on the fugitives.

"That van is just like ours—same model, same year, same color," Lukas said, looking straight ahead into the black ring of DHS forces.

"And same plate number," Raul muttered.

Laurel looked at the parked vehicle. The driver, a young man with wraparound sunglasses, had descended, hefting a large shoulder bag, and marched purposefully toward the other side of the road. The tracked vehicle with the camera turned around when it reached the ring of troops, and its arm swung to train its camera on the van the young man had just vacated. The officer who had conferred with the man in the hat marched before the line of DHS troops and pointed toward the other van.

"How do you know?" Laurel asked.

"I checked as it approached."

When the newcomer stopped, his nose scant inches from their van's driver's side, Raul reached to his door and lowered the window. "Wh-what do you want?" Raul asked, his hands back on the steering wheel at ten and two.

The man didn't answer but peered with piercing china-blue eyes at Raul's head, slowly traveling his face and chin, then panned over to Lukas, his lips blossoming into a slight pout, as if ready to blow a kiss. He sidestepped to the passenger window and leaned both arms on the windowsill, his nose inside the vehicle.

Laurel caught a slight whiff of cinnamon and something else, perhaps citrus but equally pleasant, like a warm cake.

Then the man must have caught Barandus's song, even though it had died down to a whisper. He cocked his head and narrowed his eyes in concentration for what seemed a very long time before nodding once. "Indeed you shall." Slowly he straightened, rested a hand with soft fingers on the sill, and spoke into his lapel. "Blast it."

The air burst into an earsplitting cacophony of explosions as the troops fired a never-ending rosary of high-caliber bullets into the van parked scant yards away. Windows shattered, tires burst, and the sickening crunch of twisting metal followed when the vehicle exploded in a fireball.

Laurel closed her eyes and screamed, hands drawn to her ears in a useless effort to stop the clamor of smashing bullets. Then a whoosh of hot air buffeted her face, and she threw out her hand to grasp on to something. When the roar subsided, she opened her eyes to sparkling blue eyes watching her a few inches to her left.

Outside, like a scene from Dante's Inferno, a low mist had fallen on the road. The ghostly soldiers in their black fatigues turned on their heels, moving toward their vehicles through swirling smoke redolent of cordite and burned rubber.

"Can I have it back?"

Laurel gazed, realized she was gripping his hand, and immediately let go. "I'm sorry."

"Don't be." He squinted. "The Capitol is that way." He nodded toward the next intersection and, giving wide berth to the burning vehicle, turned toward the young man waiting with his shoulder bag.

chapter 57

10:12

The view past the heavy brocaded curtains and sheers
framing the window was different from what Odelle Marino
remembered. The grass stretching past the granite monolith
of the fountain built over the Senate garage seemed dull, as
if all color had been leached from it. Even the lion-head
spouts on the fountain looked somber. In the distance, blurry
through a gauzy morning mist, the rectangular mass of the
Robert A. Taft Memorial and Carillon also appeared featureless and dull.

Yes, today Capitol Hill looked different—not so much a
place of glory and recognition but of reckoning. *I have nothing to worry about; everything is under control.* She turned
and panned slowly across the magnificent room, obviously not
an office despite its furniture: a desk with two easy chairs, and
two sofas flanking a low table framed by the backdrop of twin
windows. No doubt the room was used as an antechamber for
meetings or a sweat room for witnesses and experts to cool
their heels. That she had been made to wait for a shamefully
long time was something she had filed away in her repository
of scores to settle.

After a slight rap, the door opened and a slender, immacu-
lately groomed young man with half-closed eyes, whose
badge read *Anthony,* stood straight. "They are waiting for
you, madam."

Although both she and Vinson had been summoned, the
committee wanted them in separately. Genia Warren, the little bitch, was also supposed to appear before the committee,
but so far she was nowhere to be seen. Odelle glanced at the

orderly, then did a double take. The sleepy-lidded young man was looking around with the calculating poise of a professional killer. Only an idiot would fail to recognize a superbly trained professional. She stifled an inward curse before turning toward Vinson Duran. They had been contained for the best part of an hour in the Russell Senate Office Building. Vinson glanced at his cellular-phone screen and pressed his lips together into a thin line.

Still no news. Nikola had demanded full authority over the DHS FDU units to oversee the mopping up. Yes, *demanded* was the correct term. The man was becoming hectoring in his old age and had probably outlived his usefulness. *One thing at a time.*

"Give me a minute." *The inquisitors can also wait*, she thought.

"Yes, madam." The young man nodded and left the room, softly pulling the door behind him.

"Wait. Have the sergeant at arms come over." Odelle cocked her head but didn't turn to face the orderly. "Please," she added, as an afterthought.

"Yes, ma'am."

The device in Vinson's hands pinged and he lowered his face to it, as if closeness could speed reception. Odelle clenched her hands for an instant, eyes on the grass outside, marshalling her body language to disguise her trepidation.

"Done," Vinson said, his face creasing into a cockeyed smile. "A van was stopped at a checkpoint on Rhode Island Avenue, halfway to the ABC building."

"Spare me the geography," she snapped.

He didn't raise his eyes from the tiny screen. "From the video feed, the scanner positively identified Lukas Hurley, Raul Osborne, and Laurel Cole with over ninety percent certainty and Eliot Russo with over fifty percent."

"Why only fifty percent?"

"The man was prone on a stretcher and wrapped in blankets. Reasonable, if you ask me."

"I didn't." The tightness in her chest relaxed a fraction. "Go on."

"When the fugitives refused to leave their vehicle and reached for concealed weapons, the officer in charge had no option but to order his men to open fire. Those were Mr. Masek's exact words."

Odelle waited.

"The vehicle exploded. No survivors."

Odelle peered through narrowed eyes at the Capitol grounds. The light had changed and the mist must have shifted; in the new aching clarity, vegetation and monuments sharpened into focus. The doctor was missing, but he was of little consequence. So much for Palmer's witnesses.

"Now you can pull the plug."

Vinson's face lit up as he jabbed a code into his cell phone. Then there was a soft rap on the door and Odelle turned to find Edward O'Keefe, the Capitol's head of security, personally handpicked by her several years before. As the Senate's chief law-enforcement officer, the sergeant at arms traditionally maintained order and security on the premises and was independent of any agency or the army. But that was before the providential takeover of Capitol Hill by an extreme-left group in the fall of 2049. After taking a score of senators and other lesser officers hostage, a standoff ensued, in which it was clearly demonstrated that the resident security forces were ill-equipped to deal with such an emergency. While Thomas Corvus, then the aging and incompetent president, agonized, surrounded by his advisers, she had sent in her Fast Deployment Units. After a show of tactical virtuosity transmitted live by all the major networks, in less than two hours Odelle's team had killed all the terrorists—and only two senators were wounded in the cross fire. That the "terrorists" ranged from age sixteen to twenty-one and were armed with weapons loaded with blanks was carefully kept from the public view.

Fueled by a vindictive press and riding the crest of the ensuing outcry, Odelle had managed to change an ancient rule and substituted DHS forces for Capitol security.

"At ease."

On the sunny side of fifty, Edward O'Keefe was no sergeant but a full colonel, and he cast an imposing figure in black fatigues. The ex-marine had always refused to don any apparel more congenial with his office.

"As they tried to reach these grounds," Odelle said, "the fugitives from the Washington, D.C., suspension facility were spotted at a checkpoint. Regretfully, they're all dead."

O'Keefe didn't move or relax his stance, eyes fastened on a small print and its oversize frame on the opposite wall. Yet the man had an unnerving aura about him: the body language of someone who actually knew how to break people's bones.

"Naturally, we know nothing of their supporters—the organization that masterminded the breakout," she continued.

Vinson pocketed his cell phone. "I'll use a computer at the security center," he said, dropping his voice into the age-old lilt of the marketplace. Slipping past O'Keefe, he opened the door and disappeared, leaving a trail of laughter in his wake, like the Cheshire cat's smile.

Odelle cringed at Vinson's childish behavior and continued. "I've heard a rumor, so far unconfirmed: There's a possibility such a criminal group may attempt a repetition of the 2049 fiasco." Nothing wrong in adding a little overkill security. "Suggestions?"

"I will power the antitruck hydraulics throughout the Hill, call in additional FDU units, and place my men on maximum alert."

"Sounds good, Colonel. Seal the grounds tight. Don't let anyone in. In particular, all access to this building: Constitution Avenue, First Street, Delaware Avenue, and C Street." Then she threw him a morsel. "I'm counting on you."

When she was alone, she neared the window again and looked toward the fountain. Her eyes blurred. She treasured a hoard of private memories of Araceli's face, her voice, and her form, but none like the images of a distant morning when Araceli had danced in that same fountain and together they had to flee before the shouts of an irate gardener.

Then training took over. She swallowed hard, stepped over to the desk where she'd propped her briefcase, and marched purposefully out of the room and into the corridor where Anthony, the killer aide, waited.

372 carlos j. cortes

Partway down the hallway, he stopped before a door, reached for the handle, and opened it, standing aside.

A long line of military trucks snaked to a stop before the roadblock at the confluence of Pennsylvania and Independence Avenues.

Edward O'Keefe, the Capitol sergeant at arms, rested both hands on the back of the swivel chair occupied by Sergeant Thomas, the shift officer at the Capitol Security Center, peering over his shoulder at the computer screen on the desk.

"Zoom in," he said.

The screen filled with the cabin of the first truck and the insignia stenciled on the door: *Marine Corps. What are they doing here?* A sergeant appeared around the front of the vehicle to hand over a sheet of paper to the Capitol security platoon leader. The security officer seemed to scan the page, then shook his head.

O'Keefe's radio beeped. He tapped his ear set. "O'Keefe."

"General Erlenmeyer to see you, sir."

"Where?" O'Keefe zeroed in on the screen again. His security officer and the Marine sergeant continued to argue.

"Outside the door, sir."

O'Keefe turned to look at the solid steel door protecting the control center.

"Sir, another military convoy has been halted at Maryland and Second."

He spoke into the microphone clipped to the neck of his tunic. "Is the general alone?" A stupid question, since generals never went alone anywhere.

"Two aides, sir. A colonel and a major. All security-cleared."

O'Keefe bit his lower lip. He couldn't leave a four-star general standing by the door. Other security officers had stopped scanning the scores of screens at their stations and were looking at him.

"Open the door," he said to no one in particular as he stepped forward.

After a muted thud, the thick door swung on its diamond-tipped hinges to frame General Erlenmeyer, flanked by two officers in full uniform.

O'Keefe stood at attention and drew a rigid arm to his brow. "General . . ."

The security officers stood at attention by their stations.

Erlenmeyer looked down his patrician nose at O'Keefe. "Colonel, I am relieving you of your duties. Please stand aside."

Time seemed to slow. Sergeant Thomas pushed his chair back and was reaching for his regulation sidearm when the colonel accompanying Erlenmeyer leaped forward, slapped a huge hand on Thomas's crotch, and rammed a pistol in his neck. O'Keefe turned to the general, to stare into the black hole of a Smith & Wesson an inch away from his nose.

"Perhaps you didn't hear the order, Colonel. Witnessed by Colonel Robinson and Major Freedman, you've been relieved of your duties. I will construe any further move as rebellion and a threat and will blow your brains out. The same applies to your men." Erlenmeyer's voice remained conversational and even. "Freedman." He spoke to the major at his side. "Show the colonel our presidential orders."

A collective sharp intake of breath followed as the men reacted to the statement.

O'Keefe scanned the sheet of paper held in midair by the major, his mind in turmoil. *First Odelle Marino and now the army. What's going on?*

Freedman folded the paper and, with swift movements, removed O'Keefe's sidearm, flicked the safety catch, and checked the weapon. When he noticed there was no bullet up the spout, he snapped the action to load it and shook his head. "Slipshod."

Colonel Robinson nodded to Thomas's screen. "Order your sentries to let our vehicles through."

Pain flickered on Thomas's face as his eyes swiveled downward to the paw grinding his groin.

O'Keefe made to turn around, but Freedman rammed his weapon in his side.

"You heard the colonel," Erlenmeyer said. "That's a direct order."

Robinson removed his hand.

Thomas leaned over his console and spoke into a microphone. On the screen, the security officer at the roadblock froze. Thomas repeated the order, enunciating each word with care. After a few seconds, an obviously confused officer stood aside and the barriers dotting the ground started to lower.

"Now the convoy at Maryland and Second," Robinson said.

Thomas flicked through screens and repeated the orders.

"Take over, Colonel." Erlenmeyer nodded to the deadpan faces of the security officers, then lowered his weapon. "Let's go meet our men." At the door, he stopped and signaled to Major Freedman, who prodded O'Keefe ahead of him.

Odelle stepped into the room and froze. She'd been there before—it was a place for informal meetings, with a large oval table, its high-backed chairs now occupied by people she knew well. But she was taken aback by the level of the confederates. To one side of the table sat Senator Palmer with Genia Warren and her very much alive black-bereted puppy, Lawrence Ritter, his face curiously dotted, and Richard Papworth, chairman of the Permanent Select Committee on Intelligence. The opposite side was occupied by John Crookshank and Eugene Stem, Senate majority and minority leaders, respectively, followed by Robert Barrat, the assistant secretary of the Senate. At the head of the table stood Bernard Robilliard, the secretary of the Senate.

She stood transfixed, staring at Bernard Robilliard and his big, slightly brutish face. It could have been the light and the precise angle his face was turned, but for an instant he looked like Tomas de Torquemada—the ruthless inquisitor who ordered the burning and torture of thousands at his autos-de-fé.

She darted a glance at Ritter. So the man was mauled but in one piece, unlike her aide George Wilson, naked on a marble slab with several holes in his body and a tag around his big toe. So far, Nikola Masek had been unable to piece together what had happened to Wilson, but it was only a question of time.

She didn't believe in coincidences, but she felt a definite

clenching in her gut when Bernard pasted a genial smile on his face and turned to look directly into her eyes.

"Ah! Here you are. Don't stand there. Please, make yourself comfortable. This is not the Inquisition."

chapter 58

||||

10:32

Odelle Marino approached the table, where an obliging Robert Barrat held a chair for her, flanked by an unoccupied seat and the bulk of Richard Papworth doodling on a legal pad. She lowered her briefcase and ran a hand down the back of her skirt to sit. "If you say so. Still, I thought I caught a whiff of burning bramble."

"Nothing can be further from our minds, I assure you." Robilliard slid into his seat and ran a hand over the polished surface of the wood in front of him. No papers. "Before we start, let me clarify that this is not a committee—"

"Then what is it?"

Robilliard pursed his lips an instant. "Let's say a fact-finding meeting to decide if an inquest is necessary." He waved a hand in the general direction of the others. "You know everybody."

She stared at Genia Warren, who stared back with cold determination. "Some better than others, but, yes, I know everybody. You've not answered my question."

"I thought I had."

"There's an agreement between my agency and this House to give reciprocal fair warning and background before convening any meeting." She raised her hand a fraction to forestall Robilliard's reply. "I'm well aware that agreements are honored more in the breach than the observance, but the fact of its existence still stands. I have been arraigned before this—"

"You haven't been arraigned. You've been asked, like the rest of us, to attend a meeting, and there hasn't been time to draw an agenda we can all agree to. In fact, there is no agenda."

"Fine, let me rephrase my original question. What's the purpose of this . . . friendly gathering?"

"Ah, the legal mind. I have convened this meeting at the request of Senator Jerome Palmer to determine whether we have grounds to form a special committee."

"To do what?"

Robilliard pursed his lips again, but this time Odelle knew it wasn't an oratorical device but a ruse to delay an uncomfortable answer.

As if on cue, Senator Palmer rested a hand over a thick folder. The bastard had brought papers. "The events of the past days have raised grave questions, not only about the security of the prison system but about alleged criminal abuse of the facilities."

"Alleged by whom?" Odelle snapped.

Senator Palmer turned to face her. Dark bags under his eyes gave him the appearance of a tired bloodhound. "Alleged by me."

"Criminal abuse of the facilities? Don't make me laugh! No doubt you have depositions, documents, or the like to back your preposterous accusation." She stretched out a hand, palm up, her eyes on the folder.

"Madam Director, you've not convened this meeting. I have, chaired by the secretary of the Senate. Your role here is to answer questions, not make demands."

She lowered her hand to the table and held it there for an instant, before drawing it back. "I don't have to answer your questions."

"I'm afraid you'll have to," Robilliard said.

"Or else?"

"Or else I will presume Senator Palmer's claims have substance, in which case I will convene a special committee."

Odelle stared at Robilliard. Whatever that bastard Palmer had concocted must surely rest on his vanished witnesses. In a flash, she decided to call their bluff. "Do it, Mr. Secretary. And, when you do, summon me through the proper channels and I will gladly answer any questions. Until then, if you'll excuse me . . ." She pushed her chair back as a commotion sounded outside the door.

All eyes turned to the door and the imposing figure of Colonel Edward O'Keefe, the Senate sergeant at arms. He stood under the frame for an instant, then stepped in with curiously short steps. Odelle's gaze stopped at his empty holster; his sidearm was missing.

Two mountainous soldiers in full combat gear, their weapons trained on O'Keefe, prodded him into the room. Out of the corner of her eye, she saw her companions around the table start to rise, faces disfigured with shock. No, not everybody: Palmer, Genia, Ritter, and Robilliard remained seated.

"What's the mea—" John Crookshank, the Senate majority leader, blurted.

Another figure blocked the entrance, to a collective gasp around the table. General James Erlenmeyer, also decked in combat fatigues, waited until O'Keefe and the two soldiers stepped aside before marching into the room.

"My forces have secured Capitol Hill and all its accesses. Until this emergency is over, nobody will leave the premises." He glanced at Odelle Marino. "Or this room."

"Holy—" someone swore.

Odelle sprang to her feet. "This is high treason, General. I'll have you thrown in a tank, headfir—" Then she clamped her mouth shut.

General Erlenmeyer turned in her direction, his chin raised so he looked at her down his nose. "I'm sure you would, madam, given the chance." Then he swiveled on his heel to face Bernard Robilliard. "I have orders from the President of the United States." He slapped at his tunic top pocket. "My commander-in-chief and that of everyone in this building." He spoke forcefully, clipping his words. Then he turned to O'Keefe. "Ahead of me, Colonel," he said, and nodded toward the open door.

Both soldiers stood at attention and marched out of the room after the general and O'Keefe. Odelle gasped as, before the door closed, she spotted Vinson's ashen face peering in from the hall.

"Now that we're safely tucked in, perhaps we can resume," Senator Palmer said.

Silence.

"I will pose a few questions—"

"The only questions I will answer will be before a court of inquiry."

Senator Palmer tapped his folder lightly, his eyes unfocused. "Very well. I will lay the case and you will listen."

She had started to shake her head when Senator Palmer jerked his head in her direction, a ferocious expression on his face. "And if you refuse to listen, so help me God I'll have you placed in irons by the soldiers outside and restrained while I read the charges."

"Charges?" she growled. "Who the fuck do you think you are?"

"I'm your nemesis." Then he snapped his fingers and turned to look over Robilliard's head.

"Yesterday, at my home, Director Marino threatened my life and that of my family if I didn't bow to her demands."

"You liar!" Odelle shouted.

Senator Palmer stared at her for an instant. "A sound and video recording of the exchange is my first exhibit."

The lights dimmed as a large screen lowered from a groove in the ceiling; a tiny video projector peeked from a housing over the table and flared to life.

Over the following minutes, the only sounds in the room were the unmistakable voices of Senator Palmer and Odelle Marino, as the crisp images on the screen depicted the pair walking in Palmer's garden.

You've been a naughty boy, Senator, stealing something of mine. I suppose that, as he is your son, you have a claim of sorts on Russo . . .

Everybody in the room held their breath.

. . . But let bygones be bygones. Your driver was killed on his way to work.

Odelle stared ahead, eyes unfocused.

. . . I want Russo back. As soon as you deliver him, I will have him disappear with the rest of the center inmates without a trace; they would have never existed. . . .

Next to Palmer, Genia darted a quick glance to Lawrence Ritter.

You can hide him in a vault, Palmer, in Switzerland or Tierra del Fuego, but I will find your Timmy. And, when I do, so help me God, you'll never see him again. So don't fuck with me, and don't push me any further. I can use the full resources of the DHS to get that boy, and his mother, and his father, and his father's father, and all of your wretched kin. . . .

With a slow glance, Palmer took in the shocked faces around the table.

Don't be a fool, Senator. I could have snatched your grandson an hour ago. The snap of Odelle's fingers on the screen echoed like a rifle shot. *Just like that.*

As the lights came back up, eight pairs of eyes converged on a remarkably composed Odelle Marino.

"That's a fake. I was never near your house. I can produce affidavits from scores of people, both from the DHS and independent witnesses, who can testify under oath I was miles away from your address all morning."

"I never said it was in the morning," Palmer's voice was almost a whisper.

Odelle pointed to the disappearing screen. "The light."

"But you said it was a fake."

She pressed her lips together into a grim line.

"Say, Palmer, according to the conversation we've just heard, the only other person on the grounds was your grandson, so who shot the film?" Eugene Stem, the Senate minority leader asked.

"My grandson did," Palmer's face was impassive. "Timmy hides in his tree house and points a plastic rifle at whoever happens to be with me. To keep me covered, he says. I strapped a miniature camera and a directional microphone to his rifle."

Robilliard grimaced. "I see."

"My second exhibit will tax your patience." Palmer reached for his reading glasses and opened the folder before him. Then he nodded to Genia. She stood, reached for the folder contents—eight sets of a document stapled in one corner—and started distributing them around the table.

When she reached Odelle and slid the document before her, the DHS director hissed, "A stab in the back?"

Genia straightened. "No, love, not in the back, but staring into your eyes as you bite the bullet. Remain calm . . . and you won't feel a thing." With that she continued her rounds, placing a document before each man.

"The document before you contains photographs of two young women," Palmer said, "and another photograph of an accidental homicide by an officer of the riot police. These are old prints. There are also recent pictures of the wretch we spirited out of the Washington hibernation facility: Eliot Russo, a civil rights lawyer, purportedly dead in a car accident eight years ago. My son."

A buzz of shocked expletives spread across the table as senators reached for the document. Odelle remained immobile, staring straight ahead.

"On those pages, there's an account of a wretched love affair gone wrong and the vengeance of a spurned lover. But don't let feelings blind you. Others share my son's fate stored in a tank without benefit of trial. In addition, our nation's hibernation facilities have been turned into a kind of parking area for the Russian Mafiya. They've been storing their enemies in our system in exchange for vast sums of money."

"This can't be true," Richard Papworth, chairman of the Permanent Select Committee on Intelligence, blurted. "We would have known."

"Indeed. And you did know, Richard."

Papworth gripped the edges of the table and started to rise.

"It's over, so please spare us the theatrics. At the back of the document, there are three appendixes. Appendix One is list of the people who knew about the use of hibernation facilities to store anybody from dissidents to whoever the Mafiya wanted to keep in cold storage. Your name is there, next to a code number. The code identifies a large file containing irrefutable evidence about the individuals involved in this infamy. In Appendix Two, you will find the details of accounts Director Odelle Marino keeps in Antigua, with a balance in excess of three hundred million dollars. Blood money for services rendered."

All faces turned to Odelle when she started laughing. It wasn't a forced laugh but deep, throaty, from the belly, breast-shaking. "You're pathetic. All of you. These papers are a craftily constructed lie, full of circumstantialities and fakery. Nowhere in any suspension facility is there anyone who's not been sent there by the courts. Nowhere. You can send inspectors to all the facilities, check the identity of each inmate. Nothing. It's all a lie."

"Pulling the plug didn't work."

Her laughter died, and, like spectators at a tennis match, all faces turned toward Genia Warren.

"Less than an hour ago, a signal flashed from this building to override Hypnos's security program releasing center prisoners from their harnesses and then flushing the tanks."

As the outcome of such a maneuver registered, a sharp intake of breath echoed off the fabric-clad walls.

"The men and women who are property of the Mafiya were resettled in recent days and replaced by common inmates. To even the numbers, scores of prisoners would have been reduced to mush by the fluid-treatment turbines and flushed down the sewers once the solids had been removed for incineration. Fortunately—and I'm referring to the inmates, not you," Genia paused and exchanged a quick glance with Odelle, "we intercepted the signal and triggered the emergency status in all facilities. The nationwide suspension system is locked; it will remain thus until each facility has been thoroughly inspected and illegal prisoners have been sent to reanimation to ascertain their identities and secure their freedom or to return them to their countries of origin."

Odelle's face was frozen in a stony expression.

A sharp beep shattered the silence. Palmer reached to his pocket, drew out a slim cellular phone, and listened for several seconds. When he folded the device back into his pocket, he had to rein in a sudden urge to smile. "As I said," Senator Palmer continued in a soft voice, his eyes on the empty folder before him, "the document before you is my second exhibit, but, as Ms. Marino sagely pointed out, our technology allows us to fake almost everything. In Appendix Three, you may peruse a list of thirty-six illegal prisoners and their relative location within the system." At Eugene Stem's frown, he paused. "No mistake. Thirty-six. These are the ones left alive. In the second part of the appendix there's a long list of names, but these are long dead. Appendix Three will corroborate the document you hold and everything I've revealed so far. Providing the facilities are inspected by an independent committee, you will find twenty-six men and ten women who shouldn't be there. Scattered through various facilities, inspectors will also find twenty-four Russian and Chechen citizens, a few Chinese, and several others, all wanted by sundry governments for organized-crime activities."

Palmer leaned back and massaged his eyelids. "Naturally, that will take time, and I don't want to impose on you any more than necessary. My Exhibit Three is outside that door, waiting to testify for himself."

For several seconds nobody moved, then John Crookshank started to stand, but Robilliard arrested the movement by gripping his arm. "Oh, no, you don't. Let me claim a little glory." Robilliard stood, marched to the door, and opened it with a sharp pull, only to step back at once. "What in the na—"

General Erlenmeyer stood in the opening with a bundle in his arms—a frail figure with enormous eyes and almost translucent extremities. After a painful awed silence, the general stepped forward to occupy the vacant chair, still holding Eliot Russo to his chest like a baby. Then a man and a woman, with shaved heads carpeted with stubble, and a small man with a remarkable likeness to Woody Allen entered the room, carrying with them an obnoxious smell of excrement. Their shoes and trouser legs looked as if they had waded through something dark and slimy.

Odelle stared at the figure that General Erlenmeyer held, her face distorted by an expression of fascinated revulsion. After a few heartbeats, she reached under her hair with an almost coquettish gesture to unclip a small reddish-colored earring. Ritter started to move, but Senator Palmer reached over Genia and stilled his arm. Then Palmer locked eyes with Odelle and blinked once.

Odelle Marino smiled faintly, pushed the earring past her lips, and crunched it between her teeth. Then she leaned back and turned to look at Eliot Russo before convulsions racked her body.

Senator Palmer stood staring into Odelle Marino's lifeless eyes as pandemonium broke out.

chapter 59

||||

14:47

Senator Palmer moved to the desk and half sat on a corner, facing the group scattered on chairs and sofas in a large Congress office he'd commandeered to accommodate everybody. Eliot Russo sat wrapped in a blanket on one of the sofas, with Laurel holding his hand and Dr. Carpenter next to her. Most senators had scrounged a seat, but a few stood with the motley group stationed close to the door, the air heavy with the odor of excrement. The confederates had emptied the contents of the truck in a garage basement and trampled the stuff all over.

With Lukas and Genia stood Ritter, Harper Tyler, Raul, Henry Mayer, Antonio, Barandus, and Colonel O'Keefe, his regulation sidearm back in its holster. General Erlenmeyer sat on the sofa next to Eliot Russo.

"Now that you're all gathered, I can tell you that, within a few minutes, the President will convene a press conference to inform the world about what's happened." Palmer paused to inspect his fingernails. "Enough lies: The President will give the world a version of what's happened. It can't be any other way. The full truth would serve no purpose and would cause this nation much harm.

"In her address, she will disclose having found one illegal prisoner in the system: Eliot Russo. The rest will be given the best medical attention we can muster. Some will be returned to their countries of origin and others will be granted asylum. Everyone but Russo will remain anonymous."

"Er . . ." Bernard Robilliard cleared his throat. "The stunt all of you have pulled is remarkable, and it's obvious other agencies lent a hand." He nodded toward Genia Warren. "But I've just heard that the . . . shit tank and a van with the rest of your confederates passed through the gauntlet Director Marino had thrown around Capitol Hill. How?"

Senator Jerome Palmer glanced at Genia. "By the devices of a man unknown to most of you: Nikola Masek."

"Ah, Odelle's bloodhound. Hardly an innocent bystander," Robilliard pointed out. "If anyone knew about the atrocities within the hibernation system, he did."

Genia leaned forward. "Without his help, we wouldn't be here."

"And no doubt he's been adequately compensated," Robilliard mused as if to himself.

"The President will sign a document giving him full immunity from prosecution before the day is over," Palmer said.

"And the man from Hypnos? Will he also enjoy immunity? And the others?" Floyd Carpenter blurted.

"No, my friend. Vinson Duran from Hypnos is in custody, and, within the next few hours, scores of people—a few occupying some of this nation's highest offices—will be arraigned before the Senate."

"And then condemned to the tanks?" Henry Mayer asked.

Senator Palmer held Henry's gaze, then shook his head slowly. "I'm afraid not. A nation as large and complex as ours demands compromise. Perhaps justice will not be served in full, but all of those who knew of this infamy will be forever removed from public office. That's the best we can attain without irreparably damaging our nation's reputation. Victims will be compensated—generously—although I'm aware no compensation can ever be sufficient to erase what's been done to you." He looked into Russo's eyes. "Or any other innocent who has ever had to spend a minute in those harrowing tanks without trial."

"Just a moment, Senator." Laurel stood and stepped into the center of the room. "A moment ago you said, 'Everyone but Russo will remain anonymous.' That won't do. As you said yourself, enough lies." She turned around and locked eyes with Raul, who stepped over to her side. "We're not all gathered. Bastien Compton died."

Aside from the agency executives and politicians, the rest of the gathered gravitated to the center of the room.

Laurel looked over her shoulder and nodded before facing Senator Palmer once more. "We can't just ignore his sacrifice."

Something flashed deep in Palmer's eyes, but he didn't say anything.

"Arlington," Raul said.

Robilliard huffed. "He wasn't a member of the armed forces."

"In a way he was," Palmer said. "Acting on direct orders from the White House."

"I see your point." Robilliard ran a hand over his hair.

"What can we do about armed forces membership, General?" Palmer asked.

General Erlenmeyer adjusted a blanket over Russo's legs. "We're swamped in paperwork. Often names are misspelled, dates are absent or inaccurate—it's a miracle we can keep track of everybody. If we look carefully enough, I'm sure the service record of Bastien Compton will be found."

"That won't be necessary," Lawrence Ritter pointed out. "On June first, 2002, army rules changed, and some civilians who served the United States during wartime were allowed to have their cremated remains inurned with military honors at Arlington National Cemetery."

"Wartime?" Robilliard asked.

"How else would you describe this morning's events?" Tyler retorted.

"No cremation," Laurel said.

Robilliard sighed. "We should be able to manage a standard honor cerem—"

"Full honors," Tyler interrupted.

"And the Medal of Honor," Henry chipped in.

Robilliard opened his mouth to say something but clamped it shut and shook his head. General Erlenmeyer nodded. "Such a medal is bestowed on members of the United States armed forces who distinguish themselves above and beyond the call of duty while engaged in an action against an enemy of the United States." He glanced at Palmer. "Most fitting."

"We shall honor our departed friend," Palmer said.

Laurel turned to look into the sparkling eyes of her companions and stopped at Russo's.

He reached for his sunglasses with an unsure hand, removed them, and squinted, keeping his eyes half closed. "There's hope for us if there's still honor among thieves."

Senator Jerome Palmer stepped forward, suddenly looking much older than his years. "Now we must endeavor to recompose our lives, or whatever is left of them. I have resigned my office and, before leaving, I wanted to thank you all for your indescribable courage. Most of you have placed careers and even your lives in jeopardy to have a modicum of justice done. I'm proud of you, proud of being your countryman, and proud of having known the kind of people who have made our nation great." One hand on the door handle, he turned to face a sea of stern faces. "Nothing I can say will erase the past. Justice may not have been served in full, but the prisoner is free."

Mark Shirer, Noncommissioned Officer in Charge, from the Third United States Infantry Old Guard, glanced toward the approaching hearse with apprehension. For more than eight years he'd escorted deceased army officers and two ex-presidents to their final resting places in the Gardens of Stone. The procedure, honed through almost two centuries, was a production worthy of a big-budget Hollywood picture, combined with the precision of time-honored military code—almost a ballet, every movement, event, and detail painstakingly rehearsed with no possible departure from the established pageantry. *Until today.*

According to the schedule details supplied by the Arlington Memorial Cemetery office, the man in the approaching casket, Bastien Compton, had no military record. Of course, a Medal of Honor and sanctions by the President and both Houses of Congress went a long way toward justifying his final rest in the most hallowed land in America. Over the previous hour, a trickle of limousines had turned into a flood, as politicians, military officers, and the high echelons of government flocked to pay their last respects to the unknown man who had merited the highest decoration in the land.

By Shirer's side, the Right Reverend Shawn Ramfis, bishop of the Episcopal Diocese of Atlanta and reportedly a close friend of the Compton family, was to officiate the ceremony at the grave. The bishop's presence wasn't unusual, but the motley group of honorary pallbearers—a mix of civilians, two of them with only a faint stubble on their heads—was. With them were four military officers looking awkward in new uniforms and a four-star general behind an alien-looking man in sunglasses, wrapped to his neck in blankets and strapped to a wheelchair.

Laurel followed Floyd Carpenter with her gaze as he stepped over to Russo's wheelchair. The doctor reached into a side pocket and produced a plastic bottle capped with a thin spout, which he placed between Russo's lips. General Erlenmeyer watched the procedure and nodded. Since the gathering at Bastien's church service, the general had remained at Russo's side.

Henry, Barandus, Antonio, and Tyler looked unrecognizable in their army uniforms, their usually hunched or relaxed stances now gone, as if someone had soaked their clothes with an overdose of starch. Apparently a team of military tailors had been busy. Laurel knew nothing about insignia, but she didn't see how there would be room for any more ribbons on Barandus's and Antonio's chests.

The four previous days—following the events at Congress—were hazy, lost in a dizzying whirlwind. Laurel didn't see Floyd during that time, but they spoke often on the phone. Floyd had transferred Russo to a wing of Nyx and arranged an army of medical personnel to tend to his charge. After signing papers and learning by heart the official version of events for carefully staged appearances before the media, Laurel went home for an overdue supply of hugs, tears, and the nearness of her mother and father. She needed to replenish her exhausted soul. In four days she'd spent more time with them than in the past four years, and it felt good. Her father had explained that they were taken from the house by DHS men and locked in a room at their headquarters. They hadn't suffered any harsh treatment, only the anguish of not knowing what had happened. Three days later they were returned to their home by a nice man who assured them Laurel would be joining them soon. During Laurel's visit, Mother busied herself with meat loaf and banana bread in the kitchen but stopped every time Laurel entered her inner sanctum. They would stare an instant and smile, then they would hug and cry and laugh, and her father would join them. She'd never seen her father cry before, but now he seemed to enjoy a newly discovered pleasure. Nor did the DHS entourage escape her mother's bounty; they would return to their families a few pounds overweight.

At dawn, Laurel had flown with her parents into Washington, D.C., courtesy of the U.S. Air Force, to join Tyler and his lot at the farm. Laurel still couldn't get over her shock when she stepped out of the car to face four vaguely familiar military officers. They stood at attention before a crowd of farm workers, with Floyd Carpenter and Antonio's family, the children waving tiny American flags.

Raul had arrived a few minutes later with his family, his mother clutching his arm possessively. Then Lukas's entourage had made a grand entrance, cars disgorging cinnamon-skinned men and women in their Sunday best, hair slicked and new shoes gleaming under the weak sun. Lukas seemed taller, very serious, gripping the hand of a pretty young woman whose eyes were glued to his face.

When the limousines arrived at the church where the service would be held, General Erlenmeyer was standing at the foot of the stairs with a group of military officers and civilians. He stepped over as Henry, Barandus, Antonio, and Tyler lined up for inspection. The sound of conversation quieted, and Laurel grinned at the general's raised eyebrow when he peered at the men's chests. Then he paced to a stop in front of each of them, to draw a stiff hand to his cap before shaking their hands in turn. Henry, the fearless Lord of the Sewers, his dishonorable discharge revoked by presidential order, couldn't take it. As the general saluted him, he started to cry.

It seemed impossible that only four days separated the harrowing ride to Congress and Bastien's funeral.

Beyond the approaching hearse, Laurel eyed the media gathering endless footage and taking notes. Another group of men and women wove continuously in and out of the crowd, their eyes shielded behind dark glasses. Secret Service. She had seen Senator Palmer hugging Bastien's parents, braving the mother's angry eyes. Everywhere she caught half-smile exchanges between the politicians, obviously relieved at Odelle Marino's timely departure. But for the gravity of the occasion, many would have indulged in backslapping.

The military escort was already in position when the hearse transferring the casket from the church to Arlington Cemetery slowed to a stop and uniformed men started moving. Behind them, at Patton Circle, stood a black artillery caisson pulled by six horses. Astride three of the horses, soldiers sat straight and stiff. Behind the caisson an officer held another horse by the halter.

After the body bearers transferred the casket to the caisson, the procession moved into the cemetery.

Laurel pressed her eyes shut and wished for a human touch. Miraculously, Floyd's fingers cradled her hand. Then she felt a tentative tug on her sleeve and lowered her gaze to Russo's wraparound glasses, his bony fingers twitching as if begging for alms. Holding their hands, she stepped forward as General Erlenmeyer wheeled Eliot Russo ahead of him—the silence of the procession broken only by the rhythmic clip-clop of hooves. Behind the caisson marched a caparisoned horse, wearing an empty saddle with the rider's boots reversed in the stirrups. Laurel swallowed. Bastien, their warrior, would never ride again.

Senator Palmer joined them to walk very straight, followed by Henry, Tyler, Antonio, and Barandus. Raul and Lukas brought up their rear in dark suits and ties.

As the procession moved toward the grave site for the private service, the army band played Johann Pachelbel's Canon, and a composite battalion made up of a company each from the Army, Marine Corps, Navy, and Air Force closed the cortege.

The saluting battery fired nineteen guns, spacing the rounds so that the last one was fired as the caisson reached its destination.

Bastien was to be laid to rest in Section 260. The sod looked fresh. Laurel thought that people usually have a physical address when living and Bastien, even in death, was to have one: Arlington 260, 1346.

A crowd had gathered around the grave site. Row upon row of folding chairs faced swaths of artificial grass strewn around a rectangular hole in the ground, rigged with the contraption to lower the casket.

Friends, acquaintances, and a few members of the family had dissolved in a gaggle of bureaucrats, agency executives, military officers, Secret Service agents, and politicians, all trailed by a crowd of media reporters hauling cameras and digital recorders.

In the distance, a baby cried. Laurel turned toward the wail to see another guard unit filing into the columbarium.

Bishop Ramfis led the way to the grave, followed by the casket team. In a well-rehearsed movement, they set down the casket, stretched out the United States flag, and lowered it over the coffin.

A gentle breeze rippled the grass and shook the tops of trees. *Ashes to ashes, dust to dust.* In a few minutes the crew would tamp the churned dirt into the earth. Then they would roll up the artificial grass, fold the chairs, and immediately drive them to a different section of the grounds to set up again.

Bishop Ramfis read from the Episcopal Book of Common Prayer. The bishop, with his white surplice, reminded Laurel of a long-legged waterfowl scurrying from one place to another. A tall and gangling man, his robes rode high on his legs, baring spindly ankles disappearing into large shoes. But, Laurel had to concede, he was a talented professional. She had seen him in action at church. With the damp gaze of one familiar with the species' miseries, he'd dished out words of wisdom, handshakes, and hugs. Even so, Laurel marveled at the feeling of emptiness smothering her grief.

When the bishop concluded his service and backed away, the NCOIC stepped up to the coffin, froze, and then backed away as President Leona Hurst stood and walked over to stand beside the flag-draped casket.

"My words may not be politically correct, but this is not a rally. It is a reunion of friends to honor our departed hero, Bastien. Our nation is full of double-barreled nationalities. Seldom has a minute gone by without hearing of African-Americans, Irish-Americans, Mexican-Americans, and the like—as if being an American wasn't enough and an individual needed other signs of identity. Bastien Compton's family has African and Scottish roots, but he was simply an American, the kind forged in the trenches of Concord or Bunker

Hill." She turned to the Compton family in the front row and locked eyes for an instant with Bastien's mother. "Although not a member of the armed services, Bastien distinguished himself conspicuously by his gallant and intrepid actions, above and beyond the call of duty. The young man we honor today volunteered to serve his country and, in doing so, made the ultimate sacrifice—a devotion that cost him his life."

As the President scanned the grounds until she spotted Senator Palmer, Laurel marveled at the capacity of politicians for mendacity.

"Words are inadequate before our loss," Leona Hurst continued. "My late father would read excerpts from *Romeo and Juliet* at bedtime. As the Right Reverend spoke, I vividly remembered some of those lines:

> *"When he shall die,*
> *Take him and cut him out in little stars,*
> *And he will make the face of heaven so fine*
> *That all the world will be in love with night,*
> *And pay no worship to the garish sun.*

"I am proud of Bastien and proud to be his compatriot." She stepped back away from the coffin.

The firing party released three volleys as the sound and echo of "Taps" sounded from across the field, played by two buglers. Whispers died and everybody turned toward the music, right hands over their hearts while the men and women in uniform rendered a rigid hand salute.

The team by the casket folded the flag into the triangle reminiscent of the cocked hat from the American Revolution. The President gathered the folded flag and offered it to Mrs. Compton, leaned over to whisper something in her ear, then hugged the woman, who was now racked by sobs.

Laurel retreated into her shell and put on a brave face, zeroing in on small details like the whine of the electrical motors lowering the casket into the grave, the hands of the two very different men she held in hers, and the absence of birdsong.

The casket bearers left, pausing once to render a last hand

salute to Bastien, and a sonorous rumble echoed down the path.

Everybody craned their necks as the USAF pipe band, led by a drum major, slowly marched toward the grave to the strains of the redeeming "America the Beautiful."

Then grief welled in Laurel's chest and she wept, the sound of the drum's somber muffled beat etching into her memory.

Shortly after Bastien Compton's burial, Leona Hurst, the fifty-first President of the United States, convened a second press conference to elaborate on the abridged one served four days earlier. In this meeting with the press, she awed the nation with the outcome of her personal crusade to bring the mightiest government agency and one of the world's largest corporations to heel. In her brief, she stressed her role as the mastermind of the scheme that exposed the existence of an illegal prisoner within the system, who had marshaled her most trusted officers and advisers into a fearless thrust to dismantle the power network knitted by Hypnos and the DHS. As commander in chief, she extolled the courage of General Erlenmeyer in obeying her direct orders to secure the Capitol grounds. On January 20, 2061, she was inaugurated for a second term after winning by a landslide. Since the Constitutional amendment of 2033 had extended the number of terms a president could serve to three, four years later, in 2064, she won her third and final mandate.

In the wake of her public disclosure, 117 public servants and officers were served subpoenas to appear before a Senate special committee. Every one of them was dismissed from public office and left after having signed their confessions and sundry documents to guarantee their discretion.

Lukas Hurley received a commendation and, shortly after, emigrated to Peru, where he lives with his wife, Elena, and their twin daughters, Eva and Rosa. Elena's relatives help the Hurleys run their ten-thousand-acre estate of pastures and farmland.

After an extraordinary session of the ad hoc Special Hibernation Committee, it was decreed that Odelle Marino's ashes should be placed in a specially constructed hermetic urn and suspended in tank 913 of the Washington, D.C., hibernation facility for a period of one hundred years. Shortly after, President Hurst signed an order to confiscate all of Odelle's possessions, but it became apparent that her ill-gotten fortune had disappeared the same morning of her suicide from a numbered account at Banca Fleishmann in Antigua. Although the SWIFT organization cooperated fully to track the funds, they hit a dead end. Following six rapid transfers, the money reached Gibraltar and then branched outside the SWIFT system to accounts in Liechtenstein and the Isle of Man. Onward from these two points, the funds vanished.

Harper Tyler retired to his pig farm with Antonio Salinas and enlarged the operations by purchasing adjacent land. A month later he descended into the Washington sewers to look for a boy, whom he found suffering from a fractured leg. After a brief passage through a clinic to set his leg and diagnose his condition, Joshua—aka Metronome—adjourned to the farm, where he receives special tutoring from a score of newfound uncles and two remedial teachers. In his spare time, he helps his newly adopted father in the layout and construction of a huge 0-gauge model railway in the cellar. James Marshall—aka Barandus—runs an expanded O'Malley Cleaning Services and offers fluid-management consultancy.

The American government slapped an unheard-of two-hundred-billion-dollar fine on Vinson Duran, the owner of Hypnos. To cover the fine, Vinson had to relinquish his majority shareholding. The money, in full, served to pay compensation to the center inmates and to bankroll two foundations: Theta, for the research of hibernation technology, and HMA (Hibernation Monitoring Agency), to oversee the operation of suspension centers with an army of independent inspectors drawn from the ranks of retired government officers. The United States Congress enacted a bill, later transformed into law, to partially nationalize Hypnos and supervise its board by appointing a chief executive officer nominated by Congress. After an absence of two years, Vinson Duran returned to the limelight by founding a corporation to research full-body transplants.

Laurel Cole moved in with Floyd Carpenter after dating for more than a year. Following Dr. Carpenter's appointment to run Theta, they married, and soon after Laurel gave birth to their daughter Eryn. Raul Osborne took a year's sabbatical, during which he traveled throughout Europe. On his return to the United States, he teamed with Laurel to lead a civil rights organization.

Jerome Palmer resigned from the Senate, but his absence from the corridors of power was short-lived. Before President Hurst's reelection, she cajoled him over a bottle of excellent cognac in Palmer's study to be her secretary of state.

Inside a fortnight of her predecessor's suicide, Genia Warren was sworn in as the new director of the DHS, coinciding with Lawrence Ritter's resignation. Less than six months after Ritter accepted his congressional appointment as CEO of Hypnos, he moved into Genia's family home, but not before yielding to Father Damien's demands. The priest refused to acknowledge him as a neighbor unless he married her first.

In addition to accepting an undisclosed settlement from the United States government, Eliot Russo became president for life of the Hibernation Monitoring Agency. He lives with a remarkably attractive housekeeper at a converted light house in Maine, where he tends to his orchids under the tower's glass dome. He keeps several tiny rooms—more like monastic cells—ready to accommodate his frequent visitors.

Nikola Masek runs a security company in the Dominican Republic. In association with his in-house hacker, Denni Nolan, he offers computer security services to government and private corporations. Dennis married his woman, and the family laundry business has branched out into neighboring Haiti.

After another congressional commendation and a princely award, also undisclosed, Henry Mayer continued his interrupted trip to Honduras, where he failed to locate his friend and took to tramping the high sierras, looking for a suitable place to farm chinchillas. His carefully laid plans, however, didn't take into consideration the staff at Trujillo's Registro de Propiedad, the government office where land ownership deeds are registered. After Henry stood in line all morning to ascertain the status of a wonderful tract of land high on the Cerro San Jorge, the pretty young woman staffing the counter slipped a *Cerrado* sign on her desk and gathered her handbag, on her way to lunch.

Emilia Gutierrez must have felt a pang of guilt at seeing the bewildered expression of the giant gringo in dusty lizard-skin boots and sweat-stained Stetson, because she stopped for an instant to reassure him she would be back in two hours. Henry tagged along with her to a local watering hole for sandwiches and a soft drink to outline his plans.

Emilia, a fisherman's daughter, was aghast at the thought of growing furry things to craft into expensive coats for high-maintenance American women, and she suggested Henry should scout the coast to get other business ideas. Since it was already Friday and she didn't work the weekend, she would show him around. A few weeks later, Emilia Mayer succeeded in getting her dazed husband to buy a fish farm with her father and two brawny brothers as hired help, and Henry blesses the day he stood on line at the Trujillo Registro de la Propiedad.

bibliography

For information on sewers I'm indebted to a number of sources, the most important being: *The Mole People: Life in the Tunnels Beneath New York City* by Jennifer Toth, *Cloacina: Goddess of the Sewers* by Jon C. Schladweiler, *American Sanitary Engineering* by Edward S. Philbrick, *Paris Sewers and Sewermen: Realities and Representations* by Donald Reid, *The World Beneath the City* by Robert Daley, *Access All Areas: A User's Guide to the Art of Urban Exploration* by Ninjalicious, *Invisible Frontier: The Jinx Book of Urban Exploration* by David Leibowitz and L. B. Deyo, *Beneath the City Streets* by Peter Laurie, and *New York Underground: The Anatomy of a City* by Julia Solis.

I consulted several publications dealing with explosives, in particular: *The Longest Walk: The World of Bomb Disposal* by Peter Birchall, *The Anarchist Cookbook* by William Powell, and the superb *Jane's Explosive Ordinance Disposal 2005–06* by Colin King.

Finally, I also checked a wealth of particulars on the subject of mammalian physiology, especially: *Mammalian Hibernation III* by Kenneth C. Fisher, *Physiology of Natural Hibernation* by Ch. Kayser, *The Biology of Human Survival: Life and Death in Extreme Environments* by Claude A. Piantadosi, *The Human Factor: A Requiem for Darwin* by A. J. DiChiara, *Temperature Regulation in Humans and Other Mammals* by Claus Jessen, *Metabolic Regulation: A Human Perspective* by Keith Frayn, and *Alcor Life Extension Foundation: An Introduction* by Jerry B. Lemler.